THE HEART OF DIVINITY

EDGE CASES

4

THE HEART OF DIVINITY

SILVER LININGS

Podium

Podium

THE HEART OF DIVINITY

CHAPTER 1

A TALE LONG PAST

A long line of wagons led down the path away from Elyra, along with a long line of *people*. For all that there should have been sound—voices of people talking, laughing, sharing in their worries and their fears with one another—the whole evacuation was eerily silent. There was the occasional laugh. The occasional voice that tried to break the oppressive silence that hung over them. The occasional minstrel, even, that tried to play a song to lighten the mood.

But no one was in the mood. They were all still processing what had happened to their homes. Half of them could barely even remember those homes anymore, their childhoods a series of vaguely shaped impressions that could have been anything. They remembered the people who were important to them, remembered the things they brought with them, but so much life and beauty had been sucked out of the lives they had lived that it was all they could do to *walk*.

In the midst of all this silence, Sev sat in the carriage that carried him and his friends. Helix, Vex's brother, had retreated to the back and put up a sound-proof barrier so that he couldn't hear them; Sev appreciated the gesture, though he'd told him he didn't mind it if Helix participated.

His friends did deserve to hear this first. He just . . . didn't know where to begin. He still didn't remember it all, even if the memories were slowly coming back. There were over a thousand years of memories to sort through, and even without the effect that had erased them, he'd forgotten nearly half of it all.

Just start somewhere, he told himself. Vex was looking at him encouragingly, eager to hear the stories he had to tell. The wonderful lizardkin wizard who had been a late addition to their party. A lover of magic and the arts, he'd started out so very unsure of himself, worried for his family and unwilling to talk to them about any of it.

Now he'd stood up to his father. Convinced him to help. Saved his little brother from the torture that their family had experienced. He'd found a lover, even. Vex had grown so much.

It hadn't even been part of the plan to include him. It hadn't been a part of his plan to include any of these three.

And yet he'd come the furthest with them.

He smiled slightly, barely even realizing he was doing it, and started with the earliest thing he could remember.

"When I was first planeshifted here, I was just barely graduated," Sev said quietly. "I can't say what I was studying. I don't remember it. Most of my memories of Earth are still . . . clouded. But I remember what I was trying to *do*. I remember trying to see if there was a use for what I knew from Earth—I was hoping to be able to change the world, you know? Help people."

"Sounds just like you." Misa grinned at him, teasing.

Misa was rough but warm. She made him think of a fireplace that was intentionally just a little too hot, spitting cinders out onto a fireproof carpet and making the children around laugh and giggle with fascination. Somehow, that comforted him.

"Turned out planeshifting doesn't work like it does in the stories," he said. "I wasn't the first, I wasn't special, and all my ideas were already in place. That's what Anderstahl is, by the way—the kingdom of the planeshifted. Research, science, technology, engineering . . . it all happens there."

"I haven't seen much of that outside Anderstahl," Vex commented.

"It's the anchors," Sev said with a sigh. "It's a clever design, but it makes it hard for things to spread. Especially ideas, but not just those. Food gets lost during transportation, travelers forget what they're doing, quests disappear . . . It's not a perfect system."

"But it was the best that could be done," Derivan said. His voice had that calm, resonant tone to it, a gentleness that defied his size and appearance. "And the Guild helps where it can."

Derivan was the strangest of them all, really. The system had designated him as a monster; he was an empty suit of enchanted armor, stitched up with a broken system, powers he shouldn't have, and far too much kindness for someone who had been born with no friends or family.

He'd recruited him on nothing more than an impulse. In the previous loop, he'd caught Derivan just as he was dying, stabbed through the chest with an adventurer's sword. Sev had almost dismissed him but caught the whispers of a breath.

I am sorry. I did not want to hurt anyone. I wish . . . I wish I could have been different.

Something about that had stuck with him. He never remembered the words, but even through the universal Reset, the impulse had stayed. Find him again. Give him the opportunity to be who he wanted to be. The impression of the memory lingered, leading him to Derivan.

And Derivan had taken to that opportunity with the fierceness and ferocity of someone who wanted nothing more than the chance to be *kind*.

"The Guild single-handedly deals with probably three-quarters of all the problems generated each Reset," Sev said. "Without it, this world—Obreve—would be much worse off. We didn't have anything to do with that. The Guildmaster built it on her own dreams. She's an amazing woman.

"But like I said . . . I wasn't special. Everything I wanted to do, everything I wanted to create—it was basically already done. I could figure out small improvements here and there, but it would have been the same thing I would be doing back on Earth, I think. Building on the shoulders of giants.

"I guess at some point, I figured that I didn't need to be special. I was . . . happy. Satisfied with my life here. I tried to be kind; I tried to help everyone who needed help. I kept my head down and just lived as close to a normal life as I could for someone accidentally transported to another universe.

"And then . . . we noticed the Void.

"You have to understand—we were much more advanced back then, before half of reality began to collapse. We had devices to measure objective reality. We *knew* when it was weaker, and we could even tell when something was erased from the universe, just by measuring the shape of the hole it left behind. It's not like the Void is the only thing that can do that. There are monsters, most of which are gone now, that do the same thing.

"The Void is only unique because it cannot be stopped. It's almost a lie to give it a name, because it's not a *thing*; it's just . . . the natural decay of this universe. It's supposed to end. We've stretched it long past heat death with magic and technology, and even further still with the anchors. We see worms and creatures and beasts that eat away at reality, but that's all just reality working to comprehend the one thing it cannot: its own end. The Void doesn't have a form. It doesn't have a shape. It isn't something we can fight.

"And we tried anyway."

Sev sighed, collapsing backward into his seat. "It took a long time before we managed to invent the first anchor. We figured out ways to use the Void—ways to slow it down. Ways to preserve information, which we now call infolocks. We used to call those Vaults—people that held precious information that was lost to everyone else, because we didn't have enough energy to let everyone remember it.

"When we managed to invent the first anchor, there was a celebration. Global. All of Obreve celebrated. Every continent, every culture. We thought we solved the problem.

"And then the first anchor failed." Sev gripped the edge of his chair. "I was . . . I was there. I wasn't a healer. I was an engineer. I made little toys for people to enjoy; I didn't . . . I couldn't *fight*. I just watched the people around me die. I had a few tricks I could use to protect myself, but none of them were things I could use to protect anyone else."

Sev looked down, away. "I keep saying 'we,' but I wasn't part of the team working on all this. I only joined after that first anchor broke. We had to figure out a way to fix it, and they lost some of their best scientists. They needed people to work on the problem, and I was there. I could help, a little. I could do maintenance, fix a little code, redirect some of the anchor's subspace.

"But I was never in charge of anything big. That was always other people. Someone better, smarter, faster . . . I felt kind of useless, I guess. Like I wasn't doing enough. Like I needed to be someone more.

"And then I got the chance." Sev's voice turned slightly bitter. "Because everyone important was gone. Sucked away through their sheer metaphysical weight, because that's what the Void is drawn to. That's why we have the anchors. We create metaphysical weight, artificially, and give the Void something to eat. But when the anchors fail, the first people we lose are always the most important.

"Imagine being saved because you're mediocre."

Sev paused there. He waited for the words he always heard—for someone to tell him that he wasn't mediocre, that he'd done everything he could.

But no one said a word. Misa, Vex, and Derivan all watched him with serious expressions, and though he could tell they each wanted to speak, they did not.

Sev was grateful. He'd heard those words a million times, and they'd never made him feel any better. It was a simple fact.

"But metaphysical weight is a funny thing," he said. "It counts your actions and potential based on the raw, physical traits you have. You might be familiar with what we call those things today."

"Stats?" Misa guessed.

"Stats," Sev agreed. "We designed the system to draw the Void to the people and things that can handle it. The anchors and, to a lesser extent, high-level individuals, which is really just a measurement and redistribution of metaphysical weight . . . It's a bit complicated. I wasn't behind a lot of the design, so I can't say exactly how it works.

"We didn't even know what created what we eventually called monsters." Sev gave Derivan an apologetic glance, and the suit of armor just inclined his head in a nod; he didn't mind. "You were the one to find out, Deri. Echoes of people that were already erased . . . We could measure what was removed from reality, but I guess we missed some things."

A small, bitter smile. "A lot of things."

"How did you . . ." Misa gestured, a little helplessly, not knowing how to phrase the question.

"Like I said, I was . . . not exactly the last one standing, but pretty close. I was the last one left with any knowledge of how the system worked. I knew we could Reset it all—we had something like a save state in all the anchors. But it's costly to activate, and we can't restore *everything*.

"I won't lie; the first Reset was based on blind hope that things might be better the second time around. I didn't realize it would wipe my memory the way it did. I didn't realize an entire continent would be just . . . gone.

"It turns out your life can go pretty different when a whole continent is missing. You guys know the rest. I became a cleric, befriended Onyx. At some point, we realized what was happening. I sacrificed everything I could to try to save him. I lost everything I knew about Earth, my memories of my old friends and family . . . my love for making things."

Sev looked down at his hands. "He's been working in the background ever since, trying to guide me every time we have to perform a Reset. Trying to make sure we find the right people, the right minds. But this last Reset, we didn't even do that—all those people we've been working to find, everyone we thought would give us the biggest chance of beating this—they were all gone."

"So we're just people you took a chance on," Misa said. She didn't sound angry. "Glad I wasn't some chosen one."

"You really hate those kinds of stories, huh?" Vex asked with a smile.

"I don't *hate* them," Misa protested. "But I don't feel right being . . . chosen. I'm just me. I love my family; I love you guys. That's all I am! That's all I fuckin' need to be."

"I think that, perhaps, is what made things different." Derivan tilted his head. "You said it yourself—the flaw with metaphysical weighting is that it does not accommodate for emotional drive. Yes?"

"We're gonna fix things this time," Vex said. "Save everyone. No matter what." He stuck out a hand. Derivan placed a hand on top of his, and Misa placed hers on top of theirs; the three of them looked at Sev.

Sev stuck his hand into the circle. "Or my name's not Sev," he said, cracking a half-joke.

Everyone groaned.

CHAPTER 2

CASCADE FAILURE

Sev let himself relax. There was a comfortable sort of silence in the caravan as it rode and bumped along the makeshift path; Vex was poring over his notebooks, Derivan was watching over his shoulder, and Misa was typing away into the system, presumably talking to her family.

It was strange—for everything that had happened to Elyra, for all the chaos they had just witnessed, everything around them seemed just . . . *normal*. The dissonance was jarring. The anchors did their job well, hiding any sign that there was anything wrong with the world at all.

"Do you think we would've found out about all this?" Vex mused out loud. Sev and the others glanced at him, and he elaborated after a second. "If we hadn't done that one mission when all this began, harvesting those mana crystals . . . would we still be *here*?"

"Hitting us with the hard questions, I see," Sev joked, though there wasn't that much humor in his voice. He spared the effort to smile a small smile at Vex when the lizard glanced at him, but truth be told, he felt *exhausted*. Part of it was recent events, and part of it was the weight of all the memories that had been thrust upon him.

He had been through *lifetimes*. None of the memories had been entirely sorted out yet, but it explained so much about that odd feeling of familiarity, the flashes of insight he kept having into people he shouldn't have known. He wondered how much of that was manufactured, and how much of that was Onyx intentionally placing someone into his path.

"I don't know," Sev finally said. "I think Onyx was pulling some strings there, trying to make sure we'd find out as soon as possible, but if we didn't give him the opportunity . . ."

There were so many decisions that had led to this—small and large. What would have happened if they'd allowed Derivan to strike off on his own? If they had chosen to exile Jerome, the paladin who had tried at first to take credit for their discovery? If Misa hadn't been so determined to save her own family?

"I'd say I could find out, but I don't think my skill lets me change a decision that far back," Misa said.

"Also you probably shouldn't try," Sev said. The anchors were strained enough.

"Also that," Misa agreed.

"Regardless," Derivan said, his voice its usual quiet stoicism, "our decisions have led us here. One can only hope that it is enough."

"It will be," Vex said, injecting a bit of false cheer into his voice. "Won't it?"

Derivan smiled at his companion. "For you, I shall do my best."

Vex flushed, burying his face in his hands. Misa barked out a laugh. "When did you learn to *flirt*?"

"I have been paying attention."

"No kidding." Misa grinned. "That's still pretty tame, though. You gotta hit him with something ha—"

"Ahem," the Guildmaster said.

Everyone jumped. Of course they did. Sev physically flinched as seven different versions of the Guildmaster suddenly warred with themselves inside his head—seven iterations that had all done the same thing, building up the Adventurers' Guild to try to mitigate the effects of the anchors.

"When the fuck did you get here?" Misa demanded. "You could at least *knock*!"

"But that isn't nearly as fun." The Guildmaster smiled a serene smile.

. . . That, at least, was largely the same in his memories—though the Guildmaster didn't always have the same *class*. She just found other ways to surprise the people she worked with.

"Why are you here?" he asked quietly. She wouldn't come here herself if it weren't urgent.

Something complicated happened in the Guildmaster's face, a twisting of emotion he didn't quite recognize; she sighed, and suddenly a whole lot of life seemed to leave her, and she looked ten years older.

"We're seeing cascading anchor failures all around Elyra," the Guildmaster said. "I think that's what it is, anyway, based on your report. Dungeons all around are requiring a *lot* more delves to keep them stable, they're considerably more dangerous, and it's getting worse each time. We've already had a few close calls with dungeon breaks."

"Shit," Misa muttered. "I can spare a few clones to help out—"

"There's more," the Guildmaster said, shaking her head. "Nearly all mana nuclei are reporting severely reduced mana crystal production. We can't keep up like this. At our current capacity, we can keep things stable for only two more months, assuming things don't get worse."

"Fuck." Misa closed her eyes. Sev recognized the look on her face; she was trying to organize her thoughts. "Okay. I have some information from my mom—I was talking with her a few minutes ago. We might be able to do something about the mana crystal thing."

"What?" Sev said, surprised.

"It's news to me, too," Misa said. "You remember Fendal and Teque?"

"Hard to forget," Sev said. They'd be passing by Fendal on the way to Anderstahl, and he'd been planning to make a slight detour to break through the shield and . . . do whatever needed to be done. He hadn't actually planned anything further than *break past the shield*.

"They didn't need our help," Misa said, watching the look on his face. She wore a small smile, like she'd wanted to give him the news herself.

Sev blinked, then felt a small feeling of relief blossoming inside him. It was nice when things worked out.

All too often, it didn't.

"Apparently, Noram and Noram—the otter and the lizardkin; they're going by different names now, but Mom hasn't told me what they are—found a way to create . . . soul bonds? Through the system. It helped them both, uh, exist completely. That part's not important. The important part is that a soul-bonded pair only needs to deposit one mana crystal per week instead of two. Something about efficiency in the system.

"More importantly, they *also* found that reality slivers can replace mana crystals in a pinch." Misa frowned. "The system's been working on a way to utilize reality slivers—I think this is it. Whatever automated systems are still running found a way."

"Do they have enough slivers?" Vex asked worriedly.

"For now. It'll give us more time, at least." Misa glanced at the Guildmaster. "I think?"

"It depends on the amount, but as long as we don't have to deal with system sickness, I think we can make things last a few more months." The Guildmaster looked grim—that still wasn't a lot of time, Sev thought, and she knew it too. It felt all too much like things were still falling apart, and though he felt this was the closest he'd ever gotten, he still worried it wouldn't be enough.

Misa gave him a sympathetic glance, as though she knew what he was thinking, and Sev winced. He'd been hoping his doubts wouldn't show.

And still he had so much more to remember. There was more he'd been trying to do; he was sure of it. Right at the end of every two-century period—not that he was awake for most of it—when the system and world were falling apart and they had to hit the reset button . . . in that moment in time where magic, reality, and divinity were all exposed and vulnerable.

There was something he had *seen*. Wasn't there?

Onyx? he asked, reaching through his divine connection with his god—but there was no response. Onyx was *alive*, but the only thing he felt through their connection was a slow pulse of reassuring fire, like things were still running on track.

It didn't assuage his worries, but he did feel a little better.

"Is there anything more we can do to assist?" Derivan's question was more direct. The Guildmaster glanced at him, flicked through her system screens, and then nodded to herself.

"I'll have Max get in touch with you if there is," she said. "For the most part, your duty is to make sure Elyra evacuates safely. You four"—she glanced at Helix and amended herself—"*five* are in charge of keeping this convoy safe."

"The rebel faction is doing a pretty good job of that on their own," Vex commented. "They're . . . better leaders. I think most people trust them."

"They're all well known in their respective communities," Helix said with a shrug. "I'm not surprised people trust them. Heck, if I hadn't known half of them when I was introduced . . ."

"You would've fireballed them?" Vex asked dryly.

"No!" Helix looked affronted and then vaguely chastised, deflating suddenly. "Maybe. I dunno."

Vex snorted—but his gaze flickered to his still-unconscious father, and Sev offered him a sympathetic smile. He didn't know what his friend was going through, but he doubted it was easy . . .

. . . And it said a lot that Vex's mother still hadn't shown up.

"Are you here to recruit?" Misa interrupted his musings with a question, and the Guildmaster gave a wry smile in return.

"I am here to try," she said. "We don't predict a very good return. Most of Elyra is still scared, and your new leaders are too busy wrangling an entire moving kingdom to be able to assist much with the Adventurers' Guild. If you didn't have several anomalies in your path, I'd be sending you out to help with crystal collection and dungeon delving, but as it stands, you're probably this convoy's greatest defense."

"Anomalies?" Vex frowned.

"Anomalies," the Guildmaster confirmed. "We have a couple of [**Intuitionist**]s thanks to Charise, some adventurers with classes focused on precognition and forewarning, and a few clerics from the temples that can divine aspects of the future. Everything is . . . gray right now. You have a lot of dark spots ahead of you."

"What's that mean, exactly?" Misa raised an eyebrow, looking unimpressed.

"It means that every single one of those people *cannot predict* the outcome of events that are coming up in your timelines," the Guildmaster said. "Which I probably should have led with. Look, I have a lot on my mind."

"Do we have any idea what threats we'll be facing?" Vex looked worried. Sev didn't blame him; these were the people he had grown up with, after all.

"None." The Guildmaster sighed. "There are a lot of new dangers popping out of the dungeons, and a lot of them we've never had to deal with before. Just the other day, an adventuring team nearly died because of a snake that had poison that ate away memories. By the time Max got there, they forgot who they were and were fighting among themselves."

"Venom," Vex said automatically, then looked immediately embarrassed. "Um. Sorry."

The Guildmaster looked faintly amused. "Venom, yes," she said. "Just be careful. We're trying to contain the spread, but it's not looking easy. Keep an eye out for anything strange, including strange behaviors from people, just . . . anything out of the norm."

"What about you suddenly appearing in our caravan?" Sev asked, raising an eyebrow. The Guildmaster shrugged, appearing perfectly serious.

"Even that," she said. "Verify it with me through your systems if you can. I'm not kidding when I say what we're up against breaks all the rules. Some of the new dungeonspawned can attack your systems directly."

"Dungeonspawned?" Derivan asked.

"New term." The Guildmaster shrugged. "In light of those like you. You're not the only one from a dungeon that's turned out to be a *person*, you know? The Guild can't do all that much to change public perception, but we can spread the word a little bit. Ask people to be sure that the thing they're killing is an enemy and not someone returned from the Void, even without their memories. Least we can do, right?"

"I suppose," Derivan said. His voice was soft—almost stunned.

The Guildmaster had always been like this. In every previous iteration, she remembered the smallest things and used the Guild to enact the beginnings of change. If the world had been just a little bit different, if it hadn't been falling apart . . .

Sev wondered what she might have achieved.

"I don't suppose we get to know your name yet?" he joked.

The Guildmaster smiled. "It's Alyssa," she said.

A woman stepped out of their caravan, disappearing amongst the crowd.

Misa grumbled something under her breath, rubbing her temples. "It's so strange when she does that," the half-orc grumbled. "Especially now that I know she's doing it. It's like seeing double."

CHAPTER 3

FAMILY PROBLEMS

Vex glanced at his father, a small crease of worry making itself known between his brows. Derivan sat next to him, a comforting presence and a reminder that he wasn't alone in all this. He'd come so far in the last three or so years—he remembered how *afraid* he'd been of his father, not so long ago. He remembered how much it had scared him to leave.

Karix was responsible for a lot of that. His change of heart didn't change what he'd already done. That other version of his father, the one that Irvis had used against him and had ultimately sacrificed himself for him . . . that showed him who his father could be.

But this wasn't that version of him. This Karix hadn't made the same realization, hadn't walked the same path. He'd changed his mind and *helped*, and for that he deserved some credit, but Vex wasn't forgetting that his father had initially planned to betray him.

"It'd be so much easier if I could just forgive him," he muttered out loud. "Or if I could just hate him."

"And yet you would not be you if you found it quite so easy to hate," Derivan said. He placed a hand on Vex's chest, his touch gentle and his voice warm. "You have a good heart. It is one of many reasons I love you."

Vex felt his heart skip a beat, and he ducked his head slightly; even after all this time, he wasn't entirely used to these open displays of affection. His voice when he replied, though, was still uncertain. "Then shouldn't I find it easy to forgive him?"

"He has hurt you, deliberately and continuously," Derivan said. "That he has changed his heart now does not erase what he has already done. Your pain is real, and so is your right to feel it. If you choose not to forgive him, no one would blame you."

"I *want* to forgive him," Vex confessed. "I feel like I have to."

"You do not."

"I know that." Vex leaned into Derivan's touch, resting his head against the metal chest plate, and wondered how it was that the armor could feel so warm though his body was nothing but metal. "I *know* that, intellectually. But . . ."

"You feel it is the right thing to do," Derivan said. He stroked a hand down the back of Vex's head, gently running metallic fingers through the frills and scales. "It is not. There is no right answer here. If you feel like you *must . . .* then perhaps you are not yet ready to forgive him. Not truly. And perhaps that, too, is all right."

Vex managed a small smile. His eyes were wet—when had that happened?—and he laughed a small, affectionate laugh. "When did you manage to get so wise?" he asked, only half-joking.

Derivan leaned down toward him, close enough that their faces were almost touching. His eyes curved in his own version of a gentle smile. "When you gave me a reason to learn," he hummed.

Vex couldn't help his smile now. "You're a hopeless romantic," he accused playfully.

"And would you prefer otherwise?" Derivan's eyes seemed to glow with affection and amusement.

"Not at all."

For all his fears and worries about what would happen—with the world, with his father, with his home—he did now have one constant that would stand beside him.

For him, that meant everything.

—⁂—

It was another three hours before Karix woke.

That was a good thing. If another hour had passed, Vex would have started to really worry. Mana deprivation wasn't supposed to last this long, but nothing felt certain anymore. The system they'd all been relying on was starting to fall apart—Vex wouldn't have been surprised if the basic facts of life began to change, too.

"How are you feeling?" he asked.

It felt strange to be asking Karix that question. It was the same question Karix would pose to *him*, years and years ago, when he was first strapped into the chair to get his mana channels burned into him. There was one specific answer Karix had wanted to hear back then.

Stronger.

"Sore, but it'll pass," Karix grunted, rolling his shoulders and staring around the caravan. "Where am I?"

"In a caravan on the way to Anderstahl," Vex replied shortly.

"Did it work?" Karix tried to sit up but evidently wasn't ready for it; he swayed once, then began to tip back down. Vex caught him before he could slam his head on the hardwood floor.

"Did the spell work? Yes. We got . . . almost everyone out of Elyra. The Speaker is missing. No one realized until yesterday."

"*Yesterday?*" Karix blinked. "How long have I been out?"

"Almost seventy-two hours. You broke the record for mana exhaustion." Vex didn't meet Karix's eyes for a moment. He'd been worried for his father, and that was still strange to him; for most of his life, he'd seen Karix as this invincible, indomitable figure. It was a big part of why it had been so difficult to go against him, and why he'd been afraid to come back.

It was strange, too, to think about how he was probably now more powerful than his father.

"Damn." Karix didn't react much to the announcement. He let his head thump back down onto the floor of the caravan and stared up at the ceiling instead of meeting Vex's eyes. "I feel like shit."

"It's probably the lack of food," Vex said. "Want me to get you something?"

"*Please.*"

It was with some relief that Vex stepped away, though in the limited space of the caravan, that didn't mean much. He put a quick meal together—soft foods, mostly, bread and stew mixed in with a little bit of manavine for mana recovery—and took the time to gather himself.

He was *fine*. This was the first time in years that he was spending any significant amount of time with his father in any non-antagonistic context, where they might be expected to talk and make up. He could do this.

"I can do this," he muttered to himself. Derivan was nearby, watching him, and the armor gave him a small nod at his words; he was letting Vex handle all this by himself. Vex had asked him to.

He wasn't sure if he regretted that decision yet.

Vex made his way back, carefully balancing the bowl of stew in both hands and awkwardly carrying the plate of bread between his teeth. Karix gave him a *look* as he walked in—somewhere between exasperation and affection—and Vex felt a part of himself growing angry.

He wasn't ready for this, he was realizing.

Vex placed the bowl of soup on the ground next to his father, followed by the bread, and watched as Karix dug in ravenously—probably a little too fast to be healthy. He waited.

Karix was the first one to speak.

By this point in time, he'd managed to sit up without falling over again, and had found a chair he could sag into without looking completely undignified. "I guess we have a lot to talk about," he said.

"I guess we do." Vex didn't know if he agreed.

"With Elyra gone, I can't burn in Riss's mana channels even if I want to." Karix let out a sigh. "And Helix talked to me. I *do* understand what I've done."

"I don't think you do," Vex said quietly. "I don't think you *can* know. You aren't any of us. You don't know what channel burning did to Helix, or to Lyssa, or to Varon or Xirra. None of them even had childhoods. *I* barely had a childhood, and you gave me the most freedom out of any of us."

Karix opened his mouth. Vex could almost practically see the words forming in his throat—the same words he'd heard a dozen times before. *I made you stronger.*

Because *strength* was what had mattered then.

There was a tiny voice within him that told him that without his father doing that—without the mana reserves burned into him from childhood— he wouldn't have become the wizard he was. He wouldn't have been able to adventure with Derivan and Sev and Misa, wouldn't have been able to save them from all the dangers that he had.

But he didn't *know* that. He'd spoken to Derivan about this, and the armor had looked him in the eyes and told him with all the sincerity in the world: he believed Vex would have found a way.

Maybe it was time he believed in himself too.

To his credit, Karix swallowed the words before they emerged. He looked down and away for a moment, and when he spoke, it was with a slightly strangled voice. "I'm sorry," he said.

Vex sighed.

"You aren't forgiven," he said. It was oddly comforting to say the words. "Maybe I'll forgive you one day. I'm not taking that off the table. The world is ending, and it feels . . . petty? To care about this. But I'm also not ready to just let go of everything you've done. I want to be, but I'm not."

Karix watched Vex, silent. For a moment, Vex was afraid his father would lash out at him—that he would demand forgiveness for what he'd done. He didn't think Karix had ever handled *rejection* before. Not when he was a noble and nearly everyone would acquiesce to his whims. Not when his own children were afraid of him.

Then Karix closed his eyes and leaned back in his chair. "Okay," he said simply.

"I'm sorry," Vex added reflexively. Karix opened an eye and raised an eyebrow at him, questioning, and Vex frowned at himself. "Or . . . I guess I'm not. This is complicated."

"I made things complicated." Karix shrugged. "There's a lot I want to say. But I'll wait until you're ready. That seems like the least I can do."

"I might never be ready." The words emerged before Vex could stop them, and for the first time, Vex saw his father visibly flinch. Karix didn't respond for a long moment, and Vex didn't open his mouth to take it back.

It was the truth. He didn't know if he would ever be ready. But he was confronting that now instead of denying it, and that was . . . a start.

"Okay," Karix said again. This time, his words were softer, more tightly controlled; Vex saw the tension in his father's arms, in the lines of his throat as he forced down his reaction.

"Thank you." He meant it, too. The old Karix could have made this conversation a lot harder for him. "I'm not . . . I'm not going to ignore you completely or anything. We're still going to need to work together to fix all this."

"That I suspected," Karix murmured. He glanced out of one of the caravan's windows, looking at the immense throng of people nearby. Vex followed his gaze—the entire kingdom of Elyra was just outside. It was staggering to think about.

"Could you leave me alone for a bit, Vex?" Karix asked after a moment. "Just give me some time."

"Yeah, of course." Vex mumbled out the words, then darted out of the room, back to where Derivan was waiting for him. He collapsed into a chair, put up a silencing ward, and then let out a long, slow breath.

"You did right by yourself, Vex," Derivan said gently. Vex leaned into him as the armor sat down by his side.

"It doesn't feel like it," he mumbled.

"Would it have felt right if you had forgiven him?"

". . . No, that wouldn't have felt right either. I think . . . I think it would have felt worse."

"Then you have your answer." Derivan squeezed his arm around Vex's shoulders, and the lizardkin allowed himself to nod a small nod.

"I do want to forgive him. It's just . . . hard."

"I know, Vex. You have a good heart." Derivan paused for a moment. "Perhaps we should go speak to Riss?"

"Oh!" Vex brightened. As much as he hadn't forgiven Karix, he hadn't wanted to leave his side until he recovered. Now that he had . . . "Yes. Let's go."

Derivan smiled, holding out his hand, and Vex took it with a small smile.

At least he had *something* to look forward to.

—⁂—

Elsewhere, worried voices whispered.

"Please tell me you have good news."

"Anderstahl's stability is at 70% and dropping."

"That's not good news."

"We think there's a possibility Seven left something behind to help. He's left divine signatures all over the place."

"Do any of them lead anywhere?"

There was a long silence.

"That's what I thought."

". . . Not to interrupt, but have you guys just considered asking him for help?"

CHAPTER 4

LOSS OF STABILITY

Sev was worried.

This wasn't anything new. He was always worried. But his worry now was something that gnawed at him; he looked out at the world and he saw that it was *wrong*. Flashes of old memories ate at him, telling him how different everything should have been. Everywhere he looked, he saw dreams and ambitions and cultures that had been cut out of the universe, leaving only ghosts behind.

In a way, he was happy that he remembered any of it at all. Whatever trick Onyx had pulled with Misa's reality anchor—or whatever trick *he'd* pulled, considering some of this had been orchestrated with a more-informed version of himself—had worked. He'd been able to regain . . . some of his memories.

That didn't make things much easier. He still had no answers. He didn't know how to fix things. He knew his former self had tried to set something up, that there was a little bit that could be carried over in every Reset, although that space was rapidly shrinking. A small safe space deep within the Void, anchored to stability so that they could build *something* that would fix all this.

The problem, of course, was that he didn't remember any of what he was building. He hadn't wanted the Void to have even a conceptual link to it, and so it was erased out of his mind for him to rediscover every iteration. It was inefficient and dangerous, and it was also the only method he knew that could keep that space safe.

The Void was infectious. It raced through physical reality and conceptual links, eating away at anything that wasn't anchored—and sometimes leaking through the anchors, as Elyra's destruction had proven.

Of course, the result was that for all he knew, he hadn't been able to find a working solution at all, and he'd died before finding anything that could help in all six of his previous Resets.

But if that were the case, Onyx probably wouldn't have let him get this far. Probably.

He wondered what Onyx was up to now. Communication with the god was still sporadic; as far as Sev understood, he was following a path he couldn't know anything about, lest the Void start eating away at it. Onyx resided in the Void specifically because it was disconnected from the rest of reality—the Void did not link within itself—and with him were a few of the remaining dead gods whose echoes remained alive.

It explained some things early on. Sev remembered the moment in the first dungeon, when they'd first acquired the reality anchor. He remembered the other voice Onyx had spoken to while they were floating in what he now knew was the Void, just before they were transported back to reality.

He wondered how many of those gods were left.

"Somethin' on your mind?" Misa asked, and Sev tried not to jump at her sudden appearance. He was sitting on top of their wagon, just staring out at the scenery, and hadn't been expecting her to join him.

"Just . . . everything." Sev gestured vaguely, ignoring the way Misa smirked at him. "It all looks so normal, you know? When I look out at it all. But then I remember everything that we've *lost* . . .

"We used to have phoenixes in the sky," he said quietly, and when Misa gave him a questioning look, he elaborated. "They're kind of an Earth legend, and I think the name caught on here. They're flame-aspect birds that burn themselves to ashes at the end of their lifespans to be reborn from an egg."

"That's morbid as fuck," Misa said plainly. Sev let out a startled laugh, and she looked at him. "What? They're burning themselves alive! That's morbid! Do you think that's *not* morbid?"

"I guess I never thought of it that way," Sev admitted. "We usually see their life cycles as something beautiful. Out with the old, in with the new, or something like that. Rebirth."

"Oddly relevant," Misa observed. Sev cocked his head for a moment, then nodded in understanding, glancing out at the scenery again.

Obreve, their world, was dying. If it could be reborn . . .

But that was a big *if*.

"Does this mean you're remembering more things about Earth?" Misa asked him. Sev hesitated.

"For the most part, no. I gave up most of my memories of Earth with intention. I won't ever remember who my parents were, or what my childhood was like, or what schools I went to. I can remember general knowledge, I guess. I know bits and pieces of Earth culture from the time I was there."

"There's no way to restore your memories at all?" Misa glanced at him, and he saw the look in her eyes. He let out a small laugh.

"Not unless anyone has memories of *me*, and even then, I'd only be able to know what things were like from their perspective," he said. "It'd be like remembering the life of a stranger."

There was a small silence at that admission. Misa didn't seem to know what to say and opted instead for grabbing Sev around his shoulders in a rough, one-armed hug; Sev didn't protest. He appreciated the comfort, really, and if he had to admit the truth to himself...

He needed it.

Sev let himself relax, and his mind drifted. He considered everything they had been through together, everything they'd learned so far—

—and then he sat up with a start.

"Derivan's thing," Sev said.

Misa gave him a strange look. "His what?"

"The [**Flame of the #######**] he got after Misa's bonus room collapsed." Sev tried to put his thoughts together. "Do you have it?"

"No? I don't keep most of our loot." Misa frowned. "Is this about how we forgot to investigate it again?"

"No! I just think I know what it is— Come on; let's get Deri," he said.

Sev hopped off the caravan, his mind racing. *Phoenixes.* They'd been real here. The flame was the flame of a phoenix, representing rebirth.

Maybe—just maybe—it was something they could use.

Sev looked expectantly up at his armored friend, who cocked his head curiously.

"I do have it, yes," Derivan said. "But I do not understand. You say it is . . . the flame of a *phoenix*? A creature of Earth origin?"

"No— Well, maybe." Sev frowned, trying to figure out how to explain it. "The one on Earth is fiction. There was a similar magical species that lived on Obreve. I'm hoping there are similarities that we can use."

"I see." Derivan hummed thoughtfully. He rummaged through his belongings—he really didn't have very many of them and mostly kept them in a small bag he kept lodged within his stomach cavity—and pulled out the [**Flame of the #######**].

It looked just like it had when he first acquired it. A warm, orange glow like a flickering flame held within crystalline amber. It radiated a small amount of heat. Not enough to hurt, but just enough for Sev to feel like he was basking in sunlight, even through the dark clouds that hung overhead.

[**Flame of the Phoenix**], Sev thought. If he had it right. It *fit*. He didn't know what he could do with it yet, but if he was right about what it was . . .

"You said something about phoenixes getting reborn after burning to ashes, right?" Misa said thoughtfully, interrupting his ruminations. "Ya think that might be a phoenix egg?"

Sev blinked.

The system hadn't *called* it an egg, but that meant almost nothing. Names were arbitrary and representative. A flame could refer to a heart, a soul, a core . . .

. . . Or an egg.

An egg that hadn't hatched.

"[**Triage**]," Sev commanded, doing it out loud mostly for the benefit of his companions. Information bloomed in his mind, the system feeding him everything he needed to know about the Flame.

There was a long pause, and then Sev groaned. "Shit. I'm an idiot."

"It's an egg, isn't it?" Misa said, entirely too much smugness packed into her voice. Sev gave her a perfunctory glare and then nodded reluctantly.

"It's an egg," he echoed. "It can't hatch. There's a hairline crack in the amber that's infected with a tiny piece of Void. It's not spreading, because I think the egg is somehow fighting it off, but . . . It can't hatch while it's doing that. Let me just—"

Sev reached out with a healing spell—a system-driven one first, just to test the waters—and flinched when it backfired, divine magic exploding out of the makeshift system-rune and smacking him with enough physical force to make him lurch backward. "Ow."

"Did your healing spell just slap you in the face?" Misa asked, sounding amused.

"Shut up," Sev grumbled. He glanced at the system error screen that popped up.

<ERROR>

No matching template found. Entity does not have health. Entity cannot be healed.

"I should have expected this," he muttered. "The system doesn't know what phoenixes *are* anymore; it can't just restore them with a Shift like it would normally do with health. And the divine magic it uses as a backup suffers from the same problem when it goes through the system. I think even if I bypass it . . ."

Sev grimaced a little, calling forth the power of a god's Domain. It always stung him to channel a Domain like this—it felt like his body wasn't built for it. Fire was an appropriate Domain to call upon here, followed by Time to reverse what had been done to it, and Light for its healing properties . . .

But even the divinity he tried to pit against it was absorbed into that tiny fraction of Void, and Sev gritted his teeth in frustration. It didn't make the Void any stronger, at least, but healing didn't seem like what they needed to fix this.

"We're gonna need to find another way, aren't we?" Misa asked, as if she'd been expecting it the whole time.

"The problem is that the system doesn't know what's supposed to fill in the gap," Sev said with a grimace. "So the reality anchor's got nothing to push back against the Void with. If we had something *close enough*, we might be able to get Deri to approximate it using Shift, and I can do the rest."

"Perhaps a mana crystal or a reality shard?" Derivan suggested.

"No, those aren't . . . We need something that matches this in *essence*. Like a piece of a flame elemental or something, except I don't think we've met any of those in a while. There might have been one in Fendal or Teque . . ."

Sev trailed off thoughtfully. "I'll send Novice a message," he decided. "He or Raltis might have some idea of where we might find an elemental. We could get Vex and Helix to layer some fire magic on the thing, but I don't think that's going to be enough."

If nothing else, at least now they had a plan. Sev let himself feel a little comforted by that, even if he didn't yet know how this would help them in the grand scheme of things.

One step at a time. That was all they could do.

CHAPTER 5

HAYWIRE DUNGEON

Days passed. Sev was still waiting on a response from Novice, who had promised to get back to them and then gone silent for several days in a row. From what he'd heard from Misa, Novice was fine but incredibly busy managing the intricacies of Fendal and Teque. Apparently, their request would take about a week to process, which . . . sure.

The evacuation to Anderstahl was somehow still proceeding smoothly. Sev was surprised—he'd expected a fight to break out by now, or for the rising tensions between the nobles and the so-called common classes to turn into something ugly. The former rebels, however, were remarkably good at keeping the peace.

And also remarkably good at making sure none of their own stepped out of line.

"I think they're adopting some of the Guild's policies," Vex said, when Sev pointed this out to him. "I heard Helix talking about it with Karix—with my dad. He doesn't believe that the Guild's strategies work so well."

"Did Helix manage to change his mind?" Sev asked, raising an eyebrow, and Vex let out a small laugh.

"He made a little progress," the lizardkin admitted, his expression strangely wistful. "He doesn't get it yet. Not really. But he's . . . trying? And it's more than I ever expected from him. I almost . . ."

Vex shook his head and trailed off, choosing to let the sentence die there, and Sev opted not to press. If the lizardkin needed to talk about it, he would; there was an implicit trust there now. Sev gave Vex a small, reassuring smile, and Vex gave him a grateful one in return before hopping up to his feet.

"Wanna go see how Deri and Misa are doing?" he said brightly. "I hear they're training today. Trying to figure out more of Deri's Remembrances. They can do some pretty cool stuff."

"Why don't you go ahead," Sev said, smiling at his friend. "I'll join you guys later."

"Are you sure?" Vex looked up at him, almost pouting. Sev laughed.

"That look works on Derivan, not me," he said, making a shooing motion with his hand. "I'll just be a minute! I want to check my messages, that's all."

"Fine, fine," Vex said. He took two steps, then turned around and raised a finger. "If I don't see you in ten minutes, I'm coming back for you!"

"Yes, yes." Sev waved a hand at Vex. "Go see your boyfriend already!"

Reminding Vex that Derivan was his boyfriend always worked a treat. The lizardkin immediately darted off, weaving with surprising agility through the crowd.

Or not surprising, really. His Agility stat was monstrously high at this point.

Sev glanced over his system. He hadn't been lying, although he'd also wanted a moment to himself so he could prepare. Derivan's Remembrances . . .

Remembrance was an appropriate term. Many of them really did feel like a tribute to the cultures or the people they were from. The problem was that across his lifetimes, Sev had *met* many of those people, many of those cultures. The first time he had sat through Derivan testing his Remembrances, he'd lasted up until the third item Derivan pulled out that was a deeply personal belonging of a close friend who had since been erased.

Then he'd had to excuse himself.

"It's too damn easy to blame myself," Sev muttered into the air. "But it's not my fault, is it? I didn't fail them. I just . . . didn't save them."

There was no answer to be had for him, of course, and the weight on his shoulders did not change. Sev sighed. He knew what his friends would say to him, and he knew that they were *right*; he had done everything he could. It was too easy to fall into the trap of thinking he could have done more.

"All right, I definitely need a distraction," Sev said out loud, and then glanced to his system. He might as well check his messages like he said he would.

There was a new one from the Guildmaster. Huh.

He still had trouble remembering her by her *name*, even though she'd told them what it was. Probably an effect of her specific set of skills. He could remember it with effort if he tried—Alyssa—but for the most part, he still just thought of her as "the Guildmaster."

[You're passing by a village that could really use your help,] she had sent. [I can't spare any other adventurers at the moment or I wouldn't ask you.

We're getting reports of some really abnormal activity from the dungeon near Halis. Think you can make a small detour while the Elyrans go ahead?]

[We can do that,] Sev sent back, feeling—oddly enough—relieved. A task was a distraction, and dungeons were something he was familiar with. [I'll get my team and keep you updated. Anything we should be aware of?]

Sev was only halfway to Derivan and the others when the Guildmaster replied. [There are reports of Void-infected monsters with Void-aspect skills. You're probably the only team that can actually deal with those.]

[Is this happening anywhere else?] Sev asked, suddenly worried.

[Not that we are aware of. I'll send you an update if we get any more reports.] A short pause. [Be careful. Those aren't the only anomalies that have been reported in the area. The dungeon's boundaries are fluctuating and the geography within is unstable. We don't have any good information otherwise, because most of the people that have gone in have died.]

Well, that wasn't encouraging. [I'll keep you updated in case you need to send anyone after us,] Sev sent back, hoping his dryness would translate into text. Then he paused and added it anyway. [Assume I said that in the dryest tone of voice imaginable.]

The Guildmaster didn't dignify that one with a response, which was probably fair. Sev shifted his attention to the raucous sounds of his teammates-slash-family, who were just about now coming into view.

Somehow, Sev wasn't entirely surprised to see Vex sitting on Derivan's shoulders.

"Guys," he called out. He let the divine domain of Sound carry his voice, which was technically an abuse of the power, but the Goddess of Sound, it turned out, delighted in this sort of use of her domain. "We've got a mission."

"A mission besides the one that we're on already?" Misa asked, raising an eyebrow and gesturing to the Elyrans milling around.

"Yes," Sev said plainly. "The refugees don't need us to guard them every step of the way, and we can portal back to them with Shift if there's an emergency. But the Guild doesn't have enough people to send around, and apparently we're uniquely suited to solve this particular problem."

"What problem's that?" Vex asked. Sev looked up at the lizardkin, blinking away the sun in his eyes. It was weird to be talking *up* to Vex for once; he was used to the lizardkin being significantly shorter than all of them.

"Rogue dungeon," Sev said simply. "Something's going haywire over at Halis, and we're the best team to figure it out. It's got Void-aspect monsters and everything, so we're going to have to be careful."

"Well, shit," Misa said. Sev noted that despite her words being grave, she was having trouble hiding the grin on her face. "Guess we gotta deal with this, then."

". . . You're just itching for a fight, aren't you," Sev deadpanned.

"I haven't had a good fight in *weeks*, and the Void isn't a problem I can usually punch in the face," Misa said, folding her arms.

"Yeah! Punch the Void in the face!" Vex cheered.

Sev stared at him, then at Misa. ". . . Did you get him drunk?"

"No, he got himself drunk because Helix told him he couldn't hold his alcohol," Misa said. She looked amused.

"I've been gone for all of five minutes," Sev grumbled. He poked Vex in the small of his back, casting a sobering spell that washed over him and made the wizard sit up straight with a gasp. "Come on."

Halis wasn't far from where they'd set up camp. With a minor speed buff from Sev and Vex combined, they made it to the village in a little under half an hour, and Sev immediately realized that something was wrong.

"Stop," he ordered. Derivan had already stopped and was holding a hand out to prevent Vex from stepping forward any farther. Misa took a second longer to parse the instruction but stopped before she crossed the boundary and into the dungeon.

This wasn't a village anymore. The entirety of Halis was under the domain of the dungeon.

"This wasn't what the Guildmaster said," Sev muttered, mostly to himself. "She mentioned the dungeon boundaries fluctuating, but she would've said something if it had managed to absorb the entire village."

"It is likely to be a recent change." Derivan's eyes glowed gently as he scanned the area in front of them, presumably using Shift to determine the exact dungeon boundary. Sev could sense that something was *wrong*, because he could sense an area ahead where the domain of divinity simply cut off, like a dead zone to the gods—and even that was a problem. Dungeons were not impermeable to divinity. Healing spells had always had their full effect within a dungeon.

"The line is here," Derivan added, using a spark of mana to trace a web of lines over the dungeon boundary. "The dungeon appears to have a compromised reality anchor. I am analyzing it with Patch."

A small pause. Sev waited to see what Derivan would find, and Vex looked ahead worriedly at the village of Halis. There were still no signs of life. Misa's fists were clenched, impatience skittering across her expression.

". . . The Void is directly interfering with the integrity and self-destruct mechanism in the anchor," Derivan said. There was a clear frown in his voice. "I cannot repair it. Any repair I attempt is immediately dissolved. The infection does not currently appear to be progressing, but it is likely only a matter of time."

"Shit," Sev muttered. "Is there anything we can actually do about it?"

"I suspect delving the dungeon will only make things worse," Derivan said. He paused for a moment, scanning something that was invisible to Sev, and when he spoke again, it was with significantly more concern. "If I am interpreting this correctly, the recent domain expansion is almost certainly due to a successful delve. The Void appears to hijack the mechanism used to distribute rewards to distribute itself throughout the anchor."

"That sounds worryingly like it's intelligent," Vex said, shuddering slightly.

"I do not believe that it is." Derivan hesitated. "But the Void may be . . . echoing the intelligence of the people it has consumed. What it is doing here is not unlike some of the Remembrances I gained from my time in the Void."

"Why now?" Misa demanded. "What's different?"

"Nothing," Sev says quietly. "We can Reset the world with the anchors, but we can't Reset the Void. It's been growing, and the anchors have been breaking. The system won't be able to keep things intact for much longer."

He took a breath. "We will go in and evacuate the village, if there is anyone left to evacuate. We will not interact with the dungeon more than necessary. Do not accept any dungeon challenges; do not accept any dungeon rewards. In and out as quickly as possible. Derivan, can you sense anyone in the village?"

Derivan shook his head. "The internal geometry is greatly warped," he said. "There are signs of life but no certain location. I can barely get Shift to work within its boundaries, and I cannot open any portals."

"All right," Sev said. "Doesn't matter. If we know people are alive, we're going in. I'm going to send an update to the Guildmaster so she knows delving dungeons might make things worse. Sound good?"

Everyone agreed, and together, they stepped through the dungeon boundary.

—⁓—

Xothok stood in front of a massive steel door. Ale— *Alyssa* was beside him, making a few last-minute checks on her gear. She muttered a low complaint to herself as she realized that yet another one of her daggers had begun to crack and fall apart, small filaments of Void rendering it unusable.

Then she glanced up, as though alerted by the system, and narrowed her eyes. "Shit," she said.

"What?" Xothok asked. Alyssa cursing was almost never a good sign.

"We may not want to complete this dungeon." She glanced up at the iron door, scanning it as if hoping she could find an answer there. "The symptoms here are very similar to what Sev and his crew are experiencing, and they've reported that completing a delve can make the dungeon worse."

". . . Isn't the whole point of delves to maintain dungeons?" Xothok asked. He was pretty sure that was what he'd heard in the briefing. Then again, he also hadn't been completely paying attention during the meeting.

"Yep." Alyssa frowned, glancing back down the passage at the way they'd come. It was sealed off—this was a dungeon that sealed them into a bubble of stone as they navigated an invisible maze, the walls opening before them and closing behind them. It corralled them slowly toward the boss room, too. Xothok could sense the passageways in the earth shifting every so often, making it so that every step they took led them farther and deeper in.

There was, theoretically, no way to leave.

"Think we have a choice?" Alyssa asked.

Xothok considered the question for a moment. He thought about what he'd come here to do—to reconnect with Alyssa and learn more about how her life had gone. Alyssa had joked about it being . . . a date? And Xothok had mostly managed to keep a straight face and hide the fact that he was interested.

She'd also shown him up the entire way here, being Platinum and all.

But this dungeon was a *maze*, and he had been an [**Astral Navigator**].

"'Course we do." Xothok felt a grin creep up his expression. It had been a long time since he'd felt like he was having an adventure. Getting into this dungeon had felt like a job.

Getting out?

Now *that* felt like it could be fun.

CHAPTER 6

EVEN IN THE SHADOWS

The village of Halis was disturbingly empty.

Sev's heart sank as they wandered cobblestone streets, looking into every building to see if they could find any survivors—and more and more, it was looking like there weren't any, despite both Derivan and Vex claiming that they could sense life here. Misa's own attempts with her skills had turned up nothing. She'd tried searching all the realities generated by her alternate selves, sending them down different streets and into different houses.

The worst part was the fact that everything else about the village was perfectly intact.

There was no sign that there had been a struggle anywhere in Halis. No furniture tipped over, no scratches in the wood or damage on the stone from skills being slung around. The meals that sat on dining tables were still warm, with a gentle haze of steam and the mild aroma of spice and meat drifting over the room.

In any other setting, it would have seemed warm and inviting—but with the dungeon's oppressive domain pushing down on them, it just felt *wrong*.

"You're sure there are still survivors here?" Sev asked, for the umpteenth time.

Vex looked troubled. He traced a glyph in the air, the pattern looking something like a leaf encased in a lens, and peered through it. "I still see signs of life," he said quietly. "I just can't pinpoint any of it. It's like they're . . . scattered."

"Or Shifted," Derivan agreed. "But if they are, it is beyond my ability to sense them, and that is unusual in itself. I do not know what would allow them to hide from me like this."

"So what the fuck is going on?" Misa muttered. She scanned the air, holding her mace out as if she thought she could ward off whatever was happening here with it, which Sev supposed she technically *could*. Sort of. Misa's eyes narrowed slightly as she seemed to trace *something* across the room, and then she suddenly straightened. "I'm going to try something," she announced, and then before Sev could say anything about it, she vanished.

"Wha— Misa?!" Sev hurriedly called up the system to see if anything had happened to her, but her health readout hadn't changed; she was physically healthy but apparently *missing*.

Her mana, on the other hand, was dropping in chunks. Sev realized what had happened in the same moment Misa reappeared, panting and nearly doubling over; she steadied herself on the nearby table, trying to catch her breath.

"Misa?" Vex asked. "Are you okay?"

Rather than replying, Misa gave the lizardkin a thumbs-up, gulping down a few more breaths of air as she did so. Her skin glistened with a sudden sheen of sweat, and she retched once or twice; it took her a moment to steady herself and her stomach.

"I'm fine," Misa said. She didn't *look* like she was fine. Sev eyed her critically, and she rolled her eyes. "I *will* be fine. The dungeon or something in it is actively distorting the people here—that's why we can't track any of them. I tried to block it, but it's a constant attack, and there's so many of them that they'd just disappear again as soon as I cancel the block."

"I cannot sense what the dungeon is doing." Derivan seemed perturbed by this fact. "This is a spectacular use of Shift, if that is indeed what is happening. I cannot imagine . . ."

"It's not Shift," Vex said. His eyes glowed as he pushed his mana sense to its maximum, scanning the environment around them—and then the color of it changed as he tuned it further. "Or not entirely Shift. It's spatial magic. I didn't sense it before because it's slightly Shifted and attuned to be harder to detect."

"Do I want to know what kind of spatial magic it is?" Sev asked, already dreading the answer.

Vex closed his eyes before responding; when he opened them again, the glow had faded, and he seemed marginally paler. "The kind that splits you apart into a thousand pieces but keeps them all connected," Vex said grimly. "Misa disappeared because, I imagine, she had to protect every piece at the same time. Or however many she could without instantly dying."

"Yeah, that sounds about right for how shit it felt," Misa said. She cracked her neck and let out an irritated grumble when it refused to cooperate. "Like I was being yanked a million different ways at once."

"If it's spatial magic, can you counter it?" Sev asked Vex. The lizardkin didn't answer for a moment—he hesitated, staring at the air as if he could discern an answer from the ceiling tiles—before he eventually nodded.

"I think I can," he said, and then his eyes hardened. "I can. I'll need time to set up a ritual."

Sev nodded. He trusted the lizardkin.

"We'll set up watch in the meantime," Sev said. "Since we're technically in a dungeon. Can't forget about the monsters."

—◆—

It didn't take long for the first monster to spawn.

Dungeons challenged adventurers; it was what they did. It wasn't *surprising* that monsters began to spawn soon after the dungeon detected new delvers within it. What was surprising was that the dungeon hadn't sent these monsters after the villagers themselves and had instead held them hostage in an intricate web of spatial magic.

Sev didn't understand it, exactly, but he figured they would find out soon enough.

It was a dark, spindly thing that emerged from the shadows. Misa was the first one to spot it—Sev saw her narrow her eyes and then jerk her mace toward what seemed like a completely normal albeit unusually dark alleyway. A second later, the darkness began to pool into spidery legs and . . .

. . . Nope, it was just legs. The whole thing was legs.

<**Level 72 Legs**>

The system apparently wasn't feeling very creative either.

Sev yelped when it scrambled toward them, abnormally fast, mostly because the way it moved was jerky and unnatural; Derivan stepped forward calmly and grabbed it in one of his gauntlets, and then Misa smashed her mace into it.

Several times.

Your party has killed a level 72 Legs!

It was kind of anticlimactic, really. After all the dangers they'd encountered on the way here—the people they'd had to fight—a monster like this was trivial to beat.

"Watch the shadows," Sev instructed. Mostly unnecessarily. Derivan and Misa were already eyeing every stray alleyway cautiously, their backs to one another.

Which meant Sev was the only one in a position to see it when their own shadows melted together and something else started to emerge.

"Behind!" he called out, and he took several quick steps forward, just in case a new monster had begun to emerge from his own shadow. It was lucky that he did, too; a dark claw slashed through the space he'd been in a moment later, rippling the air as space was torn apart around it. Sev's heart seized as he looked at it—that wasn't a normal attack.

Misa and Derivan seemed to realize the same thing. Both of them had leapt back from the monster that appeared between them, and Sev glanced at the system tags.

<Level 86 Shadowskitter>
<Level 92 Shadesplitter>

The Shadesplitter was the one that had attacked him. The Shadowskitter was living up to its name—it was *small*, a tiny, buglike thing that stood between Derivan and Sev with an aura of menace. It would have been amusing if not for the fact that its entire body was rippling with spatial magic and Void.

The Shadesplitter, on the other hand, was a mantis-like thing with bladed arms that sang with spatial magic.

The increase in level wasn't lost on Sev. The dungeon had evaluated how dangerous they were and evidently decided they were more of a threat than it first assumed. A quick glance within the house they were protecting showed that nothing had spawned within yet, but it was very possible that it was only a matter of time.

Dungeons didn't *normally* spawn monsters within their designated safe spaces, but this was very far from a normal dungeon.

"Think these are the things that took out the villagers?" Sev asked grimly.

"Almost certainly," Derivan responded, his hand resting on the hilt of his sword.

"No shit," Misa snorted. "Let's take them out."

As one, they moved.

Misa split into several copies of herself. Derivan summoned a Remembrance into his hand, a pale, glasslike orb that shone with strange colors. Sev called on his bond with the God of Light.

These were shadow creatures, after all.

The Shadowskitter was *fast*. True to its name, it skittered along the floor, dodging Misa's attempts to crush it with her mace; it didn't help that it was small and none of them were quite used to fighting opponents that were that much smaller than they were. Derivan frowned, then made a twisting motion with a hand—a Shift.

The Shadowskitter disappeared and warped into the air, where it scrambled desperately for purchase. Misa didn't give it a chance—before it could land, she slammed her mace into it like a bat, sending it flying and crashing into a nearby wall.

It wasn't dead, Sev knew. There had been no notification for it. But at these levels, nothing was really going to die from one hit.

He shifted his focus to the Shadesplitter. Unlike its smaller counterpart, it was waiting and watching, almost like it was intelligent. It had eyes that glowed a soft green, and Sev tensed, waiting for it to make the first move—

Misa threw her mace at it.

The Shadesplitter blocked, of course, but that was only one of her copies; she charged up almost immediately after, following up with a kick below the blades and between its legs, then attempting to crush her mace into its skull. It raised a bladed foreleg to block that, too, and at the last second, Misa shoved herself away before her mace could come into contact with it.

Sev saw why. The first mace she'd thrown—the copy—was cut clean in half, a ripple of spatial magic keeping the two pieces only technically intact. The Shadesplitter glared at them, letting out a skittering roar, then charged toward Derivan, who threw the glass Remembrance he held at the ground.

It exploded into a sharp burst of light that glimmered with color. Sev thought he recognized it for a sharp, painful second, as a brief memory of fireworks and festival touched on his mind; he pushed it aside to stay focused on the fight, and seized upon his Divine Domain to take control of the light before the Remembrance's power faded.

Light swirled like a physical thing, a brief flash and glittering color turning into a torrent and a river. Sev felt the God of Light open the connection between them a little more, lending more power to him than he strictly should have; he felt the light he held in his grasp shine even brighter as everything around them darkened.

The shadows grew as he gathered up the light. The Shadesplitter shrank back, almost fearfully.

And then it spoke in a hissing, broken voice. "*S . . . Stop. Stop. Stop.*"

The Shadowskitter wove in from where it had impacted the wall. With all the light he had gathered, Sev almost didn't see it. It ducked underneath the light he carried, then leapt, tiny claws gathering enormous amounts of spatial-Void magic that screamed like sharp razors even to Sev's unattuned senses.

Straight toward the Shadesplitter.

CHAPTER 7

THERE CAN BE LIGHT

If there was anything that could be said for Sev's team, it was that they didn't hesitate to act when it counted.

All they needed to hear was the Shadesplitter trying to speak.

Sev directed the light toward the Shadowskitter. Misa appeared in front of the Shadesplitter, putting her back at its mercy in order to defend it from the Shadowskitter. The air shifted around Derivan as he called Shift into play, creating a layer of *separation* between the Shadesplitter and the rest of physical reality, in part to protect Misa and in part to protect it.

Then everything happened all at once, very, very quickly.

The Shadowskitter *screamed*, a powerful, resonant sound that cracked through the air and rippled into Misa, whose mace became something like a giant bowl as she blocked it. The Shadesplitter pulsed strangely, body warping as the remnants of the soundwave came into contact with it.

The light crashed into the Shadowskitter and shone so bright Sev could see it through his eyelids.

Your party has killed a level 86 Shadowskitter!

All that remained was an echoing, remnant scream. Sev took a breath, staring at the scorched section of the floor that marked where the Shadowskitter had once been. There was nothing there but blackened stone now.

The Shadesplitter was still there. It wasn't trying to fight them anymore; instead, it was making agitated, sharpening motions with its arms, sliding them against one another and creating small sparks of magic.

Spatial magic. But no Void, Sev realized. It almost looked like it was anxious; the motion was jerky and repetitive. After a few repetitions, it seemed to calm, and the motion slowed to a stop.

"Do you want to explain what's happening?" Misa's voice wasn't harsh, but it wasn't exactly gentle, either. The Shadesplitter shrank back from her words and immediately began sliding its arms against one another again, agitated just by the question.

Derivan stepped forward, crouching in front of it. "You are scared," he said. "You are confused. You are new to this?"

It nodded. It seemed to relax a bit. Derivan was large enough that he blocked the Shadesplitter from being able to see Sev or any of the other two, and that apparently helped a bit.

"Did you do all this?" Derivan asked. He nodded back toward the empty town. The missing townspeople, he meant.

Slowly, shyly, the Shadesplitter nodded again. "S . . . *Save. Save them. Save them.*"

Sev's brows furrowed. It had tried to save the townspeople? But its skills were rooted in splitting things apart with spatial magic . . .

. . . Oh.

"Did you cut them apart so they wouldn't be hurt by anyone else?" Sev asked, too shocked to regulate the tone of his voice. The Shadesplitter shrank back again, and Derivan gave him a reproachful look.

"You tried to protect them?" Derivan rephrased. It took a moment for the Shadesplitter to calm down enough to respond.

"*Save them,*" it repeated, with a little more confidence this time. "*System . . . System says. Strike. I . . . strike. But I do not kill.*"

Sev ran through what it was saying in his head.

The Shadesplitter had experienced the same System compulsion that Derivan had. Unlike Derivan, it had no way to fight against it and no friends to help, so it had done the only thing it knew how to—it *cut*. It used the only skill available to it to make sure that the people it cut stayed alive, connected to all their disparate parts, and then it made sure the pieces were too small for anyone else to harm them.

"Why?" Derivan asked. The Shadesplitter seemed to frown at the question.

". . . *Savior,*" it finally said. "*Salvation. Friends.*"

Sev had no idea what it meant by that one. He glanced at Derivan, whose eyes glowed softly as he knelt in front of it. "You were a town hero?" he asked, and it nodded.

"*Stranded,*" it hissed. This time, Sev thought he heard a note of bitterness in its voice. "*Forsaken. Forgotten.*"

"That was the Void, not them," Sev said. This time he thought he understood, and this time he managed to keep his words calm. True to his guess, the Shadesplitter didn't flinch away from him. "It erased you from their memory."

It had been trying to save a village it thought had forgotten about it; to know that they hadn't done so *deliberately* was probably a huge relief. The Shadesplitter didn't respond, but Sev thought he could see the emotion in its face; its arms trembled slightly, and it dipped its head.

"*Sorrow,*" it said.

"You cannot bring them back," Derivan surmised. "This was the extent of what you could do."

The Shadesplitter nodded mournfully.

"We have a solution for that problem." Derivan glanced back toward the home they'd appropriated for Vex's ritual, and Sev followed his gaze. The dungeon had apparently exhausted whatever resources it had spent on generating the three enemies they had to fight; Vex, thankfully, hadn't had to deal with high-level monsters mid-ritual. As far as Sev could tell, anyway. "And then perhaps a solution for yours, too."

"*Solution?*" the Shadesplitter asked hopefully.

Misa grunted. Sev glanced at her, then quickly sent a heal her way, realizing what she was doing; as soon as she understood the situation, she'd started blocking the bond the system used to control the Shadesplitter. She hadn't said a word about it, either. Her face was strained in concentration.

They needed to get the townspeople and the Shadesplitter out of this first. It was a miracle that they were all still alive—a miracle that wouldn't last once the dungeon recharged and sent even more monsters after them.

"Solution," Sev echoed. "Come on; let's get going. We gotta make what you did count."

—⟋⟍—

It took about a minute for Sev to explain everything that had happened to Vex, and their new understanding of the situation in the dungeon.

"Oh, good," Vex said, sounding relieved. "The last piece of magic this needs is some of the original spatial magic that took them apart. I wasn't sure how I was going to get my hands on that. Um . . . You should probably hide, though. When I bring them back."

Sev winced. He hadn't thought about that. The Shadesplitter drooped a little, and Sev sighed.

"Whatever your intentions were, all they know is they were attacked and torn apart. They don't know that you were trying to save them, and some of them might resent you for it anyway." The experience was probably close to torture for more than a few of them, but Sev didn't want to say it quite like *that*.

The Shadesplitter seemed to understand, though. It withdrew into itself a bit, curling up and sinking slightly into the shadow. Then it shook it off and stepped forward anyway, looking to Vex for instructions.

Vex nodded toward the center of his circle. "Cut here," he said softly.

The Shadesplitter *cut*, and magic blasted outward.

—⁂—

Sev would find it difficult to describe what happened in the aftermath of the spell. There was a coalescence, for lack of a better word—a moment where the air vibrated and sang with power, and particulate matter in the air began to draw back together. Visually, it looked a lot like people blurring into existence, except it happened all at once, together with bright bursts of light that made it difficult to see.

The Shadesplitter had hidden within a shadow as soon as the spell began in earnest. Sev knew it was only a matter of time before the dungeon commanded it to attack again—Misa couldn't protect it from the call of the system forever.

"We need to evacuate everyone as quickly as possible," he said. "Misa. Can you use your duplicates? I'll keep you topped up on health."

Misa gritted her teeth and nodded. "Just gotta be quick about it. Not sure how long I can keep this up, but it ain't gonna be long."

"Vex, Derivan, if you have anything that can speed this up and keep them safe, now's the time to use it," Sev said. He had a few divine spells up his sleeve he could use—the major one was one that would freeze Misa's health in place for a while, which would hopefully reduce how taxing all this was on her.

The other spells would create shields around each of the townsfolk and slow down time in the dungeon so they could be grabbed and evacuated as quickly as possible. There would be time for fear and panic later, after they were out of range of the dungeon.

Vex had his own magic he was casting. Sev saw streams of mana pouring out of their wizard, wrapping around each civilian as they appeared in a bubble of protective magic. Derivan pulled out a Remembrance, something that looked like a rope that pulsed with spatial magic. Anyone he touched with it disappeared; in his divine sense, Sev could feel them reappear back outside the dungeon. Misa's duplicates grabbed them and physically carried them out.

Around them, the dungeon roared to life, and new monsters started to spawn.

Their attacks bounced off the shields that both Sev and Vex had wrought, and Derivan and Misa reached many of the targets before the monsters could even get there. But Halis was a large town—it was a wonder that the Shadesplitter had managed to get to so many of them to begin with.

Darkness wrenched around one person, and Vex's shield sputtered out. The golden light from Sev's own skill faded a moment after, and it was only Derivan desperately lunging toward them and tagging them with the rope that saved them from getting torn apart.

They weren't moving fast enough.

And just as Sev had that thought, the Shadesplitter reappeared. It roared. It attacked, and Sev's heart froze for a moment.

But it was attacking the other monsters.

CHAPTER 8

THE END OF THE WORLD

They couldn't save everyone, in the end. Even with the Shadesplitter's help, even with all the powers they had working with them—there were too many to save, and the dungeon's monsters were too many in number. Creating three high-level monsters was one thing, but Halis's civilians weren't nearly as high-leveled; the dungeon didn't *need* powerful monsters to kill them.

It just needed a lot of them. Enough to get to people before either Sev or Vex could get to them with the shields, before Derivan could get to them with the rope. Enough to do it before Misa could notice it and block, because she still needed to know what she was blocking.

The Shadesplitter roared in frustration, and Sev's heart was heavy.

They had saved most, though. They were outside the dungeon now, and the townspeople were looking around in fear and concern, and there wasn't time for them to panic.

"The dungeon's boundaries are still expanding," Sev said. "We need to run. *Now.*"

There was a note of command in his voice, imbued to him by a divine presence. Sev felt a little guilty for using it, but it wasn't anything as violating as mind control; all it did was make sure the command came through clearly, piercing the veil of panic that had started to overcome a lot of them. Some stumbled, but most started to run, and Vex created a giant arrow of mana in the sky to help.

"This way!" he called. Sev appreciated it. He hadn't thought of that at all.

In this way, they were able to make it back. The Elyran refugees had made some progress in the time without them—more than he'd thought, actually, which meant it took some effort to catch up—but they *did* catch up, in the end. Sev offloaded the Halis townspeople to Helix and the other leaders of the Elyran rebellion to let them bring them up to speed; they were pretty much the de facto leaders of the expedition, anyway.

Sev had bigger concerns. Mostly the fact that the gods were pinging him rather urgently, and several of them were gods that were worshiped heavily in Anderstahl. He gestured for his teammates to wait for him in the caravan and tapped into his divine connection—

SEV!

A dozen voices screamed at him at once. Some of them were quieter, and not all of them said his name; one called him a *supplicant*, and another one just said *boy*. He was pretty sure he knew who those gods were, and he suppressed the wave of irritation that followed.

I was busy, he responded down the connection. There was a clamoring on the other side, like a dozen different presences were fighting over who got to speak—Sev rolled his eyes, though he knew the situation must have been serious to warrant this kind of response—before Tempus finally took control of the line and spoke.

Sev, Tempus said. The god of time's voice was urgent and hurried, as if he knew he didn't have much time—and that was worrying. Sev knew the man as a slow and patient speaker. Time was his domain, and he never needed to hurry. *Anderstahl is beginning to fall to the Void as well. We do not have as much time remaining as we hoped.*

Shit, Sev responded. It was meant to just be a thought, but he accidentally sent it along the connection anyway . . . *How much time do we have?*

Weeks, Tempus said.

It would take weeks for their convoy to even reach Anderstahl. The last Prime Kingdom was supposed to be a bastion for all of them. If what Tempus was saying was right, they would arrive just in time to watch the kingdom fall just as Elyra had.

You have a solution, Sev said. He wasn't sure if it was a question or a statement; his tone was pleading. He *wanted* there to be a solution.

Yes, Tempus said cautiously, and Sev experienced a wave of relief before Tempus continued, *perhaps.*

Why perhaps? Sev demanded, a touch more impatient in his mental voice than he actually wanted.

There is a contingent of humans that are looking for you, Tempus said. *They are well shielded, and they seem to know more about the Void situation than almost anyone else. We would not have found them if Onyx had not guided us—they are hidden even from divine senses.*

What the fuck?

Sev's brain stuttered to a halt. Humans? Looking for him? The people he was closest to were his team and, to a lesser extent, the Guildmaster and some of the clerks who worked at the various Guild branches he visited. He didn't know anyone else who knew him, especially not anyone who knew about the Void, and *especially* not anyone powerful enough to keep themselves hidden even from divine senses.

They may have a solution, Tempus added, unnecessarily. *We do not know much about them. Only that they are searching for you and that they know about the Void. But if there exists anyone that may know how to delay the Void's expansion...*

It would be a group of mysterious humans who happened to know about the expansion of the Void, yes. Especially if they were looking for him.

They have left a beacon for you, Tempus said. *We thought it was nothing, at first—divine noise sent out by the death of another god. It was only Onyx pointing us in the right direction that allowed us to identify it as something more.*

There was something about how casually Tempus had mentioned the *death of another god* there. Like it had been happening for a while and he'd gotten used to it. A thought hit Sev, and he searched desperately for his connection with Aurum—

—It was still there. Weaker, certainly, but still there. Aurum sent a weak pulse of gratitude down their link for his concern, and Sev brushed it aside. *Tempus, what's been happening to the gods?*

For a kingdom to be eroded, its gods must be destroyed, Tempus said grimly. *The anchors pull at us to supplement their power. If they lose integrity...*

They would eat away at all of them, trying to fuel itself to save an empty kingdom.

I did not want to tell you this way, Tempus added, his tone a touch sorrowful. He'd tried to hide it, Sev realized. He wouldn't have said anything if Sev hadn't called out his phrasing.

...How do I find the beacon? Sev asked.

Reach out with your divine sense, Tempus said. *I will guide you.*

Sev didn't waste any time.

It took him only moments to let Derivan, Misa, and Vex know what was going on; all three of them were worried, but none of them could do anything for this. He was at the center of it all, and he needed to go find out what this group of humans wanted from him. If they were lucky, they would have a solution.

If they weren't . . . they'd find another solution. They had to.

Which was one of the reasons Sev chose to do this by himself.

He was reluctant to part with his teammates, but they were being stretched thin enough as it was, and they couldn't afford all four of them to be caught up in something that didn't guarantee them a solution. There was another potential avenue they needed to explore—Teque.

The mana had been able to hold against the Void for years, in that other history. The bonus room in Elyra was gone, but Teque wasn't; the primordial river of mana there still existed. The mages there, with all their knowledge of the old ways and how mana behaved—they were still there.

Only because they had bonded with Fendal's citizens, as Sev understood it. When Elyra had started to fade away, *something* about Teque had started to destabilize, but their connection with Fendal helped them hold strong.

Misa's village had a loose connection with Fendal because of how Charise, Volaro, and Juni had helped with Fendal's rebellion. There was some kind of link there to Misa's skill that they thought could be exploited—some way to fold both Fendal and Teque into the protection of Misa's skill and, vice versa, allow Misa's skill to be fueled by the integrity of the two villages.

It would, they hoped, bolster her reality anchor, which might very well become the last bastion for them if things kept going the way they were going.

Vex and Derivan would go to Teque. The wizards in the city of magic had been working on a solution for the Void, and although their glyphs had yet to be able to fight it directly, they had apparently been able to make *some* progress by folding the magic of the Roads into their spells. The Roads, after all, had been gifted to them by the mana to allow them safe travel in the world otherwise ravaged by the Void—it made sense that the magic within could be used in some capacity to fight it off.

Even then, that ability was limited.

"Good luck, guys," Sev said firmly. It was a serious moment. They were going to split up here, and if he was being honest, he didn't know if he'd see any of his friends again. "If I don't see you guys again—"

"Fuck that," Misa interrupted. She grabbed him, then Vex, and proceeded to crush them both against Derivan. "Group hug. We're gonna do this, you guys. We're gonna fucking do this."

Sev didn't know how she managed to sound so confident, but he saw the way everyone's spirits were lifted by her. He managed a smile himself as he hugged them back, letting himself be drawn into the warmth of their companionship just for a moment.

"See you later," Misa said firmly.

"Right, right," Sev said with a small chuckle. "See you later."

And just for a moment, Sev let himself believe it. He *would* see them again, even if he had to tear down the Void to do it.

The doubt in his heart could go fuck itself.

CHAPTER 9

JOURNEY

Activating his divine sense again gave Sev a unique, dizzying sense of vertigo as a path suddenly manifested in front of him—not *literally*, but metaphorically. There was a mental map telling him exactly where to go and exactly what time he'd reach each milestone; Sev suspected this was Tempus's way of helping, as he wouldn't have been able to make time this well if he'd been going on his own.

According to Tempus, he would arrive at his destination in thirty minutes, which was a wild abuse of divine temporal magic if Sev had ever seen one. He wasn't complaining, though. It wasn't like Tempus was forcing him to experience all the subjective time he was skipping; hiking for two days without stopping would be hell.

As it was, Sev fast-forwarded through the hike, working through the pack of supplies he had brought with him at a steady pace. Healing, unfortunately, could not fully replace food and water.

His heart sank when he arrived.

"Don't judge too early, Sev," he muttered to himself. The area in front of him looked like an empty space—just a blank stretch of grass with nothing in it. He could feel the divine energy floating in the center of it all, just past the border to the Outskirts, but there was nothing *there*. The idea that this whole trip might have been a waste of time weighed heavily on him. Even if it had only taken thirty minutes, it had cost a large expenditure of Tempus's divine power, and it meant he was now separated from his friends, who might need his healing. ". . . This better not have been a waste of time."

He took a deep breath, stepped forward twice more, and almost flinched when everything changed around him.

Sev was familiar enough by now with Derivan's use of his powers to know what a Shift felt like, even if he didn't have any senses specifically tuned for it. The sky darkened, the grass around him grew a little less vibrant, and the quiet sounds of the breeze rustling through the grass dampened down to almost nothing; at the same time, two figures appeared in front of him—a human man and woman.

He sighed.

"Did you really have to do the dramatic-appearance thing?" Sev complained.

The man in front of him smirked. "You haven't changed, Sev."

"And I have no idea if you have, whoever you are," Sev said.

"We'll get to that." The man exchanged glances with the woman, an unreadable look passing between them. Sev huffed in annoyance. "First, how much of your past do you remember?"

"Some of it," Sev said. "Not all of it. Most of it is still a jumbled mess."

"But you remember *more*?" the man insisted.

"More than I did a week ago, I guess," Sev said. He narrowed his eyes. "Why?"

"Because we need you to remember if you left us a way to fix the anchors," the man said. "We're barely keeping Anderstahl stable as it is. If you don't have a way to stabilize it . . ."

"Then we have days left, not months," the woman next to him cut in. "Integrity is dropping fast. We can mask it with some of the tools you left behind, we can even stabilize it or act as pseudo-anchors, but none of those is going to buy us more time than a few days."

Sev rubbed the bridge of his nose. "Well, I have good news and bad news," he said.

"What's the bad news?" the man asked.

"I have no idea how to fix an anchor and I'm pretty sure I didn't leave anything behind that could help."

". . . And the good news?"

"I think I have a way to stabilize it anyway." Sev pulled a reality shard out of his pocket. "You should have contacted the Guild. Everyone has some idea of what's going on now. At this point, we're all working together to find a solution."

There was a long pause.

"I think you'd better come with us," the man finally said.

"Can I at least get your names?" Sev asked, resigned.

"Right. Uh, I'm Muchen, and this is Aisha. You're probably wondering how we even know you."

"I would *very much* appreciate it if you started giving me some answers, yes."

"Right, right. Well . . ."

—⁊⁊⁊—

Teque had *changed*. Derivan was startled by how much it had changed. Everything was different, from the people roaming the streets of the underground city to the very feeling of the mana in the air.

Beside him, Vex experimentally cast a spell—first a glyph-based one, and then another one through the system. Unlike the last time they'd tried this, there was no backlash; the mana didn't react violently to the system's attempt to control it. Instead, it flowed together, almost as though it were assisting the system rather than being controlled by it.

"Do you think that's because it knows we're trying to help?" Vex asked Derivan, watching the rune in the air. His hand tightened around the armor's. "Or . . . do you think it's because Irvis . . ."

Derivan squeezed Vex's hand back reassuringly. He knew the lizardkin still wasn't entirely happy with what they'd had to do to Irvis. For all that he'd done to them, his anger and hatred had stemmed from a very real torture— and that kind of torture was something Vex was all too familiar with.

"I do not know," Derivan said. He trailed his other hand through the air. The mana here was dense enough that he could call upon it to coalesce around the fingers of his gauntlet. He almost flinched at the sensation—this was the replacement arm that Gallant had forged for him, and he still wasn't used to the sparks of sensitivity it had compared to his original arm. The buzz it sent through him was the closest thing to physical pain he could remember experiencing.

Still, he did his best to ignore it, bringing his hand up in front of Vex instead as the mana danced around his fingers. "But what I do know is that the mana feels . . . happier. Kinder. It is more obvious here than anywhere else, but it is a change I have noticed ever since his death."

Vex nodded slightly, watching the mana dance through Derivan's fingers, then leaned into him as they walked. ". . . I'm glad for that, at least," he said quietly. The mana in front of him leapt from Derivan's fingers and up to Vex's face, as if nuzzling against him, and that was enough to make Vex's eyes brighten and a smile twitch up onto his lips. "Derivan!"

"I was not the one that did that," Derivan said, amused. "You may thank yourself for being so charming that even the mana loves you."

"*Deri.*" Vex laughed, some of the moroseness dissipating from him as he did.

Derivan only smiled. Perhaps he'd given the mana a small prompt—but it had not taken much more than that. He had only spoken the truth.

"We're looking for, uh . . ." Vex squinted, trying to remember. "What do the Norams call themselves now again?"

"Raltis and Novice," Derivan said, amused again. "The otter and the lizard-kin, respectively."

"Right!" Vex brightened. "Think they're at that fancy wizard tower? I still want a wizard tower, by the way."

Derivan laughed. "I believe they said they would be waiting for us at the town square," he said. "Not at the 'fancy wizard tower,' as you put it."

"Right, right." The fact didn't seem to dampen any of Vex's enthusiasm. Derivan wasn't sure if he was just trying to distract himself or if he was truly this excited to see the two again—he suspected it was a mixture of both. "What kind of new spells do you think they've made?"

"I do not know," Derivan answered truthfully. "But I am looking forward to finding out."

The town square—which wasn't really a square, Derivan noted, more of a lopsided circle—opened up in front of them. In the center of it loomed an enormous fountain that immediately caught Derivan's attention and made Vex's jaw drop. Raltis and Novice both sat at the edge of it, but Vex and Derivan were far too distracted by the fountain to immediately greet them.

"Is that a Reset Fountain?" Vex asked, his eyes wide. "It's . . . not like any I've ever seen."

"Do you like it?" Novice grinned at him. "Raltis and I made it. It's very fancy."

"I can see that," Derivan said. He could *feel* it, too—the inner workings of the Fountain were open to him through the senses of Shift and Patch. He could see the way it drew upon the mana around them and used it to open up access to the system. "This is impressive work."

What was it Sev had said? Stats were the shifting of metaphysical weight. In that context, this Fountain was a work of art in and of itself. He could see how the inner mechanisms were tuned to delicately rework those weights and balance them against one another, with virtual weights created to round out a person's existence if they chose to invest heavily in one particular stat.

Most Reset Fountains, if Derivan remembered correctly, could not go nearly so far. There was a limit to how many points they could redistribute and how many of those points could be placed into each stat.

"Was there a reason you had to make this?" Vex asked. Derivan glanced at Vex, then toward the otter and lizardkin pair, the same question in his eyes.

Raltis nodded. "The system's been distributed among all citizens of Teque at this point," he explained. "But their stat distributions are identical to whichever citizen of Fendal they're paired with. Obviously, that doesn't really work, and the normal process of just resetting the points and then slowly allocating them over weeks didn't seem prudent, considering the present situation."

"So we made a Fountain that could do it all at once," Novice continued. Derivan blinked once; the lizardkin picked up seamlessly from Raltis, almost as if he knew where the otter was going to end his sentence.

"How?" Vex asked, interested. "System manipulation isn't something any class I know of can do. Not to this degree, anyway."

Raltis grinned. "Magic of the Roads," he said. "It's why you're here, isn't it?"

The otter hopped off the Fountain and gestured for Derivan and Vex to follow along with him, which they did; Novice trailed behind the three of them, seemingly content to let Raltis do the talking. The trip they took wasn't a long one—there was a portal nearby that led almost directly to the entrance of the Roads.

"Is there a reason you did not simply ask us to meet you here?" Derivan asked. There was a faint hint of a smile evident in his eyes, though it was likely only Vex would be able to tell. Physical Empathy told him there was something here still left unsaid.

"Yes, well . . ." Novice looked embarrassed. "It was my idea. I wanted you guys to see the Fountain we made."

Derivan chuckled. Vex, evidently, related to this greatly; he stepped forward and gave Novice an unprompted hug. "You did great with the Fountain," he said cheerfully. "I'm going to need to hear how you did it in detail later!"

"You will?" Novice looked stunned at first, then delighted; Derivan allowed himself a small smile as he took a step back to stand next to Raltis. Vex saw something of himself in Novice, he knew, and Novice looked up to him. Neither of the two were inclined to actually talk to one another without a bit of prompting, though.

"Ahem," Raltis said. Derivan took note of the soft smile with which he looked at Novice, almost the way a father would look at his son. "Let us discuss the magic of the Roads, yes?"

"Right!" Vex straightened. "I know you mentioned the Roads are a kind of . . . translation magic? I thought it was fate magic."

"It's both." Raltis grinned, showing his teeth. "But the fate aspect of it isn't important here. What *is* important is that the Roads are primordial translation-aspect magic. And your system? It has a *language*."

CHAPTER 10

LOST IN TRANSLATION

"You're using the Roads to translate the *system*?" Vex asked. Derivan couldn't blame him for sounding stunned; he felt much the same way.

And maybe a little offended. Patch hadn't been the easiest stat to understand nor get used to, and the little ways it pinged at him to *fix things* bothered him even now. It hadn't proven to be a problem yet, thankfully, and with the system on the verge of falling apart, Derivan was hopeful that it never would, but . . .

He would have to be careful either way.

It was probably for the best that the Roads worked the way they did, now that he thought on it further. He wouldn't wish for others to have to deal with the same problems he'd had to deal with when it came to Patch.

"The best part is that it's a two-way translation," Novice said, beaming. "Meaning it doesn't just help us understand what the system is doing; it helps us change the system, too. We can translate what we're doing into something the system can understand. It's how we built the Fountain."

"How do you even use . . . translation-aspect mana, as you called it?" Vex asked. He flicked his fingers toward the Roads, and Derivan sensed the familiar activation of a skill—[**Advanced Mana Manipulation**]. He frowned and shook his head a second later. "Standard mana manipulation doesn't seem to cut it, and I know it doesn't respond to glyphs. I've tried casting glyphs near the Roads before."

"There's a special glyph you have to use for it," Novice explained. "We actually couldn't get it to work for the longest time. Something about new glyphs being impossible to make. But we kept trying, and it eventually just . . . worked."

Derivan exchanged glances with Vex. This had something to do with either Vex's semerit or the Grand Anchor that had been integrated with his system;

they hadn't had the opportunity or the means to explore either of those things further, but Clyde had said something about new glyphs being impossible. Vex and Derivan had both altered the fundamental fabric of things over in the bonus room, allowing new glyphs to once again be created, and that was a working of magic that was contained within Vex's semerit—what the Librarian Isolis called a representation of future change.

Seeds of your potential. Derivan remembered the words Vex had told him Isolis had said. It was the same night they'd discovered what the semerit could actually do. In their exploration of its inner workings, they found that it contained all possible futures linked to the kingdom Vex had seen contained within the semerit.

If Elyra was the kingdom of magic and Anderstahl was the kingdom of technology—planeshifted technology, to be precise—then this third kingdom, Enkiros, had been the one representing divinity. The realm of the gods, yes, but not only that. It was the realm of all creatures touched by divinity, ones that had long since been erased from the world.

Dragons were among them, and by far it was the easiest transformation for Vex to tap into, for it was a realm of divinity he was closely aligned with. As far as Derivan understood it, dragons had been curious creatures. The very basis of their magic was driven by curiosity, a form of power drawn from the gap between what they knew and what they didn't.

It did mean that older, wiser dragons became less powerful over time, but that was only power in the literal sense; there was a lot of power to be had in the knowledge they gained over their lifetimes and the ways in which they expressed them. Dragons whose innate magic was weakest made up for it with the ability to do incredible things with that limited magic: they knew their magic so well that they could do with a single unit of mana what took others millions.

"Can I see the glyph?" Vex asked. Derivan blinked, realizing he'd allowed himself to become distracted; it was strange how much easier it was to distract him these days. He was changing. Not because of his stats, though those certainly changed him in a different way—he was growing in a way he'd never been able to before.

He wondered if that was in part due to the Remembrances he now held. Mementos of other lives, other cultures, other lifetimes; in some ways, he embodied those things now. He was a suit of armor, a protector, and as what he needed to protect grew . . .

So too did he.

An interesting thought.

Novice produced Vex's magelight and began to draw the glyph into the air; he paused halfway through his demonstration and spoke, sounding a little embarrassed. "Uh, I kind of forgot to ask . . . do you want this back?"

"I made one of my own," Vex said with a laugh. "You can keep it. You've been using it longer than I have, at this point."

Derivan glanced at Vex, slightly amused but choosing to say nothing. Vex's magelight was a makeshift thing he'd built out of supplies he managed to salvage from the at-the-time-corrupted Elyran Adventurers' Guild; he'd complained more than once about having to rebuild the mana channels carved into the thing.

But it was in Vex's nature to be giving, and the way Novice's face brightened made it worth it, he was sure. Derivan would make sure to take Vex back to Anyati's shop after this, though. Giving his first magelight to Novice didn't mean that Vex couldn't get a new one of his own.

"Thank you," Novice said. Derivan could see that he meant it, too; he clutched at the magelight as though it meant something deeply personal to him, and Physical Empathy told Derivan that it *did*. "It . . . I never got the chance to thank you for leaving me with your magelight. It helped me find myself again."

"Oh," Vex said. He didn't say anything more for a moment, and Derivan reached over to place a hand on his shoulder; Vex relaxed slightly under his touch and gave Novice a small smile. "I just . . . hoped it would do something."

"It did," Novice confirmed. "Even your notebook did. I like your art, by the way."

Vex immediately stiffened, more out of embarrassment than anything else. ". . . The notebook I would like back, if you don't mind."

"Right!" Novice seemed oblivious to Vex's obvious consternation and dug in his backpack to hand it back to the other lizardkin. Derivan noted with amusement that Novice had left several bookmarks in it, which Novice refused when Vex tried to return them to him.

"You have never allowed me to look at your art," Derivan said, his voice slightly teasing.

Vex huffed. "I'll let you look at it later," he muttered, then immediately changed the subject. "You gave me something when the system took you— do you remember it? I'm not sure if you want it back. I haven't been able to figure out what to do with it."

"The Spelldisk?" Novice shook his head. "That's not actually mine. Or, uh, I guess it *is* . . . but it kinda never worked. I remember something about it that seemed different when I gave it to you, so I'm guessing whatever it is now, you're supposed to have it."

"Are you sure?" Vex pressed. "Because the system said it was important to you."

"It was, but what you gave me is *way* more important." Novice grinned. "Look at me! I'm doing magic! *Proper* magic!"

Vex couldn't help but grin at that, and Derivan laughed at the face the lizardkin made as he tried and failed to suppress his smile. "Proper magic," Vex agreed. "Still—"

"Nope," Novice said. He held up a hand. "I don't wanna hear it. Look, the system did something to that Spelldisk for you. I never got it to work, and between the two of us, you're more suited to finding out."

"If only I knew where to start," Vex said. He rummaged through his tail-bag, pulling out the Spelldisk and examining it critically again. Derivan eyed it curiously—he'd never gotten a close look at the thing. Vex hadn't had that much time to examine it in their time in the bonus room. There had been so many other things going on, and so many things about an entirely new system of magic they had to learn . . .

Novice was right—the system had altered the Spelldisk in some way. He could feel it through Patch, the way the system had attached itself to the runes inscribed along the sides. He frowned a little, stepping forward. "May I?" he asked.

Vex blinked. "Be my guest," he said, offering it up to Derivan.

Derivan reached out and took the Spelldisk, analyzing it with his senses. The system's text for the item popped up in front of him:

A sentimental item that belonged to a young would-be adventurer. He crafted this in the dead of the night, where his parents would not be able to see, each day pressing a new rune into the circuit along the edges.

On the surface, it casts a simple Light spell. But Light exists to cast away Shadow, and in the same way, the Spelldisk may bring a secret to light.

"Light exists to cast away Shadow . . ." Derivan said out loud, reading the text. "It cannot mean the shadow elementals in Mundane, surely?"

"I don't think so." Vex hesitated. "We wouldn't have wanted to cast them away, anyway."

"It is connected to the system," Derivan said. "I can sense the connections through Patch."

"Oh!" Novice bounced on his feet slightly. The glyph he'd started drawing was still in front of him, half-finished, glowing in the air. "Then you should try out the translation glyph! Perfect opportunity, right?"

"Well . . ." Vex gestured to the half-finished glyph. Novice blinked at it and laughed, embarrassed.

"Right, right," he said, bringing up his magelight once more.

Vex stared at the glyph Novice produced. It was a thing of chaos—where most glyphs were formed of beautiful, sweeping lines, an abstracted form of some artistic product, this one was . . . not. It was still beautiful, but it was a mix of the swooping curves of glyphs and the straight, jagged circuitry of the system's runes, mashed haphazardly together like they were a bad collage.

"This is the glyph?" he asked, unable to keep the uncertainty out of his voice. Raltis laughed.

"Yes. It surprised us, too," the otter said. "Novice discovered it while trying to find magic that could work on the system. Strange, isn't it? Perhaps he's the one that should be named after the ancient archmage."

"I'm still a novice," Novice muttered, embarrassed.

"If you say that in front of me again, I'm going to throw my book at you," Raltis fired back instantly—but he was grinning. Vex smiled, enjoying the banter.

"How do you use it?" he asked.

"Oh, you just kind of . . . do." Raltis waved a hand vaguely toward the glyph. "You'll understand when you try it out. It sort of connects with you and lets you see things."

Well, that was interesting. Vex blinked, cocked his head, and nodded; he pulled his improvised magelight out from his belt.

And then, eyes trained on the glyph in front of him, he began to draw.

CHAPTER 11

CAST IN SHADOWS

Vex understood what Raltis meant as soon as he completed the glyph. Tendrils of intent—not mana but *intent*, invisible to his normal mana-sensing abilities but clear as day when it was directed toward him—connected to his mind, providing him with a lens through which he could see the world.

The new perspective was almost dizzying. He saw the world weighted with history and metaphor, saw a thousand subjective realities superimposed on ontological truth.

And he saw through this perspective a means to spin one subjective reality into another. To translate the very nature of a thing from one reality to another. Not a shift, exactly, but a reworking of the rules to make those rules *possible*.

"Wow," he said out loud, blinking a few times. The rush of information would have been overwhelming if not for the experience he'd already had with this kind of thing from his Research rune.

"That's all you have to say?" Novice said, throwing his hands up. "The first time I tried that, it knocked me to the ground and I didn't get up for an hour!"

"I did tell you he'd be fine," Raltis said, amused.

Vex glanced at them. "Please tell me you weren't betting on whether or not this glyph would knock me out."

There was a long silence.

"I am glad it did not knock you out," Derivan said. He said it more to fill in the silence than anything else; Vex saw a trace of amusement in his eyes, and he also saw how the armor would have been very much *not* amused had it actually managed to knock him out.

Vex just shook his head and laughed.

Now with the Glyph of Translation active, he looked back toward the Spelldisk in his hand and watched as this new magic splintered it into a hundred disparate pieces.

One piece was the way it was originally created: by a young lizardkin Noram, who listlessly carved the runes he'd seen all the powerful mages use into the stone without knowing what they did or how to use them. The stone never worked back then, for the runic circuitry was broken on a fundamental level.

One piece was the way the system had changed it. The runes had been subtly altered and realigned into a complete, working set of runes—a set of runes that would in theory cast a [**Light**] spell.

Except . . . It was a *complicated* way of casting that spell. A standard [**Light**] cast was a single runic circuit that looped in on itself; it was one of the simplest runes in existence. The Spelldisk, on the other hand, used a network of five runes that were complicated in and of themselves. Vex recognized the runes for [**Greater Gateway**], [**Temporal Timeout**], [**Divine Dominion**], [**Purifying Presence**] and [**Shadow's Sublimation**].

All were spells a Platinum-ranked adventurer would use. They were spells that tapped into fundamental aspects of reality.

And they were being used to create a ball of light.

Vex looked closer.

The Glyph of Translation sang within him as he channeled his mana into the Spelldisk and watched light blossom into existence above it—but what he had created wasn't *light*. Not really. It had the properties of light, certainly, but . . .

"It's almost like a projected [**Truesight**]," Vex said out loud, looking intently at what the Spelldisk was emitting. He wasn't sure this was something he could have figured out on his own—even his Glyph of Research only simulated what he would do when investigating something. The complexity of this particular Spelldisk was one that would have taken him years to decode. Even beyond the five main runes he'd recognized, there were smaller ones embedded deep into the disk, and mana aspects that were altered by the system in real time when mana was channeled into it.

It was *complicated*. But then so was [**Truesight**]. As Vex understood it, the system itself had multiple variants of the spell, and it never clarified which version of it a mage had; they would have to contend with their own understanding of reality to determine how effective their variant of the spell was. Now that Vex thought about it, the Glyph of Translation he was using was not unlike what the deeper forms of [**Truesight**] were said to be like.

But the Spelldisk projected [**Truesight**]'s effects *outward*, allowing anyone who saw something touched with its light to perceive its underlying reality. They weren't exactly entirely comparable—the Glyph of Translation was a deeper magic, one that was rooted in the fundamental forces of the universe, and the Spelldisk merely unveiled truths—but truths could be a powerful thing.

Especially when, with a little bit of magic, you could decide what the truth *was*.

Vex held the Spelldisk up to his eye like it was a lens instead of a solid piece of stone; with the effects of the Glyph of Translation active, it might as well have been. He saw, overlaid upon itself, the many realities that Derivan could manipulate with Shift. Different timelines, different realities, things where one thing had happened instead of the other.

He saw echoes. Not in the traditional sense—echoes of reality, the same kind of echo that the entirety of his bonus room had been.

And though the residue was muddy and fading . . .

He *could* see what remained of the piece of reality that had been his bonus room. It was long gone by now, of course—an echo of an echo, a residual shape left behind by the nothingness of the Void rushing in to fill in what once had been a vibrant reality.

Light exists to cast away shadow . . .

. . . The Spelldisk may bring a secret to light.

"What if I just . . ." Vex muttered out loud. He saw, in the corner of his eye, Raltis and Novice both making a move to speak; Derivan, however, recognizing how Vex was lost in thought in a way that signaled he was just on the verge of an epiphany, quickly shushed them.

Vex gave himself a moment to think about how much he loved the armor, then shifted his mind right back to the Spelldisk and its effects.

Teque was still here. That was key to this—they'd never been able to find the connection between the bonus room and Teque. They knew it was there, and they knew that the Roads should have been able to connect them. It just . . . hadn't done so.

Vex turned his gaze to the Roads, still looking through the Spelldisk.

He could see the remnant link there. The entirety of that bonus room had been supported by Elyra's Prime Anchor, which had long since fallen apart; *Fendal's* reality anchor, however, hadn't. Not yet. It was unstable, but it was being supported by reality shards generated by Teque and by the unusual circumstances with which Teque had been created.

"I think . . ." Vex started his sentence slowly, hesitantly. He wasn't sure if he should say it out loud—he was worried that if he did, he would bring them false hope. That he wouldn't be able to do it. But he made himself say the words anyway.

"I think I might be able to bring the bonus room *back*."

It took some time for him to figure out the details.

The first and most important thing was that as he was right now, there was no way he'd be able to perform a working of magic on a scale quite that large. He would be asking the mana and the system together to recreate an entire world, and both entities had enough trouble maintaining just the current world without having to support a second one on top of it.

The second thing was that the bonus room wasn't the only thing that he might be able to bring back through the Spelldisk. It had been the first one to come to mind, but whatever the system had created here, it gave him the ability to tap into the residual echoes of *anything* that had been erased, provided that erasure was recent enough. Provided he still had a connection to what had been erased—as he did through the Roads here in Teque. He could . . . restore things.

Not indefinitely, and not without cost. But the ability to do so at all was so precious, Vex could have cried at the thought of it. Derivan, Raltis, and Novice all seemed to be in much the same frame of mind. As a test, Vex had tried to recreate a roll of bread he remembered eating from the little cafe situated near Clyde's inn; the resulting bit of baked good was just the way he remembered it, and he almost hugged it before remembering himself and sharing it with the others instead.

This was a reminder that he needed to find a way to help Derivan taste foods in the same way he cou—

Derivan gently plucked a piece of bread from him, and then, before Vex's eyes, his helmet just . . . split open. Melted apart as though it were liquid, with dripping slime forming teeth and a tongue.

Vex stared. His face felt hotter than usual.

"You, uh, figured out how to eat?" he asked. His voice came out sounding a little strangled, he was pretty sure, and Derivan looked at him curiously. Vex couldn't figure out if he *knew* he was flustered or if he was just genuinely oblivious.

"I believe so," Derivan said. "I am not certain that I have correctly manufactured the sensation of taste. But it is unique, and I enjoy it."

"You're using the Slime stat for it?" Vex asked. He couldn't imagine when Derivan would've had time to figure out something like this.

"And a Remembrance," Derivan said, nodding. "There are many I still have yet to explore."

"I see," Vex said. Raltis and Novice both snickered at him, and he did his best to ignore them. "I'm, uh, glad to hear that. You should tell me more about how it works. Later."

Derivan cocked his head. "Are you all right, Vex?"

"I'm fine," Vex said, probably more defensively than he should have. Was Derivan smirking? It felt like Derivan was smirking. "Anyway, we should . . . figure out the limitations of this thing. The Spelldisk. Not your mouth."

"I did not think you were talking about my mouth," Derivan said. He definitely sounded amused now.

"You're enjoying this," Vex accused.

"Perhaps a little." Derivan smiled at him.

Vex grumbled.

Honestly, it was unfair how easy it was for Derivan to make his heart melt.

CHAPTER 12

REUNION

"You've just been living two lives this whole time?" Misa asked, half impressed and half in disbelief. Her mother snickered at her expression.

"Is it that hard to believe?" Charise smirked a little. "It's not that hard."

"You're controlling two bodies!"

"Misa. You have a skill that allows you to split into an almost arbitrary number of copies of yourself, and you control them simultaneously in combat."

"I don't *control* them," Misa grumbled. "They're all me. We just know each other well enough to work together."

"And I know myself well enough to work in two bodies." Charise grinned a smug grin.

"I don't think that's how it works, Mom."

"Well, I'm the one with two bodies, so I get to say how it works."

Misa laughed.

It felt . . . good. It felt good to be able to laugh with her mother again. She'd spent some time with Orkas and Charise both after they'd been brought back from death, in that little bit of time they had before they had to set out to Elyra again—and she'd spent a little more time with her mother when she summoned her to help out in Fendal.

But this was different. The world was still at stake, yes, and there were many, *many* things they still needed to understand, but there was no ongoing crisis and no imperative for Misa to *leave*. Not yet, anyway. They did have a task, of course. They needed to figure out how to adjust [**An Anchor of Heart and Home**] so that it folded into Fendal and Teque as well as J'rokksur.

It was just that this was a part of it. Talking to her mother again, immersing herself in the idea of *home*, even though she was sitting in the middle of Fendal instead of in J'rokksur.

Many of the villagers from her home had come to visit too. The walls may have been unfamiliar—the streets weren't the trampled-dirt pathways she was used to from her childhood, and the buildings were too rigid, too *organized* to be of orcish design—but with so many of the people she knew, people she'd considered almost as close as family . . .

Well, it felt like home again, anyway.

"Do you ever think about what you're going to do once all this is over?" Charise asked. Misa glanced up at her mother, surprised at the sudden question; Charise laughed. "Don't give me that face. Come on. You've been thinking about protecting your friends. What do you want to do after that?"

"I don't know," Misa admitted. She glanced down at her hand, flexed it once, watched her fingers open and close over the shaft of her mace. "But . . . This is the life I love, Mom. There isn't an *after* for me. I mean, maybe when I'm old and rickety and stuck at home, I guess." She snickered.

"Adventuring, then?" Charise asked.

"Adventuring," Misa confirmed. "And helping people. And doing it with my friends."

"Meaning you haven't changed since you were five," Charise teased.

Misa groaned. "Mom."

"I'm not wrong."

"No," Misa admitted. "I know you haven't spent as much time with them as I have, but . . . they were my family while you were gone. They still are."

"Then why don't you tell me about them?" Charise smiled, clapping once. "I'm sure there's plenty of new stories you have to tell. Oh! Let me get your father first. He'll want to hear the stories too."

"Okay," Sev said. "Let me get this straight. You're all people I recruited in past iterations of Obreve?"

"Yes," Muchen said. Sev still wasn't sure what to make of this group of people—they didn't seem at all like the type of people he'd choose to work with. Not *willingly*, anyway. They were too serious by half.

He supposed he couldn't blame them, though, considering the circumstances. He was just used to something . . . different.

"And you've been helping keep things stable in each iteration," Sev said. "You guys keep your memories through every Reset?"

"Not entirely," Aisha said, glancing at the others. "It tends to filter in slowly, in bits and pieces. You said something about hacking the anchors so they'd restore more of our memories."

"I did?" Sev consulted his own memories for a moment. Sometimes, he felt like a stranger looking at his own history. "... I guess I did."

He couldn't remember *how*, nor did it really matter, at this point. The anchors weren't stable enough to handle any more modification of that sort, and they wouldn't be able to handle another Reset. Like it or not, this was going to be their last try at saving everyone and everything.

"But just to be clear," Sev added, "you don't actually know how we're going to solve this? I didn't leave behind some secret template or anything?"

"Really wish you did." The one that spoke up was an enormous orc by the name of Gorash; he stood in the corner of the room, leaning against the wall. He was one of the less social ones here, by Sev's reckoning. "Woulda made things a lot less confusing."

"I was probably just as confused," Sev muttered.

This was . . . frustrating, he had to admit. Meeting these people felt like it should have given him a clue—something he could go on to start fixing everything. But everyone here was just as lost as he was. He hadn't learned anything. All they had was access to a bunch of old technology he no longer remembered how to use, and a few techniques to jailbreak anchors . . .

. . . Actually, now that he thought about it, he'd initially dismissed the idea because most anchors were unstable. There was one anchor that was still stable.

Misa's.

"Okay," Sev said after a moment. "Let's break it down again. We've got three different types of anchors: The Prime Anchor at the center of each Kingdom; the Grand Anchor stored in a Vault beneath each Kingdom; and the regular reality anchors stored in every dungeon scattered roughly equidistant across the continent."

Aisha nodded. "Yes. The Prime Anchors hold together all the smaller reality anchors in the region and sustain the industry and civilization within each Kingdom. They're what allow more complex spells and technologies to operate. Smaller reality anchors can't do nearly as much. They mostly act as relays."

"What about Misa's anchor, then?" Sev pointed out. "She's got a reality anchor, and it's essentially functioning as a Prime Anchor without being connected to or reliant on one. It's not like it's being supported by the Elyran Prime Anchor anymore."

The others exchanged glances. "We aren't sure," Muchen admitted. "It's almost like it's got the function of a Prime."

"Might be all the reality shards you've been feeding it," Aisha said.

"Or just something about it being attached to a person instead of sitting in the Void," Muchen said thoughtfully.

Sev frowned, shaking his head. "Maybe the reality shard thing," he said, although he sounded unconvinced. "Or one of the system's adaptive changes."

"Or your weird friend," Gerald remarked. He'd been silent for most of the conversation—Sev got the distinct impression most of the others didn't like the guy, not that Gerald seemed to mind. He stood in the corner of the room, his hair unkempt, observing the discussion with a surprisingly keen gaze. "Metaphysically weird, that is."

"Who, Derivan?" Sev thought about it. "He might have used Patch to do something to Misa's anchor, I guess. I know he's tried to look at our systems a few times. But I think he would've let us know if he did anything this significant."

"You know him better than I do," Gerald said with a shrug.

It *could've* been a cumulative effect, Sev thought. Maybe a combination of a few different factors, along with the influence Misa herself no doubt exerted on her anchor just by being its host. The system was adaptive to a degree, and considering how often she pushed her anchor to sort through every adjacent reality and choice . . .

He could see it.

"You said I left behind manuals," Sev said eventually. "Things that explain how the anchors work, that kind of thing?"

"It's in the next room over," Aisha said, nodding toward a door. "Be careful if you go in there, though."

"Why?"

Gerald yawned. "You didn't wonder why we didn't contact you earlier about this whole thing?" he asked. "Your status effects."

Sev frowned. He hadn't thought about those in a while—one of his maluses changing to a four-letter word, still lost to the system. He still had the [**Fatebroken**] status effect, too, although he could feel its influence waning. "You know what they are?"

Gerald pointed, and Sev startled as a system window popped up at the man's command. "Don't see the point in obfuscating this one," he grunted.

[**Fatebroken**] [**Malus**]

*Applied by [**Sacrifice to the Lost**]. Modified by <ERROR>. The choices you can make in any given situation are limited by the futures you have chosen to give up. The futures you have given up have been selected by an unknown entity. You are not your own.*

"Gerald," Aisha snapped. "We're not supposed to go around modifying people's systems."

"Eh, what's the big deal?" Gerald yawned. "Sev's friend can do it. Armor guy. Name starts with a D." He snickered. "Heh. D."

"*Gerald.*" Aisha's voice was distinctly exasperated.

Sev snorted, amused; he was beginning to understand the dynamic here a bit more. Gerald was . . . definitely more abrasive than he was used to, but he didn't mind it. "What about the other one?" he asked. "Used to be called [#######]. Now it's labeled as a [**Concept**] and [####], whatever those things are."

"[**Concept**] is a new system label," Gerald said with a shrug. "Means you embody something the way an Aspect embodies something in magic, except it's more system-oriented. Uses the same system of metaphysical weight your stats do."

"Okay." Sev frowned. "That's . . . helpful, I guess. Why am I one?"

"What do you think?" Gerald flashed a smirk at him.

"Oh, come on," Sev grumbled. "Uh, let me think . . . Nope. No idea. If I did, I would've figured it out months ago when it happened and I wouldn't be asking you now."

Gerald rolled his eyes. "You used to be more fun," he accused.

"The world probably wasn't as close to being destroyed back then."

"You know what?" Gerald paused. "Fair point."

"So . . ."

"You're [**Hope**], dumbass," Gerald said. "Or [**Path**]. A little bit of [**Fate**]. System's confused on exactly which word defines you the most. You gave up a whole bunch of your independence and your possible futures to try to make sure we get to a future where we all survive. You think it's a coincidence that you found Derivan? Or Misa? Or Vex?"

". . . Huh." Sev was silent for a long moment. "I thought that was Onyx's guidance."

"*Ow.*" Gerald winced, as did a few of the other members of . . . what did he call these people, anyway? Some kind of secret cabal? "Careful with the infolocks."

"This entire conversation has been about stuff behind infolocks."

"Okay, *fair,*" Gerald allowed. "I just didn't prepare myself for that one. Okay, yes, Onyx helps a bit. Nudges you in the right direction. But he wouldn't even know that your friends were the right people if not for a little bit of your [**Fate**]."

Sev sighed. "So . . . what? They *were* chosen?"

"Nah." A few of the others in the room shifted uncomfortably, and Gerald glanced up at them and snorted. "Look, I'm going to be real with you: things aren't looking good. Anderstahl's anchor is falling fast, and I bet you anything repairing it ain't gonna be as simple as throwing some reality shards in there and calling it a day."

"*Gerald—*" Muchen tried to speak.

"There's no *point* in keeping things secret anymore." Gerald's relaxed demeanor fell away, and Sev saw something in his eyes harden. "You're worried it's gonna weaken his [**Concept**]. It's not gonna get any weaker than this. There's almost nothing left to sustain it. So we're gonna stop doing things your way and start doing things my way."

Muchen glared, then glanced at Sev, as if asking for help. Sev shrugged.

"Honestly, I think he's right," he said. "And I don't really want to be kept in the dark anymore."

"I'm not against it," Aisha said.

"Go for it," Gorash grunted.

"*Finally.*" Gerald rolled his eyes. "[**Fate**] isn't real. It isn't about true pre-destination—it's about hope. About the *idea* that things might be going the way they are for a reason. The belief that things could be better. What your [**Concept**] and Onyx were able to do together is fundamentally just give us the path that's gonna give us the most hope. It doesn't mean we're going to succeed."

"Shit," Sev muttered. "I was kinda hoping we had something there."

"Nope." Gerald shrugged. "But it doesn't matter. Only way to move forward now is to do it like we're gonna succeed."

"Right." Sev let out a breath. "So the reason Aisha was worried about me looking at the old manuscripts—"

"Is because the more you know about the future, the more it technically weakens your [**Concept**]," Gerald said. "But like I said, it can't really get any weaker from here. Not because you're failing or anything. Just that the world doesn't have that much of a future left."

Sev grimaced. "I feel like you didn't have to put it quite like that."

"I did." Gerald stood up a little straighter and stepped closer, into the light; Sev eyed the line of red, swollen flesh that covered half his face. He said nothing. "I make jokes, but I'm the only one that's taking this situation as seriously as it should be taken. The rest of y'all just think it'll somehow work out."

"I don't," Gorash muttered.

"That's because you think we'll fail," Gerald shot back. "Look, go look at your manuscripts. Tell us if you find anything that'll help. Then we're heading over to the Anderstahl Prime Anchor and seeing if your reality shards will fix it."

"Sounds like a plan," Sev said, sighing. He straightened, heading toward the door, then paused. "You guys don't happen to know any fire elementals, do you? Or any strong source of fire-aspect mana."

Aisha and Muchen glanced at each other. "We might," Aisha said cautiously. "Why do you ask?"

Sev felt the [**Flame of the Phoenix**] burning a hole in his pocket. "Need them to help me heal something," he said vaguely. "Can you get them?"

"I'll get him," Gerald said. "No reason you guys have to risk getting burned."

Aisha looked guilty. Sev glanced between the two. There was a story there, he sensed.

But now wasn't the time. Sev opened the door and stepped past it into a dusty workshop, taking in a deep breath. The scent of mahogany and ancient paper filtered in.

Old memories flared up. Memories that were *decades* old. Sev's eyes narrowed.

He could do this.

It was time to start reading.

CHAPTER 13

OLD MANUSCRIPTS

A few hours later found Sev sitting in the midst of a pile of old books and papers, slowly poring over them. Not for the first time, he wished he had Vex with him—the lizardkin would be done with all these in an instant. He'd reached out through the system already, but apparently there was something going on in Teque that Vex and Derivan had to handle first; for now, he was on his own.

There was something about flipping through these old papers that made him . . . ache. The familiarity was part of it. He had memories of *writing* these notes. He recognized the handwriting, the shaky scrawl that he wrote in when he was excited or nervous or just hadn't touched a pen in a while.

These were notes that had been preserved across the Reset. The whole place he was in right now was fortified, in a manner of speaking. Aisha had partially explained it, but he remembered building this place: a small pocket just outside of reality, not unlike a dungeon but with a wholly different purpose.

Something needed to be maintained between Resets, or the whole thing was just for naught. This was where he kept projects he thought might give them a chance. This was where he chased down every new lead, everything they found that might allow them to preserve their universe. To preserve Obreve.

He remembered, too, every time one of those leads ran into a dead end. Either because the method he thought might work didn't, or because the tools he wanted to use vanished, consumed by the Void. Even the people who might be able to help him were gone. The various species that had once populated the other continents, their advancements and their magic . . .

All of it was gone now. All the friends he'd made, the different people he'd met—all their stories, their hopes and dreams.

With his memory returning, he was the only one who remembered them all.

"Shit," Sev muttered to himself. His eyes were wet. He sniffed, leaning away from the old parchment so his tears didn't soak into the paper and damage it, and took a moment to gather himself.

So many *memories*.

He wished, more than ever, that his friends were with him now.

With a sigh, Sev got to work.

—⁂—

Hours passed.

Papers lay scattered all around Sev. His hair was a mess from how many times he'd run his fingers through it, trying to think; he was going through all the documentation he could find on his plans, and one thing stood out to him as their only chance.

Grand Anchors. They were paradoxically both his first and last attempt at finding a way to circumvent the encroaching Void. He'd started working on them early on, but the biggest problem with the Grand Anchors was that they didn't just make a passive record of reality, like the Prime Anchors and their network of smaller anchors did. The Grand Anchors were built not to maintain, but to *produce*. He'd built three of them: a Grand Anchor of Magic, of Reality, and of Divinity.

None of them were functional when he'd first built them, but they weren't meant to be. Producing a fundamental aspect of the universe wasn't a problem he could solve by himself. Each anchor was built to run its own simulations and calculations, to analyze every universal Reset: to record each contraction and subsequent expansion of their universe and observe how each aspect came into being.

There was an order to it. Divinity came first, the divine planes reconstructed and then repopulated. Magic came next, flooding into the world and infusing everything with mana. Then the raw substance of Reality, upon which everything else was built.

With each Reset, the Grand Anchors became a little more complete, a little more capable—but even still, it wasn't enough. It became increasingly clear that they would not be finished before their universe was lost entirely. He'd started looking for other ways out then, other solutions that might save the world they lived in.

Nothing else had worked. Everything led to a dead end. Not even the gods themselves had a solution for the end of the universe.

So . . . backup plan it was. The Grand Anchors still existed, and they did, in a manner of speaking, *work*. They just couldn't operate themselves automatically the way he'd originally intended. Instead, they needed a guiding mind, someone who was capable of understanding the nature of the Grand Anchor. Someone who could guide its function and embody its Concept.

Vex, in that vein, was perfect for the Grand Anchor of Magic. That left two more—the Anderstahl one would, at least, be easy enough to get to, and the last one . . .

Sev's heart dropped.

The last one was gone.

Each of the three Prime Kingdoms carried one of the three Grand Anchors that he'd made. The problem was that the third and final kingdom—the kingdom of Divinity—no longer existed. Not as far as he knew, anyway.

That was going to be a problem. It was possible—likely, even—that the Grand Anchor still existed within its Vault somewhere underneath where the kingdom had once been. The problem with that, of course, was that it would just be in the middle of the Void.

There was no guarantee they'd survive the journey to get to it, in other words. And without the last anchor . . .

Sev let his head hit the desk with a *thud*. His notes were insufferably long, and thinking about it too hard made his head hurt. Even if they were able to get the final Grand Anchor and find a host for each of them, he wasn't certain his plan would work—there was no guarantee that each anchor would be able to produce *enough* of their Concept to sustain the universe.

"Explains why and how a reality anchor got attached to Misa, though," he muttered to himself. In retrospect, he probably should have questioned how it was that the anchor had settled so easily into her; the answer now was obvious. He'd modified the system at some point in the past to allow people to bond with anchors in preparation for this last resort.

There was a knock on the workshop door. Gerald pushed it open a second later, and a wave of heat accompanied him; Sev winced and constructed a quick barrier out of golden energy so that heat didn't ignite the dry, ancient paper he was surrounded by.

"We've got the guy you asked for," he said. "The sun elemental."

"*Sun* elemental?" Sev stared. "I just asked for a flame elemental. Or, uh, a strong source of fire-aspect magic."

"Yeah, well, not many flame elementals left, and I happen to have a sun elemental as a friend," Gerald said with a shrug. "You need him now?"

"The sooner, the better," Sev said, feeling at the stone in his pocket. In truth, he wasn't sure that this would help them at all—but it was as good a bet as any.

Phoenixes embodied rebirth. There had to be something there they could use. Something there that could help.

Sev couldn't help but feel, just a little bit, like he was headed toward yet another dead end.

—⁂—

"A semerit," Raltis said. The otter stared at the center of the table, where Vex had placed the [**Semerit of the First Library**]. "You're telling me the legends are *real*?"

"Shouldn't you know more about this than I do?" Vex asked, bemused.

Raltis huffed out a laugh, shaking his head. "I suppose. But things here aren't exactly well connected anymore." He inclined his head toward the Roads. "You might've noticed those of us in Teque don't really know as much as our surface-dwelling counterparts."

"I did wonder," Derivan said.

"It's because we're all so isolated," Raltis said. "A lot of us are communities that were remade some time after the so-called end of the universe. And we lost a lot of history in the initial stages, when we were all evacuating underground. A lot of memories, too. Not just history, not just people. What little we were able to preserve is precious."

"And the stars?" Vex asked.

Raltis's smile was sad. "Not much reason for us to remember anything about the stars when we're all underground," he said, gesturing up to the mana river floating above them. "I think more of us were concerned with survival than with preserving what we could remember of the surface. Or maybe it's just that we couldn't really remember much of the surface at all. Hard to say. And we had a replacement that was just as beautiful."

The mana river above them almost seemed to respond to those words. Its hues shifted from light blues and royal purples to the lightest shade of pink and yellow, and a few sparkling drops of magic fell from above, raining down onto the rooftops below. Vex couldn't help but gaze up at it too. It was a phenomenal sight even now—perhaps especially so, with Teque and Fendal joined.

Something about that union seemed to make the mana that sustained this place almost . . . joyful. He could see it in the way the mana flowed with more energy than ever before, the way it was responding to the words of its residents.

"It is strange how the mana here acts almost like a living weather system," Derivan remarked after a moment, following Vex's gaze. "But we are getting distracted, I think. Surely there is something you could tell us about these semerit that could help us?"

"It's all myths and legends," Raltis said. "I wish I had something more concrete. I haven't even looked at those books and legends for a while; far as I can tell, half of it is just made up, and the other half is . . . probably exaggerated. Stories about the stars dancing prophecies into the sky, about new worlds being written about in books. We can try to sort it all, certainly, but . . . it's going to take time."

"Not like we've got anything else to do," Novice finally said, speaking up for the first time in a while. He'd been staring contemplatively at the semerit for a while. "I think I remember reading a bit about them the other day. In one of the older books."

Raltis narrowed his eyes at Novice. "Did you go into the forbidden section of the library again?"

". . . Maybe."

". . . What did you learn?"

"Something about how they signify change?" Novice shrugged.

"That's what the Librarian told me," Vex said. "I— Wait. You have a forbidden section of your library?"

"Not all books are *safe*," Raltis grumbled. "Although Helg . . . was the one that organized that section of the library. So it's possible . . ."

The otter fell silent, clearly lost in thought. Vex caught the spark of guilt in his expression, though he didn't call it out. There was nothing more to say about it.

"I think what I read was that they're seeds of potential," Novice said. "Normally, you'd use them to make new spells. New glyphs. Or, well, not 'you'— but the Librarians. Or whoever's in charge of that kind of thing."

"Not sure creating new glyphs helps us right now." Vex frowned slightly. "It does match what the Librarian told me, though. It's just that Change and Stability should be able to help us craft most of the spells we need, along with this translation aspect you've told me about."

"But there is more to your semerit," Derivan pointed out.

"You mean what the system said in the item description?" Vex glanced at it again. "I don't know what 'contains one temporal paradox' *means*. Or how we're supposed to use it."

"You changed the course of events in a kingdom, did you not?" Derivan asked. "Perhaps that is the paradox. An event that both happened and did not."

"That . . . makes sense." Vex paused, thinking about Derivan's words. "You think we can use that somehow? Bring the Kingdom back?"

"You believe you can use the [**Spelldisk**], along with translation-aspect magic, to restore that which has been erased," Derivan said. "But most such things are buried deep within the Void. Here, you have an opportunity—your semerit has already partially undone one such erasure through a knot written into time. Why not start there?"

Vex stared. "Derivan, I could kiss you."

Derivan paused for a long moment. "I am waiting."

". . . You know what?" Vex said. "You're not going to fluster me this time. I'm going to do it."

"Very well."

Vex stalked up to Derivan, crossing his arms; the armor stared down at his boyfriend, equal parts amusement and affection in his eyes.

They kissed. Derivan cheated a little, using the Slime stat he had to give himself just enough of a mouth and a tongue to make it comfortable.

It was a good kiss.

Across the table, one otter and one lizardkin glanced awkwardly at each other, then quietly slid out of the room.

CHAPTER 14

SUNLIT

[Misa, I need you to come meet up with me,] Sev sent. Being connected to her reality anchor was convenient—unlike most others, his system didn't suffer from the same strange glitches and stutters that plagued most others he knew. [Are you done with Fendal? I'm not sure what progress looks like on that front.]

[Uh, yeah, more or less done, actually,] Misa replied. She seemed surprised. [You got me the exact moment the system linked me up to the town. How did you— You know what? Never mind. I should be used to weird coincidences around you by now.]

[About that,] Sev sent. [Turns out I embody Fate. Or something.]

[You what.] Misa's reply was so flat, Sev could practically hear it through the text on the system screen. [You know what, never mind. We'll talk when I get there in person. I'll get Derivan to send me where you are. It's not going to tax his Shift too much, is it?]

[Not if I give him a Blessing of Travel, which I can do from here,] Sev said. [You go find him and let me know when you're ready.]

There was a long pause with no reply from Misa. Sev was beginning to wonder if he needed to follow up with another message before he got an abrupt new message from her, filled with barely concealed amusement.

[Uh, yeah, I'm not gonna interrupt them,] she said. [You get your blessing ready. I'll get back to you. Later.]

[What?] Sev sent, confused. There was no reply.

—⁂—

It took about an hour before Misa sent him a message that she was ready, which Sev privately thought was about an hour longer than necessary. He wasn't sure he wanted to question her on *why*, though; there was a grin on her face that told him she'd be all too delighted to tell him the answer.

Maybe some other time.

"Had a safe trip, I hope," Sev greeted.

"I did." Misa grinned at him, somehow completely unrepentant. "You needed me for something?"

"Yeah." Sev ignored the look she was giving him—she wanted him to ask, and she *knew* he wanted to ask—and instead brought out the [**Flame of the Phoenix**] he still held in his pocket. The cracked amber still held warm in his hand, and now that he was paying attention, he could sense the way that warmth . . . pulsed, for lack of a better word. Like the beating of a heart.

"I need to heal this, and I need a strong source of fire-aspect mana to do it," he said.

". . . And you called me because?" Misa asked, puzzled.

"Because," Sev said, this time with something of a glare directed at some corner of the room, "the only source of fire-aspect mana we have access to is so strong I can't actually share a room with him without getting burned. I can heal myself, but having to heal both myself and the egg isn't really ideal."

"Seriously?" Misa seemed bemused now. She glanced around the room, a slight furrow in her brow. "What is this place, anyway? You never said."

"It's a small basement underneath Anderstahl's main headquarters," Sev said. "Or their palace, if you're more used to that term."

"We're in *Anderstahl*?" Misa stared at the room around her. "This isn't anything like how I imagined it. And how did you even get here? The convoy's still not even halfway here. Even if you sped it up—"

"I've got divine connections, remember?" Sev interrupted, laughing. Misa was excited to go outside and see the city, that much he could tell; some things didn't change, no matter how much danger the world was in. "Blessings aren't that easy for the gods to administer anymore," he continued, a little more seriously. "So I can't just abuse it. But for things like this, for getting people to the right places at the right time . . . it's worth it. We won't make it in time otherwise."

Misa's excitement was instantly replaced with caution. "Are things that serious?" she asked.

"Yeah," Sev said, his expression settling into something a little more severe. "Uh, the people I met up with here are apparently people I recruited in past . . . Resets, as it were. They have some idea of what's going on and they've been trying to keep Anderstahl stable. It's why it's the last Prime Kingdom to fall."

"I hear a *but* coming."

"But despite their efforts, their Prime Anchor is close to failure," Sev said. "On the order of days, not months the way the Guild thought. We can probably fix it up and prolong things with reality shards, but that's only gonna last us so long."

"Shit," Misa muttered. She strode up to Sev. "And healing this thing is gonna help us?"

"Honestly, I don't know," Sev admitted. "I'm willing to try anything at this point. It's not going to *hurt*, I don't think."

"Sure," Misa said dryly. "What's the worst that could happen. We get a pet bird that's always on fire?"

"Pretty much," Sev said. "You ready? It's not going to be easy to block the sun elemental."

"You've got a *sun elemental* helping you?" Misa blinked. "No wonder you need my help. All right. I don't have enough mana stocked up, but I've got other tricks at this point." She pulled out her bow.

"Please tell me you're not going to shoot me with that," Sev said.

"I won't," Misa said, aiming her bow at Sev. "Tell you, I mean."

"Misa."

"It won't hurt!" She drew back an imaginary arrow, and Sev flinched; he felt the Concept materialize in her fingers, and she gave him a reassuring smile. It was a warm one, too, surprisingly—not a trace of the humor she might normally find in this situation. "Seriously, this is the next best thing to me sitting here and blocking. It's just going to be an arrow loaded with the concept of regulation. You ready?"

"I guess I have to be," Sev said, grimacing a little. This felt reminiscent of needles, somehow. He didn't know in what way, but the memory felt like it had something to do with Earth. "Let me just call him out. Solar?"

A door creaked open, and Sev tried not to take a physical step backward as the wave of heat nearly crippled him. It was already being suppressed as much as the sun elemental was capable of doing—that suppression was just limited.

Said elemental spoke with the cadence of a crackling fire and with a voice that sounded both like a roar and a whisper. "I am here."

"Whoa," Misa said. She stepped forward. "You doing okay there, buddy?"

The sun elemental paused, turning to her. He seemed puzzled. "What do you mean?"

"Somethin' about your fire." Misa frowned, looking Solar up and down. "Dunno how to place it, exactly, but it feels a little . . . off. Like you've got something on your mind."

Sev gave Misa a confused look. "When did you learn how to read fire?"

"I've been spending a lot of time around my mom," Misa said dryly. "You pick up a thing or two from an [**Intuitionist**]. That, and we might have figured out a new way to use [**An Anchor of Heart and Home**]."

Sev paused. "You didn't."

Misa grinned and placed a finger to her lips. "We'll talk about it later," she said, turning back to the sun elemental. "But seriously. Your name's Solar, right? Is everything all right?"

There was a long pause as the sun elemental studied her. Then he let out a sigh, the sound crashing against the walls and blasting a wave of heat at their feet. Misa didn't hesitate to fire her arrows of Regulation, planting one in herself and the other into Sev's thigh; he felt relief flood into him as the temperature around him abruptly cooled into something tolerable.

"It is not," Solar admitted, though the admittance was a little begrudging. "But there is little you or your friend could do about it. Simply let me give you the help you seek and I will be on my way."

"You don't sound like you want to leave," Misa responded. Sev could hear it too now—the note of reluctance in Solar's voice.

"It is . . ."

Hesitation. Sev couldn't help but join Misa in her worry; he saw the way the sun elemental seemed reluctant to speak, almost like he was afraid. What was there to be afraid of? It couldn't be the others here, surely; Muchen and Aisha had been nothing but kind, and Gerald . . . well, there was clearly history there. But he'd detected nothing malicious.

"It is nothing," Solar said after a long moment, clearly still trying to avoid the topic. Misa folded her arms across her chest, unconvinced, and now Sev joined her in her skepticism.

"You can talk to us," he said.

Solar sighed once again, though this time the impact of his heat wasn't felt as thoroughly. Misa's arrows helped. "It is not something that others can help with," he said plainly. "There are few of us left—sun elementals, fire elementals. The stone endures. The oceans wax and wane. But fire only grows or burns away, and we are no longer in the first phase of our existence."

Sev frowned and glanced at Misa. "You're telling me that other sun and fire elementals are . . . what? Dying?"

"Did you not find it strange that so few of us remain?" Solar asked. "How many of us have you encountered on your journey?"

"We haven't met that many elementals to begin with," Sev said. "Earth elementals and shadow elementals, primarily. But nothing of air or water or fire. We didn't think it was a trend."

"I see." Solar was silent for a moment. "Perhaps the situation is more dire than I expected. In truth, I have not been outside for a long, long time. I have been informed that this place is safer for me than most places would be."

"I mean . . . you're not wrong there," Sev admitted. This location in particular was fortified against the Void, partially by sheer proximity to the Anderstahl Prime Anchor and partially because it had to be to preserve the contents of his workshop between Resets.

"How long has it been since you've been outside?" Misa asked.

"Too long." The admittance was reluctant. "I have not seen the sky in many an eon."

". . . You mean eon non-literally, right?" Misa asked. "Because an eon is like a billion years."

"Elementals such as I experience time differently," Solar said, and then a little bit more sheepishly, ". . . but perhaps I did mean it metaphorically."

Sev chuckled a little at that interaction. "Let's do this outside," he suggested. "It'll give us more space away from the heat, anyway. And we can protect you if the Void tries to do something."

Solar shifted, clearly a mixture of excited and nervous. "Are you certain?" he asked. "I do not want to put others at risk . . ."

"I'm sure I can call in a few favors," Sev decided. A divine barrier would keep most of Solar's heat out and away from the general populace of Anderstahl. Worst case, he'd have to ask one of the gods to help him out.

A small part of him worried that there wasn't enough divinity left—that he was wasting it on trivial matters when it could be needed for something important later on. It was a genuine concern, too; there were other things he could prioritize here. But something deep within him told him that this was the right thing to do.

Maybe it was the part of him that saw the sun elemental right on the verge of guttering out. Despite the immense heat, despite the sheer *power* of the flame . . .

Deep within that flame was a candle close to burning to its end.

What was a single life in the context of the universe? Not much, surely. But Sev didn't know if they would need whatever divine power would be spent on this at all. He didn't know if divinity would help them in the end, not the way the Grand Anchors might, or the way the [**Flame of the Phoenix**] might. All he would be doing was holding on to power *just in case*, and if that was all he was going to do, then he might as well do nothing.

No. If he was going to use his power, then he would use it to be kind.

It was just who he was.

It took a bit of work. Getting Solar up to the roof of the Anderstahl castle—Sev had simply decided to just start calling the building a castle, even though it was really more of a *skyscraper*, which was a word he hadn't thought about for a long, long time—was a more time-consuming task than he'd anticipated.

It *had* taken a divine favor. The Goddess of the Inner Flame had responded to his request. Her domain didn't quite overlap with what he needed, but it was close enough; her favor granted him a Blessing he could use to turn that outwardly generated heat into an internal flame.

Which—as was often the case when it came to the gods—was really more of a metaphor for hope and life. Solar's expression when the Blessing had touched him had been a delight. There was fear and tension on his face that just melted away, and the sun elemental let out a long, low sigh of relief almost as soon as the divine power settled.

"Thank you," he said, his voice soft. "This— It will not last forever. Will it?"

"Unfortunately not," Sev said. "But you can keep it burning on your own."

"That is easier said than done," Solar said. "... But it feels possible now, at least."

"Come on, you two!" Misa called down from further up the stairs. "There aren't *that* many stairs left!"

Sev glanced at Solar. "I don't suppose I could convince you to carry me?" he said, half-joking.

Solar glanced down at his hands, made of pure fire, and then at Sev. "Will you survive?" he asked plainly.

"With the Blessing in place?" Sev considered the question with more gravitas than was perhaps strictly necessary. "... Maybe."

Solar snorted his first real laugh at this. "I am willing to make the attempt."

When they did make it to the roof of the skysc—*castle*, Sev nearly fell out of Solar's arms. The sun elemental froze the instant they pulled open the door onto the rooftop; the sun streamed in through the clouds. They'd managed to time it somehow so that it was almost exactly sunset, and the sky was ringed in hues of red and yellow, nearly the same colors as Solar's body.

"Thought you'd like the view," Misa said with a cheeky grin.

Solar swallowed. Sev carefully pulled himself out of the sun elemental's grip so they could both have an unobstructed view of the quite-frankly beautiful sunset. Truth was, there was rarely time for them to sit and stare at their surroundings, and it had been a long time since he'd truly appreciated nature's wonders . . .

. . . Seeing Solar's wonder at the sight reminded him that it was sometimes worth sparing a little time to remember what they were trying to save.

"All right," he said softly. He placed the [**Flame of the Phoenix**] on the floor, stepping back several feet to give Solar space. "Whenever you're ready. But take your time."

"I am ready now," Solar said. Something about the sight had apparently energized him, and now Sev saw him absolutely *brimming* with fire-aspect mana—so much so that he couldn't tell where the elemental ended and the mana began. He watched as Solar directed that energy to coalesce around the stone, and he brought his own healing to bear at the same moment.

Crack.

The sound echoed in the air, and something in both the mana and the threads of divinity before him yawned open.

CHAPTER 15

REBIRTH

Phoenixes were divine creatures.

Sev supposed he should have seen that coming. It wasn't something he'd thought about—there was the passing knowledge in his mind that there were species out there that belonged to the divine planes yet were not gods themselves. Angels were one such example. Dragons were another, though he hadn't sensed those threads of divinity around Vex when he'd transformed in the fight against Irvis. Something unique about his style of transformation, maybe.

Phoenixes were a third. They were creatures intimately linked to the divine, and Sev could sense that even now, with the way every thread of divinity in the vicinity suddenly lurched and pulled toward the amber-colored stone that was the [**Flame of the Phoenix**]. He had to scramble with [**Divine Manipulation**] to prevent the effect from stealing away the Blessing he'd placed upon Solar; a second later, and the sun elemental would have scorched them off the roof.

Well, probably not, actually. Misa was still there watching over them. But it would've been a very uncomfortable few minutes, and Sev would rather avoid it entirely.

He watched with a detached sort of curiosity as the phoenix began to lay claim on all the divinity surrounding it. He didn't fight that claim, except to maintain his own spells and Blessings—who knew how fighting it would disrupt the healing process? Sev didn't want to think about what a newborn phoenix would be like if detached from its own divine nature.

There *was*, however, a resonance in the link he shared with his gods. Like they all recognized something important was happening. None of them reached out to him—not yet, anyway—which was a surprise, but maybe they were simply waiting to see what happened, or they didn't want to potentially interfere or disrupt the link the baby phoenix was forming with the divine.

It took a solid five minutes. Divinity gathered, then contracted, drawing in streams of mana with it. Sev felt the healing spell draw on his power more and more, until the center of the roof was a knot of potential . . .

And then it happened, almost too quickly for Sev to see. He thought he caught a glimpse of a glimmering pool of pure possibility sitting beneath the [**Flame of the Phoenix**]. It was a multifaceted fractal of color, barely visible in the sunlight and almost immediately washed away by the pulse of power that came with the final burst of healing—

For a moment, it was like the world itself was holding its breath.

And then the stone cracked in two, and there was a little *chirp*.

"By the gods," Misa said. She sounded utterly delighted. "It's so *cute*."

"I almost feel like it's too cute," Sev muttered, staring at the baby phoenix.

It was *definitely* too cute. His visual senses warred with his divine ones; on the one hand, he could see the tiny bird with wet feathers and too-large eyes, looking around at the world with open curiosity. It hopped out of the little stone that had served as its egg, stumbled a little on the floor, then caught itself by awkwardly flapping its wings and sending a wave of heat along the floor.

Sev just barely remembered to pull up a divine barrier a split second before that wave of heat would have hit him. He wasn't sure he wanted to take his chances with the raw power of a divinely empowered baby bird.

Anyway. On the one hand, he saw a cute bird. On the other, he saw something that almost bent reality around it just by existing; the little phoenix was subconsciously laying claim to everything it touched, declaring all things its domain. It wasn't doing it on purpose, but if it were allowed to run wild . . .

Sev grimaced a bit at the thought and quickly ran forward to pick up the little baby phoenix.

The phoenix didn't fight his grip, at least—it seemed to find comfort in his hands, if anything. Sev felt the way it relaxed and stopped trying to claim dominion over everything around it. Reality unbent, bouncing back into shape, and Sev let out a sigh of relief.

The little bird purred in his arms.

Solar stared at it, evidently enraptured by its appearance. "It is beautiful," the sun elemental told him, walking up so he could peer over Sev's shoulders and at the bird he held in his arms.

"It's adorable," Misa declared. She kept a still-respectable distance away, apparently reluctant to get any closer. "I want to pet it."

"Why don't you?" Sev asked, amused.

"I have to be respectful," Misa said. "I can't just steal the baby phoenix from its dads."

"Wha—"

"I am not—"

Both Sev and Solar spoke at the same time and over one another, and they stopped almost immediately as Misa began cackling with laughter.

"I'm just kidding, guys," she said, snickering. She walked over, giving the baby phoenix a small smile. "I've been waiting to make that joke ever since you told me you were gonna heal this thing."

"Of course you were," Sev grumbled.

"Do we know how it's gonna help us?" Misa asked. "I mean, not that it has to, obviously. It can just hang around and look cute, for all I care. But is there a chance that it could?"

"I think so," Sev said. "But I don't know how."

"Yet," Misa said.

"Yet," Sev confirmed. "I'll look into it. I think it *can* help us. We just need to figure out where all the pieces fit together."

—m—

They stayed on the roof for another two hours in total. As long as it took for the sun to finally go down over the horizon, and for day to turn into night; even this, Solar was fascinated by, though his presence alone lit the rooftop up like it was daytime.

"It has been a long time since I have seen this," he said quietly.

"Is it weird for you at all?" Misa asked. "If that isn't too much to ask, I mean. I'm just wondering. Since you're a sun elemental."

Solar seemed more amused by this question than anything else. "It is not 'weird,' as you put it," he said. "My connection with the sun is different from what you believe it is."

"I just figured you were a piece of the sun or something."

"And you are not the only one to make such an assumption," Solar said. "We are . . . an embodiment of what the sun represents. Life-giving energy, to a degree. Light. Fire. Warmth. Many things, all in one."

"When we met you, you were burning," Sev noted. He reached out, noticing that the Blessing he'd placed on Solar had weakened—and yet the sun elemental's power hadn't begun to overwhelm them again. There was no wave of suffocating heat associated with the Blessing fading away. "Now you're . . ."

"Now I am calm," Solar said. "Or perhaps that is not the right term for it. I am at peace, I suppose."

"Glad we could do that for ya," Misa said. "It ain't worth it, you know. Being scared. Things are pretty seriously messed up right now, I'll give you that, but there's too much to miss if you spend all your time afraid of what's out there."

"Perhaps you are right," Solar said. He gazed out over the rooftop and into the city of Anderstahl. Sev followed his gaze—this was a first for him. He hadn't actually paid attention to Anderstahl even once he arrived in the little basement-workshop setup, partially because he'd been led there via a series of tunnels and hadn't actually gotten the chance to look at Anderstahl's landscape.

And when they got to the rooftop, he'd been kind of distracted by the sunset. And the presence of a sun elemental.

But now Solar approached the edge of the roof, and Sev followed him, staring down at the Prime Kingdom proper. Anderstahl, like many other places, presented him with a sense of aching familiarity—but this was even worse than it normally was. Sev winced a little, stepping back from the edge of the roof and feeling suddenly dizzy; concerned, Misa grabbed his elbow and steadied him.

"You all right, Sev?" she asked.

"Yeah, I'm . . . I'm fine," Sev said, trying to shake off the wave of sudden dizziness. "It's just so familiar. It's jarring."

He'd lived here for years, in one of his previous lives, but Sev didn't think that was what had triggered his nostalgia. No, the answer as to what this reminded him of was much simpler.

It reminded him of Earth.

His memories of his old home were still locked away to him, though for an aching moment he thought that perhaps this sight would be what finally triggered what remained of his memory to unlock, to give him back those memories of his original home. Yet nothing happened. His mind balanced on that razor's edge of recollection, like a word he'd forgotten was resting just on the tip of his tongue, but . . . there was nothing.

"You look sad," Solar noted.

"It's nothing," Sev said, smiling a weak smile. "Just some old memories."
Or lack thereof.

In his arms, the little phoenix chirped, having woken up from its slumber. It wriggled about, then chirped again, this time a little more demandingly. Solar's attention was thankfully quickly drawn to the little bird.

"I believe it is hungry," he said, and then, before Sev could stop him, the sun elemental coalesced a scale of pure fire-aspect mana on his fingertip. The phoenix chirped once happily, then shot forward and swallowed it whole.

Sev stared.

"Is that how we're going to have to feed it?" Sev asked after a moment.

"I believe so." Solar looked up at him. "Why do you ask?"

"Solar, have you ever thought about adopting a pet?"

CHAPTER 16

SETBACKS

A few things were immediately clear to Sev.

One was that Solar and the new phoenix had something of a bond. The bird had certainly imprinted on him when he'd picked it up—it had been comfortable enough to fall asleep in his arms, and that meant something—but there was something more in what it shared with Solar. It chirped at him, then hopped from Sev's hand into Solar's.

"I am not sure I would call a phoenix a pet," Solar said, gently stroking a finger down the back of the bird's neck. "But . . . you are offering her to me?"

"She seems to like you," Sev said. "I'm going to be honest: I don't think I'll be able to take care of a baby phoenix. Misa and I have a lot to do if we want to keep this universe intact, and that's not exactly a fight I want to take a baby to, even if it's a divine creature."

"That is sensible," Solar admitted. "I am not certain I am the right person for her."

"You are." Sev smiled a little. "Besides, I can't think of anyone else that could feed her. I guess I could ask you to come with us, but . . ."

Solar withdrew immediately, holding the phoenix close to his chest. ". . . I would rather not," he said softly. He didn't take his gaze away from the phoenix.

"There we go, then," Sev said. "You take care of her, and we'll come back if we need her or your help with something. How's that sound?"

"That is . . . acceptable." Solar took a breath, glancing around at the rooftop again. After a moment, he smiled, though Sev couldn't exactly see it in the brightness of his form. "Thank you both for showing me what I was missing."

"And now you can't keep yourself locked away, 'cause you have a baby to look after," Misa said, grinning broadly. The grin vanished after a moment. "Seriously, though, don't keep her locked away."

"I will not," Solar said, sounding a bit offended. "But . . . I still may not be able to come out frequently. Your Blessing will not last forever, Sev."

"Right." Sev frowned slightly, turning his attention toward what his [**Divine Manipulation**] skill was telling him. "It won't, but . . . I don't think it has to. The phoenix is already kind of maintaining the Blessing for you."

"She is?" Solar's words came out as a hopeful whisper.

"Yeah." It had been subtle enough for him not to notice it immediately, and since there hadn't been a change in the power of the Blessing, he hadn't noticed any increase in heat, either. "She's been slowly taking over the Blessing. Claiming it as her own divine domain, so to speak."

". . . It seems I must thank you, little one," Solar murmured after a moment, cradling the phoenix close; she let out a happy chirp, and the sun elemental smiled once again.

"We'll head back inside first," Misa suggested. "I'm guessing you're going to want to enjoy the rooftop a little longer."

"If you would not mind," Solar said. He didn't look at either of them, too busy feeding the phoenix another small pellet of fire-aspect magic. Sev chuckled a little bit, then followed Misa to the stairwell.

The door shut behind them with a quiet *click*, leaving the sun elemental staring out at the city, a small phoenix held in his arms.

—⁓—

"We've got a problem," Sev said.

"Don't tell me you want to take the phoenix *back*," Misa said. "You just gave her to the guy! You'll break his heart."

"What? No, I'm not talking about the phoenix!" Sev said, a little flustered; Misa smirked at him, and after a second, he laughed. "Dammit, Misa."

"So what's the problem?" she asked.

"It's the Grand Anchor beneath Anderstahl," Sev said with a sigh. "It's kind of a long story, but I spent a lot of time reading through my old manuscripts and trying to figure out what we need to fix things. Our best bet is going to be the Grand Anchors."

"The one Vex has?" Misa frowned. "What is that thing, anyway?"

"It's like . . . a bigger, better version of a reality anchor," Sev said, waving a hand vaguely. "I built it to permanently anchor fundamental aspects of reality. Like pinning down the corners of a blanket instead of patching up all the holes."

"I don't think that metaphor works the way you want it to work," Misa said dryly. "But I'm following you so far. I'm still not seeing a problem. Sounds like you have a way out for us."

"There's two, actually," Sev said, sighing. "One of them is that I think you're going to need to host one of the Grand Anchors, and you've kind of already got an entire reality anchor taking up a slot in your system."

"And I'm guessing switching from one to the other isn't going to be simple," Misa said, frowning. "Especially with all the people connected to my anchor so far."

"Yep." Sev grimaced a bit as he paced. "The second problem is the third Grand Anchor. I made three of them."

"One for each of the Prime Kingdoms," Misa acknowledged.

"And one of the Prime Kingdoms is missing," Sev said. "I don't know if that last Grand Anchor even exists anymore, Misa."

"Can't you just build it?" Misa asked. She stopped in the middle of the stairwell, looking at Sev with concern. "I'm guessing you can't."

"I can't." Sev shook his head. "Or, well, I *can,* but there wouldn't be a point in building another one. The way those Grand Anchors *work* is by recording and analyzing reality at a fundamental level every time we have to perform a Reset. We don't *have* any more Resets we can do. I don't know how we're going to get that last anchor, if it's even still there, and I'm terrified that after all this work I'm going to lose the last piece we need to save the universe just because I didn't—"

"Sev." Misa interrupted him, her voice strong; Sev realized a little belatedly that he'd started to panic. His breath was coming in hard and fast, and he'd been the first one to stop in the stairwell. He was gripping the railing so tightly that it left his knuckles white, and he saw Misa's gaze linger on his hand.

He let go, embarrassed.

"Sev, I'm not gonna tell you it'll be fine," she continued. "But I *am* gonna say that it doesn't matter. Either it's there or it's not. It's not our primary concern right now, even."

"It's not?" Sev asked, confused.

"No." Misa shook her head, then gestured roughly toward the stairwell that surrounded them. "You mentioned Anderstahl's Prime Anchor is malfunctioning too, right? And we need to fix it?"

"Right . . ." Sev said slowly. He looked around—he didn't see anything wrong with the stairwell. Why was Misa pointing at it?

"Which means stuff in Anderstahl is going to be *weird* sometimes," Misa said. "Because their Prime Anchor is falling apart."

"I feel like you're going somewhere with this, but I'd really rather you just told me," Sev grumbled.

"We've been walking down the same stairwell for the past ten minutes," Misa told him bluntly. "I thought maybe they just mislabeled the floor number at first, but no. We're stuck here. So whatever form of malfunction this Prime Anchor is experiencing, it's very different from Elyra's, and we gotta get to the Anderstahl dungeon *fast.*"

Sev stared at the floor number, then poked his head over the railing to try to peer down to the first floor. All he saw was an endless stretch of staircase that eventually faded into black.

He felt his pulse pick up, and he stumbled backward into Misa, who quickly caught him.

"This is kind of a bad time to realize I never really got over my fear of heights," Sev muttered. Misa chuckled a little at that, but her glance down at the endless staircase held the same amount of concern he felt in his heart.

This . . . was definitely going to be a problem.

—⁂—

Sev sat in a corner of the stairwell. In front of him, Misa paced back and forth, wearing grooves into the stone.

"It's not an attack, so I can't block it," she muttered. "We've tried breaking through the stone, and it just leads to *more stairs.* Neither of our systems are working and we can't get into contact with our friends so they can get us out of here."

"Yep, that sounds about right," Sev said. "Oh, and we have no food or water."

"And we have no food or water." Misa growled a little. "I can't even figure out what's going on in this place using Endless Echoes. It doesn't matter what I try to change; we just end up *back in the stupid stairwell.*" She punched the wall, her Strength stat enough to shatter the stone and break open another hole that just . . . led to more staircase. Sev stared at the hole, then at Misa, who sighed and sat down next to him.

"Sorry," she said after a moment. "I let myself get a little stressed there."

"I mean, you stopped me from falling off the railing," Sev said with a laugh. "What am I gonna do, complain that you're a little mad about being trapped in a staircase?"

"There's something here we're missing." Misa's eyes narrowed. "Anchors don't do things for no reason. When they malfunction, it's almost always because something *stops working*. This isn't that. This is an effect being applied here, to us."

"Right." Sev glanced up at Misa. ". . . You said earlier that you found a new function of [**An Anchor of Heart and Home**]?"

"I did." Misa grinned a bit. "Turns out that I can borrow classes from the people in either Fendal or J'rokksur. Not something I can do *easily*, but I can do it. And the last thing I borrowed was the [**Intuitionist**] class from my mom, so right now I'm dual-classing."

"And the class is telling you something."

"Yup." Misa glanced around. "I'm just not as *used* to this class as Mom is. It's easy enough when it comes to reading people, but trying to figure out what's going on here is completely different. It's like there's a damn itch in my brain."

"It's not the Void," Sev said. "We've been in that place. The Void kind of gives up on the entire concept of distance and movement, but there's a kind of logic to it—when there's nothing there, our minds dictate how it works."

Misa nodded. "Which is why we just kind of drift around in whatever direction we're thinking when we're in Void," she said. She grinned suddenly. "Remember the first time we fell into the Void and Vex just *immediately* crashed into Derivan?"

Sev snickered. "You know, I hadn't thought about that, but he must've been thinking about the big guy, huh?"

"Thinking hard, too." Misa relaxed a little bit, leaning back and using the wall as leverage to crack her spine; she groaned as it popped, then glanced around again, her eyes a little sharper. ". . . Speaking of which, I think I got it."

"Yeah?" Sev asked, glancing up at her. Something in her tone made him grip his staff warily, and he glanced around, expecting something to pop out at them.

"It's not that space is falling apart," Misa said. "Or that the Prime Anchor is failing to maintain something crucial in this random staircase in the middle of Anderstahl.

"It's that the Prime Anchor thinks this stairwell is part of its dungeon, so it's given us a fucking puzzle."

CHAPTER 17

UP AND DOWN

The revelation that they were most likely in a region of Anderstahl that the Prime Anchor had unwittingly designated *part of a dungeon* made Sev tense up immediately. Not because he expected to be attacked, although that was part of it—the dangers in any given dungeon were typically unpredictable, and assuming you were safe in any part of a dungeon was folly.

But it wasn't that danger that made the hair on the back of Sev's neck stand. It was the sudden clarity with which he saw the stairwell they were in. The slight change to the normally sleek stone that made up the walls, rust on the railings that hadn't been there before. Some pieces of the stairwell were broken, and they weren't broken because Misa had broken them. Stone had simply crumbled away at points, weakened from erosion over a long period of time.

"Not just a puzzle," he said. "It's a trap."

A trap meant to catch unsuspecting adventurers off guard, no doubt. He reached out with [**Divine Manipulation**] once again, even as Misa prepared her bow, her expression suddenly just as wary. This wasn't exactly her area of expertise, but with the way her skills had grown, she had more ways of dealing with this than he did.

Case in point . . .

"Freeze," Misa muttered, and fired two conceptual arrows into the walls— one to the left, and the other to the right. "Whatever effect the stairwell's supposed to have, those arrows should slow it down. Some kind of time-related trap, you're thinking?"

"Yeah." Sev leaned down to brush a finger against the railing, frowning at the flakes of rust that came off on his skin. "Is [**Intuitionist**] telling you anything different?"

"I regret to say that it tells me pretty much the exact same thing," Misa said dryly. "More time's passing on the outside than in here. The reverse of the time dilation you usually get in the dungeons. If we caught it any later—"

"The whole universe might be gone by the time we get out, yeah." Sev cast his gaze around. There had to be *something*. No dungeon ever had traps that were outright unbeatable; the problem was that he couldn't sense anything here that was divine in nature to manipulate. The standard threads of divinity that wove through all of existence were here, of course, but they were under the claim of no entity; they weren't being used *against* them. "Doesn't help us with what the dungeon *wants* from us before it lets us out, though. Any chance you can connect to the Prime Anchor with your own? I feel like we should be getting system messages for this."

"If one of us did know how to connect to the Prime Anchor, it would be you, not me," Misa said, a little dryly. Then she tried anyway: Sev saw her concentrate on the force that was kept nestled somewhere between the system attached to her and her soul itself.

After a moment, she shook her head. "Nope," she said, apologetic.

"It's the Anderstahl dungeon," Sev muttered to himself. "What's the Anderstahl dungeon's theme? You've seen it before, Sev, *think* . . ."

"Something to do with Earth?" Misa asked. "It's the Kingdom that represents the planeshifted, right? Made by you guys. All your technology is replicated here, sort of."

"Yeah," Sev answered, distracted. "But I don't have most of my memories from Earth. Most of the time being in Anderstahl just . . . reminds me that I lost something I can never get back."

"Do you think it was nice?" Misa asked. "Earth, I mean."

Sev frowned. "I don't know how to answer that question," he said. "I'm sure there was stuff about it that was *nice*. In fact, I know there was, because a lot of the things here in Anderstahl are really cool. But I don't feel excited or anything when I think about Earth. Just . . . sad."

"I'm sorry," Misa offered.

Sev shrugged listlessly. "Not like we can do anything to change it now," he said, staring listlessly into the stairwell. "I don't think it's missing Earth that gets to me. It's not knowing how my life there shaped me. I don't know if there's anyone that would have missed me, even. Although I suppose if there were, they're probably long gone now."

"You don't talk much about your feelings about Earth," Misa said.

"Because it's hard to think about. Because even if I figured out how I felt about it, I wouldn't be able to do anything about it. And besides, Earth is only a small part of who I am." Sev managed a small smile. "I love it *here*. You, Vex, Derivan—you guys are my family. I worry about who I might have been, but I don't need my history to know who I am now."

Misa chuckled. "We love you too," she said, staring back into the stairwell.

Click.

Misa cast her gaze back into the stairwell along with Sev, staring at the ornaments along the railing, the crumbling stone that made up the stairs. Her arrows were still embedded in the walls, actively slowing down whatever temporal effect the dungeon was trying to place on them.

She could feel the reality anchor inside herself now. That was a new development, brought about partially by Derivan attempting to repair her system and reunite the old Path system with the more modern one of stats and skills; whatever he'd done, he hadn't successfully managed to repair it, but it had somehow made her more *aware* of the metaphysical object that had been bound to her. It clung to the fabric of her existence like a living cloak wrapped tight around her shoulders.

So many people relied on this thing. If the Anderstahl Prime Anchor failed, it would be the last anchor they had left. The last thing holding the existence of tens of thousands of people.

Even now, she could feel it falling apart. Reality shards repaired it, certainly, but it was a near thing; she could tell that the shards repaired a little less every time. Not to the point where she was expecting it to become a concern anytime soon, but enough that it would be a problem eventually. And if it came down to this one anchor to support the weight of everyone that remained ...

Well, it would snap in a heartbeat.

There had to be a link between her anchor and the Anderstahl Prime Anchor nearby. Not because there was some inherent relationship between the two, but because it was how reality anchors were built to work. As far as her understanding of them went, anyway. The Prime Anchors did a majority of the work, but the anchors as a whole were designed to network with one another and sustain reality in a grid, drawing from backups that were updated with the mana crystals the system forced everyone to pay as a tithe.

The network around each Prime Anchor was a little frayed at the edges. It was the reason it was so difficult for information to travel from Elyra to Anderstahl, and vice versa. It wasn't *impossible*, by any means, but the anchors that were near the edge of each set always prioritized the nearest Prime Anchor.

That information was least likely to be corrupted, because it had to travel less through the network. Through the Void.

All of that made sense. The problem was that the reality anchor that was tied to her had originally been linked to Elyra's Prime Anchor. It had been disconnected from the larger network and now served as a sort of Prime Anchor on its own, but that made it harder for it to connect with Anderstahl's Prime Anchor, not easier—it was prioritizing *itself*.

And Misa didn't want to change that. It *needed* to prioritize itself. The Anderstahl Prime Anchor was malfunctioning; she didn't trust it to take over for the work of her anchor, especially when so many people relied on it. Including her own family.

"You're sure you don't remember what the Prime Dungeon here was about?" she asked tiredly.

She wasn't actually tired. Probably. Part of it was the effect of having nothing to *do*; Misa wasn't used to this level of inactivity. She was half-tempted to start working out just so she could have something to focus on.

Actually, she *was* going to start working out. She placed her mace against the corner and started doing pushups, much to Sev's bemusement.

"I'm trying," he said. "And, uh . . . what are you doing?"

"Pushups."

"You can't train Strength that way at your level."

"I'm not training Strength. I'm just bored."

—⚎—

It *did* look incredibly easy for her to be doing those pushups despite the amount of armor she was wearing. Sev grimaced for a bit, imagining trying that himself— Nope. No thanks. The robes he wore weren't fun to sweat in, and all the solutions for that lay in the notably missing Vex's [**Prestidigitation**].

"I should ask for a divine version of [**Prestidigitation**]," Sev muttered to himself.

He couldn't remember what Anderstahl's Prime Dungeon was like. The memory felt like a hole in his head, and it was worse given the fact that he *should* know; all the memories surrounding the dungeon had been restored. But there was an emptiness in his head when he tried to recall the dungeon itself, and for the life of him, he didn't know *why*.

Was there a reason for this, even? Or was it sheer misfortune that left a jarring gap in his memories?

Anderstahl was the Prime Kingdom of the planeshifted. It was the kingdom of technology and invention—the things he remembered of it in his memories painted an image of a beautiful kingdom. Not a paradise by any means, but it was a kingdom he was proud of living in, at least.

He remembered the little toy shop he owned on a corner of the street. He remembered working late into the night, repairing one toy or building another. Train sets were surprisingly popular with people among all age groups, though many of them insisted on seeing a real-life version of a train.

... Come to think of it, he wondered if his little inventions had anything to do with the way Anderstahl had later built exactly that—a magically powered train designed to take its passengers all across the kingdom. There had been plans to make it reach both of the other Prime Kingdoms and across continents, even, before they'd discovered the encroaching Void.

After that, those plans had been laid aside.

It was a pity, really. The train had been an ambitious project, but if it *had* been built, even just on this continent, it could have been used to help the Prime Anchors stay connected—

Sev's eyes went wide.

"It's a goddamn *train*," he said, almost hissing out the words. He jumped to his feet, staring at the staircase as if the realization would unveil whatever trick was hidden in this so-called dungeon puzzle.

Misa just stared at him. "What in the hells is a train?"

CHAPTER 18

TRAINS

"Okay, okay," Sev said. "Knowing that it's a train doesn't actually help us. Does it?"

"You still haven't even explained what a train is," Misa said dryly. She'd stopped with the pushups and gone back to leaning against the wall and tapping the head of her mace against her palm impatiently.

"It's like . . . a bunch of wagons linked up and guided on rails," Sev explained vaguely. "Powered by a mana engine of some kind, usually. There's one in Anderstahl, actually. We can go see it later. Or you'll see it when we find the dungeon."

"You're telling me Anderstahl's Prime Dungeon is a *vehicle*?" Misa asked. She sighed. "Guess weirder shit's happened."

"I mean, kind of." Sev shrugged. "It's a train and the stuff around the train. It's hard to explain. You'll get it when you see it; trust me. I'm just . . . not sure how this helps us." He squinted at the stairs, as if looking at them for the millionth time would somehow unveil the answer to him.

The problem was that in the context of the dungeon, a staircase didn't make *sense* as a trap. Anderstahl's Prime Dungeon was a peculiar one—the train was the only part of the dungeon that was safe. It stopped in stations that would require something from the adventurers delving the dungeon before the train would move on; sometimes, that was a boss fight, and other times, it was a puzzle.

In no situation that he remembered had one of those stations ever been a simple staircase. It was possible that the station itself would have a stairwell as a trap, of course, and that getting out of the stairwell would let them find something that would let the train move on. But then what would the dungeon be testing?

And also, where was the rest of the station?

"Misa," Sev said. "Let's go back up the stairs."

"Back *up*?" Misa glanced at him. "I feel like that's the opposite of the direction we're supposed to go. And we also already tried it."

"Let's try it again," Sev insisted. They *had* tried it again, to see if they could exit the stairwell from the rooftop door they'd originally entered; no surprise that the door was gone. It wasn't that easy to get out of a dungeon trap.

But. *But.*

Presumably, the dungeon wanted them to get somewhere. He didn't know what direction it wanted them to go in, but that was fine. He just had to look out for something that *changed*, in whatever direction they went.

Up was first. He climbed the steps with Misa, stopping every so often to look at the walls and the railing again. Other than the typical deterioration of the dungeon's trap mechanism, he didn't notice anything unusual.

"Now back down," he said. Misa just stared at him skeptically but acquiesced.

Sev stopped after they moved down a flight of steps. "There," he said. "This brick's different."

"The . . . brick?" Misa glanced at where he was pointing. "Sev, that's just a brick."

"It's shaped differently," he insisted. "Look. It doesn't fit in with the rest of the wall. Like it's a little smaller."

"Huh." Misa frowned at it. ". . . I guess you're right."

Sev walked over to the brick, but Misa grabbed his hand. "Hang on," she said. "I don't think we're supposed to touch it."

". . . Shouldn't it open a secret passage or something?" Sev asked. "That's how it works in every dungeon."

"I know, but . . ." Misa frowned again. She stepped forward and pressed on the misshapen brick experimentally, then winced slightly; Sev saw her health drop by a fraction. "That's not what [**Intuitionist**] is telling me. It's telling me we should turn back. And quickly, actually." She paused. ". . . The brick's leaking. Definitely quickly. Actually, *now*."

Before Sev could protest, she physically grabbed him, tucking him under her arm like he was a ball she was carrying and not a five-foot-nine human. Then she raced up the stairs—one flight, two—and stopped again.

"You're right," she said. "It's got something to do with the way the staircase changes when we go down. Almost like we're trying to find the right iteration of the stairs to go down, and it changes every time we try."

"Shifts?" Sev frowned. "I guess that makes sense. And if it's just going to be stuff like a brick being out of place—"

Sev stopped midsentence, staring at the next flight of stairs. There was an unsettling feeling coiled in his gut, and he couldn't identify what it was; the stairwell *looked* exactly the same . . .

. . . No. No, it didn't. It was subtle, but there was the faintest impression of a face marked into every brick of this particular iteration of the stairwell.

"Well," Misa said. "I guess that means we're making progress. I think."

"This still isn't the right staircase," Sev said, hiding a shudder. He didn't even want to turn back around—turning his back on the faces gave him a prickling sensation on the back of his neck. "We're going back up."

He walked backward up the steps. Misa watched him, then shrugged. "Ain't gonna hear an argument from me. I don't want to go down the creepy face stairs. Plus, you were about to step on one."

"And you didn't warn me?" Sev glared.

Misa grinned at him. "I'm kidding. But I *did* want to see your face when I said that."

Sev just grumbled. The sensation of fear slowly uncoiled from his gut as he moved up one entire flight of stairs; sighing, he turned back around, looking back down the seemingly normal stairwell.

"All right," he said. "Let's try this again."

—✦—

Sev was beginning to feel . . . annoyed. Mostly annoyed. There was some amount of fear here, and an undeniable tension that came from the feeling of being *stuck*; claustrophobia clung to his mind like cobwebs, though he wasn't normally claustrophobic at all.

But even that was beginning to fade to make way for annoyance.

Every step of progress was accompanied by four to five missteps. They kept going down every time the stairs appeared normal, and stopped and retraced their steps back up a flight every time something seemed off besides the deterioration of the stairwell itself.

Strangely, the changes made themselves more obvious, not less, the more progress they made. A sign they were on the right track, perhaps.

Sometimes the bricks began to leak. Other times, the hazards and traps were more obvious—there was at least one occasion in which the stairs simply faded away into nothing, and another one where a thing made of shadow stood there on the steps, staring at them. They'd backed away slowly from it. There was no indication that it was a monster, or that it was capable of hearing what they were saying. As far as either of them could tell, it was just a hazard placed in their path by the dungeon.

There *were* times when the changes were more subtle. A change in the smell, for example, from a musty staircase to a slightly sweet vanilla that rang all sorts of alarm bells in Sev's head. Or a shift in the distance between the steps that Sev wouldn't have noticed if he hadn't inadvertently stumbled.

"This is just so unnecessarily creepy," Sev muttered. He glanced down the next flight of stairs with trepidation, wondering if there was going to be yet another entity standing there, staring at them—and nearly turned back immediately when he *did*, in fact, see a silhouette in the shadows. But the silhouette didn't seem nearly as threatening as the other ones, and Misa placed a hand on his back, as if to stop him from instinctively turning back.

"Wait," she said. "I think this one's right. Look—there's a door next to him."

"What?" Sev squinted down, finally managing to make out the faint outline of a rectangular shape set into the brick. He stared at it doubtfully. "I feel like calling that a door is a bit charitable."

Misa rolled her eyes. "Whatever. You know what I mean. We're supposed to go through it."

"Are you *sure*?" Sev pressed, although he relented when Misa gave him a *look*. "Okay, okay. Look, I just don't want to walk down yet another ominous flight of steps without full awareness of what's going to happen—"

Misa was already walking down. "That's okay!" she called back. "I'll do it for you!"

Sev startled, then scrambled to catch up to her.

The man standing next to the door—and he was, as far as Sev could tell, just an ordinary man, although the smile on his face seemed a little too fixed for him to be comfortable with it—greeted them with a tip of his hat. "Adventurers!" he greeted. "You must be here to explore our dungeon. Congratulations for making it this far! Do you have your tickets?"

"Tickets?" Sev exchanged a confused look with Misa. "Oh, shit. This is the *dungeon entrance.*"

"This is *a* dungeon entrance!" the man corrected cheerfully. "And you have successfully completed your entrance exam! Congratulations!"

". . . Thank you?" Sev said.

"I was kidding about the tickets, by the way," the man said with a wink. "You get your first tickets for free by getting to the bottom of the stairs. Good job! Be sure to give it to the Conductor, now, or you're going to have some trouble."

With that, he brandished two silver tickets that gleamed in the dim light. Misa took them, examining them just enough to make sure it wasn't a dungeon trap before handing Sev his ticket.

"Don't forget," the man said. "You can only leave once your train has arrived at the last station. Good luck!"

With that, he waved at the vaguely rectangular outline set into the wall. The bricks receded, then moved to the side, blasting them with the scent of coal and . . . soap, somehow. Sev blinked once, then stepped through the stone of the stairwell and into the cabin of a train.

"Well," Sev said. "I guess we have to give the dungeon points for creativity."

Misa followed him through. "Guess we're just here now," she said, looking around the cabin. "This place is . . . surprisingly cozy."

"Yeah," Sev said. He glanced around too, looking at the train cabin. Plush seats lined each side, hemmed in by intricate gold frames; really, each set of seats was more like a booth, with a large table provided in the middle for an adventurer to set down their adventuring gear. He recognized the little circular device in the center of each table, actually: it repaired most adventuring gear, even up to Platinum-ranked ones, provided the adventurer had the mana crystals to fuel them with.

A twin set of metal rails glided along the ceiling. Sev recognized *those*, too; they were designed to carry food and other items that were purchased through the system. If there was anything this dungeon wasn't lacking in, it was hospitality.

Until you had to get out of the train, anyway.

"Let's get some food," Sev said with a sigh. "We're here already. We'll find the Prime Anchor, fix it, and then get out of here. How's that sound?"

"You had me at *food*," Misa said. "Where's the Conductor?"

"Eh, he'll be along." Sev shrugged. "This dungeon's very particular about how it does things. I wouldn't worry about it. I doubt he'll even show up until we've had our first meal and settled down."

CHAPTER 19

BROAD ASSUMPTIONS

The meal they had was *fantastic*. Sev regretted that he hadn't called for Derivan and Vex to join them—this would have been an incredible dungeon delve for the four of them to go on together. His memories of the dungeon were returning, and while it wasn't devoid of its dangers, the Anderstahl Prime Dungeon was a monument to flexibility and adaptation. Every run was different.

"Are our systems still not working?" Sev asked, glancing at Misa. She frowned a little, prodding at the air and then shaking her head slightly.

"It's still connected to my reality anchor, but for whatever reason the signal just won't go out beyond the dungeon," she said, sighing with frustration. "Sucks. I'd really like to check in on some people right now."

Sev grimaced. "I was hoping that would go away once we were out of the staircase."

"Guess it's a dungeon-wide thing," Misa said with a shrug. "That, or it's another puzzle and there's something we gotta do to get the system's chat function working again."

"That sounds more likely. I don't remember this dungeon not allowing system communication," Sev said. "Though that means our first challenge is probably going to be about restoring the connection."

"That's not a bad thing, is it?" Misa asked.

"*Hopefully.*" Sev shrugged. "It's been a long time since I've been here, and there have been a whole few Resets between then and now. I don't know if it's any different. But the first Challenge is usually something simple—"

Something in the train *dinged*. The door farther ahead in their cabin opened, and a tall wood-and-silver golem walked through, wearing an immaculately pressed suit. He tipped his hat toward the two of them.

"I am the Conductor. Tickets, please," he said politely. Sev and Misa both produced their silvery tickets, and the Conductor accepted them without a moment's pause; he slid each ticket into a slot in his chest, then stood there for a minute, machinery whirring within him.

"Uh . . ." Misa said awkwardly, staring at the Conductor. "Do you need anything else?"

Another short whirr, and then the Conductor bowed. "No. Thank you for your cooperation. The train will arrive at the next station in fifteen minutes. Please enjoy the ride."

Misa stared at the Conductor as he left. "You get a weird feelin' about that guy?"

"Depends on what you mean." Sev gave Misa a strange look. "What kind of weird?"

"Not *bad* weird," Misa tried to explain, gesturing vaguely. "More like . . . *important* weird. Like [**Intuitionist**] is pinging on something agai—"

Misa was interrupted by a blast of light into the cabin as the train moved outside of whatever dark tunnel it was in connected to the entrance staircase; sunlight streamed in through the windows, bright enough that Sev had to blink several times to help his eyes adjust. Outside was, as near as he could tell, open sky and a beautiful field of flowers. The only thing that indicated that they might have been in a dungeon was the strange way the flowers moved—against the flow of the grass, like they were struggling against the wind.

"Whoa," Misa said, forgetting what she was talking about. "Tell me our first stop's going to be out there."

"Probably not," Sev said. "Though it's not like we have to stay at the station we stop at. Sometimes we have to go out and explore, or gather something nearby. This might be one of those."

"It's just been a while since I've gotten to just enjoy a field like this," Misa said, still looking out the window. "We passed through a few, guiding the Elyran convoy to Anderstahl, but there were kind of a lot of people to take care of back then."

"Yeah." Sev hummed in agreement. "I wouldn't mind going out there if we get the chance. Would be a great spot for a picnic if we didn't have bigger things to worry about."

"Tell me about it," Misa said.

They both proceeded to stare as one of the flowers erupted out of the ground, a massive *creature* that looked like someone had haphazardly stuck a worm and a crab together bursting into the air. It ate a cloud, then promptly disappeared back into the field of grass, leaving not a single mark that it had ever emerged.

Sev glanced at Misa. "That didn't make you want to go out there *less*, did it?"

"Are you kidding?" Misa grinned, twirling her mace in her hands. "Now I *really* want to go out there."

—m—

Vex, Derivan, Raltis, and Novice were all seated together in the forbidden section of the tower library. Vex hadn't had an opportunity to visit this library before and found it fascinating to even enter—there was a glyphic passphrase embedded in one of the tower walls that led into a closet, only that closet was bigger on the inside and held a *massive* number of books.

Raltis had lied a little bit about the recorded history of the world. It wasn't that everything was completely gone. It was that the records they did have were unsorted, and the residents of Teque had never had the time or the interest to go through and sort everything out from the real and the fake.

Basically, at some point, someone had cast a powerful library-aspect spell to record all of history, essentially by pulling pieces of history from the minds of everyone in Teque. This was technically an incredible feat of magic, and one that had been celebrated by everyone in Teque.

They had then proceeded to ignore the library for the next few decades. After all, the information was *technically* safe. There was no need to go through and sort it until and unless they actually needed the information.

"Bet you're regretting that now," Novice commented, staring up in awe at the towering shelves of books.

"This isn't even the first time you've been here," Raltis said irritably. "Why are you looking at the shelves like it's your first time?"

"Because look at them!" Novice gestured, spreading his arms wide. "I don't want to forget how *cool* this place is!"

Vex laughed. He couldn't help it; he felt much the same way as Novice. "How did you even make a forbidden section?" he asked. "If everything in here is unsorted, I would've just assumed no one knows what should or shouldn't be forbidden."

"Helg was one of the few people willing to sort through the library, believe it or not." Raltis sighed, a note of melancholy entering his voice. He glanced around briefly. "She loved this place too. Genuinely. Could spend hours in here reading, especially when she was a kid. The reason she got so . . . passionate . . . about risks, and about forbidding certain kinds of knowledge, is because of what happened when she tried to recreate something from one of the books."

"Oh shit," Vex muttered, already able to guess where this was going.

"Yep." Raltis stared up at the ceiling. "I should've stopped it, but I didn't see it coming. Like I said, most of us don't really know what's in these books. It's not like magic is *always* beautiful and good and magical. She tried to copy a glyph to cast a kind of summoning spell—to make herself an imaginary friend, or something like that—and ..."

A long pause. Vex waited, not saying a word; Raltis seemed to be trying to gather the strength to explain what had happened. Eventually, the otter sighed, looking down at the table.

"Her parents died," he said simply. "The spell wasn't complete. It was *wrong*, even; she got some of the strokes in the glyph wrong, but she's favored by the mana so it tried to help her complete the spell anyway. That's good when you're an experienced mage. It's not good when it's a child."

"Gods," Vex said, swallowing. "The mana did that?"

"We always say the mana is alive," Raltis said. "And it is. But it's not *alive* the same way a lot of us are, and it doesn't look at the world the same way we do. It values choice, freedom, change; it loves art and history and power. It's a force of will and imposition. It doesn't distinguish between good and bad."

"Right." Vex had known this, of course, though he'd never seen such a clear example of it before. He glanced at his hands, where a few streams of mana danced between his fingers.

Still beautiful, he thought. But there was danger hidden in that power— danger he didn't usually let himself think too hard about.

"So Helg's parents died trying to save her from what she created," Raltis said. "It was a sort of ... distortion in reality that sucked away people's mana. Incredibly dangerous thing. They were able to overload it, but at the cost of their own mana."

"Explains her reaction to the Fendal thing," Vex said quietly. "... Explains why you didn't fight her on it at first, too."

Raltis looked down, guilty. "It's not an excuse, I know," he said quietly. "She was like a daughter to me, you know? I picked her up hoping to help her after what happened, and she was always so ... well, she was sad at first. Then she was angry. Then she took up a role in enforcement, trying to make sure nothing like this ever happened again. She locked up a bunch of books here in the forbidden section—everything remotely related to summoning magic, anything related to *new* magic."

"I guess I can understand it," Vex said with a sigh, leaning back in his chair.

"Me too," Novice said quietly. "I can't forgive it. Not . . . even if I wanted to. Having my sense of self taken away from me like that . . . I still get nightmares sometimes, Raltis. But at least I know where she was coming from now."

"It must have been difficult," Derivan said, not unkindly, speaking up for the first time this conversation. Vex glanced at him to see him staring at Raltis, and saw the expression in his eyes. Kind, sympathetic, worried. Physical Empathy must have been going off hard. How much did Raltis really blame himself for this?

"It was," Raltis said. His voice was small. "I should have . . . I don't know what I should have done. I should never have let it all go this far. I didn't realize how *scared* she still was that it could all happen again. I thought she had a passion for enforcement, for making sure the people were safe . . . I didn't think she would turn that passion into something that would make an entire town a slave to themselves just to try to keep us safe. And I never even got a chance to . . ."

Raltis trailed off as he spoke, and this time, even Vex could hear the choked sob in his voice. Across the table, Novice leaned over, the lizardkin putting an arm around the old otter's shoulder and pulling him close in a one-armed hug.

"I'm sorry," Novice said quietly.

Vex stayed silent, for the most part. What else was there to say? He hadn't *been* there for the fight against Helg. They hadn't even been able to stop her initial barrier spell when she was kicking them out of Teque.

"You should give yourself time to grieve," Derivan said. He didn't seem to have the same problem Vex was having. "You have been working on the relationship between Fendal and Teque in an attempt to atone for your support of Helg's actions. And taxing your magic in order to keep everyone healthy."

"How did you—" Raltis began, startled.

"But you have not given yourself time to grieve," Derivan continued, not giving Raltis time to speak. "You are pushing yourself too far, Raltis. Take some time to grieve. Honor her memory."

"But what she did . . ." Raltis faltered. "I . . . I don't even know if I *should*. What she did was awful."

"What she did does not change the way you feel about her," Derivan countered. "You see yourself as her father. Her guide. You feel you have failed her, but there are many memories you made with her that you cannot let go of. And it is that version of her, real or otherwise, that you have not allowed yourself to grieve for."

Raltis let out another half-choked sob. Next to him, Novice shook his head, his expression a little ashen. "Shit," Novice muttered. "I should've seen this. We have a [**Soul Link**], for crying out loud."

"I didn't let you," Raltis said. "I didn't— I couldn't. After what Helg did to you and your friends, I didn't want you to have to feel me grieving for her."

"I would *understand* if you just explained this," Novice said with a sigh. He pulled the otter close, dragging him into a tight hug while Raltis proceeded to quite openly cry; Vex avoided looking at the two, if only to give them a moment of privacy.

"I . . . I think you're right, Derivan," Raltis said after a moment, taking in a deep, shaky breath. "I think I need a bit of time to grieve her. I don't know if I'm grieving who I thought she was, or if I'm grieving someone she used to be . . . but she was important to me, and I failed her."

Derivan watched Raltis for a moment, then gave him a slight nod. "I do not know that I would characterize it in that way," he said. "But I will not interfere with your grieving process. You will need time to come to terms. We will still be here when you are done."

"Oh, I don't know about that." Raltis managed a slight smile, though there was no real heart in it. "But . . . yeah. I'll try to be quick." The archmage slipped down from his chair. "Novice, you stay here and help them. I'll be at my home if you need me. Just, um . . . just knock first. In case I put any spells on the door."

"I will," Novice said.

With that, Raltis walked out of the library. His steps were slow and heavy, like there was something dragging him down—Vex saw him clenching and unclenching his fists, like he was trying to keep himself steady and stable just long enough for him to get to his usual home. Vex looked up at Novice, sympathetic.

"I didn't know he felt that way," Novice said, sounding a little guilty. "I guess I should've asked. Never thought to question why he let Helg do what she did. I just thought he was being an asshole."

"What he did to enable her was wrong, just as much as what she did was wrong," Derivan said. "But those mistakes have been made now, and we are left with the consequences. All we can do is try to recover and to learn from mistakes once made."

"Wise words," Novice said, sighing. "Well . . . let's get back to it, guys. Still a lot of books to get through."

CHAPTER 20

SEMERIT DEMERIT

An hour later found them with a small pile of books about semerit. If there was anything Helg was good at, it was organization—all the books about semerit were sorted together, and it hadn't actually taken a lot of time for them to find the section and then drag every last one of those books over to their shared table.

The "small pile" probably had over a hundred books in it. It was only small relative to the size of the library.

"A lot of these books are just fiction," Vex said with a slight frown. He stared at the book he was holding. It was, as best as he could tell, a children's book about a so-called "chosen one" who wielded a semerit of courage. "And they're basically just using the word *semerit* to describe any random artifact of power. Or any item the plot has to revolve around, even."

"I don't think Helg was being very discerning when she sorted the books here," Novice said dryly. "Any mention of it was enough."

"It shows," Vex said with a sigh. He put the book he was looking at to the side into a growing pile of *books that were unlikely to have any worthwhile information*, and picked up the next one.

He stopped.

This book had mana in it. It hadn't been obvious from a distance, not even to someone with [**Advanced Mana Sight**] constantly active like he did— almost like there was a protective layer of some sort shielding the book. But the moment his scales made contact with the tome, he could *feel* it, surging within the pages. Almost . . . trapped.

Sure enough, trying to open the book did nothing; it remained stuck stubbornly closed.

Good thing he had a spell for that.

"This one's enchanted," Vex said. "And locked with an enchantment, too. You know anything about that?"

"What?" Novice looked up, frowning. "No. The forbidden section itself is already locked; none of the books inside it are supposed to have any extra enchantments on them. Are you sure the pages aren't just . . . stuck together or something? Maybe someone spilled some juice on it."

Vex gave Novice a deadpan look, and the other lizardkin laughed sheepishly. "Or maybe not."

"It is slightly Shifted," Derivan commented, glancing over to the tome. "You are able to unlock it?"

"Yeah, I got this," Vex said. He held a hand out over the book, channeling a basic [**Dispel**] on the outermost enchantment. "Just wanted to see if there was anything I needed to be aware of. [**Dispel**]ling an unknown enchantment isn't always a good idea."

"I can help if something goes wrong," Novice offered.

"As can I," Derivan said. He placed the book he was looking through down and turned in his chair to fully face Vex.

"It's probably not anything that serious," Vex said, chuckling awkwardly—mostly to hide the fact that he was actually nervous. This felt a little too much like a trap. "I'm going to [**Dispel**] it now."

It had been a while since he'd done this. Vex pulled out his dagger, cutting the system rune for [**Dispel**] into the air and targeting the book; he felt mana gather into the rigid structure of the rune, and gently modified it into something a little closer to its glyphic form so the spell wouldn't fight with the ambient mana in Teque. There was a brief pause as the mana recognized the spell he was casting, followed by a flash of light—

—and then an enormous wave of mana poured out of the book. Vex almost flinched; the power was strong enough that he could feel it, and it would have physically pushed him back if he hadn't been sitting in his chair. As it was, it was strong enough to slightly make his chair tilt. Novice nearly *did* fall over.

Derivan didn't budge at all, of course.

"Jeez," Vex muttered, opening the book. "That was a *lot* of mana stored in this thing. Why put so much mana into a book?"

Novice stared at him. "I'm almost certain you just used a basic [**Dispel**] on a Platinum-rank enchantment."

"What?" Vex looked up at Novice, blinking. "Oh, uh. Probably, I guess?"

Novice just shook his head in astonishment. Vex, who didn't quite get it, went back to the book, stopping at the first page.

This wasn't written like a traditional book. This was a *diary*.

Day 1.

I've acquired access to the Far Libraries. It's a momentous day! They don't usually let anyone visit—hard enough to get a qualified Navigator these days, and half of the Libraries are down for maintenance or something. Think it's related to what's happening all across Obreve, but I can't be sure. Going to keep a record of everything I find and discover, just in case I become part of the Forgotten. Hopefully the enchantment on this book will keep it safe. Powerful-enough magic should repel the Void . . . in theory.

The hope is that the Far Libraries will have something that can help us. They're supposed to be a record of everything that's ever happened and everything that will ever happen—if there's any solution to this crisis at all, it'll be written in a book somewhere. Normally they don't let outsiders come in and search for the future like this, but I guess they must be desperate too, huh?

. . . In retrospect, that's actually probably not a good sign. Hm.

Day 2.

The journey took a lot longer than I expected. I feel like we passed a lot of Libraries on the way to this one, but for whatever reason my Navigator wouldn't stop at any of the other ones—maybe I'm only authorized to visit this one, or something. I don't really know how the Librarians work as an organization. I'm not complaining; getting access at all is a privilege.

The problem is that there are just . . . so many books. Library magic doesn't help me sort through them. I mean, it does, but there's so much of it that library magic barely helps. I don't know enough about the book I want to narrow down the search, and looking blindly for "the future" leads me down rows of empty shelves.

Which is worrying. There shouldn't be empty shelves. Not in the Far Libraries. They're an infinite record. How could there be any empty shelves?

Whatever. I'm . . . I'm sure I'll find what I need somewhere in here. I've got to.

Day 3.

I've heard about semerit before. This is the first time I've seen one in person. It's nothing like I imagined—all glass and bone and twisted roots. I'm not actually sure how to describe it, but it's kind of . . . ugly. The Librarian says it isn't supposed to look like that, which is probably the most worrying thing I've heard while here, and I've heard a lot of worrying things.

Like new books no longer showing up. It's making me wonder if we don't actually find a solution for this in the end.

But . . . the future isn't set in stone. The Librarians say this themselves. Sometimes a change happens and sweeps through the Far Libraries. New books show up, old ones disappear. So my hope is that I'll find something here that changes things. The best part is that I'd get to see the results immediately!

So far no changes, though.

I think I'm going to look into this semerit thing. Judging by what the Librarian has said, it's going to be our best bet at beating back the Void, whatever the Void is. So the next few pages are going to be notes on everything I find out about them.

Day 4.

Okay, so, semerit are . . . harbingers of change to the mana, or something. It's all kind of technical. The Far Libraries serve as some kind of archive that the magic draws from, like a giant magical database maintained by the Librarians. I still have no idea who or what the Librarians are. People made by mana, I guess? Not sure how to feel about a group of people literally created to maintain a magical database. I need to ask Greg—I should probably mention that the Librarian showing me around this place is named Greg, or at least he says that's what I should call him—if he gets vacation days. It's kind of messed up if he doesn't.

Anyway, back to the semerit thing. They're harbingers of change. They show up when a new bookshelf is about to be filled, or when a new spell is going to be created. Sometimes it's the other way around, too. Sometimes they show up when a set of shelves is about to be destroyed, or a bunch of books are going to disappear, because of some fundamental change to time.

So that's . . . interesting. It's almost like they're stored potential. Or like . . . a waste product created when a massive change occurs, to think about it in a nastier way. It's probably not a waste product. The Librarians speak about it like they're almost divine devices, and I can feel an enormous amount of power stored in them.

Maybe it'd be more accurate to think of them as tumors. Like reality can't perfectly adjust to all the changes that magic makes to it, so the mana just stuffs all that extra change into a little ball and calls it a day. Tons of stored potential, not much use. Symbolic in nature, for the most part, but that doesn't mean they can't be used.

I'll have to run that idea by Greg.

Day 5.

Greg says he's willing to let me try just about anything, at this point, which is also worrying but kind of gratifying. I think he trusts me!

Well, that, or he's tired of me. I'm going with the more optimistic thought process on that one.

I've tried casting a few diagnostic spells on the semerit, to disappointing results. Mana refuses to acknowledge it. There's probably a way to get it to work, but I think I'm going to switch to more technological means of analysis. Theoretically, someone with a good enough relationship with mana and with a true understanding of its nature might be able to use that stored potential of change to impose any kind of change in reality that they want, kind of like a limitless spell . . . but that's not going to be me. I can barely use magic to tie my shoelaces.

Day 6.

Technology is great! I've managed to tap into the semerit, and I was right! It contains records—a whole different branch of reality stored like a tumor. The way things could have been, but trapped within a physical vessel. The Far Libraries feed on these things, almost; some of the older semerit seem to be mostly dead, their power drained. Interesting ecosystem of sorts.

As for whether that's useful . . . maybe. I think if I can find a semerit where the Void never shows up, I could maybe find a way to force reality to align to that future instead of the one we're currently in. Wish me luck!

Day 6,182.
I've searched them all. There is none.

CHAPTER 21

PARADOX OF CHANGE

"That was a little depressing." Vex stared at the cover of the now-closed book. It had been a remarkably short read, considering the size of it. The rest of the pages were blank, though Vex flipped through them all in the faint hope that one of them would contain . . . something. Some hint at who had once owned this book. Any insight into who this person might have been.

But there was nothing. They hadn't ever thought to identify themselves, or if they had, then perhaps that information had been erased by the Void, and all that remained were the first few pages. Vex somehow doubted that was the case; it wasn't like there were a hundred empty pages between the last and second-to-last entries.

Derivan gave him a sympathetic glance. "I imagine there are many in the past that have tried to spare us from this fate," he said. "The author of this journal is surely brave for trying."

"Yeah, it's just . . . none of it *worked*, did it?" Vex stared up listlessly, brushing his fingers over the cover of the book. "Um, not that the information in the book isn't important. I think I've got an idea."

"I imagine many of those individuals had varying degrees of success," Derivan said. "We have the reality anchors, after all. Perhaps this person's discoveries were important, at the very least in our iteration of reality."

Vex nodded. "We'd have to talk to Xothok to see if there's anything else about the Far Libraries that we missed," he said distantly, his mind already focused on what he might be able to do with a better understanding of the semerit's capabilities. The description of them in the diary was still helpful—it explained the dragon transformation, for example. He'd been able to tap into the potential contained within the semerit and apply that change to himself.

It also implied that that this semerit held a version of reality that had once had dragons. Vex wondered if this was related to the kingdom he'd seen within the semerit. Perhaps that unnamed kingdom had had a relationship with dragons, though he hadn't had the opportunity to see one while within it . . .

There were still some things that seemed inconsistent here. He'd acquired the semerit within a Far Library in the systemless version of reality within his bonus room, but the kingdom he'd seen *had* the system. They'd used it.

"I wonder if semerit are universal across realities," Vex muttered to himself.

"I think they are!" Novice spoke up. The other lizardkin had been buried in his own tiny pile of books until now, but he reached out and plucked out a book from the pile. "This one's mostly just a series of myths, but it includes a claim about a Librarian saying something about semerit being full of things that 'never could have been.'"

"Vague," Derivan remarked.

"I mean, it kinda makes sense anyway, right?" Novice shrugged. "Why should the semerit just contain changes caused by magic?"

"It depends on how it forms, but I think we don't know enough about how the Far Libraries work," Vex said. "This semerit was created when Derivan and I created new magic—but there's no way the creation of those glyphs caused a kingdom an entire timeline away to be erased. I sure hope not, anyway."

"Perhaps they contain changes the mana deems significant," Derivan suggested. "Or perhaps the glyphs we created did not create this change but gave the mana sufficient power to record it."

"Either way, we know what's in the semerit," Vex said. "And we know what the semerit *is*. That's what's important here. I'm thinking we can use that in combination with the translation-aspect magic you've been using and the [**Spelldisk**]. We were already gonna try this, but knowing what a semerit *is* helps. I can design a spell to unfold all those changes into reality."

"Awesome!" Novice cheered. "I think I can help. If you want me to, that is."

"Of course," Vex said. "We're going to need all three of us. Raltis, too, if he can make it, but . . ." He hesitated, glancing at the entrance to the tower library. "Well, we'll figure it out even if he can't."

"We will," Derivan echoed. He glanced over at Vex, then took the lizardkin's hand, and Vex smiled up at him.

Novice just grinned at them both.

—⁓—

Knowing what the nature of the semerit was . . . helped. The Primordial Glyph of Translation was able to take that knowledge in combination with his own Sign of Research, and with that combined spell, he was able to learn more about the semerit than he'd ever been able to before.

[Semerit of the First Library]

Contains Enkiros, the Prime Kingdom of Divinity. Their connection to the divine planes is unparalleled, but they were unaware as their gods were consumed by their Prime Anchor in an effort to sustain their kingdom; as a result, they remained unaware as their kingdom was slowly swallowed up from within. All that remains of Enkiros now is the bare, remnant knowledge that there should be three Prime Kingdoms. The name and its people were lost to time.

The results of this sequence of events were changed and altered by the actions of Vex Ashion, scion of the Ashion House. In interfering with the king's decisions and recommending an evacuation, the people of Enkiros were preserved. They evacuated the kingdom and scattered into the surrounding lands, taking their knowledge and their secrets with them.

The paradox generated by these two differing timelines empowers this semerit, allowing its wielder to draw knowledge or artifacts from either potential outcome, as well as to visit any point in time within the period contained by the semerit.

—⁂—

"That's a lot," Vex remarked, reading over the results of his magic two more times, just to make sure he didn't miss anything. He wasn't surprised that the semerit contained the third and final Prime Kingdom—he'd been hoping that was the case but hadn't wanted to voice that hope. It made sense that the Roads had led them to a way to save Enkiros and its people.

"So, how are we gonna do this?" Novice asked excitedly. "Do you need space? Because I don't think there's enough space in Teque to host a whole kingdom. Oh! Maybe if we modified the Roads . . ."

"That's more magic than necessary," Vex said dryly; he shuddered to think of the amount of mana it would take to conjure up enough space to host an entire kingdom, let alone connect the Roads to it. Granted, he was hoping to cast an even bigger feat of magic, once he had a better handle on things—but he wasn't quite ready to go *that* far yet. "We can just go to where Enkiros is supposed to be and replace what's been erased there."

"Is that safe?" Novice asked, suddenly worried. "That whole area is going to be half-consumed by Void, right?"

"Nothing is safe these days," Vex said, glancing at Derivan. "We'll do our best to make sure it's safe, but you're right. We're going to be surrounded by Void, and that spot is probably being actively consumed as we speak. But it'll make the magic less draining to perform, and it's probably our best bet to actually doing it. Recreating the kingdom in an entirely different place from where it should be is a whole other level of paradox we'd have to deal with."

"I guess you're right," Novice said, wincing a little at the thought. "Um . . . do we know where Enkiros *is*? Because I don't actually know where the third Prime Kingdom is supposed to be."

Vex shrugged, inscribing a map of the continent onto the table with a quick flash of mana. "Well," he said. He pointed to where a partially consumed Elyra was marked, then to where Anderstahl was marked, at the southeast and southwest sectors of the continent respectively. "North, probably."

Up north was a section of the map that was entirely devoid of any markings—no trees, no rivers, no mountains, no towns. Novice stared at it for a moment, then nodded.

"Yeah," he said awkwardly. "That makes sense."

—⚏—

It did not, fortunately, take a long time for them to reach the right spot—though they were still miles away from where they suspected the Kingdom proper was. It was hard to tell, but after a certain point, it was no longer safe to teleport; too much of a risk of bumping into Void, Derivan claimed.

"It is fortunate that Sev's Blessing of Travel continues to last," Derivan commented. "If only getting around was always this easy."

"We'd be able to get everyone in the convoy to Anderstahl quickly, at least," Vex agreed. "I'm a little worried about them, to be honest. We haven't had any reports of anything bad happening so far, but that doesn't mean much with infolocks and memory-eating hazards everywhere."

"Anyone connected to Misa's anchor should be well aware if something begins to eat away at the convoy," Derivan reassured Vex. "They are as safe as they can be on that journey. The best thing we can do is to continue our path—we must find a way to preserve what remains before it is too late."

"Or more," Vex said, and when Derivan cocked his head curiously at him, Vex shrugged. "We can't just stop at preserving what's left. You met so many people still in the Void, still being slowly eaten away . . . They're refugees lost to reality. We should find a way to rescue them, too."

"Ah." Derivan smiled at him, then squeezed his hand. "You are correct, of course. I—"

He was interrupted by a shout from Novice. Vex and Derivan exchanged alarmed glances as a burst of *nothing* erupted from the ground; Novice fell backward from the sheer force of it, yelping as he did.

Vex stared up. There was nothing there. But if he used his version of [**Mana Sight**], he could see a gaping hole in the mana, shaped like an enormous—

"It's a Void Wyrm!" he called out. He pulled out his magelight, already beginning to run even as he channeled mana into it. The one that Novice had triggered was far from the only one. He could see spots of absent mana all over the field, and while some of them were relatively stagnant—most likely simple empty spots that had been erased—others were actively moving. Reality's interpretation of the Void's intent to *consume*.

Fighting it directly wasn't a good idea. The system's attempt to interpret those things as monsters was only that: an interpretation. Nothing they did could *actually* harm an absence of something.

At least, nothing that was *meant* to harm.

Novice's attempted [**Fireball**] splashed ineffectually off the Void Wyrm, and Vex completed his Glyph of Transposition, pulling Novice back before the wyrm could attempt to strike him again. Derivan took his place, and the armor didn't waste a second in leaping out of the way, his sword glancing along the edge of the wyrm's hide as he did so.

Not that it did anything. All that happened was that pieces of metal were scraped off the sword, forever lost to the Void. But it bought him time—Derivan's existence, especially with his malformed stats, was pure metaphysical weight. The Void was attracted to him.

It turned and chased him, even as Vex pulled out the [**Spelldisk**] and began to draw a second glyph.

"What are you doing?" Novice asked, panicked. "What do I do?"

"Void Wyrms can't be defeated through traditional combat," Vex said tersely. "But that doesn't mean they can't be defeated. The Void is an *absence*; it's the end. To fight nothing, all you have to do—"

He finished painting the last brushstrokes in the air. With his limited understanding before, he'd only ever been able to turn *himself* into a dragon; they were one of the creatures that had lived in the kingdom of Enkiros, and evidently he'd managed to tap into that potential and apply it to himself.

"—is fill it with *something*."

But now he knew what the semerit was. He knew what it contained. He had the [**Spelldisk**], a complicated construct created by the system for the express purpose of seeing reality the way it was supposed to be; more than that, it was a construct that gave him the ability to find remnant links between reality and what had been brought into the Void.

And last but not least: he had a Primordial Glyph that represented the ability to translate things from one form to the other.

The Void Wyrm, through the activated [**Spelldisk**], was a hole in reality—but it was a hole in reality through which he could see nearly everything that had once been erased from the world. He saw the people that Derivan spoke about, struggling to survive among one another within the Void, finding comfort with each other when the world had forgotten them.

He saw, farther away but closer than ever to this part of reality, an entire community of *dragons*.

And he commanded the Primordial Glyph to link the two.

The semerit thrummed in his hand as he drew upon the paradox that connected dragons with this part of Obreve. There was a timeline in which Enkiros had never been completely erased, a timeline in which its people had evacuated and survived; that potential surged with his magic and into the Primordial Glyph of Translation.

And then he forced a Change on the result of that Translation:

There was no Void Wyrm here, only the last remaining *dragon*.

Vex felt a tidal wave of mana pouring out of him, and he gasped, collapsing halfway onto his knees before Novice worriedly caught him; even held in the other lizardkin's arms, the magic kept pouring out of him. Undoing this single piece of Void took so much out of him that he wondered if he could even sustain this change at all. Even with his prodigious store of mana, even with all the ways in which he'd grown—

But before he could doubt himself any more, something else within him responded.

He'd almost forgotten he was holding on to it. The Grand Anchor of Magic thrummed within his tailbag, calling to him insistently.

"Novice—" Vex coughed once. Derivan was too distracted to help him; he was darting around, trying to keep the Void Wyrm distracted. Vex saw more than once the way he faltered every time he tried to wield his sword in his newly replaced hand, and winced when one particular blow knocked the sword out of his grip entirely. But Derivan could handle himself. Vex trusted him. "Novice, I need you to help get something from my bag."

"I got it," Novice said, kneeling down by Vex and unstrapping the tailbag. He rummaged through it, not the least bit surprised by its being bigger on the inside. "What do you need?"

"It'll be labeled as [**Grand Anchor—Magic**] by the system," Vex said. He felt a little lightheaded; there was mana backlash happening. The spell had taken all of his reserves and was now drawing upon the part of his soul that was connected to the mana itself, constantly regenerating his stores. "Need you to be quick—"

"Found it." Novice pulled out the Grand Anchor, then stared at it. "What do I do with it?"

"Just give it to me," Vex said weakly. He took it from Novice's hands as soon as the younger lizardkin offered it to him, and he felt an immediate sense of relief as something within him connected to the Grand Anchor. He hadn't been able to do this before, but it was like something within him had just . . . unlocked.

This was his. It was supposed to belong to him. There was a part of this Grand Anchor that resonated with his very soul, with the part of him that loved magic and everything it could do.

And right now, he needed to believe it could do what he wanted the most: to bring back what had been lost. The Grand Anchor sang with that hope. It clung to him just as he clung to it, as if they were two halves of a whole, believing and wanting the same thing.

He felt the physical form of the Grand Anchor shatter as something settled inside of him.

You have merged with [Grand Anchor—Magic].

A final surge of power erupted from him, stronger than all the others. It was more mana than he had—more mana than he'd ever had. More mana than all the members of House Ashion put together.

In front of him, the Void Wyrm flickered, and emptiness became *something else.*

CHAPTER 22

HOME RESTORATION

There was a red dragon standing in front of the three of them. It looked about as confused as Novice did, though both Derivan and Vex didn't seem particularly surprised.

"Uh," the dragon said. He was surprisingly soft-spoken. Vex had expected a powerful voice that echoed through the field; instead, the words came out quiet and almost timid, and at a normal speaking volume that he would have expected to hear from a lizardkin his own size rather than a dragon several times larger than him. "Hello?"

"Hi," Vex said, waving up at the dragon. Derivan had backed off as soon as the Void Wyrm had been replaced, and came up to stand beside him. "Welcome back to reality."

"Back to—" The dragon cut himself off, looking around at the field he was in. "I'm . . . I'm back?"

"Take your time," Derivan said gently.

"But how can I be back?" the dragon insisted. "What about the others? The rest of them are still stuck in there—please, you have to get them out, too!" He took a few steps forward and stopped, swaying slightly; Derivan reacted quickly, weaving a Glyph of Force that held the dragon in place and stopped him from collapsing.

Good thing, too, because the dragon would have collapsed into yet another Void spot and it would have removed a chunk of his flesh. Not an ideal situation for someone freshly back from the Void.

There were other Void Wyrms around them still. Vex saw the way those spots of emptiness around them moved, almost as if they were waiting for an opportunity to strike—but the density of mana around them was still strong enough that the Void couldn't spread easily, so they were safe. None of the Void Wyrms would be attacking.

For now, anyway.

"It's . . . a process," Vex said carefully to the still-panicking dragon, trying to find the words that would help him calm down. "What's your name?"

"Exvhar," the dragon replied immediately. "Can you get them out? My friends and family. The other dragons. Gods, there's so much to explain—"

"We probably already know," Vex said, glancing awkwardly at Derivan and Novice both. "Look, let's catch you up on what's going on first, okay? And then you can tell us what you know, and we'll figure out what to do from there."

"Okay . . . okay." Exvhar took a few breaths, trying to steady himself; Vex noted the puffs of flame and smoke emerging from his nostrils every time he took a breath. "Okay. But we can't delay too long!"

"I know," Vex said softly. The truth was, he didn't know if he could replicate the feat he'd just performed anytime soon. He could feel the power there, lurking within his soul—the Grand Anchor hadn't been depleted at all by this act of magic. But his *link* to the Grand Anchor had. There was something within him that had been exhausted, and his instincts told him that pushing against that limit was a bad idea.

He fired off a quick message to Sev anyway, hoping that the cleric would reply to him in time. Hopefully Sev had been able to figure out what a Grand Anchor was and how it was related to him, and if there were any dangers in him overusing it.

"There's a lot you need to know," Vex said. "Let's start with Enkiros . . ."

"That's where I'm from!" Exvhar said this with obvious excitement and enthusiasm. "Let's go there! I bet the elders can help us. I don't think anyone knows about everyone going missing—"

Vex winced.

There was a *lot* to catch Exvhar up on, it seemed.

Those who dwelled within the Void did, for the most part, understand that most of Obreve was being erased. This was something Derivan had learned from his one visit to the Void when he'd been in the Roads—the erased had formed a small community of individuals, and there were no doubt many such communities, scattered throughout the Void. Within those communities, they'd been able to figure out what was happening to Obreve, even if they hadn't been able to actually do anything about it.

Exvhar, it seemed, was not part of a community that was aware of what was happening. The dragon—and he was a *young* dragon, apparently, by draconic standards—and his kin had assumed that their entrapment within the Void was something done to them by enemies of Enkiros and not a natural result of a different phenomenon.

To say that he was horrified when he learned that all of Enkiros had also been erased was an understatement. The poor dragon was curled up into a ball on the ground, and Derivan, Vex, and Novice all sat awkwardly beside him, patting his scales comfortingly.

"It's all gone?" he asked mournfully. "What about my favorite flower shop? It's gotta still be there, right?"

"I am afraid that all of Enkiros is gone, to the best of our knowledge," Derivan said. He tried to keep his words gentle, though he knew there was no easy way to break this news. "But we are going to attempt to bring it back."

"Really?" Exvhar managed to roll around back to his feet, nearly crushing the three of them in the process; Derivan quickly held out a hand so he could gently nudge both Vex and Novice out of the way before they were hurt. "Like how you brought me back!"

"Yes," Derivan said agreeably. "We will try to bring Enkiros back. But it will be difficult, and we may require your assistance."

"Anything!" The dragon was eager; Derivan would give him that. He hopped up and down once, hard enough to make the ground tremble, and then almost ran into a bubble of Void before Derivan spun another Glyph of Force to pull him back.

"Be careful," he said, his tone reproachful; Exvhar's ears folded back a little at the reprimand, and Vex couldn't help but chuckle. "You are not in trouble. But you must be careful; the space around here is filled with Void. We do not want you to end up back there."

"I don't want to go back there either," Exvhar said, shuddering at the thought. "It's dark. And lonely."

"I can imagine." Derivan's tone was sympathetic. "Are you willing to carry us to where Enkiros is? If you remember the location, it will take us less time to make our attempt."

"Oh!" Exvhar brightened. "Yes! I definitely remember. I know where we are right now, too! I used to fly here all the time to play with this girl—Cyrlea? She had the prettiest blue scales . . ."

Derivan looked on, amused, as Exvhar began to ramble. Thankfully, the dragon didn't forget what he was supposed to do: he lowered himself to the ground so the others could climb on, and Derivan helped the two lizardkin climb onto Exvhar before he hopped on himself. They were able to fix them-selves to the dragon's back with magic, and a single beat of powerful wings took them up into the air.

Thankfully, the Void-pockets were much sparser in the air than they were on the ground. There wasn't all that much to erase in the air, after all, nor did much of it have any metaphysical weight to attract the attention of the Void. It meant their flight was mostly uneventful.

They did learn a *lot* about Exvhar, though. Maybe a little more than any of them were really interested in. Derivan didn't begrudge the dragon his desire for companionship—it was likely that he'd been lonely within the Void. Even with others of his kind there, the Void was just . . . nothingness. There was nothing new there to discover, and there was nothing new there to *feel*. He'd seen that reality hanging over every person he visited while in that cursed space.

Eventually, Exvhar stopped, hovering in the air in front of what appeared to be an empty field. Derivan knew better. The area was devoid of any mana, and Shift told him that there was nothing there to shift.

This was a massive bubble of Void, almost the size of a city. A kingdom.

"It's really gone," Exvhar said, his voice suddenly subdued; gone was the cheer with which he'd told his stories. "I . . . There's nothing there. But I remember it. I remember all of it . . ."

"Good," Derivan said gently. "We will need your memories to guide us. To take us to *what should be*."

"I . . . I think I can do that." Exvhar swallowed once, landing at the edge of the bubble. He almost took an instinctive step forward but this time stopped himself before Derivan had to use yet another spell to pull him back. "Is there, uh . . . is there anything specific I need to do?"

"Not yet," Vex said. He hopped off the dragon, his Agility making the movement graceful even as he tucked and rolled to disperse the impact. The lizardkin knelt in the ground as Derivan helped Novice off the dragon and walked up to Vex. "I have to start the process. Let me just . . ."

Derivan watched. This was Vex's moment—a culmination of all the ways in which he'd grown. Bringing back a dragon was one thing, but bringing back an entire kingdom . . .

That would be a feat worthy of an archmage.

Derivan had full faith that Vex would be able to do it.

CHAPTER 23

DEFERRED DECISIONS

Vex stood at the precipice of the Void. His eyes glowed with mana. His connection with his Grand Anchor was as strong as it could possibly be, and though there was a small piece of himself that still felt a little strained, he wasn't sure they had time to let him try to recover. Hopefully, what he had would be enough to bring back Enkiros.

"Vex," Derivan said. "You are sure you are ready?"

Trust Derivan to always see through him. Vex chuckled, smiling, and gestured for the armor to walk closer; when he did, Vex took the armor's hand in his own and interlaced their fingers.

"No," he admitted. "Bringing back even one dragon was a strain on my link with the Grand Anchor. I don't know if I can bring back an entire kingdom. But . . . I want to try, Deri. I think I *need* to try."

Derivan was silent for a long moment. This was the most conflicted Vex had ever seen him. He could almost see the two sides of the argument within his partner's mind: one side insisting that Vex stay safe, to not do something if it could harm him in some irreversible way, and the other side wanting to stay by Vex's side and support him in his decisions.

"I am conflicted," Derivan eventually admitted. His voice was soft. Vulnerable. It was the first time Vex had heard the armor like this, and he felt a small stab of guilt in his heart. "You are certain we cannot wait?"

"We can," Vex allowed, hesitating a little himself. It didn't feel like something major—just a small, nagging feeling somewhere within him, like an itch he couldn't scratch. It told him that whatever he'd strained hadn't had the time to recover completely. But he didn't *know* how long it would take him to recover completely, and they didn't exactly have the luxury of time . . .

. . . They had the luxury of a *little* time.

"I could wait for Sev to reply to me," Vex said after a moment. He smiled up at Derivan. "Just so we know for sure that whatever I'm doing won't, I don't know, irreparably damage the Grand Anchor or something."

"Yes," Derivan agreed. "I believe that may be for the best."

There were many words that stayed unsaid there—many things Vex wanted to say, and many things he thought he could see Derivan wanting to say, as well. But the larger man simply drew him into his arms, and Vex allowed himself to fall into the embrace, his head leaning against Derivan's chest.

Words could be said later.

Actions, for now, said enough.

—⁂—

"Now arriving at Soulbloom Station."

The mechanical-sounding voice echoed through the cabin as the train they were in slid to a stop. Misa glanced at Sev, then stepped through the cabin doors into this so-called "Soulbloom Station."

It was . . . strange. Everything here was so meticulously crafted—it was nothing like orcish architecture or furniture, nor even like the homes in Fendal, which on occasion seemed a little haphazardly put together. Even Elyra was all about grandiose beauty more than it was about *precision.*

Soulbloom Station was precision. Every pillar was placed the same exact distance apart. The tiles on the floor were perfectly square. The benches were lined up against one another all across the station, and there was exactly one flower blooming next to each bench. There was a certain beauty to it, but Misa couldn't help but feel a little out of place.

"This place makes me feel like I need to be wearing something formal," Misa grunted, staring down at her adventuring gear.

"Can't say I'm a fan either," Sev remarked, his tone dry. He glanced around at the station, then into the air, calling up his copy of the system. "No notifications. You?"

"Nothing," Misa said after a cursory glance at her own system screen. Not even the nagging feeling that there *should* be a system notification. The train sat with its doors open behind them, though, so it was clearly waiting for them to do something. "Are we supposed to just explore?"

"Usually these stations come with some kind of objective . . . but I guess it's all up in the air now," Sev said with a sigh. "We can probably figure out what we're supposed to do, at least. You see anything that looks missing or off?"

"The only thing that looks off to me is the fact that we're the only ones here," Misa said. "This place doesn't feel like it's supposed to be empty."

"... Huh. You're right." Sev narrowed his eyes a little as he glanced around the station. "The Anderstahl Prime Dungeon usually populates its spaces a little more."

"With people, or with monsters?" Misa asked dryly.

"I mean, we've recently found out that the two are the same thing," Sev said. "Kinda. But no, I mean people. The dungeon gives them enough autonomy to act as individuals within the dungeon, even if they're not necessarily self-aware about being in a dungeon."

"That feels kinda sketchy," Misa said.

"It is." Sev shrugged, looking a little uncomfortable. "I think people tried to tell the people they were in a dungeon, once ... it didn't really go well. But it's not like it's the first time we've dealt with something like that."

Right. Her current family had been part of a dungeon's generated scenario once too. She sighed. "At least it doesn't look like I'm going to have to do that again," she said, glancing around. "But you think the station being empty might have something to do with whatever we're supposed to do here?"

"Only one way to find out," Sev said with a shrug. He walked past the line and into what Misa vaguely recognized as some kind of office, then immediately began flipping through the papers and documentation held within. As far as she could tell from a distance, it was all schematics for the train, employment schedules, things like that.

It all felt remarkably real, actually. Remarkably *detailed*. Like it was more of a snapshot of something that had already happened rather than something generated for the sole purpose of filling out a dungeon—and considering what they now knew about how the system worked, Misa was inclined to believe that it probably *was*. Maybe the schedules weren't part of anything that had happened in this time, but somewhere, *somewhen* ...

She was distracted from her thoughts by a yelp from Sev, and she brandished her mace. Sev had opened a drawer, and hundreds of replicas of the same silver tickets they'd given the Conductor had flown out. Literally flown.

<LEVEL 27 TICKET THICKET>

Her system popped up with the name of the creature before she could stop it, and she frowned in confusion to see its level. It was a swarm, first of all, and those were rare enough to begin with—the whole collective of tickets was counted as a single monster for the purposes of health. More importantly, though, it was a low-level swarm.

Level 27. Bizarre. She'd never seen a monster this low-level in a dungeon, let alone a Prime Dungeon.

She threw her mace at it.

One of the more convenient aspects of fighting swarms was that, with the way the system calculated and applied health, you only really needed to fight one part of the swarm to be counted as damaging the whole thing. It made *actual* swarms much more dangerous, and there were definitely dungeons that would produce those. This, however?

Piece of cake. She watched as the tickets flopped harmlessly to the ground, dead from a single blow, and then raised an eyebrow at Sev.

"They were only level 27, you know," she said.

"Oh, shut up," Sev grumbled. "You try having those things buzz around your face. It's like having a dozen bugs flying around your ears."

"Sounds uncomfortable," Misa said with a laugh, picking up her mace. Sev made a grumbling noise of agreement, and together, they looked around the rest of the office.

Besides that small scare, it didn't *seem* like there was anything else in here. Sev pulled open the rest of the drawers, but they had neither any more papers nor any more surprise swarms to jump them.

"Still think it's kinda weird that those were just level 27," Misa said, glancing around the tiny office. "You think that's part of a trap or something?"

"Probably, but it's not that uncommon for there to be small monsters at the start of a dungeon," Sev said with a shrug. "Prime Dungeons especially are kinda erratic when it comes to levels. For all we know, it's just here as part of a different dungeon mechanic." He stared at the corpses of the Ticket Thicket for a moment, then started picking them up and stuffing them into his pockets.

Misa stared at him. ". . . I'll leave you to that, I think," she said.

"I'm doing it just in case!"

"Sure you are."

Amused, she made her way back out of the office and stared over the station. There was something here they were missing—something here the dungeon wanted them to do. She doubted it was as simple as finding a monster mimicking some tickets, killing them, and then using their corpses as a free pass to the next station . . .

There.

Something moved in the corner of her vision, and she narrowed her eyes slightly. Up in the lights near the roof of the station, a small shadow seemed to flit around, hiding in the corners and the crevices. Every so often, it would go toward one of the lights and stop, and then that light would begin to flicker—and after a moment, the flickering would stop, and the shadow would move away again.

Acting entirely on a hunch—one of the perks of the [**Intuitionist**] class was that her hunches were much better than most people's now, and they had already been pretty good before—Misa threw her mace at the light, and several things happened at once.

The first was that the light *detached* from the ceiling, stretching down toward the ground with long legs of glowing filament; it "dodged" her mace in this way, though it still flinched as rubble from the ceiling rained down around it.

"Wait!" it called out, panicked. "Wait, wait! I'm not an enemy, I swear!"

Misa paused.

"Oh," she said, a little awkwardly. She glanced back as Sev jogged to catch up with her—he gave her a *look*, and she gave him an embarrassed grin. "Uh . . . sorry about that."

"Oh my gods, I thought I was gonna die," it said. Misa still had no idea what it was, but the system had decided to give it a name and a label.

<LEVEL 36 CEILING FIXTURE>

. . . Not a very *useful* name and label.

"Sorry," she apologized again, now feeling even more out of her element. "Not used to dungeons giving us . . . anyone friendly. Or anyone that can talk."

"It's fine," it said. "It's fine! I get it. I'm Tinsel. I'm a Soulbloom Emanation."

"You're a what?" Misa asked.

"A Soulbloom Emanation," Tinsel repeated itself. It gestured to the field outside the station—the field of flowers Misa had almost forgotten about. And she'd wanted to explore it, too. "Basically, I'm the child of one of those flowers."

CHAPTER 24

SOULBOOM

"... You're going to have to explain that one," Misa said. She took a seat on one of the nearby benches—because why not, really—and was only slightly surprised when one of the tiles beneath her feet suddenly lurched to life and launched itself at her.

She didn't even bother fighting this one. It was a level 10 Floor Tile. It could chew on her arm for hours and not scratch her health enough to take it below her default health regeneration. She just stared at it for a moment, then back at Tinsel.

"Is this one alive?" she asked. "The same way you are, I mean. I don't want to smash it and then feel bad about it later."

"Uh," Tinsel said. "No, you can kill that one."

"Cool." Misa flicked it off her arm, trying not to feel too bad about the way it shattered against the floor. "You were saying?"

"So, the flowers out there are called soulbloom flowers," Tinsel said. "It's a really popular ingredient for alchemy—excellent for magic-boosting potions. Stuff that boosts your spells or increases your connection with the mana. That kind of thing."

"Right." Misa nodded. "I'm following so far."

"The reason it can do that is because soulbloom flowers are . . ." Tinsel trailed off, struggling to find the right words to describe them. "They're really good at processing mana into something that's kind of like an artificial soul. When it's consumed by something living, it usually enhances their connection to their soul, which lets them do all kinds of stuff with mana."

"Huh," Sev said thoughtfully next to her. "I've never heard of soulblooms before, and that's saying something. I wonder if they're something the dungeon just created . . ."

Tinsel, thankfully, ignored what Sev was saying; Misa wasn't sure she knew how to deal with whatever existential crisis it would have if it found out it was the creation of a dungeon. Or, heck, maybe it already knew.

"The thing is, soulblooms don't really have a limiter on when they should *stop*," Tinsel explained. "Over the course of a few months, a soulbloom is still non-sentient; all it's doing is drawing in the mana around it and kind of enhancing it. But after a few months, the root structure becomes complicated enough to sustain a living, artificial soul."

Misa blinked. "So if a soulbloom flower isn't processed into something like a potion so it can enhance someone's . . . uh, connection to their soul, as you put it, it just . . . *creates* the soul?"

"Exactly!" Tinsel nodded vigorously, the shadows around it shifting wildly as it did so. "'Cause all of the soul-enhancing stuff has nowhere to go, and it just kind of creates a soul out of nothing."

"That's worrying for a number of reasons," Misa said. "But go on."

"Long story short, we need your help," Tinsel said. There it was— whatever they needed to do for this station. "This station's been abandoned for years. The soulblooms here have all mostly gone out of control. There's a bunch of us just . . . loose, because the soulblooms separate from the souls they create once those souls are, uh, ripe."

"So this station is haunted," Misa said, a little disbelievingly. She glanced around. "Because the soulblooms around it have been releasing souls for generations?"

"Kinda, yeah." Tinsel nodded again. "We just attach to whatever resonates with us the most. It's not like there's anything here that's more . . . people-shaped for us to possess. So we're a lot of living objects, and we can kinda move from one thing to another. Technically we don't even really die when you smash us; we just move on to possess something else."

Misa felt a little relieved by that. "But you said you needed help?"

"Right, yeah," Tinsel said. "Um, like I said, we're normally . . . released. When we're ripe. Fully grown souls."

"Right," Misa said slowly. "I feel like I'm not going to like where this is going."

"Well," Tinsel said. "Probably not. One of the soulblooms is sick. Its roots got tangled, so it can't release any of the souls it's made. None of us can get close, and uh . . . now there are more than a hundred tangled souls in there. And counting."

Ah. Misa felt her heart sink a little at the thought. The whole thing about souls went a little over her head, but the idea of a hundred souls all tangled together was uncomfortable; she couldn't imagine what it was like for them.

"Related to the giant worm-crab thing we saw in the fields, by any chance?" Sev asked.

"Yeah, that's the one," Tinsel said, wincing a little. "The tangle of souls, I mean. It's all made of dirt. If you look closely, you can see the soulbloom's roots tangled through the whole thing. It's not usually active a lot of the time, but when it *is*, it's a problem, because it's eating all the other flowers. And sometimes it attacks us and tries to eat us, too. I lost a couple friends to it before."

Sev and Misa glanced at each other. "I guess we know what we have to do here," Sev said. "I think I want to investigate these soulblooms, too. I have a feeling they're going to be useful down the road."

"So do I," Misa admitted.

"If you help us, I can help you find some fresh ones!" Tinsel immediately offered. "Ones that don't have whole souls growing in them already. Those aren't as good for the alchemy thing—they get a little poisonous, actually. You can get soul sickness from them. I know all the best places for the new ones!"

"Sure." Misa smiled at Tinsel, who had leapt to its feet and was doing an enthusiastic little twirl. What an interesting fellow. It *had* been a while since she'd had an interesting fight, and a giant rock-worm-crab thing seemed like the perfect opportunity to let loose for a bit.

"I bet it's what's interfering with the system, too," Sev said thoughtfully. "The system relies on having a metaphysical connection to your soul. But there's basically a giant soul beacon here—it's probably rerouting half the system messages to the soulbloom by accident."

"What, you didn't consider the possibility of a hundred-soul tangle when you were making the system?" Misa asked, half-joking.

"First of all, I wasn't the one that made it," Sev said, grumbling. "And second, no, we didn't! That's not something that should ever be happening!"

"I gotta agree with your friend there," Tinsel said.

"I know, I know," Misa said. "Right. So. We need a plan. How are we going to take this thing down, and what do we want to do with it?"

—⁘—

It took them a few minutes to hash out the details of the plan with Tinsel's help.

They did not, in fact, want to kill the errant soulbloom. That was the first thing they'd needed to establish—whether they were going to kill the thing or find a way to repair it. Tinsel had been insistent that as the eldest of the soulbloom flowers, its souls would have insights that few others did. Killing it would be a significant loss to the people of Soulbloom Station.

"Like I said, you can destroy our physical forms no problem," Tinsel said. "And you're probably going to need to trim the roots down so the souls don't get tangled up again. Just don't damage the petals of the flower."

"That's a bit of an ask," Misa said. "It's going to be hard to avoid damaging it if we're crushing the body and cutting off the roots."

"It's more durable than you'd think," Tinsel said. "As long as you're not targeting it directly, it should be fine!"

"If you say so." She was willing to take Tinsel at its word, anyway; it wasn't like they had many other options. They could adapt if they needed to. "So, Tinsel, you stay out of the way."

"Done," Tinsel said immediately.

"I'll be the distraction," Misa said. "And I'm pretty sure I can do enough damage to it to break it apart. Sev, you're going to try healing it?"

"Makes more sense than most of the other options I've got," Sev said with a shrug, and then he reconsidered the statement slightly. "Well, there are divinities I could try to channel that would help with this—but there's no reason to waste divine power if a regular heal is going to work. And I don't see any reason that it shouldn't."

"Besides the system trying to stop you from healing something you shouldn't," Misa pointed out.

"Besides that." Sev sighed. "Hopefully it's not going to be a problem this time. We only ever ran into that issue once, anyway; I think it was probably just that dungeon . . ."

"I have no idea what you two are talking about," Tinsel said. "But it sounds fascinating! You should tell me more. Once we've pruned the soulblooms. Soulbloom."

". . . Is there a reason you said that with a plural at first?" Misa glanced at Tinsel.

"Nope!" Tinsel said, a little too quickly, and then with a little more guilt in its voice: "Well, uh, there might be more than one. But it's okay! We haven't seen the second one for ages. I doubt it's gonna turn up now."

Misa sighed, bracing her mace on her shoulder as she began walking out of the station and into the soulbloom field.

"Believe me," she said. "It's *definitely* going to turn up now."

CHAPTER 25

BAIT AND SWITCH

The first step to their plan was *finding* the errant soulbloom in question. Despite Tinsel's words, it didn't seem eager to erupt out of the ground and attack them—in fact, if Misa hadn't known any better, she would've guessed it was avoiding them. The soulbloom flowers in the field shifted around from time to time, some of them moving away from the pair, others moving toward them.

They'd left Tinsel back in Soulbloom Station. There wasn't really a need for it to come with them—Tinsel wasn't a fighter. Really, none of the items brought to life by the soulblooms seemed to be; they were all low-level constructs at best, dangerous perhaps to new adventurers, but not to experienced ones like Misa and Sev.

The *real* danger, it seemed, lay in the soulblooms themselves. Now that they were close enough, Misa could see each of them tagged with the system's labels and levels.

<LEVEL 87 SOULBLOOM FLOWER>
<LEVEL 92 SOULBLOOM FLOWER>
<LEVEL 1,157 SOULBLOSSOM>

The last one gave Misa pause, and she narrowed her eyes, stopping in place and holding a hand out to stop Sev from moving forward. He followed her gaze, and she caught a sharp intake of breath.

"What in the hells is that level?" he hissed, suddenly on guard. Misa just shook her head slowly. She was cautious, of course, but . . . [**Intuitionist**] wasn't screaming danger at her.

Not yet, anyway.

"Guessing it's something to do with all the souls it's got mashed together in there," Misa said quietly, keeping her voice low. There was no evidence that the Soulblossom would be able to hear her, but she didn't feel like taking any chances. "A hundred level 10s added together would add up to about a thousand."

"That's definitely *not* how the system is supposed to calculate levels," Sev said with a frown, although he'd calmed a little; that explanation made more sense to him than a sudden encounter with a monster that was over ten times the known level cap, beyond even the Overseer-type monsters they'd had to fight before.

"We should still be careful," Misa muttered. "Not sure what's going to provoke it."

"We're going to need to get closer for me to try to heal it anyway," Sev said. "Let's just take it slow. One step at a time."

"Right," Misa said. She didn't protest, although she *did* make sure to lead the way. There was no reaction from the Soulblossom. One step closer, two steps, three . . .

The ground trembled beneath her feet.

Shit.

Her block was instinctive at this point. She felt herself twist through all the layers of reality she needed to to manifest the right weapon to block the Soulblossom's strike; her mace became a shield, and then something *beyond*, a manifestation of fire and rot attached to her hand. The Soulblossom struck at her, earth wrapped in roots lurching to crush them both, but it screeched in pain the moment it made contact with her makeshift shield.

Misa grinned. Good to know that skill still worked. "Sev?" she called.

"I'm okay!" Sev called back. "Working on it!"

"Better hurry!"

The worm-thing was fast, and it didn't seem particularly inclined to follow any of the laws of physics when it came to how it moved. Misa watched it pulse through the air, swallowing swathes of space like it was dirt, the entire length of its body contracting and expanding as if it was pushing that air through its body to move.

Or it was swimming in the air. One or the other.

She was already running a multitude of other selves, testing the waters with fighting this thing. One version of her charged directly for the head, wielding only her mace; that version was immediately swallowed up when the Soulblossom's trajectory abruptly changed. Another version fired arrows from a distance, loading those arrows with concepts of *order* and *untangling*—but she could *sense* how ineffective that was. Something about the sheer weight of the hundred souls within the Soulblossom acted as a kind of shield against her concepts, breaking them down before they could penetrate very deep into the dirt.

Fine. She had other methods at her disposal. Her Strength stat was high enough now that she could let loose physically and do enough damage for it to be worthwhile; the only real concern here was the level of the Soulblossom and how much health it had—

The Soulblossom roared and struck at her, veering almost ninety degrees in the air to charge directly toward her with inhuman speed. Misa gritted her teeth, glancing behind her. Soulbloom Station was there. She couldn't just dodge this or it'd smash straight into the station, along with the train they needed to get to the next part of the dungeon.

Once again, she blocked.

A visceral pain tore through her as she did so, though the shield manifested on her arm and once again repelled the worm; Misa let out a growl of pain, collapsing briefly onto her hands and knees before forcing herself back onto her feet.

"Shit, that hurt," she said. "Sev, it's doing something—part of it can get through my block!"

"I'm almost ready!" Sev called back, sounding a little panicked; Misa wondered briefly if Sev was also struggling with his skills, and then she didn't have time to wonder at all anymore.

The worm was charging at her again. She maneuvered herself this time, putting herself on the opposite side of the Soulblossom so it wouldn't crash into the station if she dodged it; this time, she leapt *over* the damn thing, using a few of her alternate-timeline Endless Echoes selves to judge how high she would need to jump to avoid getting eaten.

Then she split into several copies of herself with [**Me, Myself, and I**]. There was a jarring sensation she'd never felt before as she did it, though she didn't have time to think about it; she directed two of her copies to charge directly for the midsection of the worm, ripping into it with heavy strikes of her mace.

It did enough damage to tear away chunks of dirt, exposing tangles of glowing roots that dangled awkwardly in the air. Extra copies of her tore away at those glowing roots, grabbing them by the fistful and ripping them away from the main body of the worm, eliciting an angry roar as they did so—Misa noticed how *difficult* it was, even with her Strength stat. It was like she was ripping at cords of steel instead of plant fiber.

The Soulblossom was clearly hurt, though. It writhed about angrily in the air with no apparent target, thrashing and crushing large swathes of the ground as it did so; Misa winced when she saw several smaller soulblooms get torn up by its desperate struggles. A few copies of her tried to pluck them out of the way to save them, but they didn't quite get there in time. Those that *did* were quickly knocked away, sent sprawling in the dirt.

Misa charged in herself. The best thing she could do was to make the entire thing smaller—and to that effect, she and all her copies targeted the same segment of the worm, bashing into it to dislodge the dirt and then physically ripping away clumps of root. The worm thrashed, but Misa reacted; a half-dozen arrows of Immobility kept it relatively pinned in place.

The smaller the target, the less damage it could do.

The roots burned at her as she tore them apart. [**Intuitionist**] called to her, warning her about her current course of action—the roots were damaging her in some fundamental way, even if the system wasn't reflecting it. But her strategy was *working*. The worm was trying to turn back around and snap at her, but she was too far up its body for it to be able to turn *enough*.

She ignored the warning, though her hands burned and her vision started to blur. If she faltered here, there was every chance she would no longer have the mental faculties to properly defend Sev. She was in too deep, as he'd say; the strategy worked. It would cost her too much to switch to another one.

And she couldn't risk what happened with Irvis happening again. Not a second time. They didn't have Vex and Derivan here to pull off a last-minute rescue, and Sev was their healer. If he was the one that got hurt—

There was a dull *thud* that Misa distantly recognized as one half of the Soulblossom splitting off and crashing into the ground; the upper half continued to writhe in the air, even with no support. She glanced down at her hands, and was momentarily surprised to see not her flesh but the bones beneath. Acid-blue sludge dripped from those bones.

She didn't react. Part of her brain had trouble processing what she was seeing; the system normally replaced damage like this in a matter of a second, but it was almost like the system was operating on a delay. Like it was struggling.

A moment later, her hands were back to normal, and the sight of her own bones felt like a fever dream. Misa shook her head, trying to clear the sight from her memories. "Sev—" she started again.

"Done!" Sev called back, and she was nearly sent sprawling as a *massive* burst of divine energy suddenly flooded the Soulblossom. It was so strong she could feel the magic seeping into *her*, too, healing her from whatever malady she'd inflicted on herself by manually tearing those roots apart.

Maybe. A small part of her whispered that perhaps the damage she'd inflicted hadn't been temporary. That perhaps she'd damaged something permanently.

That part of her was silenced as the soothing warmth of Sev's magic suffused her. The Soulblossom stopped writhing, and a moment later, she felt the clumps of earth she was sitting on fall apart; the roots no longer held on quite so dearly to everything around them. Dozens of shadows split away from the roots, racing toward Soulbloom Station.

Misa stared at the sight. It was kinda pretty, in a way.

"Misa," Sev said, concerned. "What was that? I felt something weird coming from you."

"What?" Misa blinked, shaking it off. "Oh, uh . . . Nothin'. It was nothing."

A long pause. The two of them stared at one another. The only sound in the field was the sound of crumbling dirt, wind, and one no-longer-sick level 60 Soulblossom slowly rooting itself back into the dirt.

Sev raised an eyebrow.

"Okay," Misa admitted. "I *might've* pushed myself more than I was supposed to."

CHAPTER 26

RAW CONNECTIONS

"You basically did the thing you keep telling me not to do!" Sev complained. Misa groaned, already annoyed by Sev's nagging—mostly because he was *right*, dammit, and she knew that. She knew that, but she hadn't been able to stop herself, and even now, she wasn't sure that she would have.

"I didn't know what it was," she tried to explain. "It just hurt a bit! That could mean anything! Things hurt while we're adventuring all the time!"

"But you're dual-classing with a class that gives you a supernatural intuition," Sev insisted. "You have to listen to your gut! What if whatever you did is irreversible?"

"It's not!" Misa said. "I feel better now, I swear. Not even a lick of pain."

Sev stared at her skeptically. "It's not about the pain, Misa," he said eventually, and then he sighed, coming closer to her so he could give her a hug. She appreciated it, too. He didn't really like getting dirty, and Misa was covered in a *lot* of dirt. His willingness to hug her anyway spoke volumes.

"It's already done," Misa said with a sigh. "But you're right. I don't know. I don't really know if there was anything else I *could* have done. Backed off and tried a different strategy, maybe. Used arrows to shoot down the roots. But that thing . . ."

"It was a soul amalgamation," Sev said. "Those aren't easy to fight at the best of times. You saw the way it messed with the system—those things mess with your mind, too. I get it. You wanted to make sure it couldn't hurt me."

"Yeah," Misa said, relieved. "I couldn't actually see where you were while I was up there. I guess the better option would've been to stay down here and let the [**Me, Myself, and I**] clones handle it, but . . ."

"The damage those clones take still transfers to you, right?" Sev asked. "It's not a risk-free way of attacking someone."

"The only real difference is that I don't feel the pain when they get hit," Misa said with a shrug. "It still damages my health the same amount. I have to be careful with it, same way I am with blocking. That's less of a problem these days when Vex keeps lending me his mana reserves, but . . ."

"But we're stuck in a dungeon without them at the moment, so you're going to run out eventually," Sev said with a sigh. "Look, give me some time to figure out what that thing did to you, at least. That thing was interfering with our systems somehow."

"I got that impression too," Misa said. She frowned, straightening and then glancing warily back toward the Soulblossom. "Something to do with the . . . weight of the souls, or something? You said it might have been what was affecting the chat function."

"Probably," Sev mused. "We never did a lot of experimentation with souls, for reasons I hope are obvious."

"Very," Misa said.

"But we do have theories," Sev said. "A large mass of souls like this should exert a force that's like gravity, but for souls. Something about souls attracts one another. And the system operates on the same metaphysical stuff—I'd say it was made out of souls but that'd be really easy to misunderstand."

Misa shuddered a bit at the thought. "Uh, right. Yeah. Not made out of literal souls but the same . . . material?"

"Yep," Sev said. "The fact that it sticks to itself is what lets us attach the system to people. But obviously, we run into problems if there's suddenly a giant mass of a hundred souls stitched together."

"Which has never happened before."

"Which has never happened before," Sev echoed. "Uh . . . I think. I hope."

"Riiiight." Misa didn't quite keep the skepticism out of her voice. It wasn't that she didn't believe Sev, really. It was that his memories were unreliable at best.

"The point," Sev said, quickly moving on, "is that this is new territory for us. Honestly, this entire section of the dungeon is new territory for us. And we need to make sure the side effects don't carry into the next station."

"I agree," Misa said, slowly taking a step back. "Uh. Sev?"

Sev paused. He looked at Misa's face, and then he sighed a single, long-suffering sigh.

"There's another one of them behind me, isn't there," he said, utterly resigned.

"Yep."

Misa brandished her mace, and Sev turned around, divine energy already glowing around his fingers. Before them, a second Soulblossom slowly emerged from the ground, this one much slower than the first but with a much more threatening label.

<LEVEL 2,576 SOULBLOSSOM>

—◆—

"No reply from Sev," Vex said, glancing at his system and then more anxiously at the Void still waiting in front of them. Exvhar was getting antsy, the dragon trotting around in a circle and chasing after his own tail in an attempt to occupy his mind. Novice was sitting nearby going through his books.

Derivan sat beside him, holding his hand. "Is there a change in your status?" the armor asked.

"I don't know." Vex sighed. "I feel better, for sure. Just feels a bit like there's an itch I can't reach. Or a scab."

"I am not familiar with either of those sensations," Derivan said, amused. Vex chuckled a little.

"Well . . . your new hand can feel stuff the old one couldn't, right?" Vex took Derivan's hand into both of his own, admiring the craftsmanship of the newly forged arm. "Do you mind me touching it?"

"I do not mind." Derivan's voice was suddenly softer as Vex began to trace the filigree embedded into the metal of his palm. "The new arm is . . . strange. It is not the same. And it is difficult to forget that it is not the same." He flexed his fingers briefly, and Vex watched as they curled inward, one by one. "I have not yet decided if I like it, though I suppose I have little choice."

"I like it," Vex said quietly, though there was a bit of uncertainty in his voice. "Is that okay to say?"

"I am happy that you do," Derivan said. He smiled, pulling Vex a little closer and resting the base of his helmet against the lizardkin's forehead; Vex leaned into his touch, allowing himself to relax. "I find it strange still. But I am certain I could grow to love it as you do."

Vex laughed, a little embarrassed. "I mean . . . Not just because I like it, I hope."

"I *suppose* I could search for other reasons, if I were pressed," Derivan said, his tone teasing; Vex buried his face in Derivan's chest in response, and Derivan hummed, wrapping his arms around Vex. "It is more sensitive. I can feel with this arm, and it brings me closer to understanding you and many others—closer than I have ever been. I am glad for those things. The sensitivity is . . . a problem, occasionally. But it is nothing I cannot deal with."

"I'm glad." Vex resumed tracing the patterns on Derivan's new arm, and he watched as the whole thing shook slightly beneath his fingers; he paused, waited a moment, and then continued once Derivan gave him an assenting nod. He lost himself in this for a moment, and came back to himself only when Derivan gave him a gentle nudge.

"You were telling me about how your connection with the Grand Anchor feels like an itch you cannot scratch," Derivan prompted.

"Oh." Vex blinked, trying to remember. "Um . . . yes. A little bit like how your arm feels, maybe. Sort of . . . sensitive. Raw."

"I see." Derivan hummed in thought. "And you are concerned it will worsen if you strain that connection."

"Pretty much." Vex shifted a little. "It's healing, though. I can tell it's healing. I just don't know how long it's going to take to heal, and I mean . . . what if it isn't enough? Just bringing Exvhar back strained the connection. I've got a whole kingdom I need to bring back now. Even if I *let* it heal . . ."

"I would like you to be safe," Derivan said. The words were said with the same sincerity he always spoke with, but Vex was suddenly aware of the way he was being held: of the slight shake in Derivan's arms as he held him. "Though I recognize we live in times where such safety can never be guaranteed. All I ask is that we try."

Vex nodded slowly. He glanced over at Exvhar, whose trotting had become even more anxious, and then glanced down at his own hands—felt the mana surging through his channels. Deeper within him he felt the Grand Anchor, like an ocean of magic hiding within his soul.

The connection was still damaged, but just barely. Vex was almost—*almost*—certain that it was as healed as it could be. If not for the nagging doubt in the back of his mind, he would have tried it already, but . . .

"Five more minutes," he said, leaning into Derivan's shoulder. "Let's give this five more minutes. If Sev doesn't reply by then, we'll give this a shot."

C H A P T E R 2 7

ARTIFICIAL AMALGAMATION

"Shit!" Misa leapt out of the way, dragging Sev with her; she didn't want to risk another block. Not with their system skills apparently being on the fritz. The Soulblossom didn't move *that* fast, at least—that was the one advantage they had over the monster that was over *two thousand levels* currently trying to eat them.

At least, she was pretty sure that was what it was trying to do. It was a little hard to tell with most of her focus dedicated to staying alive. Sev's eyes were already closed, and his hands were clasped together in a form of prayer; she could only assume he was working on casting another heal of some kind to take care of this second Soulblossom.

She couldn't do what she did before again. Probably. She was physically capable of doing so, but despite Sev's healing, something inside of her still seemed to ache. Misa doubted she'd be able to pull off that stunt a second time, and with a Soulblossom nearly twice as strong, she could only imagine the effects would be twice as bad.

She triggered [**Me, Myself, and I**], and even the usage of that skill nearly sent her stumbling. She gritted her teeth. There was *something* pulling at her, and using the skill was like some kind of trigger: it made her vulnerable in a way she wasn't usually vulnerable.

More specifically, it seemed to open up some part of her soul—and while it wasn't by any deliberate action on the Soulblossom's part, the sheer *weight* of its existence was enough to tear away at her the moment she tried to use a skill.

But it was fine. This was fine. She'd managed to bring five other copies of herself into existence, and each of them tore away in a different direction, using every last drop of their power to distract the Soulblossom. The worm roared and spun from one to the other, confused, trying to decide on a target.

"Please tell me this thing isn't interfering with your spell," Misa hissed under her breath. She dove into the grass, her heart pounding, one hand covering for Sev while she used her duplicates to make sure the worm wasn't targeting them—it wasn't. Whatever mechanism it used to choose its victims, it evidently wasn't the number of nearby souls, or it would've targeted the two of them already.

"It is," Sev said grimly. "But I can get around it, same way as last time. I just need a bit of time. This thing is so strong it's actually taking over some of the divinity in the area—I can't cast as effectively as I could otherwise."

"Shit," Misa cursed again. "Anything I can do? Besides play as the distraction."

"Keep an eye on your system for me," Sev said. "This thing's doing something to destabilize it, and you have a whole reality anchor attached to you. The *Prime Anchor* is in this dungeon, for crying out loud—if it can have an impact on us, it can have an impact on the Anderstahl Prime Anchor. Maybe the thing isn't degrading at all. Maybe it's just this thing slowly ripping it apart, even if it is by accident."

Misa snorted. "As if we'd be that lucky," she said, drawing a breathless chuckle from Sev. She pulled up her system screen and stared at it, watching as the boundaries fuzzed in and out of existence. The reality anchor tied to her, at least, didn't seem to be degrading any faster from the Soulblossom's presence—which was proof against Sev's theory.

Unfortunately. It would've been convenient if all they needed to do to repair Anderstahl's Prime Anchor was to take this down.

"It won't take me nearly as long to connect this time," Sev muttered. Misa saw the way his eyes moved beneath his eyelids, almost like he was trying to rapidly read something. His hands moved like he was tugging on an invisible rope, and Misa suddenly felt a *presence* coalesce around them, almost like Sev had cast another Blessing.

Then a surge of divine power burst out of him again. Healing energy flooded through Misa, giving her a burst of relief; it raced through the nearby Soulblossom, causing roots to retract and clumps of earth to fall away from the body of the worm.

The worm turned around and roared once more. It was a silent roar, and the sight of it sent chills down Misa's spine; clumps of rock rained down on them as its mouth split open, and yet it was utterly silent.

"Uh, Sev," she said. "I don't think we got it."

"I noticed," Sev said tersely.

"And it knows exactly where we are and is coming straight for us." Misa didn't wait for Sev to respond—she grabbed him by the back of his robe and started hauling him away from the worm's path. This time, it wasn't distracted by anything her duplicates did, no matter how they approached it. Arrows didn't work, nor did physical blows with her mace . . . "If you've got any bright ideas, now's the time!"

"*Aurum!*" Sev called. Misa flinched and let go of Sev as he glowed bright with power—she could almost *feel* the sudden change in the air. There was an abrupt density around her there hadn't been before.

And then Sev wasn't quite Sev.

Misa felt more than she saw the power of Aurum as the God of Gold made his presence known; Sev became a *conduit*, a channel for Aurum's power. Divine power crept its way into every facet of the Soulbloom Station and the fields surrounding it, so intense Misa thought she could see cracks forming in the air as reality strained under the weight of it.

A [**Divine Mantle**]. It was a skill she'd heard about but never seen. As far as she knew, it existed only in myth and legend. The theory behind it was simple—gods couldn't manifest themselves in the physical plane without an extreme cost associated with it, but if they had a conduit, someone who could channel their power for them . . .

. . . Come to think of it, though, hadn't her projection of Sev done something similar, back when she had to defend J'rokksur against a [**Meteor Swarm**]?

Misa supposed she shouldn't have been surprised.

Aurum reached out, and Misa felt the weight of reality dragging along with even that tiny movement. It was easy to forget how much *power* the gods really held. All this time, she'd been helping to fight against their slow erasure as they were dragged into the Void and used as fuel for the anchors.

In that way, she saw them as victims—as people in need of help. But even with Sev constantly channeling their power for incredible feats of divine magic right in front of her, she'd forgotten what they were capable of when their power was wielded directly.

Or perhaps she'd simply never known it at all. After all, how many clerics could wield a [**Divine Mantle**]?

Just the one she knew.

Aurum's fingers brushed against a single dangling root of the Soulblossom, turning its entire body into gold.

—◦—

"It's not dead," Sev said. He felt exhausted. Every drop of power had been wrung out from his body. He was suddenly intimately familiar with the idea of *soul exhaustion*, and that had only ever been a theory he'd read about. There wasn't much literature on it simply because there weren't that many ways to strain the soul. The development of the system had been the furthest they'd ever gone down that route, as far as he remembered, and the system was fundamentally not able to stress the soul that much.

By design, mostly. The amount of power that was needed to do such a thing was not *trivial*, and if skills drew directly on the soul, then what they created would not have been sustainable. People would wind up hurting themselves more as they accumulated more power.

But that didn't mean it was impossible. This was only true for system skills—the ones that relied on Shift to generate their effects. Spells and divine magic were a whole other category that didn't begin to touch on the methods the system used to cast its ideas into reality; with *those*, soul exhaustion was possible, if unlikely enough that he hadn't experienced it until now.

He supposed if he had to experience it for anything, then experiencing it to defeat a monster that was over two thousand levels was probably a worthwhile tradeoff.

"Are you sure?" Misa asked skeptically. She glanced up at the Soulblossom, and Sev followed her gaze, grimacing slightly. Every single part of it had been turned to gold, up to and including the petals of the flower.

"It's not," Sev insisted, though he was briefly worried. A quick [**Triage**] assuaged that worry—the system still registered the Soulblossom as a living entity. "It's just, uh . . . petrified."

"I hope that doesn't mean all those souls are stuck in there," Misa said.

"It . . . shouldn't." Sev hesitated, then walked up to the now-massive golden statue of the Soulblossom and the equally massive wormlike body it had formed out of its roots. He placed a hand against it. It was surprisingly *warm*, and it was warm in a way that disturbed him. He could almost feel it pulsing beneath his skin.

It *was* still alive, after all. He'd requested that Aurum keep it alive. Now it was a form of living gold, sustaining the souls within it along with the life of the Soulblossom itself.

"It's a form of stasis," Sev said. "The spell I used healed it, but there's too much to heal all at once—the system isn't fully effective, and divine magic can't completely penetrate this mass of souls either. So somewhere in there, my healing is still working its way through."

"You just froze it so the healing would have time to finish." Misa sounded a little relieved as she said it. "Well, good. I'm glad we're not just leaving this thing here."

Sev paused. "I mean, we kind of *are*," he said awkwardly. "Who knows how long it's going to take for the heal to get all the way through?"

"Not too long, I hope," Misa said. "But as long as we're not just leaving it to rot, I'm fine with it." She glanced up into the air, and Sev saw her gesture as if she was bringing up the system. "I think the system's starting to work properly again."

"You think so?" Sev tried to bring up his own copy of the system but winced as a sharp pain ran through him; Misa ran over to him and caught him as he suddenly stumbled, and he gave her a weak smile. "Whoops. Think I overdid it a little."

"Oh, come on," Misa grumbled. She picked him up and slung him over her shoulder, and Sev made a squawk of protest as he was folded rather uncomfortably in half. Not that he was in much of a mind to protest—he found he was a little dizzy. "You could channel multiple gods back in J'rokksur!"

It took a moment for Sev to figure out what Misa was talking about. "That wasn't me!" he protested. "That was your projection of me!"

"Same thing," Misa grunted. To his relief, she shifted his grip on him, adjusting so that half the blood in his body wasn't flowing to his head. Her voice was teasing, and she shook her head in mock disappointment. "Why can't you channel three gods at once yet, Sev? Vex can turn into a *dragon*."

"Okay, first of all, I think channeling one god is more impressive than turning into a dragon," Sev said, laughing. "And second, I can *stop time*! I feel like that's pretty impressive."

"That *is* pretty cool," Misa admitted. Sev felt her gait change as they hit the smooth tiling of Soulbloom Station once more. Cool air blew over the two of them. Misa carefully placed him back down on the ground, holding him by the shoulders to make sure he was steady. "You good?"

"Yeah," Sev said. He shook his head slightly. "I don't think my soul's gonna recover for a while. Not sure we should head further into this dungeon without backup from Vex and Derivan."

"Good thing my system's working again, then," Misa said. She glanced at the massive statue of the golden worm off in the distance. Sev followed her gaze—there was a slow leak of shadows around it, peeling off and slipping away as the amalgamation of souls slowly healed. "I'm going to send a message to them and see if they can come meet up with us."

"Please do." Sev groaned a little as he collapsed into a chair. Tinsel ran up to them as he did, still a literal walking light fixture—Sev couldn't deny the sight was a little amusing. "Hey, Tinsel."

"You did it!" Tinsel said cheerfully. It shoved a bundle of *things* into Sev's arms. It took a moment for him to parse what he was being handed—a few golden tickets, and then a bundle of fresh soulblooms. The smell of them alone instantly made Sev feel better, soothing the fresh ache within his soul. "Here, I decided to go collect some of the soulblooms while you were gone."

"Uh . . . thanks," Sev said, a little awkwardly but not ungratefully. He glanced at Misa, who was suddenly staring intently at her screen and sending messages rapidly, then back to Tinsel. "Actually, I think we've got a little time. Can you show me how to make one of those soulbloom potions you were talking about?"

"Can I ever!" Tinsel brightened. Literally. It shone so brightly, Sev had to squint just to be able to look in its general direction. "Ah, sorry. I forget your eyes don't work as good as most people."

"I question your definition of *good*," Sev muttered, though he was more amused than anything else. "Hey, Misa, I'm going off for a bit. Tinsel's going to show me how to make one of those soulbloom potions."

Misa nodded, waving at him and not even looking away from the screen; somewhat bemused and a little worried, Sev followed Tinsel off to a corner of the station, where a makeshift cauldron had been stapled together.

"Hello," the cauldron said. Sev jumped, then sighed.

He supposed he shouldn't have expected anything different.

CHAPTER 28

CONVOY TROUBLES

[What do you mean, you can't reach Anderstahl?] Misa asked, worried. The system still wasn't operating perfectly—it took more time than she would've liked for each message to go through, and even longer for the messages to come back through to her. There were a few other messages she had to go through, but the one from her mother had struck her with its immediate priority.

The Elyran refugees couldn't reach Anderstahl. As best as Charise and the rest of the Adventurers' Guild could tell, there was a massive wall of Void in the way—or, alternatively, just some kind of reality barrier that was blocking them. They weren't certain what it was, only that the barrier was miles wide and couldn't be trivially walked around.

Teleportation skills didn't get people across, either. Even Liz, with her Platinum-ranked ability to manipulate space and interfere directly with Derivan's Shift-induced portals, couldn't break through the barrier.

[It's like there's something in front of us that cuts off all possibilities,] Charise explained. [Leaving no possible reality where we get through.]

[Bullshit,] Misa replied automatically, and then, a little more apologetically, [Uh, sorry. I just mean that it's bullshit that it's stopping you. And also that there's no way to get through.]

[I got what you meant.] Misa could almost feel her mother's brief amusement echoing through her message. [But I don't know what else to tell you. It's what it feels like to me. There are a few *types* of teleportation skills that still get through, like Max with her [**Right Place, Right Time**], but nothing that lets us get through on our own.]

[What about Xothok?] Misa asked. [He's got an [**Astral Navigator**] class of some kind, right? If there's a path at all . . .]

[That's who we're waiting on.] The reply was a little more grim than Misa would have liked. [We haven't seen him or the Guildmaster in a couple days now—not since they went into a dungeon together. Max says they're not dead and the dungeon itself is still running instead of falling apart, so we think something about the dungeon is preventing them from getting out.]

[Shit,] Misa replied. [Why does it feel like when things fall apart, it happens all at once?]

[Because we don't notice it when it happens one at a time,] Charise responded dryly. [Check your other messages. I have a feeling you'll have something important in at least one other chat.]

Misa blinked, then swapped back over to the list of chats. Sure enough, there was an older message from Vex, blinking away.

[I've managed to integrate the Grand Anchor,] Vex informed them. [I managed to bring back a whole dragon with it, too! But, um . . . it feels like it's strained something in me. Do you know anything about that? I'm about to try to bring back all of Enkiros—you know, *the third Prime Kingdom*—so if there's anything I should know about this thing, please let me know now.]

And then a few minutes later, another message: [Also, I'm kind of running low on time. The Void bubble Enkiros is supposed to be in is expanding, and the more I let it expand, the harder it's going to be to bring back the kingdom. As in *I think it's just going to be impossible in a few more minutes*. We kinda got here just in time. So, uh, I'm just gonna try it soon.]

Misa wondered briefly if she needed to expand her vocabulary when it came to cussing. It really *felt* like it sometimes; she didn't have the words to express how she felt about this situation. "Shit," she said again, which did the best job of summing up how she felt, and then she fired off a quick response. [Hang on. I'm going to get Sev.]

She didn't even see the *message not sent* text that flickered across the system screen.

"Welp, that's five minutes," Vex said. He stood up and stretched, wriggling a bit as the tingling sensation of that stretch spread through his muscles; Derivan gave him a warm smile as he did, placing a hand on his shoulder. It didn't escape Vex's notice that he chose to do so with the new arm, and he reached up to place his own hand on top of Derivan's, squeezing it lightly. "If I wait any longer, this Void's going to be too big for me to replace. So . . ."

"So you will try it now." Derivan studied him, and Vex saw the concern in his eyes. "You are healed?"

"Can't even feel the strain anymore," Vex said, which was true. He was as healed as he was going to be. "Ready?"

"If you need my strength," Derivan said, "I will be here."

"I know," Vex said. He smiled up. "Love you, Deri."

"I love you too." A gentle caress of a metal hand against the edge of his jaw. Derivan took a step back.

Exvhar and Novice gathered behind them as they saw Vex pulling out everything he needed; first the [**Spelldisk**], then the [**Semerit of the First Library**], then the magelight to draw the Primordial Glyph of Translation. Vex could already feel the magic beginning to build. Which was always the case for powerful magic like this: it was almost like the mana *knew* that something big was going to happen. Something important.

First came the [**Spelldisk**], to see the remnants of Enkiros. Then the [**Semerit of the First Library**], to make the spell a little easier to cast—to give reality a template for that which was supposed to exist here. The Primordial Glyph of Translation had been taught to him for the purposes of manipulating the system, but here he applied it in much the way the Roads translated the people going through them.

A physical change was necessary to bring something from unreality into reality. A *translation*, from a thing without substance into a thing that was.

And last but not least, Vex drew upon his connection to the Grand Anchor of Magic that resided within him.

He felt the floodgates open.

Though he couldn't see it himself, his eyes shone with a brilliant white— and where that light landed upon the Void, it illuminated a bustling city. A kingdom where there should have been none. That light began to show through not just his eyes but through his very scales, until his very body was like a beacon. A second sun whose light could touch a kingdom no one else could see.

The current of magic picked Vex up, lifted him from the ground, and drew him forward into the Void.

Around him, reality pieced itself back together.

"Vex is trying to *what*?!" Sev almost hit his head on the counter when he jerked up at Misa's words. He stood up straight. "Tell me I heard you wrong. Or, wait, no, tell me I heard you right. Shit. I don't know which option is worse."

"Explain," Misa said. Short and sweet. She wasn't angry at him, but she *was* trying to keep him focused. He could appreciate that. Sev could feel his mind running in a dozen different directions, picking up on a dozen stray memories he hadn't explicitly recalled before now.

It shouldn't have been possible to bring things back from the Void. Things that were erased were gone permanently—reality did its best to stitch things back together, but it was all still *gone*. The reality anchors had been built to preserve what remained, not to bring back what had already been erased. It was the whole reason they were slowly losing ground.

And yet . . .

Misa's family had been brought back from the dead.

No, the situation was a little different. J'rokksur hadn't been completely erased. When a dungeon failed and broke, the land it preserved would slowly be offloaded to nearby anchors; it would be *forgotten*, perhaps, as less power was now dedicated to preserving it, but it wasn't *erased*. Not erased the same way things were when they were lost to the Void, anyway.

No matter how he thought about it, there wasn't a way for things to be brought back from the Void. Reality anchors could Shift things in from different timelines, but there was a crucial *something* lost in the process when something was consumed by the Void.

"You said he already succeeded with it," Sev said. He got up and began to pace, briefly forgetting about the soulbloom potion still bubbling in the cauldron—it would be fine anyway, according to Tinsel. Soulblooms couldn't really be overcooked. "Did he explain how he did it?"

"He said something about integrating the Grand Anchor," Misa said. Sev stopped in his tracks. "And that it strained something in him. So he wants to know if it's safe for him to try to bring back the whole kingdom with it."

That made sense. That was what the Grand Anchors were designed to do, over the Prime Anchors and all the other lesser reality anchors. The Grand Anchors could create reality, not just maintain it.

The problem with that was what they'd just learned—*soul exhaustion*. Like most artifacts of the system, the Grand Anchor was a construct that attached to both system and soul, using the same substance souls were made of. It was *made* of that soulstuff, for lack of a better word for it. There was a physical vessel to house it, yes, but that physical vessel wasn't exactly necessary. It just made transporting it easier.

With what they'd now learned coupled with Vex's testimony that he felt like he'd strained something . . .

It was the same sensation Sev had experienced himself when he'd mantled Aurum. The same sensation Misa had felt when using her block to repel the Soulblossom. With the levels of power they were using, channeling it all through their souls was no longer safe.

Not that he could think of an alternative. The Grand Anchors themselves were supposed to be a last resort.

"We have to stop him," Sev said. Misa's eyes narrowed—she didn't like that answer.

"He's in danger?" she asked.

"I don't know," Sev answered, and he raised his hands defensively when Misa opened her mouth to speak again. "I really don't. Grand Anchors were experimental, Misa—they were my last resort. They're also the only way we can fix Obreve, because *everything else* has failed, which means we *do* need to bring back Enkiros no matter what. But I don't know if it's safe for Vex to bring back a whole kingdom with it. I want to at least study the phenomenon of soulstrain a bit first. And we have these soulbloom potions now. We can recover even if we *do* strain ourselves and our systems."

"I'm not sure we have the time," Misa said. She brought up her system screen and froze, her eyes narrowing a little as she read through the words—and then she cursed, typing rapidly. "Shit, I think he already started. I asked him to hold on but the system didn't get the damn message through, and he said it won't be possible to bring Enkiros back at all if he waits too long."

Sev winced, his heart sinking. "Fuck, that's not good."

"What's the worst-case scenario here?" Misa demanded. She twirled her mace—Sev could almost see her mind ticking, could almost see what she was planning to do.

It wouldn't be the first time she'd used that blocking skill to teleport. This would be the farthest she'd ever tried to do it, though; the layers of reality she would be forced through to find a timeline where she'd gone with Vex and Derivan . . .

"The worst-case scenario is that it strains Vex's soul to the point where it explodes," Sev said, because there wasn't any point in hiding it. The thought of it put a sick feeling into his gut, though. "But—but there are safety mechanisms in the system. It *should* prevent that from happening. The problem is that just preventing it doesn't mean it isn't going to do huge damage before the failsafes kick in—"

"Sev, *stick to the facts*," Misa interrupted, her jaw tense.

"Worst-case, he dies. Most likely case, he takes a little longer to die, and we have time to get the soulbloom potions to him and try to heal him." Sev glanced back at the cauldron. It was . . . unbelievably lucky that they'd happened on this right when they needed it. Coincidence? Or related to his position as the Concept of [**Fate**]? "Best-case scenario, he succeeds and will need the potions to recover anyway."

"Bottle it up," Misa instructed. She adjusted her belt, then fired off a quick message to Derivan. "Enough for both me and Vex. I'm going."

Her tone brooked no argument. Sev wasn't going to argue with her, either. He swallowed the knot of worry in his throat and nodded. "We've made enough potions for you both. Keep in contact. My system's back online now."

"Will do."

CHAPTER 29

SOULSTRAIN

Vex was dimly aware that something hurt.

But it was a dim awareness. There was a point where the pain had become excruciating, and then something had *snapped*—which was a relief, really. He wasn't sure he would have been able to tolerate the pain for much longer, and he'd grown up on pain. This was excruciating on a level he'd never had to define and that he hoped he'd never have to define again.

Whatever it was that had snapped, the pain felt lesser after that. Or maybe it wasn't that it was lesser? Maybe it was just that it was distant. He wasn't entirely sure what the difference between the two was, but whatever the case, he was grateful that it wasn't quite so mentally overwhelming anymore.

The spell was still going. That was good.

He didn't have to exert any conscious control over it anymore. He'd had to at first—the internals of the semerit were a lot more complicated than he expected when it came to restoring an entire kingdom instead of a single dragon. Even within the semerit, there were multiple possibilities, multiple different outcomes; he'd had to mentally sort through them to find the one that was closest to what had actually *happened* in reality.

It helped that he'd been inside the semerit before. His actions, too, had been recorded within it—that was the whole reason the semerit had been labeled as containing a temporal paradox, after all. Because he'd added an outcome that never existed before.

An outcome where the citizens of Enkiros evacuated before the kingdom was consumed by the Void.

It was staggering how many other possibilities existed—how many different ways that same kingdom had fallen. Not all of it was to the Void, though the Void was always what eventually consumed them. It was just that in some possibilities, the kingdom fell to infighting long before the Void properly consumed them. Disagreements about how the gods functioned, about what the gods wanted . . .

In only one of them did anyone even notice that the gods were slowly going missing, and that person had been summarily dismissed. For how could an entity so powerful as a god be erased from not only reality itself but the minds of everyone that had witnessed them?

Sorting through all those possibilities had been taxing. He'd felt something within him slowly tearing apart even while he was doing it. And then he had to push that possibility *outward*, pouring the power of the Grand Anchor into the Primordial Glyph of Translation, using the remnant fragments of reality caught by the [**Spelldisk**] as a sort of substrate for everything else to grow on. Doing all that pushed his mind to the limit, and if he hadn't experienced this sort of cognitive overload already from his use of his Sign of Research . . .

. . . Well, it wasn't worth thinking about, because it hadn't happened.

The point was that the restoration spell he was casting had eventually reached a sort of critical mass of power, at which point he no longer needed to maintain it—in fact, he couldn't stop it even if he wanted to. It dragged more power out of him with or without his will.

It was the first moment that Vex thought he might've made a mistake, because he couldn't stop this spell. Not even if something went wrong and he had to.

Even the fear of that mistake felt distant from him, though. Vex felt a little bit like he was floating in a bubble—come to think of it, he *was* floating, so maybe that wasn't all that unusual. He could still see and hear and think, at least, so things hadn't gone *that* far off course.

He could see the marble pathways of Enkiros's streets materializing before him. He could see the streetlights and the merchants walking along the streets. They weren't completely real yet; it would take far more magic than what he'd cast so far to bring them back. But they were getting there. What he witnessed now was something like an echo of the past, a moment that had already happened, long ago.

The iteration of Enkiros that was coming back was a few days before the Void had begun to spread within it. Vex wondered briefly if choosing that point in time had also strained the spell he was casting. He wasn't asking for Enkiros as it was *now*; he was asking for Enkiros as it was before the Void had ever begun to damage it.

It *shouldn't* have, he thought. As far as he could tell, most possibilities within the semerit were weighted equally and would have been equally difficult to bring back from the Void.

He had a brief, silly thought, wondering if things would proceed in the same way. Would the Void begin to expand in the middle of the kingdom again? And perhaps more interestingly—would a copy of him show up in the middle of the palace, interfering with a discussion on what to do about the encroaching Void? That was the possibility he was drawing from, but . . . he was here and not there.

The thought made him giggle a bit, so that was nice. It was good to know he could still giggle. And laugh.

Vex thought he heard a voice calling for him. It was a familiar voice, too. Derivan? He wanted to turn around and respond, say that he was fine, but . . . he found that he couldn't. His muscles simply wouldn't obey him. His entire being was still under the spell's control, and his body was a mere conduit at the moment, channeling vast amounts of reality and pouring it into the Void.

It would be fine, probably.

Vex barely noticed it, but within the spell—something that had happened at the same time he felt that strange *snapping* sensation within him—there was a tiny, errant split.

The flow of power within him was no longer a single stream. It was two, then three, tens of dozens of individual strands, split down the cracks of a broken channel.

And before him, Enkiros *Shifted*.

—◊—

[Derivan, I need you to attack something. I don't care what you're attacking—just swing your sword at the grass or something. Tell me when you're going to do it.] Misa's instructions were quick and precise. Derivan stared at them for a moment and then at the outpouring of power from Vex.

He didn't hesitate. [Three seconds,] he informed Misa.

One. Two. Three—

Derivan swung his sword, ignoring the way it nearly slipped from his grip. It *did* slip from his grip a second later as Misa appeared before him and his sword *clanged* against the shaft of her mace; he ignored the weapon too as it bounced off of him and landed in the grass.

"The spell is straining Vex too much," Derivan said. He couldn't help. He'd already tried. Their combined Sign was supposed to link the two of them, to a degree, but his attempt at using it had only forced a sort of magical feedback through the Sign and thrown him back; he couldn't interfere with what Vex was doing.

What was worse was perhaps the knowledge that if he *did* interfere, it would only make things worse. He'd gotten at least that much of an impression from the mana. There was no stopping whatever Vex had started. It would be seen through to its conclusion, no matter what the result was.

Derivan tried to quell the fear rising in his heart. He'd never felt it quite like this before. He barely noticed Misa's own appearance—her face distorted in a grimace of pain, her hair disheveled, and a staggering number of potions strapped haphazardly across her body.

He *did* notice it quickly enough to catch Misa before she collapsed, though. "Misa?" he asked. He didn't need two of his teammates to be hurt, not like this.

"Just . . . give me a second." Misa said the words in a half-growl, panting; she ripped one of the potions off and drank it down in a single gulp, then seemed to recover, straightening and catching her breath. She stared up at Vex, whose power was still pouring into the Void in front of them.

Even Exvhar was starting to look worried now. The dragon had seemed excited at first, but now he was realizing how much he might have been asking from Vex. Realizing how much restoring Enkiros might have *cost*. His tail swung nervously behind him, and his wings fluttered as he tried to control himself.

Novice, for his part, simply clutched at the magelight Vex had given him and stared. Every so often, his fingers twitched, as if he wanted to paint a glyph that would help—but he stopped himself every time. No doubt he'd gotten the same feeling from the mana, that trying to help would only hurt Vex in the process.

"Shit," Misa finally said. She stared up at Vex. "He already started, huh?"

"And something is wrong," Derivan said.

"No shit," Misa said, though her expression softened when she saw Derivan's restrained panic. "I've got potions. We can help Vex heal—"

"You do not understand," Derivan said. "Something is wrong with the *spell*."

Misa's gaze sharpened. "What do you mean?"

"I do not know how to explain it." Derivan glanced at Novice, who nodded at him; he felt the same thing. "The spell is . . . fracturing. Vex cannot contain the amount of power that this spell requires."

"Will the spell complete?" Misa asked.

"Yes, but . . ." Derivan hesitated. "The outcome will not be what we expect or what we want. I can already feel it."

He could feel it with Shift, to be specific. Vex wasn't just restoring Enkiros to reality—that was what he'd been doing at first, certainly. The moment the spell had fractured, every single possibility that Vex had been manually holding back had come flooding out. Now he could feel other versions of Enkiros layered and Shifted on top of itself, over and over and over. Different iterations of the same kingdom. Different people. Different outcomes.

This was where he *could* help. He could feel the spell trying to compress all those different layers of reality together, not knowing what to do with them; he had to reach out with Shift, hold those layers apart. Letting them merge could very well mean the end of Enkiros—some iterations were so utterly different that they would be annihilated without Shift to keep them apart.

This was the only way he could help. The only way he could make sure what Vex was doing wouldn't be for nothing.

(But he couldn't think that way, surely? Vex would be fine. *Vex would be fine.* He refused any other outcome, refused any other possibility. Vex had to be fine.)

"Derivan," Misa said. She had a hand on his shoulder—when had that happened?—and pulled him to face her, away from Vex. He almost resisted. He wanted to turn back and see what was happening, even if he knew, consciously, that it didn't matter whether or not he was looking at Vex.

He could feel it. Even looking away, his stats were active, and half of them were focused on Vex in some way. He knew exactly where the lizardkin was, knew how much power was flowing through him, could feel the state of his system.

It was . . . surprisingly intact, considering everything that was happening to it. He could actually feel the system reaching out to try to compensate for the damage the spell was doing. He almost reached out with Patch to try to help but almost immediately could feel himself being warned away. The system was *fine*. There was nothing here that needed fixing.

Only Vex.

"*Derivan,*" Misa said again, shaking him a little to catch his attention. This time, Derivan managed to make himself focus on her.

"Yes," he said, more to indicate that he was paying attention than anything else.

"We'll make sure he's okay." Misa's words were firm. It was more certainty than he felt within him, and there was a comfort in that. At least *someone* was more certain than he was.

"I allowed him to do this." Derivan said the words before he realized he was thinking them. "I should have—"

"He would've done it whether you tried to stop him or not," Misa said. She smiled at him, a sad smile, but it made Derivan's heart clench—she was right. Vex was determined. He'd already put it off as much as he could, but he was under the impression that if he put it off any longer, it would have made recovering Enkiros impossible.

And he *had* asked Vex to slow down, to wait until the last possible moment. Vex had healed in that time. That had to count for something.

"It is . . . difficult," Derivan admitted after a moment. He didn't even entirely know what he was admitting was difficult. Not blaming himself, perhaps. Or standing here and doing nothing while raw power poured through Vex, eroding at his very being. "You are aware of what is happening to him?"

"Kinda," Misa said with a sigh. She took a seat in the grass and gestured for Derivan and the others to join her—there was nothing further they could do for now. They had to wait for the spell to complete. "Funny enough, Sev and I were up against something pretty similar in the Anderstahl Prime Dungeon."

"Similar?" Derivan asked. He latched on to the story like it was a lifeline.

"We had to fight a monster, but the interesting thing is what it did to us," Misa said. Her voice was low and calm, the opposite of everything Derivan was feeling; he wondered if she was doing it on purpose. Misa gestured to the potions still strapped all across her body. "Soulstrain. These potions heal it."

"Soulstrain," Derivan repeated. It *sounded* right. If he tried to feel for what was happening to Vex—

"We couldn't use our systems, and it messed us up if we tried to use our skills directly on it. Or even if I touched it directly." Misa winced a little at the memory. "Sev had it a little easier, I guess 'cause his divine-magic stuff doesn't interact with the system as much. But it turns out that some types of power you have to channel through your soul, and our souls can only take so much of that strain."

"And this is what has happened to Vex," Derivan said. "It is his *soul* that is injured."

"Yes, but these potions will help." Misa pulled one of them off the straps on her and handed it to Derivan; he took it, cradling it like it was a precious remedy. Which it was. "They're made from the soulbloom flowers we found in the dungeon. They improve your connection with your soul—or help repair it, if it's been damaged. It helped us. It should help Vex, too."

"It will." Derivan didn't know if he was just clinging to hope or if what he felt now was rooted in reality. The vial in his hands felt . . . *right*. Like it was what they needed to fix this, if they could get it to Vex. He was half-tempted to walk over there right now and pour the potion down Vex's throat. He would have, if he thought it would help.

A long pause. Power surged around them still. It almost felt like an itch he couldn't scratch—not that he knew what that felt like. He glanced down at the more sensitive of his two arms, and remembered Vex slowly tracing the patterns on it.

Slowly, he closed his fist.

"It will," he repeated.

CHAPTER 30

WAYWARD WIZARD

"Ow," Vex said dully.

Everything hurt. He wasn't really sure *why* everything hurt, but he did know that everything hurt, and he knew that it hurt in a way that was wrong. Like deeply, badly wrong. In a "he probably needed immediate medical attention" sort of way, not that there was anyone around to provide him with said medical attention.

It took him a moment to figure out where he was and what was happening.

One, he was alive. He'd been a little afraid for a moment that he might have died trying to cast the spell. It would've been embarrassing, for one thing, but he also just . . . didn't want to leave Derivan like that. And the rest of his friends, of course. They were a factor too.

Two, he wasn't sure he was going to *stay* alive for very long. Something felt like it was twisted the wrong way inside him. If he had to put a name to the feeling, he would've said it was his soul, cracked and broken in places it should never be cracked and broken.

The system was holding him together? It felt like the system was holding him together. How did he know that?

[**DANGER: EXTREME SOULSTRAIN DETECTED. SYSTEM FAILSAFES INITIATED. PLEASE SEE A CLERIC AS SOON AS POSSIBLE.**]

Oh. That was how he knew that. Vex stared at the text floating in the air in front of him. It wasn't even in a neat little box; it just floated there, like it was waiting for him to acknowledge it.

He poked it. It went away.

"Huh," he said.

Soulstrain was probably a bad thing.

Anyway.

He was somewhere in the streets of Enkiros. He knew this because of the pristine marble that surrounded him, though the kingdom was oddly *empty*. Vex was almost certain that the spell he cast should've brought back the kingdom and everyone in it. Maybe he was just in a particularly empty sector, or it was a bad time of day?

That didn't make any sense. There weren't any signs of the streets being worn down from use—if Vex didn't know any better, he would've guessed that these streets had never *been* used. He'd seen something like that in some distant possibilities where Enkiros had been built but never used . . .

But that couldn't be right. That wasn't the possibility he'd chosen to bring back. He thought back to the spell and to the time he'd spent trying to process the chaotic rush of information, wondering if he might've made a mistake—

"*Ow,*" Vex said again, a little more emphatically this time. Thinking hurt. More than that, though, thinking about the spell he'd cast brought back some of his memories with a sharp clarity. He remembered the sensation of something fracturing within him.

To a lesser extent, he remembered the spell fracturing along with it. He just didn't know what that meant. How it had affected the outcome of the spell. The idea that he might have failed weighed heavily on him. If all he'd succeeded in doing was bringing back an empty version of Enkiros and pushing himself into a state where he was quite literally dying . . .

. . . Well, he didn't know what he'd say to the others.

Whenever he found them again, anyway.

Vex slowly pushed himself to his feet. As comfortable as the marble streets were—and they were *surprisingly* comfortable—he needed to start moving, at least. To try to make his way back to his friends. Maybe there were some people here in this empty ghost town of a kingdom that would be able to help him too. Always good to be optimistic.

"But first," Vex said out loud. Mostly to hear the sound of his own voice than anything, though it was a small comfort when he heard how weak and frail he sounded compared to the usual. "Gotta see if I can talk to my friends and tell them where I am."

Vex opened the system—

PAIN.

—then closed it again, gasping, staggering backward and leaning against the nearest wall. His eyes were wide, and he felt the cold grip of fear slowly begin to curl around him.

Nothing quite like being unable to access the system to make everything sink in.

"Fuck," he said, which was about as eloquent as he felt like he was capable of being. Vex stared down at his trembling hands, then out toward the empty streets.

A thought struck him, and he squeezed his eyes shut, trying to force it out of his head.

It snuck in anyway, an insidious whisper: what if he didn't get to see his friends again?

What if he didn't get to see Derivan again?

He wasn't sure he could bear the thought.

—⁂—

"Derivan?" Misa asked worriedly. She'd never seen the armor so . . . distant, though *distant* wasn't the right word for it. Distracted, perhaps. It was the closest thing to vulnerable as she'd ever seen him. She could practically feel the worry emanating from him, the anxiety as his gaze traced the streets of Enkiros.

"I am here," Derivan said automatically, then paused, looking at Misa. ". . . I cannot deny that I am concerned. I am trying to stay focused."

"It's okay to be worried, you know," she said. Derivan went still, then slowly shook his head.

". . . No," he said. "There is no time for it."

"Derivan—"

"I cannot allow him to be lost when I am able to find him," Derivan said. He sounded tired. "Please. Allow me to focus."

Misa sighed and said nothing.

She knew how Derivan felt, truth be told. This was nearly identical to how she'd felt back when they'd lost their first real fight against Irvis. She understood the feeling of helplessness, the thought that nothing you did could help. There was nothing she could say here that would *help*.

All she could do was be there.

It wasn't like she wasn't worried herself. Her concern for Derivan was one thing, but whatever was happening to Vex left a cold feeling coiling in her gut. Vex was a lot like the little brother she'd never had.

Come to think of it, maybe she *was* in the same boat as Derivan. It wasn't like she was doing any better at pushing back her own fears and worries.

"You said you can find him," Misa said. "You know where he is?"

"He carries a piece of me within him," Derivan said, his voice soft. "Yes. I know where he is. But he is Shifted too many layers away, and the residual magic around him is constantly and repeatedly Shifting him—finding him will not be easy. And . . ."

Derivan hesitated briefly, then glanced at the air, presumably at a system screen. He sighed.

". . . And I suspect that the Prime Anchor of Enkiros has decided that these circumstances are worthy of its dungeon," he said quietly. He sent a system window over to her for her to see, and Misa stared at it, her heart sinking.

Activation conditions for the bonus room <The Bridge Between> have been met.

Transportation not required. Participants already within bonus room.

The kingdom of Enkiros has been split into a multitude of infinitesimal fragments of itself, each harboring a different possible future.

Find the fragment at the core of the restoration spell to repair the broken Primordial Glyph.

The broken Primordial Glyph . . . ?

"Oh, shit," Misa said. She stared up at the sky, where a river of mana not unlike that in Teque hung in the sky. It took her a moment to recognize it for what it was. A small piece of a *massive* glyph.

But . . . it was the wrong piece. She didn't even need [**Intuitionist**] to tell her it was the wrong piece. Something about the river of mana above screamed at her like it was *wrong*. It belonged to a fragment of reality that had never been here, and the mana above reflected that fact—like it had been twisted through a funhouse mirror.

"In a dungeon again, huh?" Misa muttered.

"Every fragment has an entrance and several exits," Derivan said. "I cannot Shift us to the right fragment immediately—the Prime Anchor itself is holding these fragments in place now. To fight it would be to destroy the anchor."

"So we're in a maze," Misa said.

"Of sorts," Derivan agreed. "I believe the exits are conditional. They are tied to different objectives. I can sense these with Patch, to a degree."

"And you know how to get us to Vex?" Misa asked.

Derivan seemed to focus for a moment, and then he nodded. "He is close to the core fragment," he said. "A few fragments away at most. We are at the edge. It will take us time to get to him. Do we have time?"

Misa thought back to Sev's parting words as he helped her strap the potions onto her body. "With the system's failsafes, it should be at least a day before his soul is strained to the point where it's irrecoverable."

"Then let us act quickly." Derivan didn't waste any time—he strode off, and Misa hurried to catch up with him. Novice and Exvhar had been left behind, mostly because Exvhar didn't seem to want to enter this twisted maze of his former home, and Novice felt he had to take care of the poor dragon. They were waiting just outside.

There were a lot of people counting on them for this. Misa might not be able to see them herself, but she could feel them right on the edges of her perception—like a whole kingdom's worth of people were holding their breath, Vex among them.

[You probably can't see this,] Misa sent. [But just in case you can . . . hold on. We're coming for you.]

CHAPTER 31

ON THE RAILS

It had been a long time since Sev was last alone in a dungeon.

Properly alone, anyway. He'd been separated from his party before, but even then, they were always nearby. Now Derivan, Vex, and Misa were all basically on the other side of the continent—and while it wasn't impossible for Misa to get back into the dungeon, it was . . . inadvisable, at best. Sev wasn't planning to help her get back via her block-teleportation even if she wanted to; the first teleport had put enough strain on her.

Well, in theory, anyway. Calculating soulstrain wasn't exactly a well-developed science, considering how little of a problem it had been so far. The system used Shift to power its skills, and Misa's abilities were system-based, unlike the rest of them. Shift didn't put that much strain on the soul. But there were multiple compounding factors: the distance, Misa's tendency to use her skills in ways that were outside their intended usage, the barrier that was apparently blocking off all of Anderstahl . . .

. . . The perception bracelets that Vex had made for them, all the way back when they were negotiating with the Elyran nobles. Sev glanced down at the string tied around his wrist and at the little enchanted bead strung onto it. He couldn't deny that the enchantment had been useful, but the description Vex had gotten for it had described a hidden cost.

He was pretty sure he now knew what that hidden cost was. Soulstrain. Every usage of it to alter the perception of everyone else stretched the user's soul in ways it was never meant to be stretched.

Good thing they hadn't used it more frequently. Sev could only imagine the results of that would have been . . . bad.

"So!" Tinsel said. It still wasn't leaving him alone, not that Sev was complaining. He did wonder if there was a better way to refer to it in his head than, well, "it," but when he'd asked, it had just insisted he keep referring to it that way. "Off to the next station, then?"

"Maybe." Sev glanced back at the field of soulbloom flowers. As far as he knew, this was the only remedy for soulstrain that existed. The coincidence of the dungeon producing these when the problem hadn't even been known before felt strange to him. Onyx working behind the scenes again, perhaps? Or someone else? "I feel like I should collect a few more of these, just in case I can't come back here."

"What do you mean?" Tinsel cocked its head. "We're always going to be here!"

Sev winced. He wasn't even sure if the stations stayed the same between delves—he was, in fact, pretty certain that they rotated, and that the dungeon phased them in and out all the time. He'd never seen Soulbloom Station before, after all. And that was *before* taking into consideration that the universe was ending.

But maybe that was a bit much to drop onto a light fixture given life.

"You never know what will happen," Sev said lightly instead. "What if the train breaks down?"

"Oh!" Tinsel didn't have eyes, but he could hear the way they widened in its voice anyway. It flickered thoughtfully, then hopped up on light-filament legs. "Then you should take me with you!"

Sev raised an eyebrow. "Why is that, exactly?"

"Well, I always wanted to see what the other stations are like," Tinsel said, not unreasonably. "And if the train breaks down, I won't be able to. So I should do it now while I get the chance! Plus, you have extra tickets because your friend isn't here."

"Aren't you the one that gave me the tickets?" Sev asked, amused. "You could get one for yourself if you wanted."

"It's not the same," Tinsel insisted. "Besides, I want to go on a train ride with a friend! You're a friend, aren't you?"

"I suppose." Sev let himself smile, to Tinsel's delight. "But you have to understand—I don't know what's coming. I might not be able to protect you. Some stations might be dangerous."

Most of them probably were, he thought to himself.

"Yeah, but I can't die!" Tinsel pointed out cheerfully. "Well, I mean, you could destroy my body. But that doesn't count. I just possess something else."

. . . It *did* have a point there.

"Fine," Sev said. He didn't even say it begrudgingly—he had to admit he'd appreciate having some company. It helped prevent him from dwelling too much on what was most likely happening with Misa and the others. Misa hadn't yet sent him an update, and he had no idea if it was due to the peculiarities of Soulbloom Station, or if she just hadn't had the time. He hoped Vex was all right. "Let's go, then," he added.

"All aboard!" Tinsel cheered, running ahead. Sev chuckled and followed after it—though not before grabbing all the remaining soulblooms Tinsel had picked and stuffing them into his pack.

Better to be safe, he decided. They did have several potions made already, but with the way things were going, there was every chance they'd need more.

—⁂—

The train ride with Tinsel was . . . awkward. Not because there was nothing to talk about, or nothing the two of them had in common—if anything, Tinsel was all too eager to share the details of its life in Soulbloom Station. And it was very eager to learn about life outside of the station as well; Sev had a little bit of difficulty with its enthusiasm, though he did find it endearing.

He just wished it would be endearing a little bit farther away from him. Like, by a couple more feet, at least.

Beside him, Tinsel kicked its legs against the table, apparently finding the movement of the train itself fascinating. It had a full plate in front of it—a plate that was piled high with all manner of lightbulbs and tiny, glowing bugs. Apparently the train adjusted its meals for its passengers, though Tinsel still didn't exactly have the mouth to consume any of it. It seemed content to just stare at the glowing plate in front of it.

Heck, maybe that was how it ate.

"Did you hear what the announcement said?" Tinsel asked. "The next station's called *Ichoric Ascent*. I wonder what it's like!"

"It doesn't sound pleasant," Sev said. He had, in fact, heard the announcement and was trying desperately not to think about it. *Ichoric Ascent* sounded like he had to climb his way up through a mountain of dangerously unsanitary organic material.

"But it might be interesting!" Tinsel said cheerfully. Sev wondered if there was anything that could get it down, or if it was bound to be this endlessly cheerful all the time. He didn't mind it. It was sort of a comfort, in a weird way.

"I suppose," Sev allowed.

The door to their cabin hissed open, and the Conductor strode in. Sev glanced up with interest—he looked . . . a little different from before? He couldn't tell exactly *how*, though. He wasn't dressed any differently; he was wearing the same immaculately pressed suit. He was the same combination of wood and silver, and he was as expressionless as ever . . .

"Who's that?" Tinsel asked, swinging its legs.

Sev glanced down at Tinsel. "That's the Conductor," he said. "He takes our tickets to make sure we're allowed to go to the next station."

"Oh." Tinsel paused, then cocked its . . . well, its entire body. "What happens if we don't give him our tickets?"

"I have no idea," Sev said. The Conductor paused and tilted his head slightly, as if he could hear them, and Sev blinked. ". . . Let's not find out."

"Okay," Tinsel said, cheerful as ever.

Maybe it was the way he was walking that was different. There was something more lifelike about the way the Conductor moved—like he was a little more fluid, a little more organic. Gone was the stiffness of the joints, the telltale mechanical movement that he often saw in automatons and constructs like these.

"I am the Conductor," the Conductor said once again. The voice was a little smoother too, Sev noted—a slightly deeper baritone. He wondered what was changing. Misa's intuition had pinged on the Conductor as being *important*; this was almost certainly a part of it. Maybe the Conductor had something to do with how they were going to get into the final area of the dungeon. Or maybe he could give them backdoor access somehow? That seemed like something Misa would pick up on with an intuition-enhancing skill.

He'd been going through the dungeon conventionally so far, but if there was any chance he could skip . . .

"Tickets, please," the Conductor said patiently.

"Hold on," Sev said. "I've got a couple of questions, if that's all right."

"Tickets first." The Conductor's voice was firm, and there was an edge of steel in it that hadn't been there before—but it had not, Sev noticed, said *no*. Sev shrugged and handed over two of the golden tickets he'd acquired from Tinsel just a few hours before, and he saw the Conductor's shoulders relax a fraction as he fed them into the slot in its chest.

Interestingly, the silver in the Conductor's body changed as it processed the tickets, turning from chrome to gold; Sev felt the tiniest change in the air, so minuscule he almost wondered if he imagined it. There was some significance to that change, though what that significance was, he didn't yet know. Part of the dungeon's mechanics?

Tinsel didn't seem nearly as reserved when it came to asking questions. It was looking at the Conductor with fascination. "Do they taste good?" it asked curiously, reaching out to poke at the slot. "If I ate some tickets, would they turn me gold, too?"

Sev winced and grabbed Tinsel's hand before it could start randomly prodding the poor Conductor. "Maybe don't start poking strangers without their permission," he said.

"They do not taste of anything," the Conductor said politely. He didn't seem to mind the brief faux pas, though Sev could've sworn he saw a brief, appreciative glance thrown his way. "But I require them to function, and so does the train. And I do not believe they would turn you gold, no."

Interesting. So the tickets were a form of food? He wondered if the dungeon had worked that into its local ecosystem, or if it was just an arbitrary requirement put into place. Maybe the tickets held a form of mana the Conductor could consume or something.

Well, since Tinsel had established the Conductor would respond to questions—

"How many stations are there, do you know?" Sev asked. "What if we want to go straight to the end?"

He felt a slight chill as the Conductor turned to him and examined him. "There are ten stations in total," he answered. Sev's heart sank—that was far too many stations. Doing them by himself, or even with Tinsel's help . . . there was no guarantee he'd be done in time to repair Anderstahl's Prime Anchor.

He didn't even know how much time he still had. What had Muchen and the others said? Something about how the anchor had days left, not months, if it couldn't be repaired. He had a fistful of reality shards with him he was almost certain he could use to repair the anchor, but he needed to get to it first. With ten stations, accounting for the fact that some dungeons could take days to clear and the fact that there was travel time between each station, there was no guarantee at all that he'd reach the end of the dungeon in time.

"You cannot 'go straight to the end,' as you put it," the Conductor added. "We do not have enough fuel. You must acquire tickets from each station."

Sev had assumed something like that was the case, but it still made him wince to hear it. "And how long does it usually take to get from one station to the next?"

"It depends on the station," the Conductor said. "Each station is farther than the last. Ichoric Ascent is another five hours away. The tenth station is two days of travel from the ninth."

Sev winced. He supposed that explained why the dungeon had made the train so . . . comfortable, though it seemed like an arbitrary enforced waiting time. Was there a reason for it? Maybe the dungeon was taking the time to build each station while the train "traveled."

He definitely wouldn't put that past a dungeon.

"What if I just run along the train tracks?" Sev said, half-jokingly. The Conductor just stared at him for a long moment—long enough it began to make Sev somewhat uncomfortable. Apparently he'd never considered someone just trying to walk to the next station.

"It would take you far longer," he eventually said. "And you are not allowed to walk on the tracks."

"Will something happen to me if I do?"

A long pause. "No."

This was an unplanned scenario, apparently. "So I *could*, if I wanted to."

"It would be inefficient."

"You're not wrong there," Sev admitted, which made the Conductor relax slightly; apparently, the golem had been genuinely worried Sev might decide to abandon the train entirely and just start running along the tracks.

It wasn't necessarily a bad idea, even—he would have considered it if he'd had Derivan here to pull open portals between each station, or Vex's magic to speed up their travel time. Misa's stamina could carry them between stations too, he suspected. By himself, all he had that might improve his travel time were his Blessings, and his connection with the divine had been . . . quite sorely taxed by his use of [**Divine Mantle**].

Even with the soulbloom potions, it would take a while to recover, mostly because what he'd strained wasn't *just* his soul. The divine threads around him were stretched thin, and they wouldn't be repaired with just a potion; there was a *reason* gods very rarely visited the physical plane like this. It was costly in more ways than one.

"Do you have any other questions?" the Conductor asked.

"Yes," Sev decided after a moment. "If I said I wanted to get to the Prime Anchor, what would you tell me?"

There was another long pause. The light blue that passed for the Conductor's eyes flickered briefly to red, alarming Sev, then went back to their original color. "I do not know what that is," the Conductor said carefully.

Sev picked up on the note of deception almost immediately. "You do," he said, narrowing his eyes slightly. "But you don't want to tell me."

"I cannot elaborate further."

"It's *important*," Sev emphasized. "The Prime Anchor is breaking down, and I need to fix it. If we leave it as it is—"

"I *cannot* elaborate further," the Conductor interrupted, and this time, it said so with enough emphasis on *cannot* that Sev caught on to what it was saying. He frowned, scanning the Conductor from head to toe.

"Dungeon limitations," he muttered, half in realization. "You need more tickets?"

The Conductor tilted his head—not a confirmation but perhaps as close to one as he could give. "I suspect you know how I would respond, were I able. Will that be all?" he asked.

"No," Sev said. He rummaged around in his pockets. Tinsel had given him about four of the golden tickets in total rather than just two; he was starting to understand there might actually be a reason for that mechanic. "If I give these to you, will we be able to go farther? Or will you be able to tell me more?"

The Conductor stared at the additional tickets, and for a moment Sev thought he saw him start to reach out, as if he wanted to grab them but had to physically stop himself. He didn't answer Sev's question immediately. ". . . These are insufficient to skip a station," he said eventually. "But more will allow you to travel farther, yes."

How hadn't this been discovered before? He supposed it was rare that they ever had extra tickets to begin with—four were awarded for each station completion, and delve teams were typically groups of four, at least in Anderstahl. The dungeon scaled up the rewards if there were more delvers, but they very rarely had *less*, except for the occasional Platinum-ranker going in solo, and those . . . well, they were very rarely interested in sharing the secrets they discovered.

"All right," Sev said. "So there's no benefit if I give you these tickets now."

"No." The Conductor stared longingly at the tickets. Sev wondered if there was some underlying mechanic that this fueled—if there was a reason the Conductor seemed to want them so badly.

". . . Well, you can have them anyway," he decided. "It's not like I have any use for them."

The Conductor swung his head over to stare at him so quickly Sev was almost afraid his head would fall off. "You are certain?"

"Yes?" Sev said, suddenly a lot less certain and a little thrown off. "Why not?"

"Thank you." The Conductor took the tickets from him like they were precious artifacts rather than thin sheets of gold. He slotted them into his chest, then gave Sev a bow. "We will arrive at Ichoric Ascent soon. Let me know if there is anything more I can do for you."

"Will do," Sev said. He offered the Conductor a smile—a smile that the Conductor, in turn, seemed to take very seriously—and then watched as it left before turning a puzzled gaze to Tinsel. "Was that strange to you at all?"

"What do you mean?" Tinsel asked. It bounced in its chair, entirely unconcerned by the conversation. "You were nice to him! It made him happy. Maybe other passengers haven't been so nice."

Sev frowned at that thought; he hoped that wasn't the case, but he knew how adventurers sometimes treated the people they assumed to be non-sapient within dungeons. "Maybe," he agreed.

He couldn't help but wonder, still, if there was something more to it than that. The Conductor *had* mentioned that it needed the tickets to function, after all.

Sev opened his system window, then glanced at the group chat for his adventuring party. There still hadn't been an update—and the more time passed, the more he couldn't help but worry.

"You better be okay, guys," he muttered, more to himself than anything.

Tinsel, sitting next to him, responded anyway. "I'm sure they'll be fine!" it said brightly.

Sev chuckled a little. It didn't even know who he was talking about, but he didn't mind the boundless optimism.

He couldn't deny it made this trip just a little bit easier. A little less lonely than it would have been otherwise.

CHAPTER 32

LOST IN SOULSPACE

Vex *still* couldn't access his system, and it was starting to frustrate him.

The system had been the cause of a lot of problems. He'd never really liked it because of that. Half of Elyra's problems existed because of the system, and though one could argue that it was more the fault of the people who *used* the system, well . . . it didn't change the fact that the system itself did very little to discourage the problems it caused.

He didn't really blame Sev for it. It wasn't like he'd been part of creating the thing in the first place—it sounded like he'd only really had to learn how it worked and begin to modify it *after* everything began to fall apart. And he doubted the people that created it would have predicted Elyra's abuses, either.

The point of all this was that he was starting to miss being able to access his system. Not because of the spells it granted him, or even because of his stats, which he still mostly had access to anyway. He felt . . . a little slower than he would have if he'd had full access to the system, *maybe*, but even then, that was more likely a result of the ever-persistent ache in his soul than a lack of access to the system.

No, the aspect of it that he missed was being able to contact his friends. Being able to talk to Derivan or Sev or Misa no matter where he was, even if he was separated from them by a dungeon, or if he'd gone off on his own somewhere. That function of the system was part of how he knew he was never alone.

Now . . . well, now he felt more alone than ever.

It didn't help that whatever iteration of Enkiros he'd found himself in was completely empty. More and more, he was starting to suspect that this fragment wasn't even one of the possibilities that had been detailed in the semerit. It seemed more likely that this was a reality that had emerged . . . deformed, somehow. Like something had been cut away from what was supposed to be here at the last second, or like someone had tried to modify it.

"Wish I didn't hurt so much," Vex muttered. He said the words mostly to hear himself speak, but even saying them made his eyes sting. The sound echoed in the empty streets, and his voice sounded so weak, so *frail* . . .

It reminded him of the painful reality that he might die. The pain wasn't *decreasing*. The ache in his chest only grew, and Vex couldn't tell how much of it was due to injury and how much of it was because his heart struggled desperately with the thought of leaving his friends—his *family* now—behind.

Not to mention his actual family. He liked Helix now. He'd never get to see what Riss would be like when he grew up. He hadn't even gotten the chance to talk to any of his other siblings again after Elyra's evacuation, and he felt a little guilty about that—but he'd just been so *busy*, and a part of him hadn't forgiven them for the part they had to play in his childhood.

Helix had earned his forgiveness, at least. Vex didn't know where he stood with anyone else in the family, but Helix had changed his mind all by himself, and he'd worked to change things in Vex's absence. It was more than Vex could say he had done. *He'd* never gotten involved in Elyra's rebellion. He hadn't even known it existed.

"Fuck," Vex said numbly. He stared at his reflection in a nearby shop. Was it just him, or were his scales paler than they normally were? "I feel like I messed up."

The worst part was that he didn't even know if he'd change anything, given the chance. They needed Enkiros back—that much hadn't changed. If he succeeded, then this would be worth it.

That *if* felt like it was a lot more uncertain than it should've been.

With a sigh—and lacking any other options, really—Vex walked up to the door of the shop and pushed the door open, letting the sound of the bell wash over him. Warm scents met him almost immediately. He was momentarily struck by the smell of freshly baked bread and freshly brewed coffee, of toast and butter and just the slightest hint of cinnamon.

He'd walked into some sort of bakery, it seemed. Or a cafe of some kind. It seemed comfortable. Cozy. The seats were plush, and they even had a little gap near the back for lizardkin to slot their tails into; too many establishments didn't bother to provide for them that way.

It was also clean, which was a plus. Vex had lost count of the number of times he'd had to slide his tail into a gap ostensibly made for lizardkin and then realized it hadn't been cleaned for months. Cue at least an hour of scrubbing to make sure it was *clean*.

These days, at least, he had Derivan to help.

Tears pricked at his eyes again, and he did his best to ignore them. What good did crying do? He wanted—he *needed* a break, and this place seemed ideal for one. He'd take that break, and he'd enjoy warm toast and a buttery croissant.

Vex wandered over to the counter. He picked for himself a fresh loaf of bread, cut himself a few slices, then slid those slices into the nearby toaster.

A small flicker of realization. Without access to his system, he couldn't see the mana racing into the internal runes to heat up the bread. He could still *feel* the mana. His connection with magic was a part of him now. But he couldn't see it.

He didn't realize he'd miss the little things this much.

A lot of the food was still warm, so that was nice, at least. He plucked the toast from the toaster once it was done, scarcely noticing the heat that should have burned him, then grabbed some butter and some boilberry jam. He spread them on his toast, grabbed a croissant from behind the glass, and then sat himself down in the comfiest-looking booth.

Boilberry jam was the preferred jam of this bakery, apparently; it was the only one he could find. And once he ate it, he realized *why*. The damn thing was delicious. Why did all the boilberries he'd had before taste like mush?

. . . Maybe they were named boilberries for a reason and he should have boiled them.

Vex chuckled to himself, ignoring the wetness still trailing down his cheeks, and ate his toast.

It was good toast. The croissant was good too. As far as last meals went, that wasn't too bad.

What a morbid thought. A small smile stole across his face—he could already imagine Misa scolding him for it. Telling him off for giving up when he should have been fighting with everything he had to live.

". . . You know what?" Vex said. He ignored the ache in his chest, finished off the rest of his toast, scarfed down the croissant, then grabbed a random bottle of juice. "You're right, imaginary-version-of-Misa-that-exists-only-in-my-head. I'm not just gonna lie down and die. I'm going to figure this out."

He was still crying when he walked out of the bakery, but he didn't mind. The tears reminded him he still had something to live for. They reminded him he was still alive to cry.

"Now let's figure out where to begin," he muttered. He glanced up at the sky, trying to gauge how much time had passed. It didn't really help—the sun was nowhere in sight, and it hadn't been when he'd first shown up here, either.

But there *was* something there, now that he looked at it. A bright spot he'd initially dismissed as a cloud reflecting sunlight but was holding too steadily to actually be a cloud. For that matter, it wasn't shaped like one.

"Mana," he said to himself. A small fragment of the Primordial Glyph, if he wasn't mistaken, powerful enough to be seen with the naked eye. For a moment, he was a little stunned that that amount of power had come out of him—and then he remembered the price he'd paid for it.

He supposed it made sense now.

"Well, if all else fails . . ." Vex muttered. "Let's go where the mana leads me—one last time."

—♒︎—

Misa was halfway through smashing a wall when Derivan suddenly spoke up.

"He is headed toward us," Derivan said. Misa glanced at him sharply. The armor sounded surprised, but more than that, he sounded *hopeful*; Derivan had been mostly despondent up until now.

"That's more like it." Misa couldn't help but grin at the news—that sounded a lot more like the Vex she'd grown to love in all their time together. A spunky little lizard that refused to give up, no matter how much the odds were stacked against him. Truth was, the news that had made her heart drop the most was when Derivan told her Vex wasn't moving. That he was curled up somewhere, just . . . sitting.

"If he is also moving toward us," Derivan said; the armor closed his eyes briefly like he was trying to map out the hugely complicated space they were in, then nodded to himself, "then I believe I know where he is likely to go. It will be faster if we change routes."

". . . So I *don't* have to smash this wall?" Misa glanced at said half-smashed wall and sighed. "Pity. The shopkeeper was kind of an asshole."

"We will use a different exit," Derivan said. Misa could see him focusing on finding it, like he was scanning through the entire kingdom with a sense that only he had. She might have been able to pull off something similar with [**Endless Echoes**], but she couldn't imagine how many iterations that would've taken. "This way."

"Any weird conditions we need to fulfill to get through this particular exit?"

A slight pause, and then Derivan sighed; his response sounded slightly embarrassed. "Apparently," he said, "Enkiros holds a dance festival every year as a celebration of a past victory. We will have to reenact this in order to proceed into the next fragment, as it is a fragment based on that victory."

Misa blinked once. "... How do you even *know* all this stuff?" she eventually asked. "There's no way Shift alone is enough."

Derivan shrugged. "One of my Remembrances belonged to the former King of Enkiros," he answered simply.

Misa sighed. That ... made sense, she supposed.

"Let's just get this over with," she said, her tone begrudging.

"I suspect you will be surprised—there is much to learn from this festival." Derivan paused, looking a little stricken. "If we had the time ..."

"We'll have the time later," Misa said, her tone softening into something gentler. "Come on, Der. Vex is waiting for us."

CHAPTER 33

PATTERN MATCHING

To her surprise—though she really shouldn't have been surprised, at this point—Derivan was right. There *was* a lot to learn from the festival. It was called the Festival of Stolen Light, apparently, and had something to do with a divine war that resulted in light being spread all across the land. The dances and forms they had to perform to get through the exit were specific physical forms that were somehow capable of manipulating divine threads. Of casting divine spells, even without input from a god, though that was obviously frowned upon.

Misa couldn't deny that a part of her wanted to learn it just to mess with Sev. But all they had time for was the basic forms, which was enough to pull apart the divine threads that would unveil the portal to their next fragment.

She *supposed* she shouldn't have been surprised that they were stepping into a war zone, especially considering Derivan had pretty much already warned her of exactly this. Derivan certainly didn't seem surprised.

"Derivan," she called. He was walking through the streets like nothing was happening, and Misa groaned as she ducked and dashed to follow after him. He wasn't even bothering to dodge the spells! They splashed off him harmlessly—

—Oh. Right. They were pretty high-level at this point, weren't they? She could barely feel the amount of power the people here were using as part of their war, and when she let one of the spells splash against her forearm experimentally, it did . . . precisely one point of damage.

"You should've told me it was safe," she complained as she caught up with Derivan. The armor sounded a little amused when he responded, though even that amusement was still more hollow than she would've liked.

"You are, if anything, more durable than I am at this stage," he said. "I did not expect to need to clarify."

"...Okay, you've got a point there," Misa admitted.

Derivan cut a path straight through the chaos, purposeful and steady. She followed after him. Even if she didn't need to worry about the spells hitting *her*, she still needed to worry about them hitting the soulbloom potions strapped to her body—there wouldn't be a point in reaching Vex if they didn't still have the remedy for his condition.

So for *that*, she was very, very careful.

Every so often, she glanced back at her system interface, hoping against hope that there would be an update from Vex—and she noticed Derivan doing the same thing, even if he tried to be subtle about it. They had no luck there, unfortunately, and both of them knew why.

Vex didn't have system access. The effects of soulstrain would've weakened him severely, preventing him from accessing the interface and most of the skills that he'd earned through the system. He still had his glyphs, so he wasn't defenseless, but...

"It will be difficult for him to use his glyphs," Derivan said quietly, answering her unspoken question. "Mana channels exist both in the body and in the soul. His mana channels will be burned far beyond anything he has experienced before—including what his family did to him in his past."

There was a small note of anger in Derivan's voice; Misa didn't blame him. "Since when could you read minds?" she asked.

"Physical Empathy has reached a point where it is capable of more than it should be able to do," Derivan admitted after a moment. "I cannot... read minds, per se. But you are close to me. As are Sev and Vex. I can read you three more easily than I can others, and even interpret what you might be thinking."

"Well, damn," Misa said. "Kinda wish that worked on our enemies."

"It would be useful, if we had enemies we could fight." Derivan's answer was surprisingly solemn, and Misa took a second to take it in.

It *would* make things easier, wouldn't it? If their enemy wasn't something unseen, wasn't a natural phenomenon of monumental proportions. If their enemy had just been something they could *punch*...

But then, if all their enemies were someone like Irvis, she wondered where they would be now.

"I'm kind of glad, honestly," she said, surprising herself. "That we're not fighting each other still. Everything's come to a head, and at this point, if we were still fighting one another, I'm not sure we'd be able to get through this."

"I am surprised to hear this coming from you." Derivan gave her a smile— a genuine one, too. It wasn't without its sadness, but Misa felt her heart fill a little at the sight. "You are normally eager to fight."

"Yeah, well . . . fighting's *fun*," Misa said. "But I can fight whenever I want. Fuck, I've got people waiting to spar with me, and I think there's a goddamn queue at the Guild at this point for some reason."

Derivan seemed amused. "You should not be surprised. Many of your opponents like your spirit."

"Bah," Misa grumbled. "The point is, yeah, having something to fight might make things a little easier in some ways. But . . . I'm kind of glad *this* is what we're fighting. I'm glad it's not some evil jerk that's convinced a horde of people to fight for their cause—imagine the amount of collateral we'd have to deal with if we had to fight someone's *minions*."

"The thought is unpleasant," Derivan admitted.

"At least almost everyone can agree the end of the universe is bad," Misa said. "Like it or not, this has brought most of us together. Anderstahl and Elyra aren't fighting anymore. The Elyran nobles *have* to hang out with their so-called commoner counterparts. I mean, there are still some assholes out there, but when *aren't* there assholes?"

"I believe there is at least one priest preaching that the end of the universe is good and proper, and that we should simply allow it to happen," Derivan said.

"Gods," Misa snorted. "Bet his god ain't happy with that one."

"He has been cut off from his connection to the divine. But he does have a small following."

"Not one that's getting any bigger, I hope."

Derivan shook his head. "No. The Guild monitors people like these—keeps them in check. It may be comforting to turn to acceptance when it seems that there is nothing to be done, but it is only that."

"A comfort," Misa agreed. "And I think most of us want a little more than cheap comfort."

"I want a future," Derivan said. Misa thought his voice sounded a little softer—there was a note of longing in there she'd never heard from him before. "It took so many years for me to come into my own, Misa. It took even longer for me to understand what I want. Vex once asked me if I had goals of my own to pursue, outside of magic, because he believes the joy I find in magic is partly due to the joy I find in *him*."

"And is that true?" Misa asked.

"Perhaps." Derivan shrugged. "It does not matter, I think. Because magic *does* bring me joy. And more than that, I have goals of my own: I wish to restore the Scimitar people. I wish to learn the traditions of my kind. I wish to create magic with Vex and to live in a place with him that we can call our home."

"And Sev and I?" Misa's voice was teasing; she didn't mind indulging him. Derivan's thoughts on the future were anchoring him in their search, keeping him determined instead of depressed.

"You would be our neighbors, of course," Derivan answered immediately, as if he'd been anticipating that very question. "Or perhaps we could live in one big building together?"

Misa laughed. "I'm not sure about that," she said. "I feel like you two are a little loud for us. Or maybe it's just Vex?"

A very long pause. "The next exit will require us to rebuild a wall," Derivan said, apparently deciding to change topics. She smirked a bit. "There is a mural on it. It is a puzzle."

"Vex would've loved that," Misa said softly. She strode up to the ruined wall, looking at it critically. "Well . . . let's get this done, then. Maybe we can bring him back to see the wall once we're done."

"We will." Derivan's tone left no room for argument, and Misa agreed.

They picked up the bricks and got to work.

"Okay, there's something I need to do to get through this," Vex said, staring critically at the wall in front of him. There was a pattern of bricks sticking out of the wall, though *why* it had been built so haphazardly, he had no idea. If he had full access to his skills, he would've used his [**Advanced Mana Sight**] to peer at the inner workings of the wall, but . . . that path was closed to him right now.

He tried not to think about it. He had other ways to analyze walls. "Let's see," he muttered to himself, poking at one of the bricks. He jumped when it actually *moved* against his touch, wriggling a bit and then sliding out of the wall entirely, then flopping onto the ground like a fish would if removed from the water. "Uh. Weird."

Vex still wasn't sure how he felt about talking to himself like this. Every time he did, it reminded him of how weak he sounded. On the other hand, it kept him sane. Speaking out loud made him feel like he was explaining things to his teammates or to Derivan. It felt *familiar*, and that familiarity was a comfort.

Right now, Vex would take any source of comfort he could get.

Except sleep. He was pretty sure sleeping in his condition was a bad idea, no matter how comfy some of the beds he'd come across looked.

I'm not gonna give up.

The ache in his chest had only grown worse, and it had slowly begun to spread. Vex was beginning to become terribly aware of the fact that he was much worse off than he initially assumed, and he'd initially assumed that he was *dying*. But most of his spells weren't even accessible to him. He couldn't cast system spells, and glyphs didn't work, because he needed to paint them with mana, and his mana channels were seared so thoroughly he wasn't certain he could summon any without worsening his condition.

He'd tried once and then decided he wouldn't try again unless it became *absolutely* necessary. It had taken him a full minute to get up from the ground after writhing in pain.

Slowly, he bent over—moving any faster would *also* have hurt, because whatever had happened to him had damaged him in more ways than one, and the system was no longer simply restoring him instantly to prime condition—and picked up the still-wriggling brick, eyeing it skeptically.

"What do I know about my situation?" he asked himself. "One, I'm trapped in a version of Enkiros that seems to be empty, which is weird. Two, it's smaller than it should be—this place has boundaries. Three... Ow. Three, this looks like it should be an exit, and there's mana traveling through it. The Primordial Glyph goes this way. But I can't go through it myself. It's almost like the exit is contingent on something else?"

He refused to believe there wasn't a way through—that he was just stuck in some sort of empty plane-between-planes. What did the planeshifted call it? Purgatory, or something.

"The exit being contingent on something else..." Vex narrowed his eyes. "Like a dungeon. Am I in a dungeon?"

He shouldn't have been. He'd recreated Enkiros, and *part* of that was certainly the divine kingdom's Prime Dungeon, but the kingdom that sat on top of it shouldn't have been part of it. But something had gone wrong with the spell, and more than that, the system had been acting up.

"Let's assume I'm in a dungeon," Vex said slowly. He glanced at the brick. It was moving still, although much more slowly now that he was carrying it. "That means there are going to be puzzles. Challenges. And dungeon challenges are almost always based on some kind of internal logic, typically testing *something*."

He stared at the wall in front of him again, then looked around. The buildings *were* placed rather strangely, now that he thought about it. And the ones with lights in them—the ones with food and drink and water, including the bakery he'd stuffed himself in—they mapped to about half of the bricks protruding from the wall, if he assumed each building was represented in the wall itself.

So if his theory was right, and he was meant to touch the *active* buildings...

The brick he'd touched had been one of them. Vex rapidly pressed another five in quick succession, mapping them out to the active buildings he'd seen while exploring. Five more bricks crawled out of the wall and flopped onto the floor.

Then the entire wall collapsed, revealing a swirling portal behind it.

"*Yes*," Vex cheered quietly, then winced when the movement hurt. Ignoring it, he stepped through the portal.

One step closer to . . . wherever he was going.

CHAPTER 34

ICHORIC ASCENT

"This station is everything I expected it would be and I hate it," Sev groused.

"Why?" Tinsel asked. "I think it's pretty!"

"Tinsel, you don't have a mouth. Or a nose." Sev glanced at the giant waterfall of . . . well, ichor. As best as he could tell, this was in fact the divine definition of ichor, as in *the blood of the gods*, which was at least marginally better than the alternatives. Golden liquid filled with divine energy pouring down a cliff was beautiful, even if it wasn't sanitary.

Also, even godly blood still smelled like blood, so there was that. Every time he opened his mouth, he was met with the immediate, coppery taste of blood from all the ichor that was just kind of floating around in the air. It made him reconsider talking. And also breathing.

. . . But the urge to complain was so powerful, he couldn't quite stop himself.

Besides, Tinsel kept asking questions, and he didn't want to ignore it.

"What's having a mouth or a nose got to do with it?" Tinsel asked innocently.

"The ichor doesn't really taste good," Sev said tiredly. "Or smell good. And I can't really *not* taste or smell it when it's in the air."

"Ohhh," Tinsel said intelligently. "I get it. That sucks."

"Sure does."

"What do you think we have to do for this station?" it asked.

Sev stared up at the waterfall, then specifically at the rocks jutting out from it. They moved in and out of the waterfall, splashing the entire zone with ichor every time a new one appeared.

"It's a physical challenge," he said. He already felt tired, and he hadn't even started yet. "We gotta climb the waterfall."

And presumably fight whatever was on top. Or maybe heal whatever was on top. *Something* had to be producing that enormous amount of god blood, after all. Sev winced at the thought—he *really* hoped all he found up there wasn't going to be a gigantic corpse of a dead god. That . . . didn't sound pleasant.

And it would be difficult to explain to Tinsel, so there was that.

Tinsel peered up the waterfall. "It looks really high up," it said. ". . . I think I'm scared of heights."

"Tell me about it," Sev grumbled. "You and I have that in common."

He was *not* looking forward to this.

Not in the slightest.

—⁂—

The ascent took a *lot* of slipping, cursing, and falling. Sev found himself entirely drenched in ichor more than once, either because a rock burst out of the waterfall just above him and showered him in the stuff, or because the rock he was standing on suddenly retracted and left him to plummet directly into the pool of ichor below.

If nothing else, he learned a couple of things he never wanted to learn about the properties of ichor. It had mild healing properties, for instance, which wasn't surprising but was very much still disgusting. He was fairly certain that being drenched in the stuff enhanced his connection with the divine. *Technically*, if he wanted to do so again, he could probably perform another [**Divine Mantle**] now.

It took some convincing from Tinsel, of all people, before Sev finally and reluctantly agreed to bottle up some of the ichor for later use. He wasn't sure what drinking it would do, and he didn't want to find out—but it had proven useful enough that he couldn't really just ignore it as a resource. Not when this dungeon had already proven to be relatively prescient about what they needed.

Which was *still* weird.

"Nearly at the top," Sev grunted. He was doing his best not to look down, and he was balancing on one of the few rocks sticking out of the waterfall that didn't move. He was about ninety percent certain of that, because he'd watched it for a solid ten minutes and hadn't seen it move once.

There was always the possibility that it was on an eleven-minute cycle, but he was doing his best to ignore that possibility. The next rock would show up in . . .

Three, two, one . . . now.

He jumped and landed on the next rock.

He was on a timer now. This next set of rocks moved quickly, in intervals of about five seconds, and the worst part was that the next rock only appeared *after* the previous one retracted. He had to time his jumps perfectly to make it, and jumping was a precarious affair at best when every rock was slippery with ichor.

Sev leapt again, the rock below him disappearing back into the waterfall and a new one appearing just as he reached the apex of the jump. He was carrying Tinsel with him, but the fixture was fortunately quite light and didn't really interfere with his ability to move. It also had its eyes squeezed shut because it "didn't want to look at the heights."

And yet it had refused to stay behind.

Now. Sev jumped again. This time, it was ever so slightly mistimed, and the rock collided with the bottom of his feet as it emerged; he thumped into the rock with an *oof* and had to scramble to grab the sides just so he didn't fall off. On his back, Tinsel let out a small squeal of terror, its lights flickering wildly.

Five seconds to recover. Sev pulled himself to his feet with a burst of strength, then immediately leapt again. Only just in time, too. The rock had begun to retract at almost the exact moment he jumped, and the friction as it slipped away beneath his feet was almost enough to send him tumbling again. This time, he called up a quick divine barrier to steady himself.

It evaporated almost as soon as he summoned it, of course. This room didn't want him to cheat, apparently—it dispersed every attempt he made to climb it with his skills or to fly to the top. But the barriers still lasted long enough that he could balance himself with them.

Three more jumps.

Two.

One.

Sev finally, *finally* made it to the top, and he threw himself over to the first glimpse of solid land he could see before the rock underneath his feet disappeared again. There was, thankfully, a rather large outcropping right at the edge of the waterfall—presumably for this exact reason. The outcropping was attached to a small strip of land in the midst of all the ichor, and that strip of land in turn led to . . .

. . . some sort of island?

Though it was too small to really be called an island. It was maybe the size of a decent-sized home or the lowest floor of the Adventurers' Guild. There was a layer of grass over it, along with small, golden flowers peeking through the grass.

And at the center of that island, surrounded by tiny rivulets of ichor that somehow expanded as they flowed down the island and churning ichor that led down the cliffside, there was a corpse.

That part wasn't very surprising to Sev.

"The question is . . ." Sev murmured. He walked along the strip of land, careful not to fall back into the ichor—he didn't really want to repeat the experience of being dunked in blood again. ". . . who are you, exactly? And why are you here?"

"I don't think he can answer you, Sev," Tinsel quipped from his back. Sev groaned.

"I was talking to myself," he grumbled. "And why are you still on my back? You can walk by yourself now."

"Oh, right!" Tinsel hopped off his back cheerfully. Sev didn't know whether to be amused or disturbed by the fact that it seemed entirely fine with the leaking corpse in front of them—though he supposed it wasn't exactly close enough to see in detail yet.

And Tinsel wouldn't be particularly familiar with death in this form, would it? Its experience of death was seeing others get eaten by the Soulblossoms in Soulbloom Station. Not *quite* equivalent to something dying and leaving behind a corpse . . .

He sighed. He hoped he wouldn't regret bringing Tinsel along with him.

The living light fixture raced ahead, prompting Sev to do a little jog to catch up. Part of him was afraid to. He was unsure what he'd find. What would cause a dungeon to use the death of a god as the core of a station? All this was *actual* divine blood, not some poor mimicry created by a malfunctioning reality anchor—as far as he could tell, anyway. The Prime Anchor must have drawn on the true death of a god.

And this wasn't even a death caused by the Void. Nor a death caused by a reality anchor drawing on the gods to try to maintain themselves, though *that* particular feature wasn't one he'd had any part of. Automated systems gone rogue . . . He needed to try to disable it, but from what Muchen had told him, he'd already tried, a Reset or two ago. They didn't have much control over the system's automated mechanisms anymore.

No. This death was . . . what, caused by a war of some sort? A battle? Some conflict in the physical plane that had consequences in the divine?

Did he *know* this god?

Sev felt a mixture of guilt and relief as he arrived only shortly after Tinsel and found that he didn't recognize the god at all. The body had pitch-black skin and golden tattoos adorning its flesh—lightning that was the same color as the blood flowing out of the multiple open wounds . . .

"You know," Tinsel said thoughtfully, "I don't know much about blood and stuff. 'Cause I don't have any! But why's he still bleeding?"

"Gods have a lot of blood, I guess," Sev answered distractedly. He was trying to put a name to the god—he didn't recognize him at all, and his knowledge on them was fairly extensive. He'd done his research before picking Onyx, after all.

It *was* a good question, though. Why was the god still bleeding? The blood in most bodies would settle a few hours after death; things might be different for gods, but he wasn't so sure that—

"Oh god what if he's not dead." The words came out in a rush as he hurried to the side of the god that he'd previously *assumed* was dead. In retrospect, the first thing he should've done was a [**Triage**]. Not that system skills tended to work in normal ways on the divine, but it had been foolish to assume that the dungeon had just decided to use a random god's corpse as the centerpiece for a dungeon.

The test wasn't some morbid test of climbing. It was a test of *healing*.

The second one in a row. The thought came to him unbidden, and he froze, even as [**Triage**] filled his head with a list of all the injuries the god had. He was, for one, definitely still alive. He wasn't even *dying*. His injuries were keeping him in a state of stasis from which he couldn't heal, but that was because there was a curse of sorts overlaid on every one of his wounds.

His wounds wouldn't heal. Because his wounds wouldn't heal, he kept bleeding. Because the curse was specific to the wounds, his healing abilities were able to keep up internally, generating an endless supply of blood that immediately spilled back out.

He was producing just enough blood to stay alive but not enough to stay conscious.

Sev immediately charged a heal and let it ripple through the body in front of him.

He wasn't surprised to see that it did nothing. Even healing the Soulblossom in the previous station had required more power than this—mostly because he could no longer rely on the spells that cost him personally. The [**Memory Loss**] malus had more or less faded from his status by now. Each step he'd taken on his journey as a Concept, or whatever Gregory claimed he was, had restored him.

To take that away from himself again . . . it would unmake him. Undo all the progress he'd made.

That meant that healing was now a *process*.

Specifically, he had to do manually what the system had previously done for him automatically: find the right gods to make a divine connection with, filter their strength through with his own, and channel that divinity into the patient. Laying claim over the intrinsic divinity stored in every being allowed him to modify it at will, essentially giving him the ability to command that being to heal.

The difficulty came in conflicting divine essences. Everyone was just a little bit different, and though they might not worship any god personally, they were still aligned with the concepts of different gods to different degrees. Sev had to find a way to match that alignment in order for the heal to be efficient; the farther away he was, the less efficient the heal.

It would work anyway if he packed enough divine power into the heal, of course, but his goal was *not* to waste the stuff.

The problem here was that he didn't *know* what divinity the god lying before him was, and he couldn't draw on this god's own divine power to heal him when all of it was being used to keep him alive. Sev would have to approximate it, balancing a series of adjacent divinities to try to mimic whatever divinity he *thought* this god was.

. . . Time to talk to the gods and see if anyone knew this guy.

CHAPTER 35

A RAPID ETERNITY

Ixoryn was dead.

Or as close to dead as he was going to get, anyway. He was dimly aware that he was bleeding and that there was nothing he could do about it—who would've thought mortals would ever be able to do this much damage to him?

But that was the worst part of it, wasn't it? That it was mortals that had done this to him. If it had been anyone else, then at least he would be *truly* dead; if it had been anyone weaker, then he wouldn't have been hurt at all.

It had to be the strong ones. The mortals powerful enough to hurt him but not strong enough to kill him permanently. Instead, they'd left him like . . . this.

A living corpse, functionally. Unable to move, unable to do much of anything. He could think, but even that felt slow. Sluggish. He was vaguely aware that hours passed for even a single thought to form coherently; his vision, or what few glimpses of it he had, made it look like the world around him was rapidly accelerating. Clouds flashed by, and the sun rose and set in what felt like moments yet could not be.

If nothing else, Ixoryn thought, it meant he was spared the torture of living through every second as the world passed around him.

He was forgotten. He was forgotten a little more quickly than he would've liked, even, but then, he didn't know how much time had actually passed. The few mortals that worshiped him and knew of his demise eventually stopped visiting him, either because they no longer held the faith or because they were dead. Their lifespans had always seemed short to him—now they seemed like they flashed by in seconds, here one moment and gone the next.

None of them could heal him. There was an attempt or two, he thought. He sometimes felt the barest trickle of divinity enter his body, only to once again leak out through the wounds. If he could speak, he would have shouted at them to remove the curse from those wounds first. If the curse was removed, then he could heal himself. It wasn't healing he needed! It was getting rid of the damnable curse that prevented him from doing anything about his own condition.

Eventually, though, he resigned himself to his fate. Who knew how much time had passed by then?

Ixoryn entertained himself by telling himself stories—so many of them, he barely remembered which ones were true and which ones were not. He almost forgot what domain he actually held, with the multitude of fictitious realities he'd created for himself to pass the time. Was he the God of Strength? War? Order? All or none of those things? He wasn't quite as certain as he thought he should've been.

So things went for quite some time, though Ixoryn would not be able to say how much time that had been.

There was a moment when things changed, and changed significantly. He noticed it because it was one of the only times things had changed around him in the past who knew how many years; the sun vanished, replaced by a clear sky that never changed, and the sound of rushing water filled his ears.

On the one hand, he appreciated the change, and the sound of liquid rushing nearby was a more pleasant white noise than the cycle of birds that chirped with an incessant song every time the sun rose. On the other, now he had even *less* to look at, visually: the sky never changed, and he couldn't move his head.

The area around him felt different. The oppressive divine domain that had surrounded him for years no longer felt like it was there; instead, the threads he was surrounded by were free, unclaimed. No god had yet laid claim to this territory. If he'd been only a little bit stronger, he might have been able to reach out and claim those threads for himself and increase his strength that way . . .

. . . But no. All he could do was lie there, the threads staying tantalizingly out of reach. Yet another form of torture. If he could laugh, he would have; what had he even done to deserve such ire from mortals? He could no longer remember.

Hatred for those mortals came and went. He held on to that hatred for quite a while. Longer than he should have, perhaps, for a god of his stature. And then one day, he was simply too tired, and he let that hatred fall away; neither hatred nor forgiveness would free him from this state of nothingness.

All he could do was wait.

And then, for the second time, he felt something *change*.

There was the sound of splashing in the distance—far enough away that at first, Ixoryn thought he had imagined it. Then the sounds got closer, and he heard *voices*. Voices! For the first time in a long, long time, he felt excitement rise in his heart before he quickly quelled it. Just because there were others here didn't mean they'd be able to help him.

But at least it was something different. At least it was something *new*. He strained himself to try to listen to the conversation, though the words stole by too rapidly for him to process them properly. All he was able to get was that the one speaking thought he was dead, which he supposed was a fair assumption. It wasn't like he was moving. Or breathing.

And then—to his absolute surprise—he felt the divine threads around him stir.

Whoever had arrived was a *priest*.

Despite himself, Ixoryn couldn't help the hope that swelled in his heart.

—◊◊◊—

Figuring out the domain of this god was . . . a harder task than Sev had anticipated.

Part of it was the fact that he couldn't really sense it in the divine threads surrounding the god—the area around him was almost disturbingly empty. There was no domain for him to interact with and learn from. There *was* divine energy within the god's blood, but that was just raw energy, not a domain.

Then there was the matter of the curse that suffused the god's wounds. Sev struggled to even determine what type of magic it was, let alone a way to dispel it—this was one of the things he would've loved to have Vex's help for. If the lizardkin were here . . .

He tried not to think about it. There were too many things to focus on right now. Too many people in danger for him to hesitate.

Lacking the ability to dispel magic traditionally didn't mean he couldn't do it his own way. He'd been able to nullify the demigod in Elyra by laying claim to the divine threads around himself, and he'd been able to stop Jerome's spells by doing much the same. There *was* a trace of divinity on the curse itself, like another cleric had used a god's power to enhance it.

That made sense. It also gave Sev a means to counter it. If he could break that root of divinity within the curse . . .

"Hellooo?" Tinsel spoke, and Sev jumped. He'd almost forgotten the light fixture was even there. It had taken to sitting on the ground to wait for him to finish thinking, apparently not minding the fact that the grass was sort of splattered with ichor, and was now rocking back and forth to entertain itself. "You're staring a lot! What're you trying to figure out?"

"I'm wondering if I can break the curse on these wounds," Sev answered, a little embarrassed about forgetting Tinsel. "And what domain this god represents."

Tinsel blinked, then looked back down to the still-bleeding body.

"Leadership," it said.

"What?" Sev blinked. He stared at the god and then at Tinsel. "Where'd you get that?"

Tinsel shrugged, a motion that mostly just looked strange—like a full-body shake more than an actual shrug. "The tattoos!" it explained. "It's got lots of arrows leading to a circle in the center. And smaller arrows following them. Like a leader, see?"

"I'm . . . not sure that makes sense," Sev said slowly.

The thing was, though, it sounded right.

He'd tried to talk to the gods. None of them seemed aware of who this god was, or if they were, they didn't seem willing to tell him about it—which was frustrating, considering the situation. The gods he was closer with all seemed to either genuinely not know or were outright unable to tell him. Apparently, the political landscape between the gods was more complicated than he'd thought. They could create unbreakable contracts with one another, creating a complex web of obligations and favors that Sev decided almost immediately he didn't want to touch with a ten-foot pole.

All of which meant he was back to square one in trying to figure out the god's domain by himself. But if Tinsel was right . . .

The tattoos on the god's body *did* resemble some sort of leadership dynamic, though it wouldn't have been Sev's first guess. His first guess would probably have been the God of Directions or something.

It wouldn't cost him much to test it out. If he could align his magic with the god's own domain and direct it straight at the curse, the resulting spell in theory would be strong enough to crack said curse in two. It would be a bit like boosting the god's natural healing abilities and giving it direction.

"I think it makes sense," Tinsel said. "You should try it!"

"Yeah," Sev said slowly. "I think I will."

Leadership, was it? He didn't have a connection forged with any such god. But he *did* have connections forged with a few gods that might help him approximate something similar.

It started as the strangest sort of tickling sensation. Ixoryn thought he was imagining things, at first. It was only when the feeling *persisted* that he took it more seriously, because it very quickly built up into something far more intolerable than anything he'd felt for the past . . . well, who knew how many centuries it had been, really. The point remained the same.

Only a few minutes before, if he'd been asked if he'd tolerate an irritating tickling sensation, he would've said yes. Anything to break up the monotony of sight and sound. Now that he was actually experiencing it, he wasn't quite so enthusiastic.

Also, it was starting to itch, which was even worse. The itching spread to become almost unbearable, and he instinctively moved to scratch at the stupid wounds—

Wait.

He'd moved.

Ixoryn shifted, suddenly all too aware of the feeling of the grass beneath his body, the uncomfortable stickiness of his own blood soaked into the ground. He sat up, groaning at the sensation of his atrophied muscles suddenly being forced to work for the first time in ages, and then stared at what surrounded him.

In front of him was a human priest. That much was expected—*someone* had healed him, and it made sense that that someone was a priest.

There was also a thin, rectangular *thing*, standing there on legs of glowing light. Ixoryn had no idea what to make of it. It looked vaguely like what a light elemental might look like, except all the light elementals he'd met before hadn't looked nearly this . . . manufactured.

The third thing that caught his attention was what they were surrounded by. Ixoryn blanched—that had not been the sound of rushing *water* that he'd heard. It was the sound of his own blood splashing around and flowing down what looked like a cliff. Had someone made a *waterfall* out of his blood? That was disgusting. And offensive.

"Sorry about the itching," the priest offered. "Tends to happen with healing."

"That is . . . far from my biggest concern at the moment," Ixoryn said. He stared at the now-shrinking pool of his blood, then at the priest. "Thank you for healing me. You have no idea what that's been like."

"I can only imagine," the priest said. "I'm Sev. Priest of Onyx, the God of Sculptures."

"I don't remember anyone by that name." Ixoryn frowned. "I am Ixoryn. God of Navigation."

"Oh." Sev blinked a few times. "Guess we were both right, Tinsel. This is Tinsel, by the way."

"Hi!" Tinsel said. It seemed entirely unimpressed with being in the presence of a god. So did Sev, for that matter. It turned to Sev and asked, curiously, "What *did* you think he was the god of?"

"Directions," Sev admitted.

. . . Ixoryn didn't know if he should feel offended. "And what did the little one think I represented?"

"Leadership!" Tinsel said cheerfully.

Well . . . they *were* both right. "To navigate is to use aspects of both," Ixoryn said with a sigh. "But I digress. I thank you for freeing me from that . . . prison. Though I find I am now trapped in a rather unfavorable position."

"And what position is that?" Sev asked.

"I am a god," Ixoryn said plainly. "But I stand in the material world. This is not a natural state of things. Normally, the cost of transporting myself here would be exorbitant, and remaining here even more so—but it seems being nearly dead has allowed me to remain here.

"I don't know how long it's going to be before the costs reassert themselves, or if they ever will. I don't know if the divinity I have access to is going to remain stable. And even if both those things fall in my favor, the mere presence of a god in this plane will erode the very seams of reality."

"Oh," Sev said. "Well, you don't have to worry about that last bit."

". . . Excuse me?"

"Yeah, we're kinda long past the whole reality-falling-apart thing." Sev shrugged. "Welcome to the end of the world. And for what it's worth, I'm sorry."

Ixoryn paused, processing what Sev had just told him. And then he waited some more, mostly hoping the cleric would start laughing and claim that it was a joke.

He did not.

"I think you'd better catch me up on everything," he said eventually.

"Sure," Sev said. "But while I do that, do you mind walking with me? I'm just realizing where I'm supposed to get the tickets to the next station, and it's not really pleasant."

Half of those words went over Ixoryn's head, but as he watched, the priest got up from where he'd knelt in the grass and then walked into the now-exposed mud that had once held an entire reservoir of his ichor. Ixoryn's lips curled in disgust—but the priest either didn't mind or had gotten used to it. He did wince every once in a while as he stepped through the mud, but for the most part, he seemed more interested in picking out strange, shimmering pieces of paper that were embedded in the ground.

"I will help," Ixoryn decided. Strange mannerisms aside, something about Sev's countenance told him the situation was serious. He had no idea how picking up these strange items from the ground would help, but clearly, Sev knew more than he did at the moment.

. . . Stepping around in the remnants of his own blood was still really gross, though.

With a sigh, Ixoryn got to picking—and at the same time, Sev got to explaining.

What Ixoryn heard would have made his blood run cold if he hadn't lost so much of it already.

Halfway through the explanation, Sev stopped, glancing into the air as though he was reading something. Ixoryn stared curiously at him, and Sev said nothing for a moment, mouthing a few words to himself.

Then the priest turned to him, his gaze strangely intense. "Ixoryn," he said. "Do you have enough power to give out Blessings?"

"Uh . . . yes?" Ixoryn said, thrown off by the question. "Yes. I do."

"Okay." Sev nodded to himself. "I'm going to need to ask you for a favor."

CHAPTER 36

REUNION

Derivan wasn't sure how much time had passed. He was trying not to think too hard about it. He found that he was all too aware of every second and minute, and distracting himself from the passage of time seemed the most prudent course of action; it was, for now, the only thing that kept him functional.

He didn't like feeling like this: mostly helpless. Mostly a victim to the other forces at play. As much as he knew where Vex was, as much as Shift and Patch gave him an advantage in this dungeon that no other adventurer would likely have—navigating the ever-changing Primordial Glyph was still *difficult*. It was like it was actively shuffling itself as they moved through it, and although he could tell what the best path to take was *now*, it didn't mean the dungeon wouldn't later shift and ruin their progress.

Two steps forward, one step back. It seemed to happen around the time Vex had finally started moving, too. The dungeon had been mostly static until then. Apparently, Vex choosing to move was enough for the Prime Anchor to decide it needed to take the difficulty up a notch.

If nothing else, they were *still* moving together faster than they would have. Both Derivan and Vex were now tracing the lines of the Primordial Glyph in the sky, and with that shared point of navigation, they could find their way to one another.

Misa finished typing something into the system and jogged to catch up with him. "Derivan," she said. "I think I finally managed to get a message through to Sev."

"Is he able to help us?" Derivan asked, cocking his head.

"He thinks he might be able to," Misa said. "Don't worry about it for now. How far away is Vex?"

Derivan concentrated for a moment. "Not far," he said, surprised at how easily the answer came to him. They were exactly three fragments apart—each of them would only need to take two more exits each in order to find themselves in the same Enkiros fragment. What was more, he could tell that this answer *included* shifts in the dungeon; technically, there were currently five fragments between them and Vex.

But once they went through the next exit, the rooms would rotate, and they would be closer to one another. Derivan pivoted, changing directions to go for a different exit from the one he would've chosen.

"It worked, huh?" Misa said.

Derivan blinked. "That was Sev's work," he guessed.

"A new friend he made. We'll have to thank him later. Come on—let's not waste any time." Misa urged him forward, not that he needed any urging.

The next few fragments were almost trivially easy to get through. This one simply required that they do enough damage to a particular target, what looked like some form of gallows; Derivan was glad to tear it apart. Misa told him something about how they were set up to have incredible amounts of health, but fortunately for them, Derivan was still able to completely bypass the issue of health.

The room after that just required they find an obscure alchemy shop in the corner of the street and sort some potions in the right order. The moment he did, a portal opened up in the cauldron, and Derivan jumped in without hesitation.

Misa *did* hesitate, but she eventually followed him. He didn't blame her there.

The moment he landed, Derivan's eyes locked on to the shivering form of a lizardkin. He snatched a potion from Misa then rushed over to Vex, heedless of the state of the fragment they were in. To be fair, it wasn't a *dangerous* fragment, just a partially destroyed one. He had to dodge one or two traps along the way, but they weren't exactly able to do any damage to him regardless—

Vex hadn't noticed him yet. Derivan felt worry rise within him as he hurried forward. The lizardkin had his arms wrapped around himself. He was taking slow, determined steps forward, but every step looked like it cost him a lifetime of effort—like he struggled just to put one foot in front of the other. His tail dragged on the ground, and Derivan knew Vex *hated* dragging his tail on the ground.

Even exhausted, he made it a point to lift his tail enough that it didn't drag.

"Vex!" he called. He wasn't sure if the lizardkin could hear him. They were so close now, but it felt like every step took an eternity—Derivan found he was hyper-alert for every trap Vex might accidentally step into. He wanted to call for Vex to stay still, to let him approach, but the lizardkin seemed so *determined*, so desperate to live . . .

Derivan *almost* didn't catch the way the lizardkin's foot caught on a trip-wire. He almost didn't see the mana that suddenly surged into the nearby explosive rune.

But he *did* see those things.

He surged forward with speed he didn't know he had. Shift propelled him forward as he used layer upon layer of it to compress the space between him and Vex, essentially forming a series of tiny portals; his body stretched through that compressed space as he subconsciously called on his Slime stat, deforming and propelling him forward even farther. He wrapped himself into a tight ball around Vex protectively, even as they both crashed to the ground and he felt the heat of the explosive rune wash over his form.

Only when he was certain that it was over did he allow himself to slowly unwrap. Vex stared up at him, his mouth slightly agape, and then pressed his fingers to Derivan's face as if to make sure he was real.

"Deri," he said. Derivan's heart crumbled at the simple word. Vex's voice was so soft—so weak. It sounded like his partner had to summon all his strength to even speak.

"Drink," Derivan said in turn. He'd kept the potion safe within his body. Now he pulled it up, uncorking the bottle and holding the soulbloom elixir to Vex's lips. He saw Vex's eyes hazily focus, like he was trying to figure out what he was being given, but he eventually gave in and just took slow, careful sips of the proffered potion.

Derivan didn't have a breath to hold, but he certainly felt like he was holding his breath. His entire being felt still as he waited. The potion had to work. It *needed* to work.

Vex's eyes slipped shut, then opened again, a little clearer than before. The lizardkin smiled up at him.

"Whoa," Vex said softly. "That felt . . . really nice."

"It is healing you?" Derivan asked. He needed to be certain.

"Oh. Yes, the potion felt nice, too." Vex gave him a pained little grin. It was clear he hadn't fully recovered yet—but it was equally clear that he *was* recovering. Derivan couldn't help the laugh that burst from him in response to the lizardkin's joke.

"You are a fool," he said, with all the affection he could muster.

Vex smiled a smile that was already less pained. "Whatever that is," he said, indicating the now-empty bottle. "Can I have more?"

"Coming right up," Misa called out. She jogged to meet up with the two of them, then gave Vex a thumbs-up. "Phew. You really know how to scare us, Vex."

"I scared myself, too," Vex admitted. "... Thanks for being here for me, you guys. Is Sev here too?"

"He helped, but he's still stuck on the other side of the continent," Misa answered in Derivan's stead; the armor in question was still too busy holding Vex and thinking about how long he could get away with not letting go. "Trying to get to the Anderstahl Prime Anchor and fix it. I guess we've got a cleanup job here in Enkiros now, too."

"Right." Vex nodded. "Just ... let me recover for a bit. I'm going to need a few more of those potions." He eyed the number strapped on to Misa's body. "Maybe all of them."

Misa shrugged and handed them over. "You got it," she said.

"We will take as much time as you need," Derivan said firmly.

CHAPTER 37

TASKS

It took longer than Vex would've liked for him to recover, but he wasn't about to complain. Just the fact that he'd essentially been handed a miracle cure for his condition was pushing the limits of what Vex considered to be his luck for quite possibly the next seven years.

Eventually, though, he *did* recover—at least enough that he wasn't in constant pain and could once again access his system and its features—and he began to sort out their plan.

They were spending too much time reacting. They needed to move up the timetable. Using all the time they were given wasn't a good thing here; there were too many ways things could go wrong, too many ways things already *had* gone wrong. Sev had a decent idea of what they needed to do to fix things, so what they needed to do was hurry up on that timetable specifically.

Repair the Prime Anchor of Anderstahl, then fetch the remaining two Grand Anchors. Those were their priorities. Enkiros was also a priority, but it depended on the state of the kingdom once they'd fully restored things— as long as the people could be convinced to evacuate once again, they likely wouldn't be a problem.

That meant the majority of the continent would be headed toward Anderstahl as refugees, which *was* potentially a problem. A problem they contacted Sev about to see what he had to say. And also to update him on Vex's condition, of course.

Sev had been relieved to hear that Vex was all right, though they ended up quickly moving on to discussing the potential logistical issues they'd need to find solutions for. Vex felt . . . bad. Sev had clearly been worried about him. But there'd be time for a proper reunion later; for now, they had more pressing things to worry about.

[Anderstahl doesn't have the infrastructure to hold that many people,] Sev responded through the system. [Maybe for a while, but between feeding themselves and all of Elyra, they're not going to be able to sustain it for long. Even with magic and tweaks to the Prime Anchor. This Prime Anchor's behaving a bit weirdly, though.]

[What do you mean, *weird*?] Vex asked, curious.

[It's just the way it keeps giving us stuff we need.] Vex could almost hear Sev's shrug through his words. [It's not a bad thing. I don't get a bad feeling about it or anything, and neither Charise nor Misa's [**Intuitionist**] class is pinging off of it. It's just weird. Feels like there's something I'm missing.]

[Huh.] Try as he might, Vex didn't have any ideas about that, though he was grateful that *something* seemed to be helping them. Enkiros's Prime Anchor wasn't nearly as cooperative. He, Derivan, and Misa were all still trying to get to the center of what he'd decided to dub the fragment storm—all the pieces and different versions of Enkiros shifting and twisting around one another, caught in a turbulent flow of mana. [Weird. But I'm kinda glad.]

[Me too,] Sev said. [So, you need to grab the Grand Anchor and get back to Anderstahl as soon as possible. Derivan can help speed it up—just let me know if I need to refresh the Blessing of Travel. Enkiros's Prime Anchor . . . I mean, do you think you can rescue it?]

[I tried to move the timeline to just before the anchor failed, but I doubt we're going to be able to prevent it in time and also get the Grand Anchor,] Vex said with a wince. [Best bet is probably to try to kickstart the evacuation early—I might be able to combine some of the fragments once we resolve the spell so they can see they need to evacuate.]

[Don't strain your soul again,] Sev warned.

[I think Derivan would kill me if I tried,] Vex said, a little amused. Derivan's arm was still wrapped protectively around his waist, as if he could protect him from soulstrain by sheer virtue of physical proximity. Not that he minded, of course. [The magic's already there. I shouldn't need to tap into the anchor anymore just to manipulate it. In theory.]

[Vex . . .]

[And I will stop if that theory turns out to be wrong,] Vex promised.

[Good.]

[What do we do once we've got all three of the Grand Anchors?] Vex asked. [I'm assuming you have some kind of plan and that sticking the anchors into ourselves isn't the end of it.]

[A lot of stuff with the Grand Anchors is basically still theoretical,] Sev admitted. [The one in Enkiros should bond with me, I think—It'll be the

Grand Anchor of Divinity, and I've already got the most divine connections out of all of us. Maybe out of all priests, actually. If what you've already demonstrated with the Grand Anchor of Magic is any precedent, then I might even be able to bring back some of the lost gods with it.]

[Assuming you don't run into the same problem of soulstrain,] Vex pointed out.

[And I almost certainly will,] Sev admitted. [To be honest, Vex, I'm not sure. We've got so many of the pieces now, but I still feel like I'm missing something. Just because we can *restore* things doesn't mean we can maintain them—you've brought back Enkiros, but you just said the whole place is going to fall apart again.]

[And soon,] Vex said. He couldn't sense it himself, but Derivan could. The state of Enkiros's Prime Anchor was intimately linked with Patch, and now that he'd felt what it was like with Elyra's Prime Anchor, he could tell that Enkiros's was on the verge of collapsing as well. [We're wondering why they didn't evacuate when the system message went out—there must've been a warning.]

[There was a warning when Elyra's Prime Anchor was collapsing, too,] Sev pointed out. [They didn't evacuate without a lot of convincing. It's not an issue they're familiar with. Weren't you there when they were arguing about it? When you went into the semerit?]

[Yeah,] Vex admitted. [It's still kind of hard to wrap my head around.]

[The point is, even if the Grand Anchors can restore things, they clearly don't fix them permanently,] Sev said. [The Void is still a problem. It'll continue to be a problem.]

[We could get stronger,] Vex said. [Make soulstrain less of a problem. Keep bringing things back.]

A short pause. [Is that really a solution, though?] Sev asked. [Even if you were right and it was possible to train the soul—which isn't a guarantee by any means—is that what you want to spend the rest of your life doing? Because I don't think that's sustainable. We'd have to spend every spare second restoring villages, kingdoms, people. We'd be fighting a losing battle against the Void, just the same as before. The only difference is that we'd have a little more time before everything falls apart.]

Vex sighed. He knew Sev was right, really. More than that: he didn't think it would be possible for them to train their souls enough to handle the strain fast enough for this to *matter*. The soulbloom elixirs would help, but the supply of that was limited.

[Right,] Vex said. [So you think there's a missing step. We can't just maintain the anchors—reality shards won't be enough to keep them sustained, and restoring things with the Grand Anchors doesn't fix the underlying issues. Mine doesn't seem to be able to sustain this part of reality the way a reality anchor can.]

[Which is weird. It should be able to. We might need something that makes the Grand Anchors self-sustaining, without you having to consciously channel your connection with it,] Sev said. [If we could repair the reality anchors completely, combining that with the Grand Anchors might be a solution—but even reality shards can't sustain the anchors indefinitely. Unless . . . Hm.]

[Will the Grand Anchors wear down, too?] Vex asked curiously.

This time the pause before Sev responded was even longer. [Uh, shit,] Sev said eloquently. [Okay, I take it back. Even if reality shards *could* sustain the anchors indefinitely, we'd still be fucked.]

[So we need a third thing,] Vex said.

[We need a third thing,] Sev agreed. [Or we need to fix whatever it is that's stopping you from sustaining reality with yours. Let's worry about it later. For us to even get close, you guys need to get the Grand Anchor of Divinity out of Enkiros and to me, and Misa needs to get over here so she can connect with the Grand Anchor of Reality.]

[No Grand Anchor for Derivan?] They'd already known this once they learned there were three of the things, but Vex couldn't help teasing Sev anyway.

[It's not like I *knew* we'd be a party of four,] Sev grumbled. [A fourth Grand Anchor might've made things easier. I don't know. I want to see how they react when they're together, first. We can make a decision from there.]

[Sounds like a plan.]

Vex looked up from the system interface, sighing as the faint blue light faded from his eyes and he stared up into the sky. The light of the Primordial Glyph's mana still shone above them, a strange source of light in the distorted fragment of reality they were in.

How strange it was to think that this was a result of his own magic.

"I don't think I regret it, you know," he said, a little listlessly. He felt Derivan tighten his grip on him slightly, felt the weight of the armor press into him.

"I know," Derivan said.

"Do you think we'll do it?" he asked. "Fix everything, I mean. Not just Enkiros. I want to try to fix Enkiros, but . . ."

"It does not feel like we can," Derivan said. His tone was somber. "I can feel the Prime Anchor at the heart of Enkiros. There is a small part of Patch that screams at me to fix it—but that same part of me tells me that it can no longer be fixed and that I should not try." He was silent for a moment. "And the cost to bring it back to even this state was too great, I think."

"If I could sacrifice myself to fix it permanently . . ." Vex trailed off, unable to finish the thought. Derivan shook his head, though Vex felt the movement more than he saw it.

"No," Derivan said. "We will find another way."

He could hear the unspoken thought. Derivan was the only one of them that didn't have a designated Grand Anchor. Misa would connect to Reality, and Sev would connect to Divinity. If they sacrificed themselves to fix reality permanently, Derivan would be alone again.

Right back where he started.

"I won't leave you," Vex said, his voice soft.

Derivan's response was smaller than Vex had ever heard.

"Thank you."

CHAPTER 38

TICKETS, PLEASE

The hum of the train's engine was the only sound in the room. Sev was lost in thought. Ixoryn seemed too busy absorbing everything he'd been told—he'd barely said a word after Sev explained the situation to him. Instead, he sank into himself and spoke only to ask where they were going.

Tinsel—who had also heard the same explanation, given Sev hadn't been able to think of a good excuse to *not* tell it—was similarly and uncharacteristically silent. A slight flicker of its light told him that it was feeling distressed by the information, but little more than that.

Sev didn't blame either of them.

It didn't help that Derivan's news about the Enkiros anchor made things worse. When Sev had first learned that Vex had brought back their missing Prime Kingdom, right down to its anchors . . . he'd felt *hope*. When he'd learned that those anchors were on the verge of destruction, just as they had been before they lost the kingdom—well, that hope had been very quickly snuffed out.

He'd been through all the options. Bringing back each Prime Kingdom with a Grand Anchor as they were lost, then repairing each Prime Anchor with the reality shards that they'd learned could help the system sustain itself. It seemed like such a good idea on paper. Both the system and magic itself couldn't battle against the Void alone, so perhaps with both of its strengths put together, they'd be able to rebuild the world they once had.

On paper was the key part of that thought. The practical truth of the matter was that reality shards were few and far between. Helg had used up the majority of Teque's store of them, and the creation of new ones, while possible, didn't happen fast enough for them to keep the anchors maintained indefinitely.

It didn't help that the cost to maintain each anchor was increasing. Even Misa's reality anchor was requiring more and more reality shards, and the rate at which it decayed grew by the day. She never spoke of it, but Sev knew she thought about it—he caught her constantly checking her system whenever she thought no one was looking, staring at the invisible bar that was slowly ticking down.

He wanted the Grand Anchors to change things. There was every chance that they *could*. If they were capable of restoring things from the Void—things that should, in theory, have been erased forever—then they were surely capable of simple maintenance. He just needed to get all three of them together so he could examine how they worked in close proximity, with hosts to boost their capabilities.

He clung to that hope. Vex hadn't been able to sustain Enkiros alone with his Grand Anchor. Maybe he didn't know how yet, or maybe it simply wasn't possible until all three Grand Anchors were active. The universe did, technically, require all three to function—it made sense that a single Grand Anchor alone wouldn't be able to sustain things. It could only prop up one of three pillars.

Sev was shaken out of his thoughts as the door to the cabin hissed open and the Conductor strode in. "Tickets, please," the Conductor said politely.

"Here." Sev dumped the armful of tickets he'd picked out of the mud at the end of the last station onto the table. The Conductor stared at Sev and then at the pile of tickets on the table.

He carefully, questioningly reached out and took three. Sev shook his head. "Take all of them," he said.

"Really?" the Conductor sounded surprised. "But . . . you are aware you can trade these? For more prizes. Later, at the final station."

He had not, in fact, been aware of that. "It doesn't matter," Sev said, shaking his head. "We're not here for rewards. Prizes. Whatever you call them. We need to get to the Prime Anchor."

The Conductor observed him for a moment. Was he being evaluated? Sev shifted uncomfortably under the mechanical gaze. "I am unfamiliar with the term," the Conductor lied again.

"The dungeon core," Sev said. It was close enough to the right explanation, and he was getting the impression that the Conductor just needed an excuse; something that would let him interpret the request correctly. There would be a path from the dungeon core down to the Prime Anchor anyway, so that would work just as well.

"I see." The Conductor processed this statement for a moment, then began to feed the tickets into the slot on his chest; a slight *whirr* emerged from his components as ticket after ticket began to . . . almost *flow* into him.

Sev thought he caught a glimpse of the ticket turning into liquid as it poured into the slot, but he couldn't be sure.

He was beginning to sense more coming from the Conductor, too. Like he was absorbing something from the tickets, *gaining* something from them. He gained more substance with every ticket that went into the slot, and Sev thought he felt a glimpse of divine power, even, flickering dimly within the automaton.

What *was* the Conductor, anyway? He was a part of the dungeon's mechanics, clearly, but the Anderstahl dungeon had been extraordinarily intentional with every one of its mechanics so far. There had to be something that the Conductor represented. He was more than he seemed; that much was certain—even Misa had said as much.

Once half the tickets had been absorbed, the Conductor paused again. "Is the dungeon core your only destination?" he asked, his tone once more polite and indifferent—yet this time, Sev got the distinct impression that he was hiding something.

"No," Sev said slowly. "We're also looking for the Vault."

The Conductor wouldn't have any reason to know what a Grand Anchor was, any more than he knew what a Prime Anchor was—but there *was* a chance he would know where the Vault was.

"I see," the Conductor said again. He stood there for a moment, completely still, then gathered the rest of the tickets into his arms. "I will return shortly. Please give me a moment."

Sev blinked, then stared after the Conductor as he left.

"Was that interaction kinda weird to anyone else?" he asked.

Tinsel spoke for the first time in a while. "A little," it said. It sounded a little less cheerful, but Sev was relieved to note that not all of the cheer had disappeared from its voice. "I dunno. It kinda seems like he wants to help but he can't be open about it."

"I concur," Ixoryn said shortly, and then fell silent again.

"Yeah, that's kinda the impression I got," Sev said thoughtfully, looking at the cabin door that the Conductor had disappeared through. "You know, we never bothered exploring the rest of the train. Maybe we should— *Whoa!*"

The train *lurched.* Sev was thrown nearly face-first into the table. Tinsel went flying entirely, though Ixoryn reached out and casually caught it before it could smash itself into the ceiling. Ixoryn himself was the only one of the three that seemed relatively unaffected by the sudden movement. He stayed utterly still, as if the laws of physics were a slight annoyance that he'd chosen to brush off for the moment.

"Okay," Sev said, catching his breath. "First of all, that's not fair."

Ixoryn didn't respond, but Sev could swear he saw the god give him a ghost of a smirk. It vanished as soon as it came, though, and Sev was left wondering if he'd just imagined it.

"Second," he continued, "what *was* that?"

As if on cue, the door to their cabin hissed open once again. The Conductor walked through, though Sev only really knew it was the Conductor due to the uniform he wore. He was otherwise completely changed in appearance. His outer shell appeared to be made of shimmering, golden liquid, and beneath that liquid swam traces of light.

And there was *very much* a divine presence here, though Sev wasn't certain he could attribute it to any specific god.

"Hey, uh," Sev said. "Weird question. But what are you, exactly?"

The Conductor cocked his head at him, then glanced at the god that was still sitting in the booth.

"I am the Conductor," he said. "And I am a guide. A navigator, if you will."

Ixoryn reacted to this. He sat up straight and narrowed his eyes, staring more closely at the Conductor. "What is your name?" he asked.

A long pause. When the Conductor answered the question, he was almost reluctant.

"... I prefer to be called the Conductor. But my name, if you must know, is Ixoryn."

—⁂—

Vex stared hesitantly at the storm of mana in front of him.

It wasn't that it intimidated him, although perhaps it should have. What shocked him was how he could feel the remnants of his original spell swirling within the chaos. He hadn't really expected anything of that spell to remain, but here it was; the lines of the Primordial Glyph in the sky all led to this.

A manastorm. The first of its kind that he'd ever seen. Lightning crackled at the edges of it, though it wasn't truly *lightning*; it was formed out of all sorts of mana aspects. One or two of them might have been actual lightning bolts. The others, as far as he could tell, were about as liable to turn their victims into frogs or drench them in gallons of water.

"So all I need to do is walk into the middle of that," he said. He could practically feel Misa's skepticism radiating from her. Derivan wasn't nearly as doubtful, but then, the armor had always trusted what he said pretty much immediately.

"Are you sure?" Misa asked doubtfully. "That thing looks like it's going to try to kill you."

"It won't." Vex said the words with more confidence than he felt. "It should be just like any other spell I cast. It's my mana. The fireballs I throw don't burn me, so this manastorm isn't going to hurt me, either."

"Right," Misa said. She stared at the storm again. "And walking into the middle of it is going to do what again, exactly?"

"It's going to realign the spell." Vex sighed—he knew how ridiculous it sounded. The only reason he knew it would work was because the Grand Anchor within him resonated with its knowledge. This *would* work. It was how the mages of old would realign their broken spells. It was just happening on a much, *much* larger scale.

Most spells didn't go awry outside the spellcaster's body.

"Look, just trust me," Vex said. He slipped his hand out of Derivan's, then took a step forward, wincing a little as wind buffeted him from the force of the spell. He was not, unfortunately, immune to the physical effects of the manastorm—just the impact of the mana hitting him directly. "I know what I'm doing. We're at the core of the spell. This is the last thing we need to pull it all together."

"We trust you," Derivan said before Misa could respond. Misa huffed.

"Yeah, we do," she said reluctantly. Vex smiled at her—

—Misa disappeared and reappeared at his side, and Vex flinched as a rock burst into pieces next to his head, blocked only by Misa's mace. She grinned down at him.

"You still need us to look out for you, though," she told him.

"I guess I do," Vex admitted. ". . . Don't get too close, though."

"We will not," Derivan said. He came forward too, though he wasn't trying to block anything in particular from hitting Vex; he just wrapped the lizardkin in a tight hug. Vex noticed a few rocks pinging off of the armor's back. It was more incidental than anything, but it *did* still feel like Derivan was protecting him. He wasn't about to complain.

Vex took a deep breath and—with Misa and Derivan both providing backup in the form of shielding him against the debris picked up by the manastorm—walked into the center of said storm.

The moment he did, everything calmed. He felt the mana above and around him come into alignment once more. For a single moment, the Primordial Glyph of Translation shone above them in the sky, as large as the kingdom of Enkiros itself.

Then the spell completed, and the streets around them burst to life.

C H A P T E R   39

ENKIROS, CENTERPIECE OF DIVINITY

Even without being specifically tuned to divine energies the way Sev was, Vex could *feel* how much influence the gods had here. It was in the air, in the ground, in everything around them. It was . . . almost uncomfortable for him, even, though that was mostly because Vex couldn't quite shake the feeling of being watched.

Enkiros was a beautiful kingdom. Whatever their connection with the divine was, it enriched every aspect of the city. The air felt fresh and clean, the streets felt . . . good to walk on, for lack of a better term, and the temperature was neither too hot nor too cold.

"Damn," Misa said. "This place is cooler than I was expecting."

"Yeah," Vex agreed.

"There is something strange." Derivan seemed a little less enthusiastic. He glanced around, a slight frown evident in his eyes. "It is almost as if some elements of the city are . . . competing with one another. They are not in harmony."

"You think?" Vex cocked his head. "I don't feel it."

"[**Intuitionist**] is pinging strangely," Misa admitted. "I don't know why, though."

"Perhaps not all conflicts are those we can see," Derivan suggested. "In any case, it is unimportant. We must find the Vault. Sev has indicated to us that it is located beneath the fountain in the center of Enkiros, accessible via a passphrase."

"Hopefully this one hasn't been subverted by a group of nobles," Misa grumbled. "Think we'll run into any problems?"

"My hope is that we will not," Derivan said.

Vex glanced up ahead. He could see the fountain in question from here—it was *enormous*, with the central jet of water stretching almost thirty feet into the sky, if he was judging distances correctly. Each jet was illuminated by streaks of divine power that danced through the water and diffused into the air as tiny droplets.

No doubt this was part of what made the air feel so fresh. The whole kingdom was practically overflowing with divinity.

"Wish we could get more time to explore this place," Vex said regretfully. "It looks beautiful."

The people of the kingdom were interesting too. It was nothing like Elyra, where there was a clear disparity between the nobles and the commoners—but it *was* very clear when different citizens were the followers of different gods. Followers of a given god wore very telling outfits, down to the small items of devotion on their persons.

And then there were the ones that followed multiple gods. Those people tended to wear bright, clashing colors, and they were probably Vex's favorite to observe. They were all so different! And they all got along with one another, too, though he did catch a few of them being given dirty glances every once in a while . . .

. . . Huh. Actually, now that he was paying more attention, he caught more than a few of those dirty glances—and not just directed at the ones who worshipped multiple gods, either. There was a clear tension between the followers of different gods that he just hadn't noticed before.

"Hi!" Before they could go any farther, someone stopped in front of them—Vex blinked once, staring at the beautifully dressed dragon-like monk standing in front of them. He didn't recognize the species. He was pretty sure she wasn't a lizardkin. "You're new here, aren't you?"

"Uh . . . yes?" Vex tried. The dragon—*was* she a dragon?—beamed in response.

"Wonderful! I'm surprised you were able to get this far into Enkiros without someone offering to guide you. Would you like a guide? My name is Xelil, by the way!"

"Vex," Vex said automatically. "We don't need a guide, I'm sorry—we're here on business. Adventurers' Guild business."

"Oh!" Xelil brightened. "I've always wondered what the Adventurers' Guild is like. Tell me more! What kind of business is it?"

Oh boy. Vex glanced to both Derivan and Misa for help, only to find two amused faces staring back at him. He sighed.

Hiding what was happening didn't exactly help either, he supposed.

"It's actually very important we talk to someone in charge of the kingdom about it," Vex said politely. "I'm not sure if you've heard the news, but Elyra has fallen."

Technically, he *knew* she hadn't, because Enkiros had only just been restored. But he couldn't exactly say that. To Xelil's credit, her chipper attitude melted away almost instantly, and Vex could've sworn he saw a hint of fire in her eyes.

"Elyra has *what*?" she said. ". . . I'll take you to speak to the king and some of our other leaders. This sounds important."

"What, you aren't even gonna question it?" Misa piped up. Xelil's glance toward her was perfectly serious.

"I can tell when someone lies, among other things," she said simply. "That wasn't a lie *or* other things. Which tells me that Elyra has actually fallen." She peered a little more closely at him. ". . . And it's a little more serious than you're saying, isn't it?"

Vex squirmed a little under the intensity of her gaze. "Not a *little*," he admitted. He glanced back to the fountain—they needed to go and get the Grand Anchor, but evacuating Enkiros was on their list too. It didn't necessarily matter which one they did first, as long as both were done before the Prime Anchor started to fail. "Deri, how much time do we have?"

Derivan closed his eyes briefly, the lights in his helmet flickering out as he did so. ". . . A little more than two days, I believe."

"Not a lot of time." Vex grimaced. It was more time than they'd had for the Elyran evacuation, though—that had been *very* last-minute. They'd saved as many as they could, but the thought of how many must have slipped into the cracks . . . it was a fear of his. How could they know if they'd missed someone, if their entire history was wiped from reality? "Enough to get this done first and then get to the Vault."

"The Vault?" Xelil tilted her head, curious.

"We'll explain that later." Vex took a deep breath. "Can you take us to the king?"

"Right this way," Xelil said, injecting a little bit of cheer into her voice. Vex caught the hint of worry in it, though. He wondered who she really was. A random dragon approaching a group of adventurers and then immediately being able to tell that they were here for something important? They couldn't have been the only tourists in the kingdom when it went down, nor the only group of adventurers.

. . . Speaking of which, he needed to get the branch of the Adventurers' Guild located in Enkiros to reconnect with the Guildmaster. Once she got out of whatever predicament she was in.

"Who are you, anyway?" Vex asked suddenly. "I mean, I know your name, obviously, but you're not just some citizen, are you?"

"Very astute!" Xelil's cheer was a little less forced this time. She smiled down at him, and Vex was struck with a strange sense of familiarity. "I'm the head priestess of the Church of Navigation. We're followers of the god—"

"Wait," Vex interrupted. "Do you know an Exvhar?"

Xelil stopped in her tracks. "You know my little brother?" she asked, sounding dumbfounded for the first time in this conversation. Unmoored, even. "He's—he's been missing for days. We couldn't find him even with the strongest tracking spells we had. Do you know where he is?"

"He's waiting right outside of Enkiros with a friend of ours," Vex answered truthfully. Come to think of it, they probably should have gone back to fetch the two once the spell had resolved—but they'd appeared right in the middle of the city, so Vex had forgotten.

Xelil's eyes hardened. "I need to see him," she said immediately. "I understand your business is important. I can take you to go see the king first if you tell me where he is."

Derivan observed her for a moment and then spoke. "You believe he is involved in something that is also integral to the safety of this kingdom."

Xelil glanced up at him, surprise flashing across her face. "Yes," she admitted. "It's very serious. I doubt it's related to what you three are here for, though."

"Oh, believe me," Misa said, "you'd be surprised."

Xelil blinked. "I never got your names."

"I am Derivan," the suit of armor said.

"Misa." The half-orc waved.

"Pleasure to meet you," Xelil said. She looked between the two, then turned to Vex. "You guys are being serious, aren't you? If what we're both here about is the same thing, then what are you here for? Can you help us fix it?"

Vex shook his head. "No," he said softly. Gently. As if saying the words more quietly could somehow dampen their impact, though he knew they couldn't. "We're here to warn you to evacuate. What happened to Elyra—it's about to happen here, too."

It took a while for them to sort through everything they knew, largely because Xelil's information was incomplete at best. That they had noticed Exvhar's disappearance at all was an artifact of the way both he and the kingdom of Enkiros had been brought back from the Void. There was a gap in reality there—Exvhar hadn't been brought back with everything else. So reality had twisted to compensate, building a new event into the timeline that had never actually happened.

That disappearance of one of the kingdom's dragons meant that they'd investigated the failing reality anchor a little more thoroughly. They'd questioned the gods more heavily, too, and they'd begun to notice the gaps in their knowledge, the little discrepancies created by the disappearance of one god or the other.

The way reality anchors compensated for something being erased wasn't perfect, after all. It left jagged edges that could be identified if someone looked carefully enough. If they had the right skills and noticed the right things, which was a feat in and of itself.

Fortunately, Xelil said, that was the specialty of the God of Navigation. His domain was a broad concept that could be applied to many things; *navigation* wasn't even really the right word for it, although that was the word he'd chosen. He was also sometimes called the Guide, or the Mantle of Leadership. He didn't embody the concept of finding one's way through physical space as much as he did the general, metaphorical idea of guidance and finding one's way.

Eventually, she frowned. "I was supposed to bring you guys to the king before we went into detail about this," she complained, mostly to herself. "I got caught up in things when you told me Exvhar was alive. Look, if what you're saying is true, let's go fetch and bring him—it's going to be easier to convince everyone of what you're saying if you've got two dragons backing you up."

"Speaking of which," Vex said, "you and your brother are *very* different."

Xelil grinned at him. "What, never met a dragon before?" she said, flexing her wings and splaying them out to her sides. "We're all capable of shifting. Kinda. Exvhar's bad at it, so he hates doing it. Says walking on two legs makes him feel all wobbly. We keep telling him he'll get used to it, but he doesn't want to."

"He seems young, for a dragon," Derivan observed.

Xelil just shrugged. "He's not *that* young," she said. "A few decades old. But he doesn't want to grow up, because if he does, he has to take on more responsibilities. We're letting him figure it out on his own. Anyway, you said he was right outside the kingdom?"

"Yep," Vex said. He opened his mouth to elaborate, but Xelil held up a hand to shush him, and with her other hand, she traced a symbol in the air. A point of light shot out from her finger, zipping through the city's streets; a few people let out startled yelps, but most of them just stepped out of the way, as if they were used to it.

Xelil grinned. "*Finally* that spell works," she says. "All right! This way, then."

She led them through the streets and past a number of street stalls that caught Vex's eye—Enkiros had a *lot* of handcrafted goods. He couldn't help his eyes from wandering, taking in every craft he could see. There were things from pottery to handmade jewelry to accessories that seemed specifically made for dragons. He wondered how much they were embedded into the culture of Enkiros; Xelil had implied they all held fairly important positions within the kingdom's hierarchy.

He wondered also if the reason things had gone so far off the rails in the iteration of Enkiros that he'd seen was that the dragons were gone. He hadn't seen them at all when he interfered with the king's decision and advised them to evacuate—hadn't even heard that they existed. Yet they were present when he tapped into the semerit for the first time, and the transformation it had subsequently induced had been entirely involuntary until he'd learned to control it.

Lost in his thoughts, Vex almost didn't notice when they reached the gates of Enkiros. The guards took a single glance at Xelil and then hurried to open the gates, and Vex blinked at the non-interaction.

Weird.

"Little brother!" Xelil exclaimed the words happily as soon as she saw Exvhar patiently waiting outside. Novice stood next to him, leaning against his flank and reading a book; he nearly fell over when the large dragon immediately lurched forward to hug his sister. "Exvhar, *no*! Transform first! Hugs after transformation, not before!"

If she thought Exvhar was going to listen to her, she evidently thought wrong. Vex watched in some amusement as the dragon's younger brother bowled them both over in the force of his attempted hug, missed entirely, and then managed to hit his snout on the ground.

"Are you, uh . . . all right?" Vex asked. He wasn't even sure who he was asking. Misa snickered behind him, and Derivan looked on, mostly silent.

"I'm fine," Xelil said with a sigh. "And so is he. He always does this."

"Sorry," Exvhar said, sitting on the ground. If dragons could pout, he was definitely pouting. "I just missed you."

Xelil's gaze softened. "I know," she said. "I heard a lot from these kind people. But why don't you tell me what happened to you? From your perspective."

CHAPTER 40

DRAGON TALES

To say that Xelil was worried after hearing Exvhar's story was an understatement. Vex wondered if she simply hadn't processed everything they'd told her properly until she heard it from her brother's own mouth. One thing he'd almost forgotten was that Exvhar had *kept his memories of the Void.* He knew on some level what was happening, even if he'd been rather ignorant of it all compared to many others. He could recount the experience of being in there, of what it felt like to have your very essence slowly stripped away.

That, along with the news from Enkiros's branch of the Adventurers' Guild as they got in contact with the other branches and caught up with what was happening, was more than enough to convince Xelil that they needed to evacuate *immediately.*

"I don't care if the king agrees with me," she growled out. Vex had explained to her what happened in the first iteration of things—the one time he'd been here within the semerit, and how the king had refused to evacuate, insistent that the gods would save them. "We're going to get our people out of here *before* we get another Elyra. What did those stupid fucks think they were doing? Creating a fucking *god?* Who do they think they are? If we'd still been around at the time—"

"—it would have been an act of war, wouldn't it?" Vex asked. The realization came only as he said the words, and a small piece of horror bloomed in his heart at the realization of what they'd only just avoided.

"Yes," Xelil said shortly. "It's damn lucky you guys cut it off when you did, and frankly, I'm still tempted to give them a piece of my mind. No one goes around just trying to create gods. Do you know what would have happened if they succeeded?"

"Nothing good?" Vex said. It wasn't exactly a hard guess.

"Nothing good," Xelil confirmed. "If you're making a god out of the small piece of divinity within everyone in your kingdom, you're going to make a god that defines your kingdom. And then, guess what? Gods can't sit around in the physical plane! It would have to ascend! And your entire kingdom would lose its spark of life just like that." She snapped her fingers. "Whole kingdom of robots, that's what you'd get. Uh, no offense." She glanced at Derivan.

"I am not a robot," Derivan said, a little self-consciously. Vex looked up at him, his eyes widening a little when he realized that his partner was clutching the amulet that the Guildmaster had given him—the one that was supposed to help him stop others from realizing that he was, technically, a "monster." As designated by the system initially, anyway.

"Yeah, yeah, I know," Xelil said, waving her hand dismissively. If she knew that she'd just casually bypassed a piece of perception-altering gear, she certainly didn't indicate it. "I didn't mean anything by it. You seem cool enough. Kinda weird, but cool. Aren't we all?"

Derivan shifted uncomfortably. "I . . . do not know how to respond to that."

"You're cool, is what I'm saying!" Xelil said. "Look, don't worry about it. You have something that's supposed to stop people from noticing, right? Keep that; it works well. Took me way longer than I should have to notice."

". . . Thank you?" Derivan tried. Vex walked over to him to take his hand, and Derivan gave him a grateful squeeze as he did so.

He still felt awkward about being a "monster," evidently, and though he'd made a ton of progress past that, he still wasn't . . . open about it. Not to the world. He was open about it with them, felt comfortable with them, but Vex hadn't thought about how he never introduced himself as armor—never made mention of what he was.

"Hey, Deri?" he said softly, once Xelil's back was turned and she was leading them forward again, navigating a path through the crowd and directly to the palace. Derivan glanced down at him, eyes curious.

Vex couldn't help himself. He tiptoed, planting a small peck on the part of Derivan's helmet where his mouth would've been if he had one—where his mouth *had* been when he chose to manifest one using Slime's limited shape-shifting capabilities—and then gave him a small smile. "Once all this is over, let's introduce you to everyone?" he said. "Properly, I mean. To my family, and all our friends too. I bet Max would be excited! And Novice! And Raltis. And—"

Derivan chuckled, interrupting him by placing a hand over his mouth. "Sometimes, I wonder which of the two of us has that Physical Empathy stat," he said, amused. He was smiling now—all discomfort gone, replaced by a look of pure affection. "I would appreciate that. You would stand by my side?"

"Always," Vex said immediately. "If anyone doesn't like you 'cause you're a suit of armor, I'll fight them."

"I'm still here, you know!" Misa interjected with a laugh. She was walking along behind them, and Vex yelped when she spoke. "I'd fight them too."

"I'd fight them harder!" Vex stuck his tongue out at her. Just because.

Derivan just laughed. "I am glad to have you both as friends," he said. "But let us speak to the king and hope that he favors our plan. We do not have much time left."

That . . . was true. Vex sobered up a little at the realization. Time was relative, to be fair—but there was a lot that needed to be done before he could live the life he wanted to live.

What he *did* know, though, was that he couldn't see a future that didn't have Derivan in it. It wasn't that he needed to have the armor with him for every second of every day.

It was just that when he pictured *home*, Derivan was always a part of it.

"Okay," Vex said. "Let's get this done and grab the Grand Anchor. We're almost there. Two more Grand Anchors, and then we've saved the world."

"Two more," Derivan agreed.

Misa didn't speak, but Vex felt her grasp his shoulder reassuringly. She smiled at them both, and the message was clear—she was with them, and they'd save it all together.

The palace loomed ahead.

Time to meet the king of Enkiros for the second time. Hopefully, this time, he wouldn't get a death bolt thrown at his face.

"You're both named Ixoryn," Sev said slowly. He glanced between the Conductor and the God of Navigation. "And I feel—you're *both* divine. How is this possible?"

"I would like to know the same thing." Ixoryn—the god, not the Conductor, and Sev decided he'd keep referring to them by those names just to avoid the headache for now—said. "You carry a piece of my divinity."

"Yes." The Conductor didn't flinch at the accusation.

"*How?*" Ixoryn pressed.

"I do not know." A slight tilt of the head, a *whirr* in his mechanisms. The Conductor was distressed, if Sev was reading him right—but not so distressed that he wanted to evade the conversation entirely. No, he was uncomfortable? Or curious. "I only know what I am. I am a guide for this dungeon."

"And I'm sometimes known as the Guide," Ixoryn muttered. He glanced at Sev. "You know anything about this?"

"I'm the one that asked!" Sev protested. "I mean, I know a bit about Prime Anchors and what they can do, I suppose. If I had to guess, something happened and it tried to incorporate you into the dungeon instead of just absorbing you for . . . whatever reason. Maybe because you were on the verge of death?"

"And I was not worth absorbing?" Ixoryn said dryly. "Though I appreciate that I wasn't erased as you've described."

"All of the anchors have to have some level of intelligence so they can make decisions," Sev said. "And that kind of includes decisions when it comes to building its dungeons. I'm not sure why it would take you in unless—"

Sev cut himself off, a foreign memory suddenly piercing through him. He winced. It was one of his own, yes, but separate from the others. Something he'd hidden from himself. What—what was this? He saw himself working on something in the dark. Not even in the dark. In the Void. Like he had to work on it separate from all of reality. There were very few things that had to be built outside of reality. The anchors were one of them, but what he was building . . . it didn't look like an anchor.

The memory of what it was—its shape, its function—that was fuzzy. It was a blur in his mind, a blur he was moving around and working on, muttering to himself in a tone that almost scared himself. He sounded borderline obsessive.

The machine *clicked*. The memory ended.

"What the fuck," Sev said. "What was that?"

Ixoryn glanced at him, and Sev felt the remnant threads of divine power around him. Anger briefly flared within him. "You used divine magic on me!"

"To guide you, yes," Ixoryn said, unrepentant. "To a memory that would assist."

"That didn't *help*!" Sev said. "It just hurt! I don't even know what that memory was!"

"What was it?" Ixoryn asked.

"It was— I don't know. I saw myself building something. Don't know what it was; don't know what it was for." Sev scowled, his heart still racing— the memory had genuinely hurt. Something fought against it being revealed to him. He'd built something in secret, even from himself. Why? The only reason to hide anything like this was to tear conceptual links away from it; the less links there were, the slower the Void could eat away at it.

"But it's relevant to my condition," Ixoryn said. Then he frowned, tilting his head slightly. "Or to your future."

"Or both," Sev said. "Fuck, that hurt. Don't do that without warning next time."

"I will endeavor to warn you," Ixoryn agreed, though he seemed uneasy. "Unless it is an emergency. It should not have hurt."

"Apparently I hid that memory from myself for a reason." Sev rubbed at his temples—his head still ached. "Look, if I had to guess—and you should *not* take what I'm saying as definitive—then the only reason I can think of for the dungeon to do this would be because it's trying to save you. It wants you *here*, for some reason, instead of in the divine planes. If you were complete, you'd be forced back into them, right?"

"I didn't think of that." Ixoryn frowned in thought. "You're correct. It exacts a cost to remain here if one is a complete god. I am incomplete, which makes me mortal, but that mortality has the benefit of allowing me to participate in this realm."

A pause. "More gods should do this."

The Conductor chose this moment to speak up again. "I feel I should have input on the matter," he said. "I am, at present, a servant to the dungeon's needs."

"Oh." Ixoryn blinked, then frowned. "That won't do. Can't have a piece of myself as a slave. Let me just—"

"Do *not* sling divine power around," Sev barked before Ixoryn could try to sever the Conductor's connection with the dungeon. The Conductor, to his credit, had also taken several steps back and lifted both of his hands as if to defend himself.

"I do not wish to be disconnected from the dungeon at the moment," he said. "*Servant* was a poor choice of word, perhaps. There is a symbiosis—a mutualistic relationship. I am provided with experiences divines could not normally have in exchange for my service."

Ixoryn paused, his hands still practically glowing with power. "...I see," he said, though not without a small amount of suspicion. "We'll have to join with one another again at some point."

"I am agreed on this," the Conductor said. "I cannot remain here forever. Or even for much longer, if what you have said about this dungeon is true."

"You overheard?" Sev asked, surprised.

"I listen to everything that happens within the dungeon." The Conductor shrugged. "It is part of my job."

"Speaking of which," Sev said. He glanced out of the window—whatever the Conductor had done, it had clearly changed routes. Mostly because he was pretty sure the train was now headed *down*, and it was doing so fast enough that it felt like his ears were about to pop. "You did something when I gave you all those tickets."

"Yes." The Conductor nodded. "When a team is delving, I am restricted in what I can do for them until I am fed with tickets. More tickets enable me to do more for them, at the cost of less tickets being available for rewards later in the dungeon. But you are not interested in rewards, correct?"

"No." Not really, anyway. The rewards could be helpful, but they had more important things to worry about.

"I am therefore taking you directly to the dungeon core," the Conductor said. "And to the Vault when you are done. They are not far apart, though the Vault would not normally be accessible to the dungeon."

"You can do that?" Sev blinked.

"I have done so." The Conductor gestured—with what Sev thought was a small bit of smug grandiosity that he allowed himself, which was completely fair—toward the windows. "Next station: *dungeon core*. Good luck, my friends."

CHAPTER 41

DUNGEON CORE

The core of a dungeon wasn't a place that was normally accessible to delvers. They existed as a kind of grounding point for reality anchors—a storm of unstable reality and crumbling debris, often both able and willing to defend itself from delvers. And that was *if* they could be found. They were hidden in obscure and unlikely places, always close to the end of the dungeon but never easily reached.

The fact that this one had a train station attached to it was surprising.

Though that wasn't entirely accurate. Whatever the Conductor had done, it allowed the train to move through stone like it was water. Sev was certain he could feel the train *wriggle* as it moved through the dirt. It was one of the few memories he immediately wished he could erase, because he did not need to know what it felt like to be inside a creature wriggling through the dirt.

The "station," therefore, wasn't really attached to anything resembling train tracks. The entrance to it was covered in solid stone, and Sev suspected that the appearance of the dungeon core's room was more for aesthetics than function. Even if it felt like a standard Anderstahl train station.

Except for the storm of reality throbbing in the center of it, of course. Sev did *not* like that he had to use that word to describe whatever was going on there.

"That . . . thing . . . is what you're going to try to fix?" Ixoryn stared at it warily. "It looks like it wishes to explode. And it is throbbing."

"*Please* don't say that word," Sev deadpanned. "It's bad enough that I thought it; I don't need you saying it."

"Pulsating?"

"That isn't any better."

"Quopping."

"I—" Sev stopped. "That's not a word."

"It is."

"There is *no way* that's a word."

"You are arguing with a literal god."

"... *If* that's a word, I somehow hate it even more than the other two." Sev stared at the still-throbbing . . . whatever it was in the center of the station, and then sighed. "Anyway, no, that's not the thing I'm going to try to fix. It's nearby, though. That's the grounding point for the anchor."

"And it is . . . supposed to look like this?" Ixoryn sounded skeptical.

"I didn't design it!" Sev threw his hands up into the air. "I don't even know if *anyone* designed it! I think it's just the natural result of having a reality anchor tied directly to a spatial matrix that consolidates—" He interrupted himself. "—Never mind. The point is that that's a natural phenomenon and we shouldn't look at it."

"I think it's pretty!" Tinsel quipped. The light fixture—Sev *really* wished he had a better mental name for it, but it refused to give him a different one, and "Soulbloom Emanation" was unwieldy—had mostly recovered from its momentary depression, to Sev's relief. It seemed, if anything, even *more* determined to see as much as it possibly could before the end of the world. And to help with preventing it, if possible. Sev really didn't know if there was anything Tinsel could do to help with that, but he appreciated the sentiment.

"I . . . suppose," Sev said after a moment, only barely remembering to actually respond to what Tinsel said. Beside him, Ixoryn snorted.

"It is not," he said. "It is an ugly thing full of chaos. Impossible to navigate. And I don't say that lightly."

"But chaos is pretty!" Tinsel argued.

Sev waved a hand and spoke, trying to head off this argument before it could escalate. "We need to get down to where the reality anchor is," he said. Then he frowned. "Well, *I* need to get down to where the reality anchor is. I don't think either of you need to follow me. Or should follow me."

Ixoryn shrugged. "All right," he said, leaning back against a wall and crossing his arms.

"I want to help!" Tinsel insisted.

"And you'll help the most by . . ." Sev paused. ". . . taking care of Ixoryn. Make sure he doesn't do anything stupid."

"Oh." Tinsel thought about this for a moment. "Okay!"

Ixoryn glared. "I know what you're doing."

"Listen, it works; don't ruin it for me," Sev said. To his credit, Ixoryn didn't say another word, even as Tinsel walked over to him and mimicked his exact pose, leaning against the same wall. Sev snorted a little at the sight, then turned back to the dungeon core in front of him.

It was time to do this. All he had to do was feed the anchor a couple of reality shards. That wouldn't be so bad, right? The Void was pretty accessible from here. All he needed to do was . . . fall.

Sev *hated* heights.

—⟋⟍—

"We are evacuating this city." Xelil's tone brooked no argument—she stood with her arms crossed and her eyes burning with fury. The king had tried to argue with her. *Tried.* That attempt had lasted for all of ten seconds, and now he was positively crumbling beneath her sheer force of personality.

Well . . . he was still trying, to be fair. He just wasn't doing it successfully. Vex had to admit that he wouldn't have imagined Xelil to be capable of this level of persuasion when they'd first met her.

"You are asking me to empty our kingdom," the king said, gritting his teeth. His name was . . . something. Xelil had introduced him, but Vex had gotten a little distracted by all the artifacts that were just stored in the Enkiros palace, apparently. There was at least one cloak on display with enchantments that he'd never seen before, and *that* was a feat worthy of investigating in and of itself.

Enkri? Something like that. King Enkri.

"You are asking me to abandon our walls. To empty our homes. To leave behind our gardens!" Enkri was clearly worked up, and yet he couldn't be quite as forceful as he wanted—he flinched under the force of Xelil's glare. Vex kept an eye out, worried that Enkri would try to cast a spell, but so far he seemed too afraid of Xelil to even try an attack. "All on the delusions of—"

"Finish that sentence," Xelil said coldly. Enkri gulped.

Vex had learned that Xelil was *very* protective of her little brother and did not take kindly to insinuations about the other dragon's intelligence. Or any kind of insult toward him, for that matter.

"—of some adventurers!" Enkri blustered, trying to recover.

"Our information is verified by the Adventurers' Guild," Derivan said calmly. "By the High Priestess of Navigation, and by both the Elyran and Anderstahl governments."

"It's not your information I'm questioning," Enkri said, exasperated. "It's your solution! How can evacuating possibly be the solution? Enkiros is the product of generations of—"

"Everything we have accomplished will mean nothing if we lose the people of this kingdom," Xelil hissed. "Do you understand, Enkri? Your responsibility is to your people. The gods may guide you, but you must *listen.*"

Enkri winced and fell silent. It was clear that he'd heard these words before—they struck a chord within him. The spiderlike man hesitated.

And then, very, *very* slowly, he nodded.

"Fine," he said. "If . . . if that is what the gods desire, then it shall be done."

"Good." Xelil's attitude brightened almost immediately. She clapped once, then gathered the trio of Vex, Misa, and Derivan into a small huddle with her wings. "You guys said you needed to do one more thing, right? Something about a Grand Anchor. I won't pretend to know what that means."

"It is complicated," Derivan said.

"We're hoping it'll help us fix all this," Misa said. "No promises, though. By which I mean you should still evacuate."

"I'll handle the evacuation," Xelil said dryly, glancing back at the king. "Trust me. You guys go and get whatever you need. Do you need me to authorize anything for you?"

"Depends on whether we need permission to get into the center fountain or not." Misa grinned. Xelil raised an eyebrow.

"I should not be surprised that that's where it is," she said. "No, you won't need my permission. Just pretend you know what you're doing. It'll be fine."

To everyone's surprise, Xelil was right. It was not, in fact, difficult to get into the Vault—nor was it difficult to lay claim to the Grand Anchor that lay within. The fountain responded to the passphrase easily enough, and no one seemed interested in stopping them when they simply walked into the now-parted water. Everyone just seemed to sort of . . . assume that was what they were supposed to be doing.

Vex wasn't about to complain.

The Grand Anchor was warm in his arms. It sat in the middle of the Vault, accompanied by strange threads of golden webbing that stretched from wall to ceiling to anchor. The pedestal it sat on was worn with dust—it had been a long time since anyone had been in here, clearly. Unlike Elyra, no one had tried to force their way in.

Vex spared a moment to be thankful that Wisfield hadn't found *this* Grand Anchor instead of the one for Magic. They'd tried to create a god using its power. With the Grand Anchor of Magic, that was a difficult task at best, and one that required the combined effort of several of their elders. If they'd had access to the Grand Anchor of Divinity instead . . .

... Well, it didn't bear thinking about.

"I'm surprised getting the Anchor was this—" Misa started, and then she stopped mid-sentence, looking around surreptitiously. ". . . You know what? I'm not going to finish that sentence."

"Probably a good idea," Vex said. He'd reflexively clutched the new Grand Anchor close, wrapping both his arms around it and curling defensively around the glowing orb.

"Think it's about time we get this to Sev." Misa glanced around the empty Vault and frowned. "He needs to grab the Divinity Anchor and bond with it, right? And he needs to get me the Reality Anchor . . ." She paused. "Maybe I shouldn't call them that. I feel like that last one is confusing."

"*Grand Anchor of Reality* is a mouthful, though," Vex said with a laugh. "I'm sure we'll figure it out. It's not like you've got both a reality anchor and the Reality Anchor bonded with you."

Misa scowled at Vex, though it was a playful scowl. "Now you're just making fun of me."

"Just a bit." Vex smiled.

"I have informed Sev of our status," Derivan said. "I may need his assistance with another Blessing for us to rejoin him—the distance is great for Shift alone, and there is a barrier in the way."

"Right. The Anderstahl barrier." Misa frowned. "What's up with that, anyway?"

CHAPTER 42

FINAL FRONTIER

The Void felt cold around Sev.

It wasn't *really* cold, of course. The Void wasn't really anything. It was an emptiness that ate away at everything of substance within it—the result of the natural decay of the fabric of reality itself.

But it felt cold. That was the nature of the Void. In the absence of reality, the mind would fill in the blanks; it was a dark, featureless space, so his mind expected it to be cold.

So it was.

Sev pulled his robes a little tighter around himself, shivering. He'd been to the Void before. Long before his first encounter with it in this life, he'd been down here, trying to learn about the reality anchors. Trying to understand what they did, how they worked, why the people in charge had chosen *this* system to preserve reality and not any other.

He suspected he knew the answer, though he didn't like it: they didn't have time to come up with any other solution. This one was the one they came up with first, those scientists and mages and all the other brilliant minds that invented both the anchors and the system that was linked to them.

All of reality a game, because it was the first solution they'd thought of.

He sighed.

Onyx was here somewhere. So were many of the other erased gods, and a million other lives that were still *present* but slowly decaying. There was really only one thing that separated him from all the others, that prevented him from simply being erased from the minds of everyone that had ever known him. It was the fact that he was still linked to the system. He was linked to Misa's reality anchor, and it kept him whole and *present*, even in the dead reality that was the Void.

Others who were pulled in here were not nearly so lucky. Sometimes, their connection to the system was ripped apart—other times, they had simply fallen victim to system sickness. It wasn't uncommon. When a dungeon broke and the reality anchor maintaining it was destroyed, it could no longer maintain the system links that every person in the vicinity had. If that person didn't travel and relink to a new anchor . . .

Well, it was a moot point, because anyone who stayed put in the event of a dungeon break would die from the swarm of monsters, anyway.

Which made him think about those so-called monsters and what created them.

Mana overload. The system stripped away life and memory from all the mana it processed to keep itself running, to keep the reality anchors updated and stable. It gave them the information that they needed, but it was the equivalent of putting a living being through a form of torture. Of stripping away everything it had and leaving behind nothing but anger and resentment. It left behind an echo of mana overloaded with pain.

That echo of mana was what became monsters—or, in other words, the system's way of controlling the anger and the hatred it created through its methods. It generated these monsters using those lost in the Void as templates. They were, in a sense, the raw friction of mana struggling against the system. A byproduct of its design.

That was technically what Irvis had also been. A byproduct of all this accumulated friction—an Aspect that represented the anger of every single monster that had ever been created.

An Aspect that wanted nothing but destruction, including its own.

Some part of him almost felt like he was to blame for everything Irvis had done and for what they'd had to do to him. He hadn't designed the system, nor had he helped to build it—but he'd come in afterward. He'd had access to its inner workings, been able to learn about it.

It had taken him so long just to learn, and longer still to understand how to modify it. He'd tried more than once to alter that underlying mechanism for how the system processed mana, and he'd never succeeded.

His last attempt had been . . . well, it had been *this*. The Grand Anchors. They didn't rely on mana in the same way.

"I really hope they'll be enough," Sev said quietly.

It was one of the few fears he'd never voiced. It somehow felt okay to say it out loud here—the Void absorbed everything he had to say to the point where he could barely hear his own words.

Here, he could speak the words he felt he couldn't voice anywhere else.

The Prime Anchor shone beneath him. It was his guiding light, giving him direction and altitude in a plane of nothingness. Strings of power stretched upward from it, both into the Anderstahl dungeon and toward every reality anchor in the vicinity. It was like he was floating toward the center of a cobweb made out of pure metaphysical weight.

That cobweb was torn in places, though. The closer Sev got, the more he could see all the places where reality anchors had failed, leaving a gaping hole in the web. More than that, the thing at the very center of it—the Prime Anchor he was headed toward—was flickering and fading, like the source of its power was dying.

He could sense it trying to reach out into the divine plane, trying to hook into another god so it could consume it. That would repair it, for a time, just like mana crystals did: divine power was one way to simply override reality and command it to be whatever you wished.

And yet the more he watched, the more he thought the anchor was . . . reluctant. Like it was holding itself back. Waiting.

Sev slowed to a stop as he floated toward the Prime Anchor, and he stared at it for a moment, his expression contemplative. "You guys are supposed to be almost alive, aren't you?" he muttered, brushing a finger against it. It was a crystalline-looking thing, several times larger than a standard reality anchor—Sev knew from experience that within that crystal, spatially compressed, was a network of runic circuitry so complicated that a dozen magical experts would take multiple lifetimes to even begin to understand it.

Because the Prime Anchors, unlike the others, could grow. They could reroute and change their own programming into something that better suited the survival of reality. This one, for whatever reason, appeared to have decided it was best to preserve the divine plane, and it was suffering because of it. He saw the hairline cracks in the crystal.

It was on the verge of being irreparable. Not even days, like Muchen had estimated—this thing had *hours* left.

"I hope this helps," Sev finally said, retrieving the reality shards from his pocket. Not knowing what to do, he pressed them against the Prime Anchor, hoping against hope that it would know what to do. Misa's reality anchor certainly seemed capable of absorbing them just fine.

For a moment, nothing happened.

Then the crystalline anchor *rippled*. The reality shards fell out of Sev's hands, disappearing into the surface of the crystal like it was water. Sev watched as the hairline cracks healed, saw the Prime Anchor visibly *shudder*, like it was shaking itself awake. The cobweb of power around it flickered, then glowed a little brighter—

—and a system window popped up in front of Sev, startling him.

> **Integrity partially restored. Protective barrier removed. Query: Data indicates a large influx of sapients headed toward A-00. Confirm?**

Sev stared for a moment, speechless. How was he even supposed to respond? Verbally?

"Confirmed," he said. Whatever had happened with this Prime Anchor, it had clearly grown a little beyond the other two—or maybe it had *learned* from the destruction of the other two. Or something.

The window in front of him disappeared, and there was a slight pause. Then a new one popped into existence in front of him.

> **Warning: Increased load will increase rate of anchor degradation.**

"I know," Sev said grimly. "We don't have much choice. The other two Prime Anchors have already failed—you're the last one. At least, I'm assuming I'm talking to you right now."

There was no response.

"We're working on it," he said. "I need to get to the Vault after this, and then hopefully I can rig something together to use the Grand Anchors. Just ... try to hold it together in the meantime. Do you know how much longer we have once everyone's here?"

Another long pause. For a moment, Sev thought it wasn't going to respond to him at all, and he prepared to leave so he could avoid putting as much strain on Misa's reality anchor.

Then, finally, it responded.

> **At the current rate of degradation, complete failure will occur in 3 months, 7 days, 12 hours, and 14 seconds.**

"And at the increased rate of degradation?" Sev asked. "Assume all remaining sapients on the continent will be in the vicinity and that we keep feeding you with all the reality shards we have. How long can we keep them all safe?"

> **You will have 24 hours once all sapients are within the effective radius.**

The response was so direct and so immediate that Sev almost physically flinched away from the window; he waved a hand as if he could ward off the response with a physical gesture alone. "That can't be right," he said, fighting the panic rising in his voice. "We're supposed to have more time than that. Twenty-four— That's *one day*. That's barely any time!"

No response. Sev's mind raced. Twenty-four hours. But that timer started once everyone was in range of the Anderstahl Prime Anchor. Both the Elyran and the Enkiros refugees were headed toward Anderstahl, with the anchors behind them slowly collapsing and the dungeons breaking apart as they began to spin wildly out of control without that region's Prime Anchor holding them together.

The Elyran refugees were right at the edge—that was why they encountered the barrier. That barrier existed for the sole purpose of keeping them out so that the anchor didn't fail before he had time to repair it. Now that barrier was down, which meant that the Elyran refugees would soon cross that line, which would at minimum cut the time he had left in half.

"It's down to Enkiros," Sev muttered, mostly to himself. "The journey would take a few days at least, normally, but they're going to have to speed up depending on how fast the dungeons collapse around them. Need to figure out how much time they have since Enkiros was technically restored after being erased—"

> **There are 37 hours left before the complete collapse of all dungeons outside of Anderstahl.**

Sev froze at the unexpected answer.

That gave them a total of sixty-one hours. Marginally better than the twenty-four the Prime Anchor had first indicated, but not by much.

"I need to go get the Grand Anchor," Sev muttered. "Hey, listen, I don't know how . . . uh . . . alive you are. But thank you. And thanks for holding out for so long. We're gonna try to fix this."

There was no response, which left Sev feeling a little awkward. He shook it off quickly, though, and dove back toward the entrance to the Void, where Ixoryn and Tinsel were still waiting.

One last step before he reunited with Misa, Derivan, and Vex.

> **Congratulations on completing—**

> **You have been awarded with—**

The windows flickered past his vision, too fast for him to see. But he didn't miss the small black stone that appeared in his palm, or the item description window that popped up as he glanced at it.

> **Void Conduit**
> *Opens a portal to a location within the Void. A necessity for any adventurer.*

CHAPTER 43

REUNITED

Sev raced back toward the train, pocketing the stone. He'd think about it later. "We need to hurry," he said, pulling a startled Ixoryn and Tinsel with him. "Not much time left."

"Were you not repairing it for the express purpose of having time?" a perplexed Ixoryn asked.

"We had hours left when I repaired it. The estimations we had were off, and we didn't account for the increased load of refugees being offloaded onto the Anderstahl anchor," Sev said. He leapt into the cabin and searched around for the Conductor—there was no time to waste, no time to wait for him to show up. "Sixty-one hours. Give or take a bit. Misa's anchor is technically separate, but it's got the exact same issue—it's going to degrade faster and faster the more people it's supporting, and need even more reality shards to maintain it."

He ducked into the next cabin, which was also empty. He kept running. The Conductor always showed up through the same door toward the front of the train; he had to be in this direction somewhere. Maybe in the first cabin or something.

"Can you not offer it more of your—" Ixoryn began. He was keeping up with Sev, though he wasn't *running*; it was another one of those instances where he broke the laws of physics. Each step he took carried him farther without him having to run. Sev interrupted him before he could finish.

"I can't," Sev said. "Sixty-one hours is *with* us feeding it every last reality shard we have. I'm going to need to send someone here to keep it going as it is." Sev found the next door locked—he pounded on it with a fist, desperation fueling him. "Conductor! Are you there?"

The door in front of him slid open. The Conductor took him in and then came to an immediate conclusion. "Next destination," he guessed.

"Fast," Sev said. "Please."

The Conductor nodded. To his credit, he worked as quickly as he promised, in the sense that he *disappeared*, and then the train began to move; pretty soon, it was barreling through dirt and stone at ludicrous speeds once again. Sev collapsed into a nearby chair, exhausted, and Ixoryn and Tinsel sat opposite him, clearly concerned. The Conductor reappeared beside them a moment later.

"I hear we have little time left," he said without preamble. "We will arrive at the Vault in three minutes. Please hold on to ensure you do not get hurt."

Sev grabbed the table in front of him. Ixoryn reached out and grabbed Tinsel. The train sped up again and again, until the force of the table pressing into his chest made Sev certain it would leave a mark. The God of Navigation, on the other hand, was entirely unaffected—and Tinsel, likewise, was kept safe by him.

"I don't suppose this train can pick up my friends, too?" Sev asked. "They're outside Anderstahl. Big ask, I know."

"Not without straining the Prime Anchor even further," the Conductor said, which was . . . more or less what Sev expected. He winced—he'd have to rely on Blessings and Derivan's Shift to bring them here, then.

Three minutes. He used the time to perform his Blessing of Travel and to fire off a quick message to the rest of his party. They needed to meet up with him as soon as they could, so they could all bond with their respective Grand Anchors and just *fix things*.

The train jerked to a stop. "We are here," the Conductor said plainly, and Sev leapt to his feet, running for the entrance of the Vault. This one was protected by a keypad that was locked behind several layers of identification magic. Sev allowed it to identify him, typed in the ten-digit code, and stepped back as the doors to the Vault yawned open.

Then he ran in, grabbed the softly glowing Grand Anchor sitting on the pedestal in the center, and began to run back out—only for a portal to split the air in front of him. Sev nearly tripped over himself in his attempt to avoid running straight into Derivan as the armor stepped through the portal, followed shortly by Vex and Misa.

"You guys got here fast," he said, surprised.

"The Blessing is effective," Derivan said simply. The portal rippled shut behind him, its power spent—Sev could feel the faint threads of divinity on it fading away.

"You said we don't have much time left," Misa said, getting down to business. "How much time do we have?"

"Sixty-one hours," Sev said. "Give or take. Not a lot of time." He handed her the Grand Anchor he was still holding; it felt strange in his palms, like it wasn't quite suited for him. At the same time, Vex pulled out the third and final Grand Anchor and handed it to him.

Misa and Sev stood there, holding their respective anchors awkwardly.

"Vex," Sev said after a moment. "How did you merge with your anchor?"

"Uh . . ." Vex blinked, trying to think back to the moment it had happened. All he remembered was that he resonated with it—some strong sensation of being *aligned*, not only with the anchor itself but with the entity of mana as a whole. The mana wanted to restore the world too, after all; in another timeline, it *had*, even if its methods were flawed. "It connected with the part of me that loves magic and art. And I guess we both wanted the same thing? I remember how much I hoped bringing something back from the Void would work, and I remember feeling like the Grand Anchor wanted the same thing. Or that the mana did. And then it just . . . happened."

Misa frowned a bit, staring at the anchor she was holding. A small spark of understanding appeared in her eyes. She nodded once, and Sev watched as the Grand Anchor she held just . . . disintegrated.

A small shudder passed through Misa's frame. "There," she said. "I'm connected too. Actually, I think having a reality anchor tied to me already kind of helped. It just sort of merged with it. Sev?"

Sev concentrated on the Grand Anchor he held.

There *was* something about it that resonated with him. He could feel it. He'd forged a connection with so many gods at this point that he couldn't imagine *not* resonating with this anchor. But at the same time, there was something he felt like he was missing. Some small piece of understanding he didn't have.

He knew a lot of the gods. He was *friends* with a lot of them. He understood the framework for divine power, how reality was abundant with threads of divinity that could be claimed by any god, and how control over those threads granted a form of power that wasn't quite the same as what was granted by mana. On some level, it was reality manipulation—but unlike Shift, there was no source, no cause and effect. It was a simple alteration commanded into reality by a combination of willpower, imagination, and alignment with the god's domain.

But he still didn't really understand what all that *meant*.

The connection was there. He could feel it, almost like it was waiting to be formed—but he couldn't quite bridge the gap. He looked up helplessly at the others. "I'm . . . not sure," he said. "I can't—I can't connect with it. Derivan, maybe you should try."

Derivan tilted his head slightly. "I have neither the knowledge nor the connection with the divine planes that you do," he said, though he did accept the Grand Anchor from Sev. After a moment, he shook his head, passing it back. "Sev, perhaps—"

"We don't have time for me to figure it out," Sev insisted. "Maybe Ixoryn can do it. He's not far from here—he's the God of Navigation. I'll talk to him."

Derivan, Vex, and Misa all glanced at each other. "Navigation?" Misa asked hesitantly.

But Sev was already running.

This was *his* plan. He'd made these Grand Anchors, had pinned all his hopes on them—he didn't know what he'd do if it failed. It couldn't fail. If he couldn't connect with the Grand Anchor, then he'd have to figure it out, or someone else would have to connect with it.

And yet . . . something within him told him that he was the only one that *could* connect with it. That the connections he'd forged with so many different gods weren't easily replicated, and that those connections were what drew the Grand Anchor of Divinity to him. If he could just pass it on, he would—Velykos would be a good candidate, for example, considering the earth elemental had done an excellent job in reaching out to the gods and warning them in Sev's stead—but for better or worse, he was the one best suited for the anchor.

He dreaded the thought that he wouldn't be enough.

CHAPTER 44

THE LAST ANCHOR

Twenty-one hours had passed.

Sev and the rest of his party members were housed in a small building in Anderstahl—formerly a small industrial workshop, now converted into a temporary residence. It had originally been for the refugees, but Sev and several others had insisted on taking it and giving the refugees their beds in the Adventurers' Guild instead. No one argued with them. The people of Elyra had lost their homes, after all, and even though they'd escaped, that loss still hung heavily over them. The small bit of relief they felt over having a real bed to sleep in, a roof over their heads, and a *variety* of available food . . . well, it was worth a day or two in a glorified warehouse.

Ixoryn hadn't been able to help him, but he *had* confirmed that Sev was the only one who could even hope to link to the Grand Anchor. Velykos was the second closest, but he was far behind still. Years, according to Ixoryn. Sev's connections had been forged not only over this Reset but all the ones in the past, too. There was a small piece of him that *remembered*, and that memory forged a connection with the concept of Divinity itself that no one else truly had.

"Fuck," Sev said with a groan. His head thudded into the table in front of him. The Grand Anchor wobbled a bit with the impact, and he clutched at it before it could fall off the table.

Then he just stared at it again, trying to will it into merging with him. He could feel how close he was. He could almost feel that the anchor *wanted* to connect with him, even. But whatever piece he was missing, it was large enough that even their aligned desires weren't enough to bridge the gap.

He needed to understand Divinity, and the problem was that he didn't. He understood the gods. He understood their domains, even the nature of the relationships they had with the material world. But he didn't understand the underlying power that was *divinity*—not the same way Vex understood the mana, or the way Misa's skills and constant exploits helped her understand every layer of reality.

He'd tried speaking to Velykos, even. Enough time had passed now that the Elyran refugees had all made their way into Anderstahl, and the other branches of the Guild were slowly filtering in too. Velykos and his team had joined them in the warehouse, the small crew of skeletons citing that they didn't want to scare the Elyrans, and also that many of them simply weren't ready to face their friends and family again. Not when so much had changed about them.

They had been relieved, though, to know that the nobles of Elyra had been stripped of much of their power. It wouldn't stop those nobles from trying to regain that power, of course, but right now, they were all united in their desire to not be consumed by the Void.

Partly because the system had sent out warnings again. It told them exactly how much time they had left. This time, no one doubted it—they'd all seen it for themselves, after all. Sev was privately appreciative that it had given them the sixty-one-hour timer and not the three-month one. It hadn't gone out of its way to explain that their time would be greatly shortened by the arrival of refugees from Enkiros, either; he did *not* want to deal with a war breaking out because people wanted to squeeze out a week or two of extra time.

Especially since a war would only make the Prime Anchor deteriorate faster.

Though a week or two *would* have helped take some of the pressure off. Sev stared at the Grand Anchor in front of him again, as if just staring at it would somehow lead him to a breakthrough.

"Sev." Misa's voice was quiet. She sat down in front of him, all the usual cheer gone from her face—he saw only concern in there. Concern about *him*. "You need to take a break. You're not going to figure anything out just sitting there and staring at the anchor."

"I *can't*," Sev said. "We have— We have *forty hours left*, Misa. Forty hours! That's not even two days! If I sleep, then I'll only have thirty-two hours left, or even less if I oversleep, and I'm not going to be able to take a nap without oversleeping—"

"We'll wake you up," Misa said. "But you know as well as I do that bashing your head against this isn't going to make it any better."

"Maybe I *should*," Sev grumbled. He knew Misa was right, it was just . . .

There was so much at *stake*. What if the last minute was the one that he needed? Or the last second? If he spent even a single second doing anything else, who was to say it wouldn't be the second they needed to avoid doom for their entire world?

"I should sleep after," he said listlessly. "I *can* sleep after. I can't just take a *break*, Misa, the whole world is—"

"Do you even know what you're going to do after you connect to it?" Misa asked—not unkindly, although the words stung. "Do you know what *we* have to do? Because I've tried to use mine, and it's not exactly intuitive. I can't figure out how to restore things like Vex can."

"Vex can do that because he's anchoring the whole concept of Magic," Sev said. "Magic's supposed to be able to do the impossible. It's not the right use of the anchor at all, but he can strain it to do that."

"And what about Divinity?" Misa asked pointedly.

"I don't know." Sev thumped his head into the table again. "It does the impossible too, I guess. But in a different way. Magic has cause and effect, energy and expenditure. Divinity doesn't. Stuff just . . . happens. I mean, it uses up divine power, but not the same way magic uses up mana. If Magic's like a battery, then Divinity is like . . . I don't know, a bag. There's only so many things you can put into it at once, and you need to take something out before you can put in a new thing. Right now, the gods are doing everything they can to preserve themselves and the Prime Anchor. It's the reason I'm trying to minimize any divine magic I cast—because it'll necessarily lessen the power they have for *their* thing."

"Okay," Misa said patiently. "But that understanding isn't enough yet. I know you're feeling the pressure, but bear with me. Let's assume that it is. Let's assume that explaining that to me was the last step you needed to be able to connect with your Grand Anchor. Once you're connected, all three of us will have one. Then what?"

Sev groaned again. "If the point you're trying to make is that I have a lot more stuff to do even *after* connecting to the thing, I don't think that helps with the time pressure."

"The point I'm trying to make is that you're putting everything on your shoulders, and that's not what the reality of the situation is," Misa said, sighing; she spoke more gently than he was used to, and he folded inward a little at her tone of voice. "We're in this together, remember? You're not alone."

"I know," Sev said. "I—I know. It's just— There's so much relying on this. I don't know if I can sleep. Even if I wanted to. I keep thinking about everything—about what I might be missing about Divinity. Did you need to have some kind of realization about Reality? I know Vex's: magic is about art and expression. Mana is memory. It's a record of everything we've ever achieved, every moment of joy and beauty. But I don't know if Divinity is anything close to the same thing. Or what Reality is supposed to be."

Misa paused. "I don't think Reality is *like* the other two," she said. "It's not a force that requires understanding. It just is. It's the fundamental substrate of the universe. The bedrock. There's nothing *to* understand."

"Sounds like you understand it just fine, to me," Sev said with a little laugh.

Misa sounded a little embarrassed. "Maybe," she said. "I don't really think of it that way. But maybe you're right."

"It's that kind of insight that I'm missing about Divinity," Sev said. "Is it just the power of belief? That doesn't feel right. Or, I mean, it doesn't feel *complete*. It's something close, maybe. I don't know . . ."

He leaned back in his chair and sighed, gazing up at the ceiling. "You're probably right," he admitted. "I need to get some sleep. And maybe I'll figure something out in the morning."

"Get some food first," Misa said. "You can't go without eating, either."

"Yes, ma'am," Sev grumbled.

—⁓—

Forty hours had passed.

Three hours earlier, the refugees from Enkiros had entered the protective boundary of Anderstahl's Prime Anchor, along with every adventurer who had been out delving and trying to keep the dungeons stable. Xothok and the Guildmaster were back too, from what Sev had heard. Max, the guild clerk. Jerome and the partially recovered Elyran researcher—Kestel. Sev remembered the name, and he felt a pang of guilt for not being able to heal him. He'd brought him back, but between everything they'd learned and had to deal with . . .

Fortunately, the Adventurers' Guild had picked up the slack; from what he heard, Jerome had gone out to get the mana crystals Kestel needed to be healed himself. And that healing was going slowly but surely.

Sev had to admit he'd been impressed to see Jerome wheeling Kestel in. The lizardkin sat in a wheelchair, tail braced on a sort of plush hook Jerome wore around his waist so it didn't drag on the floor. They were chatting animatedly with one another, and Jerome even gave him a friendly wave when he saw him.

Not a hint of resentment.

"Hey, uh, this is gonna sound kinda weird," Jerome said once he was a little closer. "But . . . thanks for kicking my ass, I think? I kinda learned a lot. Because I was forced to. Which is annoying, but whatever."

"You're welcome, I think," Sev said dryly. Kestel seemed amused by the exchange—he lifted a hand to wave at Sev, and Sev nodded toward him, glad the lizardkin was doing better.

They spoke for a short while, and the two left afterward. Apparently, they'd only come to see and talk to them—and, to Sev's surprise, to offer him encouragement. Jerome didn't have any particular insights on the nature of divinity, but he seemed confident that Sev would get it.

Sev wished he felt that same confidence himself.

He wasn't any closer to connecting with the Grand Anchor, and the doubt in his heart was only growing. His friends never pressured him, but he could see the worry in their eyes, too. He didn't have another solution. All of reality rode on this. On whether or not he could figure out what he was missing.

And try as he might, for the life of him, he couldn't figure it out.

He'd spoken to the gods. To Aurum, to Tempus, to a few of the other ones he'd made friends with. He'd sat alone in his bed and said a small prayer to Onyx, hoping against hope that his first friend would find a way to respond to him and give him the insight that he needed.

Alas, there was nothing.

Forty-eight hours in, with exactly thirteen hours left, Jerome showed up again. His face was uncharacteristically serious.

"Hey," he said. Sev glanced up at him, his gaze questioning, and Jerome continued, "I was talking to Aurum. The time we have left—the thirteen hours—it's because Anderstahl's Prime Anchor has to support so many people?"

"Yes," Sev said. He didn't see any point in trying to hide it—not if Aurum had been the one to tell Jerome. "It's . . . It sucks. It's not a good situation."

"So if people leave, you're going to have more time?" Jerome pressed.

"We can't make people leave, Jerome," Sev said tiredly. "We can't—we can't choose who gets to live. I can't make that decision. You can't force people out. And fighting is just going to degrade the anchor even more."

Jerome gave him an affronted look. "What makes you think I was gonna make people leave?" he asked, and then he paused. ". . . Huh. I guess I would've done that a while back, huh?"

"You *weren't* going to?" Sev asked, blinking.

"No, I just . . ." Jerome trailed off. ". . . Listen. The level of the person leaving. It matters, right? Higher levels drain the thing more?"

"That should be how it works," Sev said cautiously. People with higher levels had more metaphysical weight to them; they drew the attention of the Void. Metaphorically speaking. They could *withstand* more of the Void, too, which was why the system worked to increase that weight. More stats, more weight, more resistance.

"Okay." Jerome took a deep breath, looking a little uncomfortable, and then finally he shook his head. "Don't worry; I'm not going to make anyone leave. Thanks for letting me know. Try to get this thing working, yeah?"

"Believe me, I've been trying," Sev grumbled. ". . . Thanks, Jerome."

Jerome gave him a thumbs-up before leaving, and Sev wondered what that had all been about.

Hopefully Jerome wasn't about to do something stupid.

CHAPTER 45

MORE TIME NEEDED

There was one hour left, and Sev didn't feel like he was any closer.

Derivan, Vex, and Misa had all left the building to try to help calm people's nerves and to see if there was anything they could do to make this bit of reality last longer. Vex and Misa were trying to channel their Grand Anchors into *something*, even if they were missing the key piece of Divinity—and even though Sev knew those anchors didn't quite work like that, he couldn't bring himself to stop them.

After all, they'd pulled off the impossible before.

Just . . . what was he *missing*?

Before he could think on it further, there was a knock on the door, and Jerome strode into the room once again. He spoke before Sev could get a word in edgewise. "I'm going to leave. It might give you a bit more time."

"Wait, what?" Sev asked, alarmed. He stood from the table, nearly knocking the Grand Anchor off of it—it was Jerome that reached out to steady it, actually. The paladin caught Sev's arm a second later, his expression perfectly serious. Sev still tried to protest. "You can't just—"

"I have to do it now," Jerome said. "If I wait, it's just going to be worse, right? It'll give you even less time. I just . . . wanted to make sure. You know. That it would work. That's why I asked."

"Jerome," Sev said. There was a rising panic in him, and try as he might, he couldn't quite seem to stop it. "Jerome, don't—we still have time. You can't—"

"I think I gotta," Jerome said, shrugging. "Look, you guys have brought people back from the Void before, right? It doesn't have to be permanent."

"Jerome, if you get erased, we aren't even going to *remember* you." Sev swallowed. "Misa's been protecting us against that, but we're in the final stages of collapse. The anchors are barely working to maintain what's here, let alone keep our memories perfectly intact."

"System," Jerome said. "If I leave, how much extra time is Sev gonna get?"

"The system doesn't just respond to people like that," Sev began, although even as he said it, he realized it wasn't true. Whatever was going on with Anderstahl's Prime Anchor, it had been able to use the system to do exactly that.

As if to emphasize that point, the system window that popped up was visible to *both* of them.

Offloaded weight will allow anchor integrity to remain stable for an additional 3 hours.

"Three hours sounds like a lot of time," Jerome said. "Three times more than what we have right now."

"I might not even need that amount of time!" Sev said, trying not to raise his voice too much—he was clutching at the table, his fingers digging into the grain of the wood. "I might figure it out in the next hour. I don't want you to sacrifice yourself for nothing."

But there was more he had to do even if he *did* figure it out, a traitorous voice whispered inside of him. Jerome considered this for a moment. Then he shrugged.

"You know, before I met you guys, I didn't really care about anyone else," he said. "I mean, I wanted to be a good guy. That's why I wanted to protect Aurum and stuff. But thinking about other people wasn't really a default for me. Now it is, and I gotta say, it kinda fucking sucks.

"But I also wouldn't go back. Can't go back, but even if you gave me the choice . . . I'm way happier this way. Weird paradox." Jerome paused. "I guess my point is that I'm gonna do this, and if you don't remember me, that's okay. It's probably better if you don't blame yourself or anything."

"Jerome—"

"Nah, I'm doing it," Jerome said. "I've thought about it. We've got an hour left. If I'm gonna do it, it's now or never. Any later and you'll probably just get an extra minute or something. So . . . I'm choosing now. All right?"

Sev closed his eyes. ". . . Thank you."

When he opened them again, the paladin was gone.

—✸—

Fifty minutes left. Jerome hadn't made it to the Anderstahl border yet, evidently, and Sev was desperately trying to figure out this last piece he needed before that happened. His eyes burned. The table below him was wet.

Why was this last piece so hard to *get*?

Sev glanced at the timer on the system. Three hours and fifty minutes.

Time was running out.

—⚬—

Thirty minutes.

Velykos strode into the makeshift home, his steps weary and ponderous. The earth elemental observed Sev for a moment. "You have not made progress," he said.

"I don't know what I'm missing," Sev said quietly. There was an ache to his eyes, though he didn't know why. Maybe it was because he'd been staring for so long. He didn't dare to take his eyes off the Grand Anchor.

"You will," Velykos said with a confidence Sev didn't feel. The human felt solid rock against his shoulder and glanced up, surprised, to see Velykos offering him a warm smile.

He walked back out. Sev saw the skeleton crew following after Velykos, saw the giant elemental bend down and hug each and every one of them slowly, with a care that belied his size.

It . . . it looked like a goodbye. Why did it look like a goodbye?

Sev's eyes burned again. He stared back down at the Grand Anchor, reached for the connection he shared with the gods to give him comfort. Thirty of them, all tied to him, all with different domains. He'd spoken to each of them and gotten to know them even in the limited time he'd had.

Belief. Divinity had something to do with belief. But that answer alone wasn't complete.

What was it he was missing?

He glanced at the timer. Two hours and thirty minutes.

Not much time left.

—⚬—

Fifteen minutes.

"Hey, Sev!"

Sev looked up tiredly, then blinked. "Max?" he asked, unsure. He didn't know how long he'd been awake, at this point. If Misa hadn't made him get some rest earlier, he would've fallen asleep already.

Max grinned at him, the receptionist her usual bright and cheery self, despite the circumstances. "Are you asking me if that's my name?" she teased. "Because you should know my name. Don't tell me you've forgotten me already."

"I haven't," Sev said. "Why are you—"

"I just wanted to drop in and give you some encouragement," Max said. She swept forward, pulled him into a hug he didn't expect, and he found himself automatically hugging back. He found himself shaking. He was . . . more emotional than he expected himself to be, and it wasn't just from the stress. "I think you need some. I should know."

"Because you're always in the right place?" Sev asked, smiling weakly.

"And at the right time." Max winked. "You'll do great, Sev. I trust you. And I'm counting on you, okay?"

"I know you are," Sev said. "I just . . ."

"Not like that," Max said. She shook her head. "Eh, don't worry about it. You'll get it. I won't keep distracting you."

She smiled at him and ran back out of the warehouse. Sev shook his head, then glanced back to the anchor and to the timer above it.

One hour and thirty minutes left.

—⟨∞⟩—

Sev lost track of time. He was trying not to even look at the timer anymore. The sight of it alone made bile rise up in his chest, and he didn't know *why*. It wasn't purely because he was stressed—there was something else to it, an ache he didn't quite understand nor could name.

He'd felt that feeling before, though he didn't know where. It made a knot of dread tighten in his stomach.

Xothok and the Guildmaster were the next ones to arrive strode up through the door. They were holding hands. Sev blinked at the sight. When had that happened?

"Fuck you," Xothok said eloquently. The Guildmaster—Alyssa?— elbowed him, and he sighed. "And thank you. You and your friends."

"I . . . What?" Sev asked, perplexed—but Xothok was already walking out, hand lifted in a wave.

"Alyssa says I have to find your friends and thank them, too," Xothok called back. "Good luck with that Grand Anchor shit. Glad I ain't the one dealing with that." A little softer, but still loud enough that Sev could hear it, he added, "We're counting on ya."

"What'd I tell you?" the Guildmaster said. Her voice faded as they walked farther into the distance, but Sev could still hear them—maybe because the rest of Anderstahl was . . . surprisingly quiet. Like a city holding its breath. "It's not *that* hard to say thanks."

"The fuck it isn't," Xothok grumbled. "And just because I've got [**Navigator**] skills doesn't mean you can use me to find whatever you want."

"You're complaining a lot for someone who does it anyway."

"Yeah, well . . ." Xothok grumbled under his breath even as the sound faded away from Sev's ears. His mind drifted back to how *quiet* the city was. Even this warehouse should have been full of adventurers, and it . . . wasn't. Something about that unsettled him: there were more beds here than there were people.

But he didn't remember there being more people here. Just him, Vex, Derivan, and Misa.

CHAPTER 46

AND THEN THERE WAS ONE

Derivan, Vex, and Misa sat just outside the warehouse Sev was in.

The ground crumbled away in front of them. Their legs dangled off a sheer cliff that dropped down into nothingness, dangerously close to the Void. Vex leaned into Derivan's side, and Derivan wrapped an arm around his boyfriend's shoulders, marveling at the feeling of having someone care about him in such a manner. Of caring *for* someone in such a manner.

He hadn't really ever considered it, not even as he and Vex got closer and closer in their adventures together. Oh, he'd certainly noticed that the lizard-kin's gaze would linger on him, especially if he thought Derivan wasn't paying attention—but he'd initially assumed that to be a matter of discomfort with the fact that he never took off his armor.

Then he'd revealed himself to them—told them what he was. He'd been forced to reveal his true nature as part of what he needed to do to protect his friends. Derivan remembered that small, foreign piece of himself that screamed at him to defend himself from those who knew what he was. The piece that had been inserted into his soul by the system.

Strange, now, how they were now relying on that very same system to keep them all alive.

Not that there were many left *for* the system to keep alive.

But if he had to face the end of the universe with anyone, he was glad it was with these adventurers he'd come to call his friends. His family, even. The relationship he'd developed with Vex was the most precious of all his memories: he'd never believed that he could form a bond so close with someone so different.

Partly because even after all that time, there was a part of him that had thought of himself as a monster. But when he was with Vex, that part of him was just . . . silent.

But he wasn't, he'd learned. He'd been a part of a whole people—the Scimitars—and one of them had even forged him a new arm.

Gallant had chosen to leave the protective boundary willingly, along with many others, when the Guildmaster made the announcement. Others were simply consumed by the Void as the "safe" land grew smaller and smaller. The Prime Anchor was trying to hold things together, even after the timer expired. The gods were all focused on supporting it, on lending the essence of their very selves to the Prime Anchor.

"If this is the end," Derivan said, "I am glad to be with you all."

"Oh, come on." Misa snorted. "Don't say that. We're going to figure it out. We always do."

"Derivan's right, though," Vex said quietly. He seemed a little lost in thought, staring out into the nothingness as if there was an answer that could be gleaned from it. Derivan glanced down fondly as the lizardkin eventually just leaned into him again, placing his head in Derivan's lap. He stroked his fingers down through Vex's frills and over his scales. "I'm still glad I met you guys. No matter what."

"We should probably go talk to Sev soon." Misa sighed, glancing back at the door to the warehouse. "Not really looking forward to it. So much shit I want to say but can't."

"We're trusting what Ixoryn said, right?" Vex asked.

"Not just Ixoryn." Misa glanced back down. "Mom, too. Everyone with a precognitive or an intuitive skill, every god that's supposed to be able to predict the future—this is all that gives us even a sliver of a chance. Divinity can do things both Magic and Reality can't."

"And we're okay with this," Vex said. It wasn't really a question. He just looked . . . sad. Derivan hummed a soft song, hand tracing small circles on Vex's back in a gesture of attempted comfort.

"I am," Derivan said. "But this will not be my first time in the Void."

"What am I gonna do, leave you two to do it alone?" Misa snorted.

"Just checking." Vex smiled faintly. "Let's go talk to him. Don't really think we have much time left."

"How much time will we give him, do you think?" Misa asked.

Derivan glanced back out into the Void and considered his response.

"Enough," he said. "And that is all that matters."

—⁜—

Sev stared at the orb glowing on the table in front of him.

For some reason, he was having trouble remembering what he was supposed to do with it. He knew it was important. He knew there was something about it that was *critically* important, and that it had something to do with him. With a task that only he could do.

He knew his heart ached and his face hurt. The table in front of him was wet.

Sev reached out, brushing his fingers over a material that wasn't quite glass.

What is Divinity?

The question came to him unbidden, but he clung to it. It grounded him. He wanted to answer that question. *Needed* to answer that question. It was his job, his duty.

Right. The Grand Anchor. I have to connect with it. It'll save … things. Important things.

Darkness closed in around him, the Void trickling in through the walls and the floor. There was so little of reality left.

There was no one left who could help. No one else who could assume the responsibility of connecting to the Grand Anchor.

After all, this was all that was left: a small slice of reality, and a human clutching an invention he couldn't understand.

CHAPTER 47

NOTHING

...

CHAPTER 48

TO REMEMBER

Sev's mind caught on a thought he'd had a moment before. He struggled to pull it back.

There was no one left to assume the responsibility of connecting to the Grand Anchor. No one but him.

Responsibility.

The Grand Anchor grew warm in his arms. The area around him, so small it had begun to press into and erode his very existence, began to widen once again.

That was the piece he'd been missing. It was the small bit of understanding that had eluded him, time and time again, because—because a part of him had kept on hoping that someone else would figure it out. That someone else would be able to connect to the Grand Anchor.

He'd assumed a lot of responsibility in trying to save the universe, but he'd only done it because he was the only one left, and on some level . . . he didn't quite believe he could do it. He believed in everyone else—in Misa, in Derivan, in Vex—and he believed that they'd be able to find a solution where he could not.

What is Divinity?

Divinity was a form of power that operated through the domains of the gods. To cast a divine spell was to lay claim to all the divine threads he needed to and to assert his authority over anyone else that might use them.

To assume responsibility for those threads, in other words.

Each and every one of the gods was responsible for their own domains, for every priest and cleric and paladin that chose to worship them.

And he . . .

He was responsible for his team.

They weren't here. He'd forgotten them. They'd stepped away, allowed themselves to be taken by the Void—a thought that made horror curl up in his heart.

Unbidden, a memory that should no longer have existed rose, flickering with the warmth of Divinity.

They hadn't done it without speaking to him first.

—⟋⟍—

"Hey, Sev." Misa smiled a small smile as she stepped into the warehouse. Derivan and Vex were behind her, holding hands; they wore the same expression, a small hint of a smile but too much sadness in their eyes. "Things going okay in here?"

"No," Sev answered. He fell silent. What else was there to say?

Derivan, Vex, and Misa all glanced at each other—they didn't seem to know what to say either. Misa came forward and placed one of her hands over Sev's own, and he flinched and moved it away; she didn't try it again, though she looked at him with concern.

"I don't know," Sev said, answering the unspoken question. "I think . . . comfort isn't what I want right now."

"Because you feel like you shouldn't have any?"

"Yes." It just made him feel worse.

Misa watched him silently, trying to find the words. It was Vex that piped up next, to his surprise. "I don't suppose it would make you feel better if we said it was okay if it doesn't work?"

Sev laughed at that—and it was a genuine laugh, too, despite himself. Not bitter, not pained. "No," he said. "I don't think I could believe that even if I wanted to. But . . . thank you. For the sentiment."

"I grew up with a lot of expectations on me," Vex said. "It's like walking around with weights tied around your ankles."

"That sounds about right," Sev agreed. There was a weight on his shoulders here, and it felt like it was pressing down on him with every second that passed.

"I don't really know if there's anything I can say that would help," Vex admitted. "I had to figure out which expectations were my own and which ones were just my parents'. I did figure it out. Eventually. It's not that I walk around without weights now. But the weights I have are the ones I've chosen. Like hanging out with you guys!"

Sev found himself smiling, in spite of himself. "I love you all, you know," he said. "Platonically."

Misa snorted. "You didn't need to clarify that," she said, amused.

"It was funnier if I did." He smirked a little, then glanced back to the orb in front of him, his humor falling away. "… What would you guys do, in my position? Would you really think it's okay if it doesn't work?"

"I do not think it is in your heart to believe that," Derivan said.

"Yeah," Sev said. He picked up the Grand Anchor, examined the softly glowing inner core. He couldn't really remember how he'd built this. "You're right. It's not."

"There are many people that believe in you," Derivan said. He examined Sev for a moment. "But there is one that does not."

Sev glanced up at Derivan. "I know what you're going to say."

"Then do you need me to say it?"

"… No."

—✺—

He knew the answer. Even after all this time, there was a part of him that didn't believe in himself.

Even his main method of healing for the longest time … it involved self-sacrifice. It was powerful, but he'd never looked for another solution. Another method. Another skill. He kept it in the back of his mind, like a button he could press to sacrifice himself if needed for somebody else.

It had been easy to throw a part of himself away like that. Easier than believing he could find another solution. But he *had* been able to do it—both with the Soulblossom and with Ixoryn himself, in the Anderstahl dungeon. The one time he hadn't even considered that he might not be able to do it. The one time it hadn't occurred to him to not believe in himself.

Belief. But not only in the gods.

The second part of the equation to Divinity.

The Grand Anchor grew even warmer in his hands, sparking another memory. The Void receded yet again.

—✺—

"You can't leave." Sev's breath caught in his throat—he felt like a child again, begging not to be left behind. Fuck. The memory was too familiar. He felt like he'd been through it a dozen times before. Echoes of the past lodged in his throat and burned his eyes, and he struggled to see, to speak. His mind raced for anything he might be able to say that would convince them to stay—

But warmth enveloped him. It took a moment before he recognized it as Misa, and a moment longer before he realized both Vex and Derivan had joined in.

Sev had lost more than he could remember at this point. Every Reset, he gathered a team that slowly became family to him. Every Reset, he lost that team—lost his memories of what they meant to him. He'd met some of them again this Reset, even. Aneryn, the shadow elemental and battlemage dying in Vex's bonus room . . . he'd saved him, the last Reset, though at no small cost. Sylix, the Platinum-ranker fighting under the name of Illyr, who lost his brother to a powerful illusory skill he hadn't known how to control at the time.

More still that he could no longer remember.

He cried. He couldn't help it. They were the last ones left. This was the last Reset, the last try, the last family he'd been able to make ever since coming to Obreve.

"How did you do it?" he asked Misa quietly. She'd experienced just as much loss as he had. She'd regained her family, sure, but for years, she'd dealt with the thought that her family, her entire village was completely gone. And she'd been lost in the rage and pain of that knowledge until she found herself again.

Misa closed her eyes. She seemed to understand the question, even without him explaining. "Honestly?" she said. "I just didn't have any other choice. Sometimes, that's what it takes."

"Not very encouraging." Sev chuckled, though the sound was small and broken. Misa just smiled a sad smile.

"Not everything is," she said.

—⚭—

That was where he was now—with no choices left to him, no one else left to help. Misa had said they were all in this together, but they were gone now.

But they'd left for him. To give him more time. And so had everyone else, though some in Anderstahl had likely simply been lost as the Prime Anchor chose what it needed to keep safe.

The other two Grand Anchors were somewhere in the Void now. But if he was right . . .

No one had left him. Not really. Not if they'd done this *for* him, because they had faith in him. Because they believed in him.

It was all a matter of perspective.

Perspective and connection.

The warmth of the Grand Anchor grew until its physical vessel shattered; Sev felt something in his soul respond, reaching out in tandem, and at the same time—

You have merged with [Grand Anchor—Divinity].

The realm of the divine was the realm of perspective. Every domain was different, and every god viewed the world through a different lens. It was through that difference in perspective that they assumed responsibility for each of their domains, and it was through their connections with the material plane and the people who followed them that they could affect that material plane.

There was a reason those divine threads appeared as *threads*, after all. As a symbol of connection.

And knowing that let him grasp the last piece he needed: a change in perspective, imprinted onto reality. He tugged on all the connections he'd ever had, all the connections he'd ever made.

It wasn't about leaving. It was about giving me time because they had faith in me. In a way, they're all still here with me. Each and every one of them.

They're my responsibility now. I won't let them down.

Divine power flooded out of him with shocking force. He wasn't just using what was already there, like ordinary divine magic—he was *generating more*, the Grand Anchor within him doing exactly what it was meant to do. There was a momentary strain with his soul, but he almost didn't even feel it, he was so lost in the rush.

If reality wasn't so broken and the divine planes weren't so drained, this would almost certainly have been an Ascension. Power kept pouring out of him, and it was so bright, he couldn't even see. All he knew was that he was bringing his perspective into reality.

No one ever left.

Sev only noticed anything was different when cool glass touched his lips, and Sev blinked to see the light fading and Misa standing there, feeding him a vial of Soulbloom potion.

At the sea of people standing past her. Derivan and Vex were the first and closest, but he saw everyone else behind them—Jerome, Velykos, Max, Xothok, all the members of Vex's family, all the members of Misa's—

Vex's hand caught his own, even as Misa held him.

"We're not done yet," he said firmly.

Reality stabilized every one of them as Misa's Grand Anchor got to work. Magic poured out of Vex, and his [**Spelldisk**] caught the brunt of it—Sev saw the connections Vex was pulling on. He wasn't just bringing back everyone that had been lost this Reset.

He was bringing back *everyone*.

Sev reinforced what Vex was doing with his Divinity, helping the magic seek out connections that were nearly entirely gone. All he needed was the smallest remnant—a loose divine thread connecting what *was* to what *had been*. No continent, no corner of Obreve, no *timeline* was barred to them.

Aneryn came back, blinking into existence. All the Scimitars—all of Derivan's people. Clyde and Belle and Elliot, the three shadow elementals they'd grown close to in their time in Mundane.

"No one left behind," Sev said.

Reality flooded out from Misa, turning the blank Void they were in into stable flooring. Magic poured out of Vex, restoring memory and culture and everything that had been lost. Divinity tied everyone together, powered by Sev's perspective and his new sense of responsibility, anchoring them to this new half-reality they had created as shelter from the Void—

Until they tried to bring back *more*, and a sharp pain lanced through all three of them. Sev collapsed to his knees, wincing, and Derivan spoke up, concerned. "You cannot keep going," he said. "The strain on your souls—we do not have enough Soulbloom potions. And we cannot make more."

Sev, Misa, and Vex glanced at one another.

"You're right," Sev said. "We've brought back all the people. That's going to have to be enough."

"What, you want to have a whole world's worth of people just living in a mostly empty Void?" Misa asked, frowning.

"No," Sev said. He brought out the [**Void Conduit**] Anderstahl's Prime Anchor had rewarded him, staring at it—thinking about the memory Ixoryn had forced him to remember.

He'd built *something*. A last resort. But that last resort wasn't about saving the world.

"Derivan," he said. "I think I have something for you."

Derivan looked down at the stone, uncertain. "What is it?" he asked.

"Something that will bring us somewhere important," Sev said.

He crushed the stone.

CHAPTER 49

CHARACTER ARK

Click.

Derivan watched curiously as they were brought to a new place within the Void. There was nothing here, technically—nothing except a small pedestal built into the ground. Not that there was any ground here either. A visible gear poked out of a slot on the pedestal, *clicking* periodically as some sort of internal mechanism shifted within and caused it to rotate.

Or Shifted within. He could feel it, the subtle changes in reality as it moved through one layer to another.

"What is it?" he asked.

Sev walked up to it, brushing his fingers over the grooves in the matte-metallic surface, then over to the gear. He pulled his fingers back before they could get caught in the next *click*, then sighed. "Hard to describe," he said. "I'm not sure I knew what I was doing when I was building this. I think I was desperate. Scared."

". . . It's not going to attack us, is it?" Misa asked, lifting her mace warily and eyeing the pedestal as if it was going to attack them. Sev snorted.

"No," he said. Then he paused, considering the question. "Well . . ."

"Sev," Misa warned.

"No, I'm just kidding," he said, a ghost of a smile crossing his expression. "It's harmless. It's basically . . . it's one of those things I made because I didn't trust myself. It's basically a computer."

"The hell's a computer?" Misa frowned.

"It's . . . Anderstahl tech, isn't it?" Vex asked, eyeing the pedestal. "It doesn't look like anything I've seen in the books, though."

"It wouldn't," Sev said. "It's made to hook into the system and use it as a display, though I'm willing to bet most of that functionality's been degraded by now."

"It has," Derivan confirmed. He felt around with Patch—he could feel where the pedestal was *supposed* to connect to the system, only those connections had been frayed and eroded. The only thing was . . . "It is recent, however."

"Recent?" Sev's brows furrowed, puzzled. "I would've expected it to break ages ago."

"It appears that the Prime Anchor was able to connect to it," Derivan said. He could feel the remnants of that connection, frayed though they were. Sev had built it to attach to the nearest living person's system—but evidently, the Prime Anchor had managed to reach out to it on its own.

". . . Huh. I guess that would explain a lot." Sev frowned in thought. "It's supposed to be a possibility engine. Searches through everything that's possible, makes an informed guess on what our best options are. Makes sense that the Anderstahl Prime Anchor was so . . . intentional about things."

Derivan's eyes widened slightly within his helmet. Every *click* of the gear gave him a strange, fuzzy feeling through the Shift stat. He'd assumed it was just an artifact of their presence in the Void, and that each Shift he felt within the pedestal was just the movement of the "computer" going from one layer of reality to the next.

But no. Now that Sev had explained it, he understood the feeling.

It wasn't moving through one layer of reality. It was moving through hundreds of thousands of them. Sorting through infinite possibilities.

"I gave up on it because . . . well, it was kind of a flawed concept," Sev admitted. Derivan noted that despite his words, he didn't seem like he'd given up hope—on the contrary, he seemed animated and energetic.

Which he was glad for, Derivan admitted to himself. Sev's difficulties with leadership hadn't gone unnoticed, but it seemed like he was finally embracing the role.

"The system already does what this thing does," Sev continued. "It just doesn't look as far as this can. The farther you try to Shift, the more expensive it is—I'm sure you've noticed this, Derivan."

"It takes more power to Shift farther away," Derivan agreed. "The divine planes are near-impossible to reach, though I feel I might be able to reach them if I were to pull sufficient power from the Slime stat."

Sev stared at him for a moment. ". . . Okay, we'll unpack that later," he decided, muttering something to himself about the absurdities his friends were capable of. "Actually, it might be helpful. This thing searches possibilities too far away from baseline reality for the system to be able to Shift it into being. I was going to suggest combining your capabilities with the system's, but the Prime Anchor is barely functional right now."

"There is a possibility you wish to Shift into reality?" Derivan questioned. He rarely used the stat in that particular way—not the way the system did it, anyway.

"Yes." Sev nodded. "I'm going to need you to connect our systems to this thing so we can search for it, and then I need you to bring it *here*. Or, well, not here—back where everyone else is."

"You wanna tell us what the plan is?" Misa said, raising an eyebrow. "Because it sounds like you've got a plan."

"I do." Sev's expression settled into something serious, and he took a deep breath. "We're not going to bring back all of Obreve like this. We could try to just bring back the dungeon—enough for us to be able to harvest more Soulblooms—but I felt how much it was straining our anchors just to maintain that amount of land."

"I did, too," Misa said, frowning.

"It's too much," Vex said. "We could maybe maintain Anderstahl if we pushed it, but Anderstahl can't handle the amount of people we've brought back, and . . . it'd be a small world."

"Right," Sev said. "We're not going to make everyone live in a world with one city and a few plains outside of it. I hate to say it, but Obreve is dead. I don't think there was ever a way to bring it back. Not to what we had before. So we're not going to try."

"What do you want to do instead?" Vex asked.

"Go somewhere new." Sev shrugged. "This isn't the only universe out there. We've been trying to save the world, but it's like you said to the king of Enkiros, Vex—it's not the world that's important. It's the people."

Misa was silent for a moment. "You want us to leave Obreve behind," she said. There was something sad in her voice, and yet . . . she didn't argue.

Neither did Vex. "Where are we going to go?" he asked softly.

"That's where you come in," Sev said, glancing to Derivan, who had remained silent until now. Derivan inclined his head in a slight nod— whatever Sev needed, he was ready. "If you can get this connected with our systems, we'll be able to get it to start a new search. I want you to find something that will bring us to a new universe, Derivan. All of us. And I want you to choose that universe."

"Me?" Derivan blinked, the lights in his helmet flickering.

"I should have made a fourth Grand Anchor," Sev said. "I think I would've named it the Grand Anchor of Life. It would've been perfect for you."

"But I am . . ." *Not alive,* he wanted to say. Not in the traditional sense, anyway. Sev shook his head before he could finish.

"You've spent your entire life trying to understand us," Sev said. "Trying to understand people that are fundamentally very different from you. You have an entire stat that defines it as a part of who you are as a person." He gestured broadly, as if pointing to all the different forms of life they'd met thus far—and they *had* met a variety of different life forms, from elemental beings to organic creatures to magical entities to living concepts. "This computer can help us find a layer of reality where someone's invented something that will take us to a new universe. We'll probably have to keep it stable with our Grand Anchors. But we need someone to find a universe that can accommodate all of us, and the rest of us grew up with all manner of preconceptions and biases about life. You, Derivan? You didn't."

"I . . . did not." He'd always been curious about the different forms of life. He remembered how fascinated he was by the world the first time he'd been allowed out of his dungeon. "I am willing. But how will we do this?"

Sev shrugged and glanced at the pedestal again. "Let's find out," he said.

Derivan nodded, reached out with Patch, and made the connection. Sev tapped into his system interface, glancing back occasionally at the others; Derivan sensed that he was privately making sure they were all still there, that all this was *real*.

He offered Sev a small smile, and the priest seemed grateful for it. He tapped in a final command.

Click.

Click.

Click.

Clickclickclickclick—

"Found it," Sev said at the same time Derivan *felt* the possibility blooming within this . . . "computer." It was a large one, but it was surprisingly distant—there were countless realities where they tried to save the world they were in and failed, and far fewer where they had simply tried to *leave*. More than that, in many of the ones where they tried to leave, they *failed*.

But there *was* one where they succeeded in building something that could traverse the Void.

"Can you bring it here?" Sev asked.

"Yes," Derivan said, with more confidence than he felt. Vex's hand wrapped around his own. "I can."

Slimes in Obreve were essentially cultivators of mana. His growth of that stat had meant much the same thing—he now had a mana pool rivaling Vex's. And while Shift didn't necessarily draw on his mana pool, he *was* fundamentally a being that was only alive thanks to mana-driven enchantments engraved within his armor; the energy it pulled from him came from the same source.

Alone, he wasn't that confident. But with Vex's help . . .

"Let's get back to the others, first," Derivan said.

Misa reached out and offered him a bit of Reality, and he used it to Shift a portal into existence. The four of them stepped through. All of Obreve was milling about on an empty plane of land—Derivan was almost surprised that no fighting had broken out yet, but he supposed the rather chilling reality of the situation was enough to make most people focus.

He ignored them for now, focusing instead on the spark within himself that allowed him to see between the layers of reality and pull them into focus. He borrowed from that power within himself, fed it all the mana he had, and felt Vex's strength flow into him.

He found the layer of reality that matched what he'd felt and then performed his largest Shift yet.

A massive ship slipped into existence, hovering just above them. It was made of gleaming metal, with massive sails that would've blocked out the sun if they still had one.

Misa stared.

"Seriously?" she said. "That's . . . that's just a really big boat."

Before Derivan could respond, however, all three of them—Sev, Vex, and Misa—staggered. Misa in particular winced, her breathing heavy. "Holy shit, never mind. Guess that's not just a boat. That thing is *heavy*. Metaphorically speaking. It's weighing on my Anchor."

"We can handle it," Sev said. "But I think I might've been wrong about us being able to maintain Anderstahl. That's . . . This is probably going to be our limit."

"We could try to get a soulbloom garden going on the ship," Vex suggested. "I think we're going to need one."

Sev winced again, then nodded. "You're probably right about that," he agreed. "Tinsel should be around here somewhere. I really hope it saved some soulbloom seeds . . ."

He sighed, then began to walk forward, toward the ship. "But first, let's get everyone on the boat," he said. "It's going to be a long day."

Derivan followed, his mind already lingering on the choice he would have to make. He would have to find them a new universe to live in.

What an interesting thought.

CHAPTER 50

NEW BEGINNINGS

No one really knew how long the journey ahead of them would be. The best they could do was take that journey one step at a time—even as that one step became a hundred, and a hundred steps became a thousand.

What they were trying to do had never been done before. It wasn't just that they had to cross the gap between realities with nothing more than an admittedly massive ship. It was the fact that they had to manage dozens of clashing cultures and species, from mundane ones to gods and demons and angels. It was the fact that they had to navigate through the wrecked ruins of realities not their own.

It was the fact that every single person that boarded that ship still had to contend with the idea that their home was gone, and that they would never see it again.

None of those facts stopped them, of course. It was nothing the Guild hadn't dealt with before, and while the *scale* of the problem was far larger than it ever had been . . .

—〰—

It wasn't long before the Guildmaster showed up, Max by her side and Xothok . . . pretending to be aloof in the distance? Sev eyed him curiously, wondering what was up with him.

"Guessing you guys have a plan?" Alyssa asked. "And I'm guessing you're going to need our help."

"Would be nice," Sev said, grinning at her. "Even with help, it's going to take a while."

"You'd be surprised how good we've gotten at logistics," Alyssa said. "Especially with Xothok here finding us the best path. Speaking of which: is that boat for what I *think* it's for?"

"We're evacuating this universe," Sev confirmed. "We can't fix Obreve. This universe is . . . it died a long time ago, and we can't keep bringing it back. We have to move on." He glanced around and gestured around them. "We've saved the people. It'll have to be enough."

Alyssa nodded, approving. "I would've done the same," she said. "Though I don't think it's going to be quite so easy for a lot of people."

"Easy for you, though?" Sev raised an eyebrow at her. Alyssa shrugged and smiled.

"The Guild is my home," she said. "It's the home I built for myself. And it's coming with us, isn't it?"

Sev glanced back to Derivan, Vex, and Misa. "Yeah," he said, smiling. "I think I feel the same way."

—⁂—

Everything was ready.

Getting everyone onto the boat had been . . . a process. Without the use of skills and magic, it probably would have taken them weeks. *With* those things, and with the help of a little bit of divine magic, it "only" took them a couple of days.

Sev was exhausted at the end of it all, but he was happy. The ship supported a few farms, important cultural artifacts and touchstones that they'd been asked to recreate, museums, a village or two.

It was a *really* big ship.

There was also a train. On the ship. Mostly because it was so big, it had required one to get around in a timely manner.

This was going to be their home for the next . . . however long it would take them to get through the Void. As far as temporary homes went, it was a pretty good one.

Derivan eyed the ship's console with some wariness. It was a glowing orb attached to the ship—suspiciously similar to the Grand Anchors Sev had built before. It even gave him the same feeling. He wouldn't have been surprised if it *was* one, albeit one that Sev hadn't personally built.

Or maybe he *had* been the one to build it in the reality he'd Shifted this from.

Derivan placed his hand on the orb and focused.

He didn't know what kind of universe he wanted. But that was, according to Sev, the whole point—everyone else *did* have some kind of idea on the way the universe needed to work, and their biases would make them find a universe best suited for them. Derivan had a true and vested interest in all forms of life, and he wanted . . .

He knew what he wanted, actually.

He wanted a world where he could keep exploring and adventuring with his friends. A world where everyone here could thrive.

The orb beneath his gauntlet grew warm, responding to that desire, and he felt it set a target.

"Done," he said.

He was smiling. He wasn't sure why. A part of him thought it was maybe because he caught a glimpse of where they were going, though the memory was so immense, it came and went in a fraction of a second. Still, it made a sort of warm contentment bloom in his chest.

What a pleasant feeling.

Now the choice was made, and their destination was set.

Even knowing where they were going, the journey wasn't *easy*. The Void wasn't as empty as it could've been—there were other universes here that had been consumed. There were dead stars and empty libraries, islands of strange matter floating in the dark. In the end, they needed Xothok's help to navigate their way through the Void. Derivan had given them the destination—Xothok and his crew would handle the navigation.

"Raise the damn sails already!" Xothok called out.

"Fuck you!" Byrrhon responded, making a rude gesture at Xothok—but he went to raise the sails anyway. Xothok grinned at him.

Whatever those adventurers had done, it had brought back the old Byrrhon. Sort of. It hadn't brought back the one that lived a life as a cruel and callous bandit, nor the one that had lived a life as a [**Navigator**]. This Byrrhon had both sets of memories, and he was . . . *calmer*, for lack of a better word. He had a sense of perspective he didn't have before.

Xothok was just glad he had his best friend back and didn't need to have Byrrhon's blood on his hands. He was glad for a lot of things, really. Having a place he could call home, no matter how temporary; being reunited with Alyssa; no longer having to worry about his crew being able to eat their next meal . . .

Xothok knew there were things he had done he could never take back. But that was why he'd decided even before this journey had begun that no matter how far the people on this ship needed him to go, no matter how long they needed his services as their [**Astral Navigator**], he would be there to fulfil his duty.

So he led their journey through the Void. The direction and hope that had once been given to him were now his to give to others. Though he grumbled about the work, in the quiet space between false dusk and illusory dawn, he searched tirelessly.

And in that search, he found strays and stragglers. He found survivors—remnants of universes and times long gone. The Void was not quite as empty as they had thought. Others had tried to fight it. Others had failed.

But they would not. And they would carry on with the legacy of all that remained. Xothok found a new goal for himself before he quite realized it.

No one left behind.

—◆—

Sev would—in the following months and years—reflect on how the final segment of their journey felt like it both took too long and yet took no time at all.

—◆—

"Finally, some *solid fucking ground!*"

Misa seemed . . . very pleased with herself for someone that had literally just thrown herself off the ship and onto solid land.

"We did it, guys," she said with a broad grin. "We made it. Whole new universe. One we don't have to worry about decaying."

"Well," Sev said awkwardly. "All universes decay. We'll probably still have to figure something out. It's not like we can keep running from the Void *forever.*"

"But we have *time,*" Misa argued. "Billions of years! And so much to explore, and time for our Grand Anchors to grow, and ourselves to grow with it . . ."

"Are you *planning* to live for billions of years?" Sev raised an eyebrow at her. Misa just grinned at him.

"I mean, I am," Vex said, perfectly serious.

"We have a whole universe to explore," she said. "You think a billion years is enough?"

"That depends, I suppose," Sev said, smiling a slight smile. "Hope you brought us somewhere interesting, Derivan."

Derivan considered the remark.

"I believe I have made a good choice," he said after a moment. "But there is only one way to find out, yes?"

His hand wrapped around Vex's, and the lizardkin smiled up at him happily. Vex spoke next. "I can't wait to explore this one with you guys," he said. "I wonder if there's new magic here! And if the Grand Anchors are going to behave any differently. Oh, and I should do some research to see if this universe has its own unique forms of power . . ."

Derivan laughed, pulling Vex close. "We will have plenty of time for this," he said. His voice took on a slightly teasing note. "But I suspect the Guildmaster will want us to help unload the people from the ship."

"We could disappear," Vex said mischievously. "Just for a while. We can come back and help after. But I kinda want to have an adventure with you guys. We'll be the first ones to explore this place!"

"We *should* be responsible . . ." Sev said, glancing back up at the ship—but his lips twitched. He was tempted.

This was, of course, the moment Max popped up. "You guys have done plenty already," she said with a grin. "Go! Explore. I'll cover for you."

Sev laughed. "You really know when to show up, don't you?" he asked the receptionist. She grinned at him.

"It's my job!" she said cheerfully. "Seriously, though, it's fine. We'll handle it. Go check things out and tell us if anything dangerous is out there. Have fun! And one more thing."

"Yes?" Sev raised an eyebrow.

"Thank you." Max grinned at all of them. "Seriously. Lots of people are gonna be pissed that our old world is gone, so I want to get this in before any of them get it in their heads to come give you shit. Also, call me if they show up; I'll kick their ass."

The four of them couldn't help but laugh at that.

"Well, how about it, guys?" Sev said once the laughter had died down a bit. "You heard her."

"Let's kick things off with a new adventure."

HOME

"Commune time!" Max cheered. Xothok stared at her, and the Guildmaster just grinned; she stared with pride at the network of homes they'd built. It was better than a traditional branch of the Adventurers' Guild by far. Building, it turned out, was a lot easier when everyone was on the same page about needing shelter.

It was *also* much easier to get adventurers to help with building when it was their own homes they were building. Of course, they'd end up being shared—this was a new universe that needed exploring, and those homes didn't really need to go unoccupied for months on end—but that didn't mean they didn't explore ways to personalize each home.

A little bit of experimentation with Shift, now that the inner workings of the system were more transparent and easier to work with, and they managed to recreate a sort of layered housing system where Shift could be used to swap between versions of a home with just a press of a button.

Alyssa couldn't deny being a little excited about that.

They all needed a home to be proud of. Their entry into this new universe hadn't been without hiccups—whatever universe Derivan had chosen was one that still had its dangers. Within the first few hours of landing atop the empty, grassy plains that had seemed to be a good landing spot, what could only be described as snakes made of pure shadow sneaked out of the nearby forest to investigate the new disturbance.

It was a *good* thing that they'd refused to allow the many eager civilians aboard the ship to disembark first. Alyssa did wonder why Derivan had chosen a universe with these dangers, but she suspected it was simply a matter of what options had been available. A universe with the right conditions for life invariably would also have hostile life on it; a universe *without* the right conditions for life would simply be uninhabitable, and a universe with an already-dominant civilization would struggle to accommodate a second one.

She approved of the choice, of course. And not only because it seemed there was more to this universe than was immediately clear. Though she *was* excited about that part. It had been a long time since she'd been able to just . . . well, adventure.

Delving dungeons with Xothok was the most fun she'd had in a *while*.

"We will . . . live in one of these?" Xothok stared at one of the newly built homes. Alyssa glanced at him and had to hold back a laugh at the look of sheer suspicion on his face—he looked like he was about to try to punch a house for looking at him the wrong way.

"They're not going to stand up and attack you, you know," she teased.

"This is a different universe," Xothok said, eyes still narrowed at the house. "The rules may be different."

Alyssa smirked. "Do you actually think the house is going to be dangerous, or are you doing the thing where you're simultaneously excited, scared of being vulnerable, and trying to make me laugh?"

Xothok paused, and a look of guilt flashed briefly across his face. "It's, uh, probably one of those three. At least."

Her grin became a little more teasing. "Want to break the new home in?"

"I am standing *right here*, you two!" Max complained. "Let me be excited about the commune without your flirting, dammit!"

"What do you mean, 'you two'?" Xothok complained, though he was obviously flustered. "I did not participate in this . . . this flirting!"

"You were *thinking* about it," Max accused. "You have a whole team of ex-bandits to take care of, don't forget! And also that Byrrhon guy."

"Right." Xothok's expression settled almost immediately at the mention of Byrrhon; Alyssa wondered if he still felt guilty about killing him. As far as she knew, Byrrhon didn't blame Xothok for what he'd done, but the memory seemed to haunt Xothok still, sometimes. "I mean, he's doing okay. Without me."

"Yeah, but he wants you around, you idiot," Max said, rolling her eyes. "Guy is desperate to be forgiven, *you're* desperate to be forgiven. Talk to one another a bit more! You've been avoiding each other since you got off the ship!"

"Playing impromptu therapist already, I see," the Guildmaster said, amused. Max looked at her and scowled.

"It's so weird when you do that," she complained. "I know you're Alyssa, but I just look at you and my brain goes 'Guildmaster.' You don't even have to do it anymore. You're just doing it to mess with me."

"The skill is still useful for *some* things," Alyssa said with a laugh. "But yes. I'll try to mess with you a little less, Max. You want to help me get people settled in here?"

"*Do I!*" Max's eyes lit up. She grinned, then instantly vanished as she activated her skill; Alyssa's arm slipped around Xothok's waist, and the lizardkin promptly froze.

"Knew that would get her to leave," Alyssa said cheerfully.

"I hate you so much," Xothok grumbled.

"No, you don't." The grin hadn't left Alyssa's face.

". . . No, I don't."

PROPOSAL

"Derivan!" Vex called. He hopped down the stairs, nearly tripping—seriously, these stairs were *way* too tall for his height, but also they were too short for Derivan's height, so they both kind of tripped on them sometimes—and then glanced around their shared living room. No sign of the living armor. Scimitar? Maybe he needed to get used to thinking of Derivan as a Scimitar. "Derivan? Are you there?"

"I am here." Derivan's response was slightly muffled. Vex peeked around the corner to find his partner halfway inside the cabinet under the sink, apparently trying to fix some piping. He stifled a laugh.

"Deri, what are you doing?" he asked. "We have spells for that."

"I was curious if I could fix them without magic," Derivan said plainly. His helmet was wet, although even as Vex watched, the liquid was quickly absorbed into the so-called metal. Part of his Slime stat. Vex still hadn't really gotten used to the sight. "It is interesting. How they function, I mean."

"I'm sure it is." Vex's expression settled into a softer smile, and he came up to Derivan to give him a hug; the Scimitar's arms wrapped around his back after a moment, and he felt a metal chin resting on the top of his head. A *squishy* metal chin. Derivan had learned from the last few times he'd tried and the metal poked him just a bit too much.

"You were looking for me?" Derivan questioned. Vex nodded eagerly.

"Yeah! You know how I asked to borrow your forge, and then also told you not to use your forge?"

Derivan chuckled. "It is difficult to forget. I had to put several projects on hold for you," he said. He didn't sound annoyed by it.

"Right." Vex had the grace to look a little bit embarrassed anyway. "And, um, you know how I've been having lessons in blacksmithing and forging with Gallant, right?"

"I do indeed." Derivan's eyes sparkled with amusement. "Your lessons are right after mine. I am unsure why you wished for our sessions to be separate."

"I had to keep a secret," Vex said. He brandished a box from behind his back—or, well, he tried. Apparently, he'd dropped it when he almost tripped down the stairs. Vex scurried away abruptly, found the box, picked it up, and then brandished it again to a Derivan who watched him with fond exasperation. "I made you something!"

"A box?" Derivan teased.

"No," Vex said, and then he blinked, staring again at the box. It *was* fairly ornate, and he'd made it in accordance to the Scimitar traditions as Gallant had taught him. "Wait, no, actually, the box is part of it."

"I am impressed by it," Derivan said. He reached out, brushing his touch over the ornate carvings that decorated the box. Their fingers touched briefly, and Vex shivered at the contact.

. . . It was so unfair that Derivan could still do this to him.

"Okay, no, but the gift is *inside* the box," Vex said, trying to collect himself. He almost let Derivan take the box before remembering that he was supposed to be the one opening it—Misa would definitely make fun of him for this later—and managed to click it open.

Scimitars didn't use rings for proposals. Not that many species did, really. Scimitars in particular, though, typically gifted their intended bond a set of cloak clasps to fasten around their shoulders. Into it would be inscribed a symbol that held meaning for both of them.

Vex, of course, inscribed one clasp with the Glyph of Change, and the other with the Glyph of Stability. He'd considered using their Signs, but those were variable—they'd changed over time and would almost certainly change again.

These Glyphs, though? They'd created them together, almost. And he knew that moment of creation had been meaningful for the both of them.

"Vex . . ." Derivan took each clasp from the box with his characteristic gentleness. "These are—"

"Scimitar bonding clasps, yes," Vex said with a smile. "I'd like to go through the bonding ceremony with you, if that's okay."

"You are proposing to me." Derivan knelt so he was closer to Vex's height, bringing the lizardkin in for a close embrace. "And here I was certain I would get to it first."

"I *have* been getting more confident," Vex said, grinning. As if to emphasize his words, he kissed Derivan, and the Scimitar kissed back, laughing.

"Yes, of course," Derivan said. "I would be honored. May I ask when you knew you wished to do this?"

"Oh, before we even left Obreve," Vex said with a laugh. "I didn't realize it at the time, but . . . I thought of home, and I just couldn't imagine one without you in it."

"That is . . . very sweet." Derivan smiled. "And you wish for us to cement this bond through the Scimitar bonding ceremony?"

"I know how much restoring your people means to you," Vex said. "And I know how much your culture means to you. I would be honored."

"As would I." Derivan hummed, holding him close. ". . . You are terribly precious to me. I hope you understand this."

Vex squeezed Derivan as hard as he could, feeling like his heart was overflowing. "Likewise," he said softly.

EPILOGUE 3

CHESS

"I forgot how bad you were at this," Onyx said, amused.

"Shut up," Sev grumbled.

He sat across from Onyx, staring intently at the board in front of him. Every chess piece was intricately and beautifully carved—even the board itself was made from an immaculate slate of marble. He would've been in a much better position to appreciate it all if Onyx hadn't been so thoroughly beating him.

"I feel like you could move that piece," Aurum said, pointing.

"Or that one," Tempus suggested.

Sev groaned. "Why did I agree to live with you guys again?"

"You said something about needing to teach us how to interact with mortals," Onyx said. "And also, we didn't want to live with anyone else."

"I visit Jerome sometimes!" Aurum said. "But he's got too many people living with him, and they all get weird when I'm there."

"Velykos is a good companion," Tempus noted. "But he has other gods living with him already."

Sev sighed. "This is what I get for letting Derivan choose a new universe," he grumbled. "Of course this one doesn't have a divine plane."

"Is it really so bad?" Onyx teased.

"No," Sev admitted, finally moving a piece. "I think it's a good thing, at the end of the day. People need to see that you guys aren't . . . I mean, they need to see that you guys are still people. And I mean, you three are fine, but I think a lot of the others need to remember what it's like to be mortal."

"The gods have been disconnected from the material plane for a long time," Onyx agreed. "Many of them no longer remember their original reasons for taking responsibility for their domain. Checkmate, by the way."

Sev groaned. "You made these pieces too pretty. It's very distracting."

Onyx rolled his eyes. "It's not my fault you like a good carving more than you like men or women. Or anyone else."

"Hey! Low blow."

"Don't make me go lower." Onyx smirked at him, and Sev sighed, leaning back in his chair; he was smiling, though.

"Well, you guys are going to have the house to yourselves for a bit," Sev said. "I'm gonna get Derivan and Vex and Misa and go explore the ruins someone discovered up north. Apparently it's haunted."

"Magic haunted, or haunted haunted?" Aurum asked with interest.

"Both?" Sev wrinkled his nose. "I dunno; I'd have to read the reports again. I don't know if ghosts are *real* here, still. Non-magic ghosts, I mean. I *could* go ask Vex . . ."

Sev paused, glancing at the nearby house where Vex and Derivan lived. "Think today's a big day for them, though," he remarked. "I'll check in and get everyone ready tomorrow— Hey!"

A certain phoenix flew in through the window, setting the curtains on fire. A second later, an entire sun elemental tumbled in through the same window, chasing after it. Sev stared in a mixture of amusement and horror—material damage wasn't *that* worrying when he had the God of Time living with him— as the two proceeded to set half the living room on fire.

Very casually, he slid the chess set into part of that fire. Onyx raised an eyebrow at him, amused.

"You know that's made of stone, right?" he said. "And I still won."

Sev laughed. "Had to try," he said. "Besides, I wouldn't *actually* want to damage these carvings."

PROGRESS

Misa lived in a little mockup of J'rokksur, a little far from the outpost where Sev, Derivan, and Vex had their homes. She felt a *little* guilty about that—but she missed her home, dammit!

Well, also, she had a copy of herself living there, anyway. So it didn't *really* matter.

And a portal. Portals were very convenient.

Clyde, Belle, and Elliot had all chosen to come check out her village and live in it for a while, which delighted her. They'd never lived in a village before, apparently? Mundane didn't count; it was meant to be a template, and being a template, the people of Mundane had never really had that much of an opportunity to develop a culture of their own.

That was their primary focus now, as Misa understood it—trying to decide for themselves what kind of society they wanted to be. And part of that was experiencing what all these new, burgeoning societies had to offer.

Misa was just glad her friends had chosen J'rokksur as their starting point.

"The others miss you, you know," she said with a grin, over her bowl of fish stew. "You should visit them, too."

"We will, we will," Clyde said. "We just wanted to come here first! See if it'd be a good spot to set up an inn— *Ow.*"

Elliot hummed innocently. "Now might not be the best time to be talking about your dream of building a new inn, hon. Although I do think it's very cute."

Clyde folded his arms over his chest and grumbled, even as Elliot tugged him closer affectionately. Meanwhile, Belle leaned forward, fingers tapping on the table in thought.

"Can I just say again how *weird* it is that you managed to bring us back?" Belle remarked. "I still don't believe it sometimes. It's never actually happened.

I would've believed it if you brought everyone *else* back, but we shouldn't have enough single-echo coherence for you to be able to call out one specific iteration of us."

"Am I . . . supposed to know what that means?" Misa asked, blinking at her friend. What the hell was *single-echo coherence*? She glanced at the still-steaming bowls of soup in front of them. "You guys should try the stew."

"Don't change the subject!" Belle pointed her spoon at Misa, then reconsidered and dipped it into the stew, taking a sip. "Okay, this is actually pretty good. But don't think I forgot what you did."

"I can't really explain it," Misa said with a shrug. "We saw an opportunity to fix things, and . . . I mean, honestly, I can't claim that things are *better* because we brought everyone back, so maybe *fix* isn't the right word."

"Second chances, right?" Clyde asked. Misa mulled over the question for a moment.

"We didn't know we'd be looking for a new universe at the time," she said. "So I'm not sure we were *consciously* thinking that. But yeah, I think that was the spirit of it. It was the end of the world. Sometimes that changes people."

"It changed a few, from what I heard," Clyde agreed.

"Made a few people worse, too." Misa shrugged. "I hear the attempts to rebuild Elyra keep going wrong in more ways than one. Vex doesn't want anything to do with it, and a lot of people are kind of splitting off to make their own nation, too. Just a few of the nobles really want to rebuild Elyra . . . you know, as it was."

"Planning to do anything about it?" Belle asked curiously.

"Right now? No," Misa said, shaking her head. "They don't have enough people interested in their regime to actually form any kind of nation, so they're just wasting their own power and resources on it. The Guild and other kingdoms—I guess *kingdom* isn't really the right word anymore, actually—make the process of moving to them pretty easy, so no one really has to stay in Elyra to survive or anything."

"So you're just letting them build an empty city?" Belle smirked, chuckling. "Evil."

"Hey, they're making their own bed to lie in, as Sev would put it," Misa said with a shrug. "Actually, he probably wouldn't say it like that. Where *did* I hear that before?"

"I use it sometimes!" Clyde said. "Only when my guests don't make their beds, though."

Misa laughed. "I don't think that's supposed to be that literal."

"No, but it's funnier that way." Clyde grinned. ". . . Okay, I'm going to ask you a dumb question, and you're free to say no."

Misa raised an eyebrow. "Really?"

"I'll be *very sad*, but you can still say no!" Clyde laughed. "Look, I think we want to live here for a while. You're hosting the Anchor of Reality, right? Everything here feels more . . . *solid*. It's comfortable. And I like the people here a lot—this is your village, right?"

"Yeah." Misa smiled. "J'rokksur. Grew up here, and everyone was like family to me. They still are; I just have a second family now." She glanced meaningfully at the portal hovering in the back of the room.

Clyde followed her gaze. "You don't feel like it's a little weird to just . . . have a hole in space open in your room?"

"Nah." Misa walked over to the portal, stuck her head through it, and called out with a wave. "Sev! Clyde is here!"

"Little busy at the moment!" Sev called back.

Misa pulled her head back through the portal. "His house is on fire," she reported. "Don't worry! They've got it handled."

"Does his house . . . get lit on fire a lot?" Clyde asked, blinking. "The stew is amazing, by the way. I'll need to learn the recipe so I can make it myself."

"Yes," Misa said cheerfully. "And I'm sure my mom will teach it to you. You were saying you wanted to live here for a while?"

"If that's all right." Clyde nodded. "I actually do want to build an inn, and these two tease me about it sometimes, but—"

"We support him and we actually do miss how cozy his inn was," Elliot said cheerfully.

"I also need to start a new skull collection," Belle muttered, mostly to herself.

"There are ruins nearby, too, I think? I want to start recording history again. I know these were all just jobs the mana gave us, but we do love them, so . . ." Elliot trailed off.

"Say no more." Misa held up her hand and smiled. "You're welcome here, and what's more, I'll get some of the J'rokksur residents to help you build your inn. How about it? Want some orcish architecture to spice things up?"

Clyde brightened. "Sounds brilliant."

EPILOGUE 5

RUINS

It was rare for the Adventurers' Guild to call upon pretty much every active-duty adventurer they had, and rarer still for Sev and his team to be the ones to lead a delve. These ruins were dangerous, though. They'd learned as much when they walked in range and the first system window appeared.

> **Unknown power source detected.**
> **Scanning for compatibility.**
> **Attempting to link with local knowledge database ...**

> **Link successful. Ruins identified. These are the ruins of what was once known as the Restless Abyss Sect. It houses a Calamity-rank Formation. Activation threshold at seventy percent and climbing due to ambient qi levels.**

"You really chose somewhere special, huh?" Sev said, glancing over the window again. "Seriously, qi?"

"It did seem strange that my Slime trait was absorbing a new form of energy, though I did not have a name for it," Derivan said thoughtfully. "But my options were limited, and I could not know every detail of the universe I chose—I only knew it could accommodate all of us."

Vex tugged his new cloak tighter around his shoulders, brushing his fingers over the clasp with affection. "Guess you ended up finding a new adventure for us after all."

"I want to know what this Calamity-rank Formation is." Misa grinned. "Sounds like something that could fuck us up."

"... You don't have to sound *that* enthusiastic about it," Sev said dryly. But he laughed a moment after, and the four stared down into the crater housing the ruins below.

"Well?" Sev said. "We've got new discoveries to make. Let's make this a good one."

ABOUT THE AUTHOR

Silver Linings has been writing for over two decades and has finally decided to direct that creative energy into authoring complete books, preferably ones about kindness and compassion. He is also attempting to spread across all the clouds in the sky and give them a silver lining. This is not a metaphor. Do not panic, and stay indoors at all times.

Podium

DISCOVER MORE

STORIES UNBOUND

PodiumEntertainment.com